D1144432

Falling Uphill

Also by Nan F. Salerno

SHAMAN'S DAUGHTER
(with Rosamond M. Vanderburgh)

NAN F. SALERNO

Falling Uphill

PRENTICE-HALL, INC.
Englewood Cliffs, New Jersey 07632

Book Designer: Linda Huber
Art Director: Hal Siegel

Falling Uphill by Nan F. Salerno
Copyright © 1981 by Nan F. Salerno
The plot and characters in this novel
are entirely fictional, and any similarities
to persons living or dead are coincidental.
All rights reserved. No part of this book may be
reproduced in any form or by any means, except
for the inclusion of brief quotations in a review,
without permission in writing from the publisher.
Address inquiries to Prentice-Hall, Inc.,
Englewood Cliffs, N.J. 07632
Printed in the United States of America
Prentice-Hall International, Inc., London
Prentice-Hall of Australia, Pty. Ltd., Sydney
Prentice-Hall of Canada, Ltd., Toronto
Prentice-Hall of India Private Ltd., New Delhi
Prentice-Hall of Japan, Inc., Tokyo
Prentice-Hall of Southeast Asia Pte. Ltd., Singapore
Whitehall Books Limited, Wellington, New Zealand

10 9 8 7 6 5 4 3 2 1

Library of Congress Cataloging in Publication Data
Salerno, Nan F., date
    Falling uphill.

    I. Title.
PS3569.A4594F3 1981 813'.54 81-5839
ISBN 0-13-301804-0 AACR2

CONTENTS

For Henry, Michele and David

ONE

The Auction

The auctioneer's tent was set up in the front yard of an old farmhouse. It was not a tent so much as a canvas roof elevated in the middle and at the corners by poles set at angles into the earth and held fast by guy ropes. Under its shade people sat on folding chairs; beyond it, they sat on blankets spread on the grass or stood about in small groups. Nearby was a mobile canteen, its side propped up like an awning. Behind the narrow counter two girls in striped caps and aprons handed out pop, cups of coffee, and hamburgers wrapped in paper napkins. In the field between house and road, cars, vans and pickup trucks were parked in crooked rows, the intense early summer sun flashing off their metal hoods. The gathering might have been for a garden party or prayer meeting were it not for the furniture, cartons of household goods, and farm equipment strewn on the grass before the gutted house, all the accumulated debris of several generations. People strolled about, musing over tarnished brass bed frames, ruptured chairs and crazed mirrors. Hoping to find a treasure whose value only they recognized, they pawed through boxes of old clothes, yellowed sheet music, moth-eaten family albums, whose subjects, gazed at by strangers, knew a second and final death.

Vivian hadn't expected such a crowd. She herself had found in the newspaper listing only one item, a silver inkwell and pen, to be of interest. "I think I'll drive out to this auction," she had remarked at breakfast. Her husband and daughter had responded simultaneously.

"But I have to get to the farm after school! It's my riding day!"

"Just don't spend your last cent."

Harry's response was routine; he never minded what she spent. But at the belligerent alarm in Corinne's voice, Vivian had glanced coolly across the top of the paper and said, "I've always gotten you there, haven't I?"—a reminder that she had, and had done so despite her own disapproval. Corinne had nodded once in reluctant agreement, and Vivian had gone back to reading the classifieds.

When Harry had stooped for his routine kiss, Vivian had smiled automatically and tilted her cheek. She nodded absently at Corinne's "I'm going now." So absorbed was she by an inner fancy that she scarcely noticed their going.

As if she were viewing a film with the sound turned off, Vivian saw herself in a long blue dressing gown, descending the stairs, moving through the quiet, dreaming house. It was her house but enhanced, seen through a lens that softened and glorified. She glided across the polished floors and scattered rugs to a small study, where she pulled back the draperies, allowing the gentle air of a summer's morning to billow the filmy curtains. She sat down at the desk, her sleeves falling gracefully back from her arms, took up a quill pen and dipped it into an old silver inkwell whose rich patina shone against the dark wood of the desk. Dear . . . , she wrote, tracing a delicate line on ivory paper. Pausing, she gazed out the window, a thoughtful smile on her lips. Then her mind's camera drew up and back and she saw the scene whole: the tranquil, sunlit room, her red-gold hair, the Grecian folds of the blue gown, the sculptured roundness of her arm with one hand poised above the inkwell, the inspiration of the scene, the centerpiece around which everything revolved. Without it, all the rest would vanish. Vivian set down her coffee cup. She would have that inkwell!

Seeing the tent, Vivian swerved her MG into the dirt lane with a flourish. Stones spurted from under her back tires. She bumped across the field and jerked to a stop beside a black van on whose side was painted the pie-shaped rays of an orange sun. She tossed her keys into a capacious straw bag with the careless gesture appropriate to a woman free to follow her whim and drive an MG about the countryside on a summer's day. Even though she had had this car for nearly three weeks, she was still satisfied with it, in tune with it. Its qualities complemented her own, made her sharply aware of herself as independent, eye-catching, fast-moving. Stepping across the furrows in her flimsy, high-heeled sandals. Vivian could hear the auctioneer chant.

"Twenty-four fifty! Would you go twenty-seven? Twenty-seven! Would you go thirty? Want 'em at thirty? Thirty over here! Thirty-five? Would you go thirty-five? Thirty-four? Thirty-four? Sold at thirty! To number 27!"

A dry, dusty odor rose from the unworked field, its furrows gone to weeds turned brittle from several weeks with no rain. Vivian was glad she had worn a light, sleeveless dress and had remembered her new, rose-tinted sunglasses. She hoped she wasn't too late. Hurrying, she caught a piece of stubble in her sandal and stooped to remove it.

Under the shadow of the canvas roof, Marvel Gibson stood behind a lectern on a low platform. He pointed the handle of his gavel at the people gathered before him. "Let's have a little quiet here, please," he demanded, "a little quiet." At his stern tone, the crowd lowered their voices and paid attention to his assistant, Calloway Claude, who stood in a cleared space at one side of the platform.

"What d'you have there, Calloway?" asked Gibson.

Calloway held up an old rusty black typewriter and turned it about. "Look at that now! All the keys go up at once! Don't often get one like that! Gimme five! Would you give five? Would you give ten, ten! Would you give twelve, how 'bout twelve? There's twelve! How 'bout fifteen? Fifteen? Going at twelve! Sold for twelve to number 43!" Calloway handed the typewriter to a helper. "Here, put it in the security area. That was 43," he reminded a woman recording sales at a table behind him.

A teenaged helper in jeans and sweat shirt brought forward a carton, which Calloway seized with gusto. "Lots of goodies here!" Rummaging about, he held up the head of an old croquet mallet stuck on the end of one of his thick fingers—"There's a dandy!"—then an old ladle, a drugstore calendar with the months torn off, a metal spoon with a cord through a hole in its handle. "And here, a salt and pepper! Very unusual! They almost match! Want 'em? Put two dollars on it! All one money! Gimme a couple of dollars to go! A dollar where! A dollar there! Everything goes! Number 4's the buyer! Mark it two dollars."

As he reached for the next item, an odd-shaped tool of wood and metal, Calloway's wide, loose mouth fell open, his eyes widened comically behind steel-rimmed glasses. "Here's an oldie! Don't know what it is, but it'd sure be handy to have around! Gimme a dollar! Gimme a quarter!" He paused, gazed speculatively at the audience, his spiky gray hair sticking out from under the narrow turned-up brim of his straw porkpie hat. "Who," he suddenly shouted, "has never been to an auction before, raise your hand!" The experienced smirked as several hands went up. Instantly Calloway pointed at one young woman and yelled, "Sold! Sold to number 34 for fifty cents! Half a dollar!"

The rising, falling wail of a police siren sounded in the distance, and Calloway glanced toward the road. "Here they come! Hope none of you parked on the highway! For a price you can get in the cemetery—don't cost much more. Here's somethin' now!" He held up two large framed pictures, their faded colors all variations of brown. One showed an old family doctor, watch in hand, taking the pulse of a child at whose bedside he sat while the anxious family stood in the shadows; the other, a thatched cottage with rose arbor, a winding path and woods, all bathed in the light of a brown sunset. "Just what you need to hang in the shop to inspire the help!"

Vivian, skirting the tent, paused to glance at the frames. Seeing they were crudely made, she moved on. Walking leisurely, she examined the piles of household goods, a broken churn, a split salad bowl, rusted springs, stacks of chipped dishes, old piano rolls, kerosene lamps, worn leather straps with sleigh bells and mud-caked farm tools. Not until she had worked her way around the yard did she find the inkwell. With a few other choice articles, it was on a table within easy reach of the auctioneer's left hand.

Marvel Gibson had observed her progress as he observed every detail of the auction. A tall, slim man wearing a Kentucky colonel's hat and a smartly tailored tan suit, he stood commandingly above the crowd. Occasionally he joined in Calloway's fun with a witty remark and a grin that dimpled his left cheek. Like Vivian, he wore sunglasses, dark ones that hid the sharpness of his eyes. He missed no flicker of interest among those assembled. Naturally skilled in the art of cagey deception, he intuitively recognized a feigned indifference and delighted in pursuing and ultimately proving in a profitable way the correctness of his judgment. He rarely lost a sale or a poker game. He understood pace. He knew how long to let Calloway josh the crowd, selling cheap items, and when to take over himself and sell expensive ones. With unblemished self-confidence, Marvel sometimes thought he would have made a great teacher or an even greater preacher.

When the police car went by, he had glanced beyond the tent, toward the road, and his attention had been caught by a woman out in the field, bending over doing something to her shoe; she was too distant for him to see her face, but her hair shone like pale gold in the sunlight and her airy dress floated about her as she straightened and walked gracefully toward the tent. He saw her glance at the pictures and noted her immediate loss of interest. Moving on the periphery of his vision, she circled the yard, disappearing, reappearing, never pausing for long.

Marvel tapped the lectern with the gavel handle, a signal to Calloway, and said, "Let's move it along now, move it along! Have to break soon!"

Calloway held up two mailboxes. "Here we go! One for alimony, one for whatever! What are bid? Eight, eight anywhere, do you give eight? Eight over here! Sold to number 62! Now here's a nice little wedding present!" holding up a shovel. "And a pick to match! If one doesn't get you, the other one will! Do you want 'em at five, at seven, at ten, ten, do you want 'em at twelve, going at twelve!"

Marvel, having snapped the reins, turned his head and saw her. She had come around to the table at his side. She came to a full stop, stretched out her hand and touched an old silver ink-well. Marvel, shrewdly watching, knew she had found what she had been hunting for.

Vivian, feeling herself observed, suddenly raised her head. For a moment they stared at each other, sunglass to sunglass, eyes obscured and darkly pink. Then Vivian withdrew her hand and moved away toward the mobile canteen.

Marvel banged his gavel and declared a fifteen-minute break.

A few people kept their seats, but most got up and milled around, looking over items yet to be sold. Across his coffee cup Marvel studied Vivian, who was speaking with an acquaintance. He wondered if her hair, like gold that deepened or lightened in color depending on the angle of light, were natural and decided it was since the skin of her arms and bare legs was that delicately tinged white he associated with red hair whatever its shade. Her dress, unlike the cotton prints, shorts and shirts of those around her, was dressy, expensive no doubt; and after meeting the self-possessed appraisal of her glance, he didn't need the flash of rings as she gestured to tell him that she was married or that her husband made good money. He would like to have observed her face, but however he shifted his ground, she seemed always to have her back to him. Deliberately? Marvel decided it was, because he liked such games and flattered himself as being attractive to women.

Calloway resumed the sale by holding up a large gray crock. "It's an oldie! See that crack there? Goes all the way to the bottom! It's the real thing! A dandy! Six dollars! Would'ja go six?"

Vivian succeeded in getting a seat under the tent, near the center, and settled herself to be patient. She crossed her knees and sat sideways, turning her shoulder toward the man on her right, whose gross stomach took up all his lap, in an effort to diminish the odor of stale beer that hung about him.

"See this," Calloway invited, displaying a white chamber pot, "would you believe there's people don't know what this is? Fact! One young lady thought it was a casserole!"

There were smiles and laughter. Marvel had withdrawn his attention from the crowd, bending down to consult with the woman recording sales. When he straightened, he surveyed the audience soberly, his straight sharp nose keen for every bid.

Calloway had lifted a CB set out of a carton. Squinting, he read off the model number. "Means nothing to me! Must have been left over from the last auction! But it's a dandy!"

"How many channels?" called out someone.

"How many you want?" demanded Calloway, poking about in the carton. "Also got some nice legs in here—wheelbarrow legs."

Marvel tapped his gavel and said, "Let's sell it!" As Calloway took bids, Marvel gestured for his helper to move up several large tools.

"Here's a practically new saw," said Calloway. "This saw's got real compression—it poops! I know, we tried it out back."

"Thirty dollars!" called out one man.

Calloway's slack mouth opened in a grin that displayed his large buck teeth. "You just bought the case! Now, what am I bid on this fine saw!"

When the hand tools were sold off, Marvel took over and began selling the items from the table beside him.

The fat man heaved himself up and left. A young woman holding a baby took his place. "Did you see that crystal bowl?" she asked Vivian. "What do you suppose that'll go for?" Vivian smiled and shrugged. "Probably for more than I can pay," said the woman. She glanced again at Vivian, more sharply, then settled back, jiggling her baby and looking pensive.

"Now here," said Marvel, finally holding up the inkwell, "we have a fine old piece, a silver inkwell, complete with quill pen. Very unusual, as those of you who've examined it know. Who'll start? What will you give?" He extended both arms like a choir director summoning up golden notes.

"Fifty," said a gray-haired man standing to one side at the edge of the tent. He was tilted slightly forward, and braced himself with both hands clasped over the head of his cane. He seemed to Vivian to be grinning until she realized that his mouth was drawn back in a compulsive constriction.

"Fifty! Fifty for this lovely old piece! You're not even in the basement! Come, who'll give eighty, ninety to start?" Marvel flipped one hand upward, demanding more volume.

"Eighty," said Vivian.

"Eighty," repeated Marvel. "That's a start. Who'll give eighty-five?"

"Eighty-five," said a woman to Vivian's right. Stout and middle-aged, she wore half a dozen necklaces around her neck, a ring on every knotty finger. Across the bridge of her nose was a large Band-Aid.

"Eighty-five, who'll make it one-o-five, one-o-five," chanted Marvel. He gestured again, encouraging, boosting.

"One-o-five," said the elderly man, helplessly showing his teeth.

"One-fifteen," said Vivian, miffed.

"One-fifteen," said Marvel, holding aloft the inkwell, "only one-fifteen for this valuable antique! Who'll give one twenty-five, one-thirty? One-thirty?" His hand, palm up, moved toward the woman on the right, drawing out a response.

Moved by invisible strings, she said, "One-thirty."

"One-thirty! Now," said Marvel, "you're just beginning to appreciate the quality of this piece, its fine old workmanship and design. Impossible nowadays at any price!"

"One thirty-five!" exclaimed the elderly man.

Vivian sucked her full lower lip in against her teeth. She felt the inkwell was hers by right; she had already in a manner possessed it. She should have had it at eighty. He was deliberately pushing this one item, forcing her to offer more and more. She should never have let him catch her looking at it. "One-forty," said Vivian. Her voice had a determined, final ring.

The older woman, hearing the challenge, turned to look at her, then said, "One forty-five."

"One forty-five," said Marvel smoothly and, turning the inkwell over, studied its bottom. "There's a date . . . no, a name, can't quite make it out, but who knows what unexpected find you might have here, just how valuable this item might be."

"One-fifty!" said the old man hoarsely.

"One fifty-five!" cried the woman, her eyes intense above the Band-Aid.

Marvel's dark glasses focused on Vivian. He raised his eyebrows slightly. "One fifty-five," he said. "Do I hear one-sixty?" Vivian stared back at him. He saw the anger in her face and said softly, "One fifty-seven?"

Certain now of his intention to force her, and angered by the sly condescension of the lowered figure, she determined to be the one to end it and at her own figure. She said clearly, "Two hundred."

There was a stir; several people turned to stare.

"Two hundred," said Marvel calmly. He held out his open, inviting hand toward the other woman. "Do I hear two-o-five?"

She shook her head irritably, several times, as if to shake loose the Band-Aid.

"Two-o-five?" he asked again, politely, this time of the elderly man, who, with an effort, drew his lips closed to signify no, then immediately grimaced again.

With the faintest of satisfied smiles, Marvel banged his gavel. "Sold to number 71 for two hundred!"

TWO

Dreaming Foxes

Vivian drove home too fast. Angry at having let herself be drawn into such a contest, she skidded around the ninety-degree corners that accommodated the endless plantings of corn and soybeans. Field after field of ruler-straight rows flashed by. In the immensity of flat land, the usual cluster of farmhouse, barn and silo was dwarfed and solitary. Occasionally small, isolated patches of woods had been left untouched, oases, where the trees grew close together in solid, compact masses. To Vivian's right, approaching on a course that would bisect hers, a truck skimmed through the fields, a cloud of dust twirling behind it. Belligerently, Vivian pressed the accelerator. As she sped past the crossroad, the driver, seeing her, braked and threw out his arms toward her in an expansive, theatrical embrace. Vivian laughed. Her anger suddenly drawn, she drove on into Warrenville at a more moderate speed.

For a stranger driving across country, Warrenville, the county seat, would be distinctive for two landmarks visible for miles in any direction. One was the courthouse clock tower, a square but graceful red brick structure that rose above the trees of the town. The sun, on a clear day, struck sparks from its gilded weather vane that would catch a distant eye as tiny flashes against the blue sky. The other, on the far side of town, was the ash-gray stacks of the iron works, two slender columns, taller than the clock

9

tower. Day and night smoke puffed from their flared mouths, geneally trailing eastward with the prevailing wind. Not visible from a distance were the four bridges straddling the Bursey River, which separated the town roughly in half. The Bursey, cutting through rich farmland on its way to the Mississippi, had created river bluffs that gave Warrenville a slight elevation. For most of the year its brownish, slow-moving surface hid a disposition for violence that broke out under the pressure of melting snow and spring rains. Then it rampaged through the town, overflowing its banks, flooding roads, undermining buildings, tearing loose whole trees, their branches raised above the swirling water. Spun by the swift current, raft-like masses of debris piled up against the bridge supports and hung there, to disintegrate gradually and float piecemeal downstream.

Vivian crossed one of the outlying bridges, a narrow steel structure with angular black girders whose boards clattered under the car wheels, and turned left, toward the older residential section. Here elm trees had once turned the summer streets into leafy, green tunnels and shaded the deep front lawns. But by the mid-1960's all had succumbed to Dutch elm disease, leaving only buckled sidewalks above their dead roots and an unbroken view of the large, solid, upper-middle-class houses that lined the straight streets.

At the corner of her own block, Vivian braked to let a woman jogger cross. Never did Vivian leave the house without seeing her, sometimes in shorts, sometimes in baggy pants and a long, woolen scarf, always jogging and staring ahead, oblivious to her surroundings. At crossings she never paused or turned her head. Vivian wondered why it was that a middle-aged woman with short, ragged hair should invariably remind her of Corinne. Corinne did sometimes wear similar socks with pompoms sticking out at the heels, but it suddenly struck Vivian that it was their expressions which were similar. There was no animation in the jogger's face, nor in Corinne's when she took her riding lessons, only a driving seriousness as if both were performing a duty.

Down the street Vivian could see the imposing, grandly ornate Victorian house she had lived in since she was married. Until recently, the sight had given her satisfaction. It had expressed permanence, stability and an income sufficient to keep its bricks well pointed and its elaborate trim beautifully white. When

Warrenville's House and Garden Club held its annual tour of the town's select houses, this house was designated as "a highlight" because of its old, rose-colored bricks, its double front door with cut glass panels and a tower room that rose above the second floor directly above the front entrance. From its windows one could look straight down at the front step for an amusingly foreshortened view of anyone approaching, or across the roofs of neighboring houses for glimpses of the river. The roof above this room was high and steep, its wide eaves curving slightly upward at the corners like a cap, its top decorated with a small black iron fence. Vivian had first seen it when she and Harry were househunting several weeks before their marriage. She had wanted the house passionately, her desire for it merging with her desire for Harry. She had rushed excitedly through its empty, high-ceilinged rooms, Harry's footsteps echoing behind her. She didn't see stained, irregular floors, peeling wallpaper, falling plaster and boarded-up fireplaces, but a house transformed—as she was certain she could transform it—to its former grand state. She saw herself and Harry living together in Victorian elegance: lamplight glistening on polished furniture and glowing softly on gilt-framed mirrors, richly-patterned rugs and velvet draperies. Built around such a home, their lives would be purposeful, gracious and charming. Their five children, two boys and three girls, in any order, wearing short pants and ruffled dresses, would fill the house with life such as it had known in years past. She had heard their laughter, seen them playing in the tower room and sliding boisterously down the long mahogany bannisters.

Harry had followed her from room to room, responding with monosyllables. She remembered his dogged expression, his puzzled blue eyes with their incredibly thick, black lashes and how she had felt in trying to arouse his enthusiasm that she was straining to lift a great weight.

Then she had been twenty and utterly confident. Now she was thirty-eight and displeased, though she wasn't sure with what. Restive and unsettled, though she couldn't explain why. She turned into the driveway and parked the car in front of the barn. Getting the inkwell, once such a compelling idea, now seemed totally unnecessary, even foolish. Marvel Gibson's image suddenly intruded upon her thoughts, but she pushed it irritably aside. She entered the kitchen, its mechanical and electrical devices camouflaged under a Victorian veneer, and surveyed with distaste all its perfectly worked out details. Seen with the objectivity of a stranger, the kitchen had all the overdone preciousness of an advertisement for kitchen flooring. Detached, she said to herself, that's what I am—detached. The word sounded like a knell. Frowning, she left the kitchen and walked slowly through the house, pausing to study each room as if she were seeing it clearly for the first time. She saw that she had indeed made of the house what she had intended. The inkwell, when polished and placed on the desk, might well be the last touch possible.

In the front hall, midway between front door and staircase, stood a large piece of furniture, a combined seat, umbrella stand and hat rack, backed by a long, oval mirror. The beveled glass panels in the front door refracted bands of blue, rose and yellow aslant the wall and mirror. Drawn by the vivid colors, Vivian came close to the mirror. Seeing her own face, she fell to studying it, lips slightly pursed, hoping to discover the reasons for her state of mind. It was a face she took good care of, monitored daily for signs of stress and coddled with lotions and creams, normally a lively, animated face, saved from bland prettiness by a decisive nose and a squarish jawline. Despite her familiarity with it, it told her nothing. She could see only an intent thoughtfulness, a slight constriction of the brow. The eyes, with blue irises outlined in black, gave no hint of what lay behind their shiny, reflective surfaces. Made uneasy by this mask-like secretiveness of her own face, Vivian shrugged involuntarily and turned away.

Standing there in the quiet, waiting house she herself had created, Vivian understood only that she was suffocated by it, by everything in it. It was complete, but its inspiration was gone. It no longer held any dream for her to inhabit. She felt an overwhelming desire to raise her arms, put her palms against the walls and push so the walls would fall outward like those of a cardboard house. Then she could breathe. She would be free again.

Corinne, thin and straight as a slat in blue jeans and plaid shirt, sat astride Masie, a plump bay mare, and squinted down at her mother. She always squinted in the sun because she refused to wear sunglasses, and she refused to wear them because her mother did. They had arrived late. The class was mounted and waiting. Now her mother stood surrounded by horses, as she spoke with the stable owner, Mr. Farley. She was delaying the class still longer, but Mr. Farley didn't mind. Nobody ever minded what her mother did. That was so, Corinne thought with bitter admiration, because she was so pretty and always knew exactly what to say. And do. She always took over everything and made it her own. She wished her mother would go. Impatiently she jerked the reins. Masie, wakened from her afternoon drowse, stomped her feet and bumped into Mr. Farley's big white horse.

"Here now!" exclaimed Mr. Farley. "Let's fall into line! Knees in, heels down!" He flicked his crop and started off. The others fell in behind, Corinne, as the oldest in the class, coming last. Feeling her mother's eyes on her back, Corinne held herself stiffly, seeing herself as she imagined her mother saw her, awkward and ungainly. But when the group passed out of sight beyond the barn and headed toward the woods, Corinne relaxed and fell easily into the rhythm of the canter that Mr. Farley, at the head of the line, set them to. The breeze created by the horse's motion lifted her hair, cooled her face. Exhilarated, Corinne felt the strength and power of the horse become her strength and power. She felt herself racing gloriously forward and wished she could ride on and on and never turn back.

Vivian leaned against the fence and watched them go, down a path designed to bring them back to their starting point in exactly half an hour. She was amused by the horses. Mr. Farley's white was really a dirty gray and its deeply curved back cradled Mr. Farley's thin frame like a rocking chair cradling old bones. Its feet were exceptionally large. The others were less heavy-footed, but something about their girth, the rhythm of their flanks as they took each plodding step in the path of their leader, suggested a close association with farm work. No nervous shying or prancing on delicate legs here or any high-spirited rearing and bucking. And just as well, thought Vivian, her eyes on her daughter's stiff back. Elbows braced on the rail fence, she watched until they rode out of sight beyond the barn.

Harry tipped back in his swivel chair and rocked gently, his feet tapping the floor. His dreamy gaze rested on the back of Jenny Blair's neck. In his private office he was separated from her by a glass partition. Still he could almost feel the triangle of neck showing between the collar of her blouse and the long black hair that parted above it and fell forward over her shoulders. Tender, that's what it would be, smooth and delicate. She suddenly tossed her head and flipped back her hair as she twirled out a finished page from the typewriter and inserted an envelope. She was hurrying to finish before quitting time.

Harry had already quit, had, indeed, done little or nothing all day. At noon he had very nearly asked Jenny to come and have lunch with him but had been diverted by Logan Gamble, who had come along with a proposition to talk over. All afternoon Harry's thoughts had been divided between Logan's proposed real estate deal and Jenny. He wished his father were still alive to advise him. He would have known in a minute if the deal were a good one. He had been one smart man, and he hadn't ever stepped out on his wife. Well, not so far as Harry knew, he hadn't. Harry laughed to himself. A man smart enough to take over three farms, a filling station and a grocery store and set his son up in the insurance business would be smart enough to get away with anything he wanted to get away with. He had been fond of Vivian. And he would have liked Jenny, Harry was sure. He thought of offering Jenny a ride home but indecision weighed him down. She was covering the typewriter, slamming drawers, getting her purse. Would she turn and look at him before she left? Ah! A quick, sideways glance! Harry raised his hand in a comradely salute and smiled—a reflex gesture. Just so he used to salute the stands when he trotted off the field after a high school football game. Then it had been for the general effect and for Vivian in particular, and always he had been answered by an enthusiastic roar in which he fancied he detected Vivian's clear voice.

Driving home in his Camaro, he thought briefly of his wife, seeing her still as she was in the snapshot he had carried with him during his year and a half in Korea, smiling endlessly at him over the bundle that was Corinne. Then she had been twenty-one, he twenty-two. Now he was thirty-nine. He was uncertain exactly how Vivian had changed, though he was certain she had. He could not now see her clearly but only through the blur of years. That she had become a presence as close to him as the back of his hand yet also as remote from him as a stranger was frightening, and he put that thought aside. He was positive he had not changed at all. But he was bothered by an inexplicable discontent, though he couldn't say with what, an unaccustomed lassitude all the more troubling in that he, always certain, never questioning, was bedeviled by indecision.

Turning onto his street, Harry passed a jogging woman. Had he not seen her, elbows working, chin pushing ahead, he would have felt something was missing. Only in the most severe weather did she not jog. Then he saw her bundled and booted, striding doggedly ahead. He figured she must spend her whole life jogging. Maybe she would rather jog than go home. He cast a jaundiced eye at his own house, forbiddingly stiff and with all that damned trim. A money-gobbler. He shuddered to think how much he had poured into it. Probably never get it back. Not that Vivian would ever give it up. It was her house. Always had been. For him home still meant the farmhouse he had grown up in, a comfortable, rambling house with a wide front porch, a side porch off the kitchen, and several tacked-on additions descending like steps at the back. As a boy he used to climb out of his second-floor bedroom window onto the roof above the kitchen, then onto the roof below that, then onto the last roof, where he could slide down the sloping lid of a large bin onto the ground. He could even, if necessary, climb back up to his own room, and, if he were very quiet crossing the kitchen, not even old Shep would know he'd been out.

Once he had foolishly assumed he and Vivian would live there. He had pictured Vivian, beautiful and aproned, at home in his mother's kitchen, serving dishes he loved on familiar china at the round kitchen table. Their daughter would play with her dolls on the porch swing as his sister Dolly had done. Their sons would use the barn, as he had, for a clubhouse, hiding place, playground, and he would pretend not to hear when they climbed out of their bedroom window. He hadn't recalled these dream memories in a long time, not since his widowed mother had died and the farm had been sold.

The possibility that he might now buy it back crossed his mind. A furtive, rebellious thought it was, yet it drew him more strongly than the back of Jenny's neck. Harry pulled in beside the MG and, because of this sudden notion and the necessity to smother it, entered the house in a grumpy, preoccupied manner.

He acknowledged Vivian's presence in the kitchen and went directly upstairs. He would take a good cold shower before dinner. That would set him straight.

The late sun shone through the dining room curtains, falling in slanted oblongs on the oak floor and patterned rug. The room was harmonious in itself, filled with a mellow light, its serenity accented by the unhurried tick of a clock. Harry, Vivian and Corinne sat together at one end of a long cherrywood table. Vivian was as conscious of every inch of its length, of the lace cloth, the dishes and the silver as if she carried their collective weight on her back. The solidity she had worked for had become a burden. The food she had prepared was tasteless and stuck in her throat. She wondered at Harry, that he could sit there and be so totally unaware of what she felt.

Harry, the deep waves of his hair sleek and shining after his shower, was pursuing his dinner with a good appetite. He had his Irish mother's coloring, deep blue eyes, black hair and brows, and a ruddy complexion as if his rich blood ran close to the surface of his high cheekbones. His shoulders were broad and muscular, his hands wide with a powerful grasp. Vivian could still see him, running with a sideways, dancing step, looking back over his shoulder, one arm upraised, hand grasping the football. No one had been able to throw it as swiftly and as far as he had. He was listening to Corinne, nodding with interest as she told him about her lesson.

". . . and we'd have had more time to practice if we hadn't gotten there late." Her tone was broadly accusing. Harry glanced mildly at Vivian.

Vivian said nothing and stabbed her fork at the salad. Corinne's childish attempt to show her mother at fault only increased Vivian's deep impatience. In six months, she knew, this passion for horses would be replaced by another, equally transitory. Meanwhile they were increasingly at odds, and she wondered, as she now more frequently did, how she ever came to have a daughter so unlike herself.

Having voiced her resentment, Corinne went on to tell with growing enthusiasm—self-generated enthusiasm, Vivian thought—of having taken a small jump. ". . . the stream wasn't very wide, but Masie jumped it . . . really great, and Mr. Farley said . . ." Corinne's face was decidedly square-jawed, wide and rather flat, her eyes hazel, her short, wiry hair a straw brown. And she was stubborn—persistent and stubborn.

". . . and after I graduate there's this place in Kentucky where I could go and learn how . . ."

Vivian laid down her fork. She cut off with a kind of strangled gasp an impatient, inarticulate protest and clasping her hands together exclaimed before she fully realized herself what she was going to say, "I am so tired of all this! Of this house and everything! It's . . . oh, we've lived here too long! Let's sell it, Harry! What do you think? Couldn't we sell it?"

Harry, caught with his fork halfway to his mouth, stared at her in astonishment.

"*Sell* it!" cried Corinne, too shocked to resent the interruption.

"Why not?" demanded Vivian, addressing Harry. "We could get rid of all this!" She made a sweeping gesture that encompassed the entire house. "We could find . . . oh, something interesting! Something exciting for a change!"

Harry regarded Vivian intently, even suspiciously, as though she had presented him not only with a difficult but an alarming puzzle.

"We can't sell this house!" cried Corinne, dismay causing her voice to turn high and reedy like a child's. Her wide mouth trembled. "This is home! We've always lived here!"

"*You've* always lived here," corrected Vivian tartly. "You think we weren't alive until you were born?"

"But I thought," said Harry, sticking to the point and picking his way carefully, "that you *wanted* this house, that you would never. . . ."

Corinne struck the table with her fist and cried out protests which her parents heard but for the moment ignored.

"I did! It was a challenge! I wanted to make it into something! And we have! But that doesn't mean we have to be stuck with it for the rest of our lives! Besides, you've never really liked this house anyway!" This long-buried conviction suddenly surfaced, less as an accusation than as support for her argument. Once spoken, it became the very bedrock of her determination to effect a change.

"When I think," said Harry, eyes narrowing at the thought, "how much I've invested here. . . ."

"Of course!" exclaimed Vivian, leaning forward eagerly, her eyes shining. "That's just what it is! An investment! We had all the fun of restoring it. . . ." Harry closed his eyes in painful memory, and Vivian hurried on. "Now we can sell it at a good profit! I'm sure of it!"

Harry raised a speculative eyebrow. Seen from this new point of view, the room's charms were suddenly apparent to him. "You're probably right," he said thoughtfully. "Houses are selling well right now."

"Arrgggh!" wailed Corinne, knocking back her chair, her eyes spilling copious tears that wet her cheeks and ran into her mouth as she struggled to speak. "You don't care, do you! You don't care about me at all!"

Her outcry having at last reached that particular pitch that both Harry and Vivian recognized as requiring their attention, they both turned to her, truly concerned, their hands outstretched.

"Why, baby! What's the matter!? We *do* care!"

"Of *course* we care! You *know* we do!"

"I'm not a baby! And you *don't* care! Or you couldn't sit there and talk like that! Not of selling our . . . our. . . ." Unable to speak that all-encompassing word, "home," which at that moment reverberated through her with almost religious overtones, Corinne was overwhelmed by a fresh onslaught of tears. Vivian reached out to embrace and comfort her, but Corinne jerked awkwardly away. Stumbling back, she felt a fresh sense of outrage which steadied her, and she turned on her mother.

"You know I wanted the barn for my horse! But you don't care! You don't *want* me to have a horse! You don't even *like* horses!"

"Corinne, that's not true! I *do* like horses, but you can't keep a horse inside the town lim. . . ."

"You keep saying that! But that's just an excuse! If *you* wanted a horse, you'd find a way! You don't even want me to be a trainer! You think I can't! I know you do! The way you look at me! You think I can't do anything right! But Mr. Farley says different! He says I'd be good at it! And I will, you just wait and. . . ." But at the prospect of the obstacles yet before her and the sight of her parents' sympathetic faces, Corinne's mouth opened in a prolonged wail.

Vivian turned to Harry. She drew her brows together and gave a little nod.

Harry instantly understood. "Baby!" he murmured, and put his arms around his daughter and stroked her hair.

"I'm not a baby!" cried Corinne, her eyes squeezed shut. But she leaned into the warm security of her father's embrace and sobbed comfortably against his chest.

Corinne went off to bed early, reassured that their home would not be sold overnight or perhaps ever, although she did not believe the "perhaps ever." Propped up against her pillows, she opened her diary and contemplated the page, ten red lines in all, allotted for that day. Often she had difficulty filling ten lines. Many days were shuffled off with: "Nothing much happened today. Talk to you tomorrow." But tonight, petted and soothed by both father and mother, she had a sense of excitement, of imminent change. Her chest muscles were tired but pleasantly relaxed. Her eyes, washed clean of resentment, were bright and wider than usual, her small, unconscious smile expectant. Masie's bold jump was proudly recorded in green ink with many flourishes of the pen. The scene at the table was translated into brief exclamations: "We may sell this house! Our whole lives may change! Who knows what might happen!" Corinne raised her head, her glance darting swiftly about, seeing not the familiar room or the home for which she had professed such violent attachment, but the unformed possibilities of the future. Happy from sheer suspense, she firmly added two more exclamation marks.

Left to themselves, Harry and Vivian had talked very little. The prospect of change and their daughter's tears had made them both quiet and contemplative. All day Harry had been in a strange mental state. He had not been despondent—Jenny's presence had kept him from that—but he had lacked his usual sure sense of direction. For Harry, that in itself was disturbing, for he needed to know always exactly where he was going, to see ahead a definite goal as distinct as the posts on the football field. Now as he emptied his pockets of coins and keys and flung his trousers across a chairback, he felt the excitement of anticipation, of having a rough outline of the future to perfect. He scrubbed his teeth with unusual vigor, splashing foamy blobs on bowl and mirror.

Vivian's proposal had startled him, but he was pleased by how swiftly he had perceived the possibilities. One change heralded many, and the expectation of action made him strong and decisive. He was ready now to make difficult decisions. He saw clearly that Logan's idea of buying the old skating rink, tearing it down and building an apartment complex was a good one. He would tell him so tomorrow. Sidetracked by his own image, Harry leaned forward and bared his teeth. Good teeth. Straight. Still white. He slewed his jaw to one side. Still a clean line. No trace of a jowl. He padded back to the bedroom, aware without really looking that Vivian, in her nightgown, was stooping over near the closet door. The full satiny curve of her hip brought to his mind Jenny's swing and swish as she walked about the office, her high heels tapping out: look at me, look at me. Not wanting to be distracted from this pleasurable train of thought, Harry got quickly into bed and turned on his side.

Vivian sat at her dressing table languidly brushing her hair, the electricity of it crackling softly as fine strands flew out and clung to her cheek and hand. A small lamp with a ruffled shade cast a flattering light on the silver-backed hand mirror and on the crystal perfume bottles, herded together on a glass tray with a tiny silver fence. Vivian's reflection in the oval wall mirror was as mellow as an old photograph. Beyond her the room was dim; the foot of the bed and the elongated ridge that was Harry were barely discernible. Her gown, designed to set off her firm rounded arms and small breasts, was Harry's favorite. She had worn it to attract his attention, and hearing him come out of the bathroom, had expected as she bent over to feel his familiar, caressing slap on her bottom and, when she straightened in mock indignation, to be closely embraced. She saw in the mirror that he lay quite still. She fussed about, made a small clatter, but he didn't stir. Sighing, Vivian rose and went to stand at the window.

There was no moon, but the pinkish downtown lights cast a soft glow against the dark and, beyond, the spotlighted smokestacks were luminous, eerily disembodied in the night sky. Down the block a street lamp shed a cone of light. A prowling cat sniffed its edges, then disappeared. A faint mist was rising through the trees along the river, and from its banks the tireless night singers filled the dark with pulsing life. The night air was soft, beckoning.

It filled Vivian with a longing to go outside and walk through the damp grass.

She turned, glanced down at Harry. He appeared to be asleep, but he was shamming. She knew his face asleep. It would be slack and vacant, not firm and with the trace of a smile on his lips. At that moment she knew he thought of someone else as surely as if his eyes had popped open and he had grinned in agreement.

She turned off the lamp and got into bed. Lying straight and separate, she gazed into the dark and into her emptiness stepped Marvel Gibson. All day she had deliberately kept him out, but now, unhindered, there he was, confronting her. She was surprised by how strongly his presence invaded her memory. His expression was enigmatic, disposed to be both challenging and gentle. Recalling him at leisure, she admired his style, suave yet commanding, the angle of his hat, the flash of gold watch and diamond ring. She heard with pleasure the quality of his voice, incisive but with a subtle Southern tinge that suggested warmth and tenderness. She was no longer angry. She even admired his cleverness. Their contest of wills, in itself, was unimportant. What was important was that they had clashed. With one long look they had been drawn together. It was only natural that they had taken each other's measure.

Vivian settled into a more comfortable position. She was growing drowsy, but her thoughts circled round and round Marvel, his stance, his gestures, his quick, unexpected smile, imbuing him with ever greater depth and charm. She turned her face contentedly against her pillow as her fading consciousness began spinning a new dream.

THREE

Accidents

If Marvel Gibson hadn't honked at her, Vivian would not have hit Wilder Fulford's dog. As she glanced into the rear-view mirror at the sky blue Lincoln Continental looming behind her, she felt a thud and heard a scream. She hit her brakes, and the Continental swerved past and pulled into the curb. A little girl followed by a man frantically waving his arms rushed toward the front of her car, the little girl crying out, "James! James!"

For one breath-stopping moment Vivian thought she had hit a child. But there, struggling to rise, was a small, marmalade-colored dog. Head extended, he strained forward on his front legs, trying to walk, but one hind leg jerked convulsively and the other dragged disconnectedly behind him. Sobbing, the little girl knelt beside the dog and tried to hold his head. The man, in rolled-up shirt sleeves and suspenders, bent over them both, making inarticulate noises. Vivian first felt an unspeakable relief that it was not a child lying there, then remorse and compassion for the dog, obviously in pain, and the crying child.

"I am so sorry!" exclaimed Vivian, "so terribly sorry! He must get to a vet at once! Come on! I'll take you!"

"Nothing a vet can do for him," said Marvel. "He's a goner." Marvel had come up behind them and stood at ease, one thumb hooked into his belt.

22

They all turned on him, the little girl with fresh and louder cries, the man with shock, Vivian with anger.

"I'm *sure* the vet can help him." She spoke positively and with that peculiar emphasis which meant she was really saying two different things at the same time. Harry would have recognized it instantly and understood she was trying to ease the child's distress. But Marvel merely raised his eyebrows above the rim of his glasses.

"I don't have a car," said the man, helplessly.

"I will take you," said Vivian firmly. "Get a blanket or something to wrap him in."

"I'm going too!" declared the child.

"You don't have enough room," said Marvel. "Park your car. I'll take everybody."

"I said I would take him and I will," said Vivian flatly. "She can squeeze in the back."

"Then I'll come with you," said Marvel. "In my car."

Guy Leatherwood, D.V.S., was a quiet, unassuming man of lanky build and uniform color, hair, eyes, complexion, all a faded, washed-out brown. He was having a busy day because his assistant, in a fit of impatience, had tried, with striking results, to remove a cat from a cage by its tail. The assistant was now being treated at the hospital, and Dr. Leatherwood was left by himself to care for the animals in the kennels, answer the phone and handle incoming patients. He had been measuring out food for an assortment of frenziedly yapping dogs when the buzzer in the waiting room sounded.

Entering the office, he was confronted by a tearful child, a woman with striking gold hair and two men. One, wearing dark glasses and a wide-brimmed hat, reminded him of the riverboat gambler he had seen on the late show the night before. The other, in a battered flat-crowned hat, stared at him through wire rims like a Saint Bernard with glasses. He also held a bundled-up dog whose dulled, pain-filled eyes were a familiar sight to Dr. Leatherwood. They all began speaking to him at once. Only the dog was quiet, and he, intimidated by the furious yapping still to be heard through the inner door, hid his head in the folds of the blanket.

Dr. Leatherwood held up his hand. "Please. One at a time." In a watchful silence punctuated by the little girl's sniffles, he got out a form and inserted it in the typewriter. "Who is the owner?"

"I am," said the man holding the dog.

"And your name?"

"Fulford." His voice was hushed as if he were giving out confidential information. "Wilder."

"Fulford Wilder," murmured Dr. Leatherwood, typing with two fingers.

"No, no. Wilder Fulford." Wilder's eyes, enlarged by his lenses, appeared startled.

"Your address?"

Vivian leaned forward. "I want the bill sent to me at. . . ."

"No, no," protested Wilder.

Dr. Leatherwood looked up. "You're not Mrs. Fulford?"

"No, I'm Mrs. Fox. I'm responsible for what happened, and I want the bill sent to me at. . . ."

"It was really my fault," interrupted Marvel smoothly, "and I will take care of the bill."

"That's perfectly silly!" exclaimed Vivian.

"If I hadn't honked at you. . . ."

"You're not Mr. Fox?" inquired the doctor, regarding them all with interest.

Marvel's left cheek dimpled as he smiled broadly and glanced sideways at Vivian. "Unfortunately, no. I'm Marvel Gibson. Real estate. And auctions."

"Ah yes," said Dr. Leatherwood. His eye fell speculatively on the little girl, staring solemnly at him across the desk top, her eyes and nose reddened from crying.

"I'm Rilly," she said. "Rilly MacGregor."

Dr. Leatherwood looked up at the others and almost smiled.

"The bill," said Vivian insistently, "will be sent to me. And please hurry!"

When the form was completed, Dr. Leatherwood invited Wilder and James into his examining room.

"I want to go too," said Rilly.

"I'd rather you stayed here," said Wilder, and the door closed behind them.

Often, during the past week, Vivian had imagined encounters with Marvel, but never like this. Where they met, or how, was never clear, was indeed unimportant. They were simply together, in a soft, dim nowhere. Because neither of them was free, an aura of sadness heightened the poignancy of their meeting. They spoke little, having no need for words. Marvel, who completely understood, would hold her close despite her faint protests and comfort her, just because he *did* understand. Always she gently touched the hollow in his cheek before he bent to kiss her. And always, just before his lips touched hers, the dream itself swooned away, only to recur, tantalizingly, again and again. Though they were close together, his face lacked definition, the features so vague and indistinct as to be unrecognizable. Still she knew him by the warmth and strength of his presence which were dearly familiar to her and filled her waking dreams. Somewhere within the actual man there existed, compelling and irresistible, this emotion, which they shared, which was as yet unacknowledged.

Now, unexpectedly, she was confined with a strange child and the real Marvel in a bare room reeking of antiseptic and resounding with the clamor of hungry dogs. Without the bolstering presence of others or the protective front of dispute, Vivian was quite unable to turn her eyes naturally in Marvel's direction. Like James, she wished dumbly to avert her face, afraid that it would betray her, that behind his smoky glasses Marvel would perceive the degree of familiarity she had reached with him. Soberly, in keeping with their reason for being there, Vivian sat down on one of the straight chairs that lined the wall, crossed her knees and smiled at Rilly.

Rilly was a small child with delicate wrists and bony knees. But her face was not babyish. Her curved forehead, straight little nose and, when closed, her small, perfectly bow-shaped mouth might have been those of a lovely eighteen-year-old. Her fine brown hair was held back on one side by a barrette. Her serious, prolonged scrutiny was unnerving. She sidled over and leaned against Vivian's knee. "I know a pome," she said, her brown eyes never wavering.

"Do you?"

"I can say it too. Want to hear it?" Vivian smiled and nodded. In a pronounced sing-song, Rilly recited:

> *Mr. Finney had a turnip,*
> *and it grew behind the barn,*
> *and it grew, and it grew,*
> *and the turnip did no harm.*

Then she pursed her mouth and cocked her head, awaiting comment.

"That's a fine poem," said Vivian, rather surprised. Seeing Rilly expected more, she asked, "Did you learn that in school?"

"I don't go to school yet. I'm not old enough. Mr. Fulford taught me. He lives downstairs with James. We live upstairs, Lena and Pete and me." Rilly paused, then said confidingly, "Lena and Pete are my mother and father, but they want me to call them Lena and Pete, so I do."

Marvel sat down beside Vivian, and Rilly shifted her gaze to him.

"Lena says you should fix the kitchen sink. It drips and makes her mad."

"Well tell your mommy I'll send one of my boys out to fix it."

"Lena," corrected Rilly.

"One of my rentals," said Marvel to Vivian, confiding in his turn. "Three apartments in it, Fulford, Mitchell and one vacant. Wouldn't like an apartment, would you?"

Vivian reached out and smoothed back a strand of Rilly's silky hair. "No, but we *are* looking for a house," she said casually.

Instantly Marvel leaned closer, laid his arm across the back of her chair. "Come around to the office! I've got several listings. Great buys, just on the market. One I know you'd like. It's just your style." His voice glinted with admiration of her style. "When can I show it to you?"

His voice sounded much too close to her ear. Rilly, staring cat-like at them both, pressed uncomfortably against her knees. Feeling hemmed in by the two of them, Vivian rose compulsively, like Venus from the sea, without answering, and was relieved to hear the murmur of voices in the examining room become suddenly clear as the doctor opened the door.

". . . and you can call tomorrow, after one. He should stay here a week anyway, depending on how he comes along."

Wilder backed out, attending to the doctor's words and nodding his understanding.

Rilly rushed over and tugged at Wilder's arm. "Where's James?"

"He'll be all right," Wilder assured her. "He has to have an operation, but he'll be all right."

"I'm so glad!" exclaimed Vivian. "I'll drive you home now."

Marvel followed her out. "I'll call you," he said, and without waiting for a response turned away. He was gone in his sky blue Continental by the time Wilder and Rilly had fitted themselves into Vivian's MG.

All the way back, Wilder was silent. His permanently chapped face was buffeted by the wind, yet he faced resolutely toward the window, so uneasy did he feel sitting beside Vivian. He clasped his hands together on his knees. Only once he reached up to settle his hat more firmly on his head lest it blow off and plunge him into untold embarrassment. To Vivian's suggestion that he could roll up the window, he quickly murmured an apologetic, "No, no. It's fine."

But Rilly complained. "I'm scrunched! I don't like this car! My grandpa's is nicer. I can lie down in his and watch the poles go by."

Vivian didn't answer, but she heard. Rilly's words only confirmed what she already felt, that everything had gone all wrong. She and Marvel had met again, as she had hoped, but how dreadful it had been. He had been unfeeling, tactless. The understanding that should have materialized between them had failed to do so. If only he had behaved differently, or she had been less strident. Disappointed with herself and with him, she screeched around a corner.

"Eeeeeeh!" exclaimed Rilly, gripping the back of the seat. Wilder, transfixed, leaned hard against the door.

Even the car was wrong! It was obviously too small! After all, it didn't really suit her. The pleasure she had experienced in its handling was now lost in the sense she had of its cramped inadequacy. She swerved abruptly in to the curb before Wilder's house and braked to a stop that threw them all forward. Cautiously, Wilder climbed out; Rilly squirmed like an eel after him. Vivian, preoccupied, promised to pick them up when it was time to fetch James home and drove off with a wave of her hand.

While driving the few blocks home, Vivian imagined the car she wanted. Almost immediately she saw herself at the wheel of a large and spacious car, the sunshine glinting off its long, sleek hood as she drove it effortlessly along a winding road above a sheer drop to the sea and across desert flats where jackrabbits bounded across the highway and distant mountains faded into the blue dusk. She saw herself—hair tossed back, a scarf around her neck—opening the door and stepping gracefully out, one shapely leg extended. Vivian knew exactly what she wanted. She wanted a car just like Marvel's.

That evening Vivian told Harry about hitting James.

"James. That's a crazy name for a dog."

"His name doesn't matter. The point is, I hit him. I could have killed him and. . . ."

"Didn't you see him?" inquired Harry, regarding her over the top of the newspaper.

Vivian sighed. "The man in the car behind me honked, I looked up, and in that instant. . . ."

"Why'd he honk?"

"I don't *know* why he honked! He just honked!" Vivian frowned, feeling deceptive. "It was Gibson, the real estate dealer. Do you know him?"

"I've seen him at Kiwanis. Wears a cowboy hat."

"A colonel's hat, I believe," said Vivian pensively. "Anyway, I had to take this man who owns the dog—I'm sure you've seen him. I see him every time I go out. He's always in a hurry, has a funny walk, carries a paper bag."

"Oh yeah," said Harry, his voice full of recognition. "He's knock-kneed, that's why he walks funny. I see him every day. Wears crazy hats. Lives a couple of blocks from here. Never saw a dog with him though."

"That's just it," said Vivian. "He keeps him in. Today he got out and ran into the street. I took him and the dog and a little girl with him to the vet's. Next week I have to take them to pick the dog up." She paused. "Harry, I think the MG is too small."

Harry crushed the newspaper down on his lap and regarded her sharply. "Too small? I thought you wanted a small car."

"I did. But it's *too* small, no good for more than two people. And it's a nuisance to get in and out of when you're carrying something like a dog or the groceries. I want a big car, like a Continental."

"But you've had this one only a month!" protested Harry, still shocked.

"Well, in a month I've found out it's too small." She cocked her head at him. "A tan Continental, that's what I want, tan inside and out." Her smile was a friendly challenge "Why not? After all, we're going to sell all this," waving her hand to include the entire house, "and get a new house. We can trade the MG for another car at the same time! Why not?"

Offhand, Harry couldn't think of a reason, and while she had his attention, Vivian said, "Mr. Gibson says he has some good houses to show. Should I take a look at them?"

"Sure," said Harry, returning to the sports page. "Why not?"

The big blue Continental rolled along the country road with all the cushioned ease of which Detroit was capable. Vivian sat well over on her side, her arm pressed against the door, an expanse of empty seat between her and Marvel. He had called, and she had agreed to meet him at his office, from where they would go to look at a house. As she had parked her car, the heat, unusually intense for mid-June, rose in shimmering waves from the softened macadam and made her wish, in her uneasy state of mind, that she hadn't come. Now, in the insulated coolness of the air-conditioned car, she felt a nervous chill.

They weren't going directly to see a house after all. He had, Marvel explained, maneuvering the car smoothly through traffic, a bit of business to take care of first with an antique dealer in the country. He had been sure—with a sideways glance—she wouldn't mind. Vivian had assured him she didn't, just so she was home by three-thirty, she added firmly.

"Husband's orders?" inquired Marvel playfully.

"Not at all," said Vivian haughtily. But she did mind. And because this unexpected move struck her as high-handed, she declined to explain and sat in composed silence all the way.

The antique dealer lived in an old farmhouse, a frame building with a steep roof, narrow windows and a lower addition at one side with a recessed front porch. Corn fields stretched away on either side, and hanging lopsided on a sagging wire fence was a weathered sign: ANTIQUES and a faded finger pointing down the dirt driveway. Marvel drove past the house and stopped beside a small one-story building whose low-pitched roof extended forward and rested on wooden posts. Under its shelter old chests and dressers were backed against the front wall. Crowded against them were wooden chairs encrusted with coats of chipped paint, part of a spinning wheel, old buckets, pails and jugs and broken-down bushel baskets full of assorted bottles and glass insulators, some clear, some sea green. A tinny bell rang as a woman opened the screen door. Her hair was pinned in a loose knot on top of her head, and she came forward smiling. She and Marvel immediately began discussing an auction, and Vivian bent over to examine the bottles.

A strong sun filled the wide, cloudless sky. It drew a sharp line between light and shade and threw Vivian's shadow on the dry, bare earth in front of the low porch. The murmur of voices behind her was the only sound other than the energetic buzz of blue-green flies, looping in and out of the shade. A fine, powdery dust coated everything Vivian touched and made her fingers grimy. She was examining a little bottle with the date 1915 raised on its base when the noonday quiet was torn by a maniacal scream. She dropped the bottle as another scream, both terrified and terrifying, tore the air. Aghast, she turned in alarm to the others, but the woman smiled, unconcerned, and Marvel grinned. His teeth were very white and sharp in the shade of his hat brim.

As Vivian stared, speechless, Marvel stepped close to her and, sliding his hand around her upper arm, held it against him. "Don't be alarmed," he said, still amused. "That's only the peacocks."

Vivian looked to the woman. "Peacocks?"

The woman nodded pleasantly. "Yes. See, up on the house roof. They fly into the trees and up to the roof. You know, they're better than any watchdog."

"Yes," said Vivian faintly, "I can imagine." To remove herself from Marvel's grasp, she went to stand apart, gazing upward at the peacocks. Their long tail feathers flouncing, they strutted along the ridge of the roof, extending their necks with each step, their sharp beaks partially open.

"We can go now," said Marvel after a few minutes. He took her arm familiarly, as though having once done so, it was natural to do so again. Vivian was affronted by his laughing at her. He might, she felt, have warned her. Now, in his close shepherding of her there was a touch of proprietorship that made her glad when they reached the car, and again she sat as far away as she could. His touch on her arm remained like a lingering burn.

"You're upset," said Marvel, turning onto the highway.

"Not at all," said Vivian coolly, looking out at the rows of corn passing like the opening and closing ribs of a fan.

"You're angry at me," said Marvel shrewdly, "because I laughed."

At that Vivian had to smile. They glanced at each other and laughed. She thought it a tie, he a victory. But their laughing together brought about a relaxed sense of comradeship.

Later, when Vivian tried to recall what they had spoken of, she could remember only scraps of conversation. They had arrived, very quickly, it seemed to her, at a house in a new development on the western edge of town. The newly paved streets, looking somehow whitewashed and full of curves and turnabouts, were confusingly alike. When Marvel pulled into a driveway scarcely longer than the Continental, whose bumper nudged the embossed two-car garage door, Vivian could have been anywhere. Or nowhere. The entire area was raw, unfinished, the earth scoured out. The street was already cracked. Torn cement bags lay in the gutter. The front yards were seamed with strips of sod clumsily laid and withering in the sun. The houses, whose roof levels alternated regularly like the cogs of a wheel, were characterless. The added touches of a brick planter, a cunning lattice, or a panel of opaque glass blocks, like different wigs on identical plastic dolls, only pointed up the sameness of their pastel-tinted fronts.

Together they toured the house, a large, expensive split-level. Marvel stayed very close to her, reaching in front of her to open doors, from behind her to open cupboards, then again to shut them. Moving soundlessly on the wall-to-wall carpet through the sunny, empty rooms, he seemed to surround her, all but embrace her. When they stood at the kitchen window, his suit coat was against her shoulder as he raised his arm to point out the view, a patch of terrace, a brick grill and some bumpy strips of sod. Thirty feet beyond, like a mirror image, were more sod, another terrace, grill and kitchen window. Vivian's mind registered these facts, but she found it more and more difficult to speak because of his closeness and his scent, which brought him closer still. When they went up the padded stairs, his silent presence was a bare step behind her, and her sense of his eyes upon her so filled her with torpor that her legs moved as if weighted with lead. After an endless moment of dream-like slow motion, she reached the landing safely and stepped with as much unconcern as she could muster into the master bedroom. Again Marvel directed her to a window, where, with a clever twist, he snapped out what had seemed to be wood stripping dividing the window into six panes.

"See?" he said, holding it up, "plastic! Removable plastic! Makes it easy to clean." He snapped the form back into place and turned, his face very near hers. As he studied her through his glasses, in which she saw herself darkly reflected, she felt herself blush. Raising both hands, Marvel gently smoothed back her hair, removed her sunglasses and with a bemused smile, leaned forward and kissed her. Lifting his head a fraction, he paused thoughtfully, then kissed her again, the brim of his hat shading them both.

Dazzled by this relatively close approximation of her dream, Vivian stood perfectly still as he carefully replaced her glasses, then followed as he led her through the other rooms. As if nothing out of the ordinary had occurred, he pointed out to her all the advantages of the house to a couple with only one grown daughter. Vivian had not been so led since she was a child, trailing at her father's heels. She barely responded to his remarks, moving all the while in a daze, her senses spellbound. Her face was still warm, and her lips quivered slightly, wanting to smile. She avoided looking directly at him. But that was not difficult, for Marvel was entirely business-like, concerned only with selling a house.

Downstairs, he glanced at her, then at his watch, ushered her out and locked the door.

"Have to get you home before too long," he remarked with a quick smile.

He zoomed out of the driveway considerably faster than he had pulled in, and instead of turning toward town, drove south along the river.

"I own this whole section along here," he said, waving his hand. "I'm going to cut down the trees and package it. Build houses and sell house and lot together. Pretty good view from the bluff." He turned off onto a dirt road whose weed-grown ruts even the Continental couldn't altogether smooth out. They bounced along, turning abruptly this way and that as the road accommodated the slope, then came to a stop beside a grove of trees on one side and a view, partly obscured by bushes, of the river on the other.

"Great spot, isn't it?" inquired Marvel with a deep, satisfied sigh, seeming to inhale the sweet country air though the windows were closed. He dropped his hat on the back seat, placed his glasses on the dashboard and turned to Vivian.

It was the first time she had seen him without hat and glasses, and for a moment he appeared drastically reduced, like an actor who had taken off both mask and shoe lifts. His straight, brown hair was combed smoothly back from a high forehead, which bore a faint red groove from his hat band. His stone-gray eyes were neither large nor small. His nose was straight and sharp, his mouth rather thin. Like his clothes, his face had a finished, polished look, neat and symmetrical. And, a great asset, it was readily adaptable, reflecting instantly what the occasion required. But behind every expression, however sober, amused or tender, was a bright, hard core.

Vivian had little time to react to Marvel revealed, for he smiled winningly, put his arms around her and drew her close. At once her dream burst into life. Overwhelmed with an emotion very akin to relief, Vivian eagerly took up her part. She leaned into his embrace, transported. Slowly she reached up to touch his cheek. But Marvel, misled by her response, pressed his mouth to hers with such fervor that his teeth cut her lip, and her hand landed on the back of his head. She attempted to stroke his hair, her fingers surprised by its softness. His embrace tightened, hurting her ribs. Marvel, delighted with her pliance, mistook her gasp of pain for passion. Nuzzling his face against the curve of her neck, he began to caress her breast and side. Startled, Vivian opened her eyes wide; filled with growing alarm, she felt his hand stroking her thigh and herself pushed backward. Their meeting was not to be like this! Their profound but restrained affinity for one another, their graceful gestures, the sweet-sad ambiance in which they met—all were lost in this awkward, panting struggle. Dismayed, Vivian stiffened, pushed away and swerved her knees to one side. Surprised, Marvel raised his head. Vivian averted hers.

Seeing the shine of tears in her eyes, Marvel was instantly contrite. He put an arm around her shoulders and drew her head gently to his chest. He stroked her pale gold hair and laid his cheek against the top of her head.

After a time, her agitation allayed by his paternal comfort,

Vivian recovered and sat up, though still within the circle of his arm.

"I'll take you home now," murmured Marvel. His long, slim fingers held her chin. He smiled into her docile eyes with understanding and kissed her twice. The first kiss was wistful and sad. The second was hard and firm and spoke of future promise.

That morning Belvedera Gibson (Belvedera Carlino before her marriage to Marvel) had flexed her long agile body, every joint, starting with her toes and ending with her fingers, stretched above her head. Rising swiftly, she had thrown on a robe and walked barefoot into the bathroom, where Marvel was shaving. Without shoes Belvedera was just his height. Their eyes met briefly in the long, rectangular mirror. Attentive to his face, Marvel rolled the electric razor carefully over his skin, thrusting out his chin and curving his lip inward. Belvedera thrust out her chin and curved her lip. Her whole face took on an expression of insane concentration, her brown eyes staring; with elbows sharply bent she mimicked his gestures: distending her cheek with her tongue, pulling up the skin along the jaw, pausing to check for a missed bit of stubble.

"Bel!" growled Marvel, flashing her a look.

"My father never used one of those things," she remarked, dropping her arms and her act. "He made a good lather, then shaved it off with a good blade."

"This is a good blade. It's double."

"Bah," said Belvedera. She moved to the other twin bowl and, making a suds, applied blobs of soap to both cheeks. Marvel glanced over, then splashed cologne on his face and began combing his hair, eyeing himself at an angle to be certain every hair was neatly in place. Bel watched him, then dabbed another blob in the middle of her forehead and one on her chin.

Shirt on and tie knotted, Marvel patted his pockets and turned to his wife. "Okay, Bel. Don't bother with breakfast. I'll pick up something." Her long black hair disheveled, her face streaked by blobs of foam, she regarded him like a mournful clown, and he had to grin. "Wash your face, Bel. I'll see you at dinner."

Belvedera and Marvel had no children but they had a very large home, visited often by Belvedera's aged parents, brothers and sisters accompanied by their husbands, wives and children and more uncles, aunts and cousins than Marvel had ever been able to remember. But he was a generous host and enjoyed having them fill the large dining room on Sundays. Belvedera was proud of Marvel. He worked hard. With shrewdness and finesse, he had built his realty business into one of the largest in the state, and for that Belvedera respected him. She also loved him, though when she wondered why—as she quite occasionally did—the only answer was that he suited her perfectly, his face, his voice, himself. Even the presents he brought her she treasured, though she recognized them as penitential offerings marking the end of an affair he supposed her ignorant of. She loved the innocent way he presented them, with immense self-satisfaction, never doubting they would please her. Always they were expensive and entirely unsuitable, so that she could honestly laugh with delight and amusement as she put on the beads that went with nothing, the blouse that made her look gawky, or hung up the painting whose incredibly bad taste made her smile each time she passed it.

She knew all the signs of an awakened interest, and this morning she had seen them, not just the infinite pains with his appearance but a certain detachment, a figurative brotherly clap on the shoulder as he went off for the day. She would be ready for him when he returned.

Marvel spent some time pondering Vivian's behavior, unusual in his experience. First, no response but also no protest. Then, strong response followed by strong protest, and that was followed not by rejection but a most agreeable harmony. In the end he credited her with temperament, a quality he fully appreciated. She was more complicated than he had imagined, more challenging, and he enjoyed a challenge. He was to take her to see another, better house next week, and he never doubted the outcome.

Belvedera was indeed ready for him when he came home. He entered the kitchen, which was redolent of tomato sauce, directly from the garage and at first thought some stray relative was helping Bel. A woman in carpet slippers, long skirt and apron stood at the sink; the ends of an old bandana, knotted at the back, flared out above her shoulders.

"Ah!" she said, turning. "It is you! Me, I am the pasta lady, and the pasta," holding up a long, pale strand, "is al dente! You will please take your seat!"

"Bel, what the hell. . . ."

"Never mind hell. We are not there yet. Please sit."

Belvedera was a fine cook and, knowing her own worth, expected prompt attendance at the table. Marvel sat. Belvedera removed the bandana, shook loose her hair and sat opposite him. Solemnly, she watched him eat, trying to divine what sort of woman he had spent the afternoon with. When he looked up at her, she picked up a limp strand of pasta, draped it across her forehead like a string of pearls, put her elbow on the table and leaned her chin forward on her hand, gazing at him through half-closed eyes.

Marvel laughed. "Bel, take it off!"

Not moving, Belvedera spoke in an affectedly langorous voice. "Take off . . . what?"

"Come off it, Bel!" But he was grinning and began telling her about his plan to sell one of his old apartment houses.

After spending the evening calculating returns on investments, taxes, mortgage rates and loans, Marvel was settling back in his favorite armchair, his mind free to think of Vivian. He recalled the feel of her and her extraordinary hair against his face. Then into his line of vision came Belvedera. She wore a long nightgown and negligee, purple, with white boa trim around the neck and down the sides. It was his latest gift to her. The negligee hung open so that as she crossed the room toward him with a curious, cat-like step, it parted in graceful folds, rippling behind her as she walked. The gown outlined her long legs and slim, boyish hips.

She stopped directly in front of him. "Like it?" she asked. With her arms out from her sides, fingers pointed, she pivoted, causing the gown and negligee to whirl out from her ankles.

"Mmmmn," said Marvel, "very nice."

"You gave it to me, remember? Just last fall."

"Mmmmn," said Marvel.

In one smooth movement Belvedera sat down at his feet, crossed both hands over his knee and rested her chin on them. Calculatingly she gazed up at him.

Marvel smiled down at her, his dimple gradually deepening.

Cupping the back of her head, he leaned forward and kissed her. Rather tentatively, Belvedera thought. It crossed her mind to reach up and touch his cheek, but that was the obvious thing. She shut her mind against the thought of how many women had done just that. Instead she held up her face, inviting another kiss. This time it was warm and lingering.

"You're asking for it, Bel," murmured Marvel.

"I am," agreed Belvedera.

That night Marvel never thought of Vivian, not even fleetingly. He breakfasted well, and all that day she never once occurred to him.

Harry's day had not been a good one. Jenny had called to say she would not be coming to work. No, she was not ill (Harry had a sudden vision of going enthusiastically to her rescue, she alone and helpless, he holding her up so she could swallow, painfully but gratefully, the medicine he had brought); she simply had things demanding to be done. She would make up the time on Saturday. Instantly Harry's day lengthened and lost its spark. Her chair with the shiny rollers and padded, arched back support was pushed under her desk; the desk itself was lifelessly neat. Where Jenny should have been, where he counted on her being, was an intolerable emptiness. Disappointment on two counts turned into irritation. Harry abandoned his own office, swung Jenny's chair out, sat down hard and spread papers all over her desk. He transacted the day's business in a brusque tone surprising to his older clients.

At the Kiwanis luncheon he approached Marvel Gibson, who had handled the sale of his parents' home, to ask about the present owners. "Think they'd be interested in selling?"

"Doubt it," said Marvel, eyeing Harry with special interest. "They just bought an expensive tractor and spreader." Seeing Harry's face darken, he asked, "You folks changed your minds? I thought you were interested in a *new* house. I'm showing one to your wife this afternoon."

Harry shook his head. "Just wondered." Then, needing to express his feeling, added, "It's the old homestead, you know. Some day. . . ." He let it drop, shook his head again. "It's not the kind of house Vivian and I want at all."

But Marvel never closed the door on any possibility. Studying Harry and scenting two sales, he said, "I'll ask around. If I hear anything, I'll let you know."

Harry, appetite gone, abandoned his apple pie a la mode, leaving the ice cream to melt into a puddle around the sugared cardboard crust, and returned to the office.

Logan Gamble was a man with a jaunty walk and a quick grin, and when he grinned, his eyes crinkled together until only a shiny line could be seen between his lids. He generally acted on impulse; nevertheless, having once taken a position, no matter how rash, he could not be shifted an inch. Only for Harry would he think twice. If Harry asked him to reconsider, he would do so earnestly, running his fingers through his tightly curled brown hair. As a high school freshman, Logan had been awestruck watching Harry play football. He had seen Harry as lithe and agile but bruisingly strong, quietly modest yet commanding the entire team. Harry, standing on the field, with huge, humped shoulders, hands delicately placed on hips, one knee forward and slightly bent in a stance both graceful and menacing, had been more than life-size. He had thrilled the stands. He had thrilled Logan, who stood in the rain, in snow and sleet and shouted wildly through a rasping throat. For him, Harry off the field was a hero still, only thinly disguised, and Logan had dogged Harry's footsteps until Harry had accepted him as friend. When Harry married, Logan was his best man. When Harry went into the insurance business, Logan became his partner as a matter of course.

When Logan strode into the office, his airy heels hitting the floor at an angle as if on the point of executing a dance step, he found Harry sitting at Jenny's desk.

"Where's Jenny?"

"Where've you been all day?" Harry's tone was aggressive. He disliked hearing her name spoken familiarly by another man, even his best friend.

Logan, arms and legs all angles, folded like a loosely jointed puppet onto a chair. He leaned one sharp elbow on the desk and grinned at Harry. "God, but it's hot! Let's close up early and get a beer. We've got to talk."

"About what?" asked Harry, his eyes steadily on Logan. "What's wrong?"

"How d'you know anything's wrong?"

"Just by looking at you," said Harry flatly. "And because everything has been wrong all day."

"Well!" Logan slapped his thigh. "Seems someone else is interested in buying the rink. The price has been upped."

Harry's jaw set. "Who?"

"Don't know. Joe said the owner called him and said a friend had offered five thousand above our price."

Harry stared intently at Logan. His lips curled inward. Just so had he looked on the field when confronted by the treachery of an opposing team. Logan waited, his eyes bright.

"We'll go ten."

"Ten! Have we got it?"

"We've got it," said Harry, "and more. I *want* that property!"

"Okay," said Logan. "Great. You'll get it. Maybe we won't have to go ten, maybe only seven or eight."

Harry demurred, slowly closing and opening his eyes and giving the tiniest shake of his head. "Ten," he repeated.

Logan grinned, delighted by Harry's style. "How about that beer?"

"Sorry, Logan, not now. I've got a little matter to see to for Vivian on my way home."

Harry's stop at the car dealer's only deepened his gloom. He had not been happy about the extra ten for the rink. Now, in trading an almost new MG for a Continental he was out another four.

Three blocks from home he passed Wilder Fulford. Wilder was puffing along, mouth open, glasses barely on his nose. Though hurrying, he never took time for a full stride. His knees brushed each other as if he were constantly going upstairs. His tight suspenders caused his shirt to bulge out over his hunched shoulders, and from under his squashed hat his hair lay in limp strands on his forehead. Man looks overheated, thought Harry, and wondered what was in the paper bag. Bottle of bourbon, most likely. And dog food. It struck Harry, who rarely drank, that a drink was what he himself needed.

Vivian was extremely agitated. She had driven home in a daze, her hands and feet performing as if programmed. A block away she stopped to let the jogger cross. Because of the heat, the woman wore a tank top and red shorts whose side seams curved like petals over her thighs. Her thick socks and running shoes dwarfed her legs, making them appear dangerously thin, susceptible to snapping like dried sticks. For the first time Vivian experienced a fellow feeling for her. She labored to lift each foot, yet on she went, chin forward, mouth gasping, like a wound-up toy bound to run whatever the direction until the mechanism itself ran down and stopped. Vivian felt herself impelled on a course whose eventual outcome she had not considered and did not even want to anticipate. She could not fix her mind on two consecutive thoughts. As she focused on one, others crowded forward in bewildering confusion. Her mind circled round and about her experience with Marvel, trying to recapture those few moments that coincided with her dreams, skirting others that brought only a shudder.

The house, high ceilinged and curtained, was quiet and cool. Still Vivian wandered restlessly from room to room. She went upstairs, found no reason to be there, came back down. She adjusted a lamp shade, checked the mantel for dust. So ambivalent was she toward Marvel, so alternately repelled and attracted, that she yearned for Harry to come home. She longed to see his face, to look into his eyes and be reassured. Harry was strong and steady. She dismissed the recently widening distance between them. That was trivial, surely, a matter of routine, or preoccupation or tiredness. Thinking of Harry gave her a sense of direction, and in a sudden burst of loving gratitude for so stable a man, she rushed to the kitchen, resolved to please him. For the next hour or two she worked in an almost happy, excited frame of mind as though she were preparing for a party. For the moment, Harry's arrival was itself the solution, and her thoughts went no further.

When the screen door banged, Vivian turned from the stove, eager but surprised. Harry never let the door bang. He strode into the kitchen. His eyes, exceptionally hard and blue in the gloom of his face, barely flicked her a glance. He muttered a greeting and went on to the dining room, where he began opening and banging doors. Puzzled, Vivian followed him, a forgotten hot pad in her hand.

"What are you looking for?"

He turned angrily. "A bottle! What else!"

Without a word Vivian opened a cupboard, took out a bottle

and handed it to him. She watched him pour the liquor, swirl water into it, take a gulp and grimace. She knew that he didn't like it, that he considered alcohol an insult to mind and body.

"What's wrong?" she asked.

"What d'you mean, what's wrong? Can't a man have a drink in his own home?" He rolled his head back and took another swallow as if he were downing medicine.

"Dinner is ready," said Vivian. Her expectation that Harry's presence would be restorative was gone. This was a strange Harry, disturbing rather than reassuring. She went to summon Corinne, studying for finals in the tower room. Vivian walked pensively up the two long flights of stairs instead of calling from the second floor as she normally would. Coming down, she took each step at a thoughtful, even pace.

Corinne clattered behind her on wooden clogs, almost stepping on Vivian's heels, talking volubly of how many equations she had memorized and exclaiming over the endless number she had yet to cram. When they reached the downstairs hall, she was struck by her mother's persistent silence. When they joined Harry at the table and she saw the glass in her father's hand, she was immediately apprehensive.

"What's wrong?" she asked.

Harry paused, glass raised. He squinted suspiciously at Corinne, then at Vivian. In the face of their questioning stares, he rose, refilled his glass, and sat down again in stony silence.

Abashed, Corinne began to eat, trying to make as little noise as possible, the slightest clink a magnified crash in the silence that oppressed them. Now and again she ventured a puzzled glance at her parents. She caught her mother studying her father with an expression that made her still more uneasy. Finishing quickly, she excused herself and hurried upstairs where the atmosphere was lighter.

Vivian was indeed studying Harry. She wondered with grave concern what could have happened to so upset him, then noted resentfully how he chopped at the food she had taken such pains with just for him. She worried that perhaps a deal important to him had fallen through, then saw with disgust how ostentatiously he removed a piece of meat from his mouth, placing it on the edge of his plate as if she had deliberately offended him. She was moved by a deep sympathy as his hand reached out for his glass, paused, and took up his fork instead, then observed, bitterly, that he had no care or interest to spare for her.

Thrown back on herself, Vivian made a pretense of reading the evening paper. She stood for a time at the back door and noted that the grass needed cutting. She wandered back and forth and watched Harry watching a baseball game on television. And all the while Harry and Marvel jostled each other in her thoughts.

As the sports announcer's voice waxed and waned, now excited, now hushed, now rising with the roar of the fans to a crescendo, the silence between Harry and herself weighed more heavily on Vivian. Harry was stretched out in his chair, his head resting against its back. He had not stirred in an hour. The announcer might have been talking to himself. Restless and increasingly anxious, Vivian settled on the edge of a chair near Harry and leaned slightly forward in an attempt to catch his eye. The game was over, and he appeared to be either watching the news or dozing. Actually he was holding very still, so the pounding in his head would not reach blinding proportions, and dreaming of Jenny, sweetly innocent, girlish Jenny. At the moment Vivian spoke to him, he was leading Jenny by the hand through the old rink, explaining his plans for a beautiful apartment complex, the Fox Apartments. And she was listening, face upturned, her eyes glowing with admiration, her mouth. . . .

"Harry," said Vivian again. "Harry . . . . Marvel Gibson showed me a house today, in that new subdivision west of town. Harry?"

"I heard you!" exclaimed Harry. "I'm trying to listen to the news!" In his irritation he jerked his head, causing its insides to spin in an opposite direction. He squinted with pain, and speaking slowly so it could settle, he said, "I know. He told me he was going to and I said okay, go ahead."

"Oh," said Vivian, somewhat put out that they should have discussed it. "Why didn't you tell me?"

After a pause he grumbled, "It was just in passing. We were talking about something else."

"What?"

Harry closed his eyes. "Just business."

Vivian contemplated him a moment, then asked, "Don't you even want to hear about the house I saw?"

"Mmmn," said Harry.

Vivian began to describe it, saw he was not listening and stopped in the middle of a sentence.

After a brief silence filled by the over-jovial tones of the weatherman, Harry cleared his throat and spoke at random. "Guess you'll have to go on looking." He raised himself carefully out of his chair, tested his knees and flexed his shoulders. "I'm going to bed."

In the dim, roseate light of their bedroom, Vivian stood by the dressing table, one hand loosely holding her hairbrush. But she had no interest in brushing her hair. A dreadful sense of loneliness filled her chest and constricted her throat. The night was surprisingly hot and humid for mid-June, and she had put on without thought or guile a filmy nightgown with tiny straps (seen in magazines in full color on models whose bared breasts and arch smiles seduced both imagination and pocketbook). Despite the still, warm air, she trembled from an inner chill, and the reflective top of the dressing table blurred as moisture suddenly filmed her eyes.

She turned and went to Harry, who was pulling his arms out of his shirt sleeves. "Harry," she said softly, "Harry, please. . . ." Unable to put her feeling into words, she touched his chest lightly, imploringly, with her fingertips.

Tossing aside his shirt, Harry, unheeding, looked at her and frowned. With sharp distaste, he said, "Why don't you put something on. You can see right through that thing." Then he sat down and bent over to untie his shoes.

Vivian stood as if struck. The blood seemed to drain from her face. Her nose and mouth felt pinched. Dumbly, she stared at the top of his head until, overwhelmed by the need to escape his presence, she went swiftly up the stairs to the tower room and shut the door.

In the dark, she stumbled over Corinne's books and half fell onto the large floor pillows. Sitting with her knees drawn up, she pressed her fists against her face, her mind too stunned to think. A tremor shook her, and reaching around, she pulled an old cotton quilt up over her shoulders. With no sense of the passage of time, she sat hunched over, eyes tight shut, while the shame she felt slowly subsided. She raised her head when she heard soft footsteps on the stairs and Harry's cautious whisper.

"Viv?"

She made no sound, and after an interval she heard the footsteps fade away. She could just see him, going away shrugging his shoulders, thinking she would sleep it off and be fine in the morning. Her lip curled with scorn. His voice had awakened her anger and resentment. Anger was stabilizing. She was no longer inclined to cry. He had, after all, solved her problem.

Corinne had left open the windows that framed three sides of the small room. The night air, heavy with the scent of rain, billowed the thin, ghostly curtains. To the east the glow from the town and the foundry lights illumined the underside of low-rolling clouds. A distant thunder vibrated, and for an instant the edges of a vast cloud bank flashed out in vivid rose and were gone, only to reappear at fitful intervals.

It would rain before morning. Gazing out into the soft, moving dark, Vivian relived her afternoon with Marvel, viewing it like a film against the background of the night. So conjured up, everything about Marvel was enhanced. His features were distinguished, his eyes softer, his manner almost courtly. She held her arm where he had held it. His amusement at her fright now turned into fond indulgence. Another time she would understand. Indulgent in her turn, she smiled to herself at his self-assurance and his attempts to impress her with what he knew and what he owned. Her moment of panic now seemed foolish. She was, after all, an experienced, married woman and should not have behaved like a silly girl. What had made her shudder earlier in the day was now excised altogether, as if it had never happened. She remembered that he had understood and been gentle, comforting. She imagined she had never felt more protected, more secure.

Reaching up, Vivian partially closed the windows, then adjusted the pillows and settled down under the quilt. The damp air was pleasantly cool against her forehead. A few advance raindrops pinged against the glass. Marvel had said he would call next week. As she drowsed off, the pillows assumed the contour of his chest, the quilt his encircling arm. She fell asleep wrapped in her dream.

FOUR

Puppy Love

James came home on three legs. Only Wilder was forewarned. He had been to visit James twice in one week, taking him some of his favorite vanilla wafers to keep his spirits up. Wilder had walked the four miles to the vet's and the four miles back, saying nothing to anyone. For Wilder, walking eight miles was far easier than being near Vivian.

A knock on Wilder's door was rare. Only Rilly knocked. Her parents walked right in on the heels of their greeting. When Wilder opened his door to Vivian he thought, for a split second, that this figure in a full-skirted flowered dress and shining red-gold hair was an apparition, so out of place was she in the narrow hallway with its dun-colored walls. When she jingled her car keys and spoke, he knew she was real.

"Mr. Fulford? I've come to take you to pick up your dog. Dr. Leatherwood said he's ready to come home." When Wilder, flustered and uncertain whether he should ask her to step in or he should step out, didn't immediately answer, she said with a rising inflection meant to jog his memory, "I'm Mrs. Fox . . . last week I. . . ."

"Yes, yes," said Wilder, hastening to stop further explanation. "I'm coming. I mean I'm ready. Or would you like to. . . ." he stepped back and extended his arm as an invitation to enter.

45

"Not now, thanks," said Vivian, smiling. "If you're ready, we can go."

Dazzled, Wilder followed her to the car and sat perfectly still all the way, elbows in, hands gripped together on his knees.

Dr. Leatherwood handed James over, wrapped as before in his blanket, but a different, ecstatic James, who wiggled and whined and strove, with forepaws against Wilder's chest, to lick his chin.

"The others didn't come, I see," remarked Dr. Leatherwood, somewhat disappointed. "Keep him in until he's completely healed. If you have any trouble, call, or," he added, raising his eyebrows at the bright possibility, "come back. All of you."

The house Wilder lived in was the house in which he had been born. His father, a man whose only extravagance was a large number of children, had built it in the most practical way he could, wasting no lumber on prettifying with Gothic trim or bay windows. The halls were long and narrow, the rooms square, the windows uniform in size and evenly spaced. Wilder's mother had had little time to swing on a front porch, so her husband had extended it only half the width of the front of the house, and he had placed the house closer to the sidewalk than were the other houses on the block, which favored deep front lawns. Its token plot of grass was a mere tip of the hat to his neighbors and a constant irritation to them. He would have placed his foundation at the edge of the walk if he had had his way, wanting, as he did, all the ground possible at the back for a garden to help feed his large family. Twelve in all he raised, the thirteenth, the only one to fail him, having wisely come too early, thus avoiding what may have been a life of untold mishaps.

Now the front of the house was obscured by a large, scraggly hedge, left untrimmed, to the despair of the neighbors, by its landlord, Marvel Gibson. The front porch had been enclosed by a partial wall, then set with windows all around to make a "sun room." There were three black mailboxes nailed between two front entrances—one, the original entrance, leading in to the two downstairs apartments; the other, a Gibson addition, leading to the upstairs apartment. There were other, inner changes—rooms cut up to provide extra kitchens and baths—which would have confounded Wilder's father but have earned his respect as a practical man.

For many years Wilder, the seventh child, had watched his brothers and sisters depart; some joined their father in the cemetery north of town, some moved to distant cities. At first he had been too young to go; then he became too old.

"Look!" his mother had cried, pointing an accusing, trembling finger as each of her children in turn departed. "Look how they leave me! Abandoning their mother!" If she could have gotten hold of her husband, she would have given him a hard shake. But she had Wilder, and to him she had clung until her fingers slipped and she could hold on no longer. She had left him the house and her savings, which were substantial.

Grown accustomed to living in rooms whose blinds were never opened, Wilder withdrew still further. He sold the house to Marvel Gibson, keeping the smallest, front apartment for himself. Finding those three rooms too empty with no one to care for, he had gone to the pound and rescued from the killing tank a sickly, abandoned pup. And he had named him James, after his father.

Rilly was sitting on the front steps, waiting. Seeing her, Wilder said, more to himself than to Vivian, "I'm afraid she'll be upset."

"Why should she be?"

Wilder looked mildly surprised that she should ask. "His leg was amputated."

Vivian had planned to drop Wilder and go on her way. Instead, she turned off the ignition. "I'll come in with you."

Rilly came running. "Put him down, Mr. Fulford, put James down!"

"Inside, Rilly," said Wilder, "he's still recovering."

When the blanket was removed and James stood in the middle of Wilder's faded living room rug, Rilly yelled and grabbed Wilder's trouser leg. Startled, James twitched, took one stumbling step and stood still.

"His leg's gone! He'll fall! He'll fall!"

"Speak quietly, Rilly. You startled him," said Wilder.

"But he can't run!" protested Rilly, on the verge of tears.

Before Vivian could comfort her, Wilder said, "You run and you've got only two legs. He's got three."

Struck by this comparison, Rilly paused, then glanced up roguishly at Wilder as if she'd caught him out. "But I'm *supposed* to have two!"

"All the same, remember he's still got one more than you've got. The doctor said that in a week or two he'll be as good as ever. Here, why don't you give him a vanilla cookie."

"Can I have one too?" asked Rilly.

From his pocket Wilder gave her several, and she sat down beside James and offered him one on the palm of her hand. "Please . . . ," said Wilder, turning toward Vivian, "please sit down. Here, sit down here," and he swept a newspaper off an old, shabby but comfortable-looking easy chair.

"I really should go, I've got. . . ."

"No, no, not there. A spring's broken . . . I've meant to . . . just haven't gotten around . . . here, sit here." He pulled forward a straight chair whose seat was covered in needlepoint and whose carved back formed a right angle designed to fit into corners.

"What a lovely needlepoint," exclaimed Vivian.

"Mother made it. She always said this was a chair for a lady."

"Well," said Vivian, sitting, "just for a few minutes."

"You must have a cup of coffee! I mean . . . I'll make . . . you will have a cup of coffee, won't you?"

Vivian, on the point of saying no, smiled and said, "Yes, I will, thank you." She could not have said no to anyone in such an obvious dither. She was touched by the anxiety in his enlarged eyes, swimming behind his glasses, his rough, weathered face and the way he stood, his knees bent toward each other, waiting for her answer. For years he had stood just like that, waiting for his mother to decide between soup or a fried egg, a peeled apple or a piece of cake. He gave a little nod and disappeared into the kitchen.

The room appeared smaller than it really was because it contained both living and dining room furniture. A large, dark-stained oak table with immense knotty legs was pushed into an inner corner, a massive buffet into another. A variety of chairs and small tables with curved legs and clawed feet stood about at random. The flowered wallpaper was almost completely covered by fading pictures, landscapes and portraits, all framed in heavy, dark frames. Through a door into the glassed-in porch Vivian could see the foot of a brass bedstead. Near the easy chair with a broken spring was another small chair with a deeply concave seat upholstered in worn red velvet.

Rilly, observing Vivian observing, said, "That's James' chair.

He always sits there." She stroked the dog's head, then asked, "How long is your name?"

"Very short. F-O-X."

Rilly shook her head. "I mean how lonnnnnnng is your whole name?"

"Oh. Well, I have three—Vivian Margaret Fox. Four, if you count my maiden name, Kearns."

"What's a maiden name?"

"A woman's last name before she marries. Your last name is Mitchell and. . . ."

"No, 'tisn't," said Rilly, sticking out her lower lip. "My last name is MacGregor."

"But your father's name is. . . ."

"I don't care! I have my *own* last name. It's from Peter Rabbit."

"Oh. Well, when you marry, your last name will be whatever your husband's last name is. My full name is really Vivian Margaret Kearns Fox."

"That's only four," said Rilly scornfully. "I know a name lots longer than that. I bet you never heard such a long name!"

"Can you tell me?" asked Vivian, smiling.

" 'Course I can." Rilly tilted her chin pertly and recited. "Hannah Maria Kaziah Kasander, Isabel Klinglesmith Comfort Fry."

Vivian's eyes widened in exaggerated amazement, her mouth in speechless wonder. Pleased with her reaction, Rilly said proudly, "Mr. Fulford told me that. It was someone he knew!"

The dark aroma of fresh coffee wafted in from the kitchen, and in a moment Wilder appeared carrying a tray with an old silver coffee pot, cups, saucers, cream and sugar.

"You brewed it!" exclaimed Vivian. "Instant would have. . . ."

"Oh no. Mother . . . that is, we never used instant." Wilder poured two cups of coffee, then one of milk, to which he added a thimbleful of coffee. That he handed to Rilly, sitting cross-legged on the floor. "You'll have yours later," he said to James, picking him up and placing him on his chair. James tucked himself up comfortably and looked from one to the other with bright, expectant eyes as if he had just come to a party.

Vivian had scarcely taken a swallow from the fragile, flowered cup when they heard the outer door slam and excited voices in the hall. The door into Wilder's apartment burst open and two voices, a man's and a woman's, called out at the same time: "Wilder! Are you there? Wilder, we just got back! We must tell you what we found!"

James gave one sharp bark. Rilly put down her cup with both hands and said to Vivian, "That's Pete and Lena."

Though only two people, they entered like six, their words overlapping, their excitability and sweeping gestures filling the room. Lena was a compactly built young woman in a jersey top, long, full skirt of paisley design, and clumsy, leather sandals. Oblivious to all else, she crossed the room toward Wilder, tossing as she went a floppy leather bag onto one chair, a soiled fringed shawl onto another. Her several long necklaces, glittery and tarnished, swung against her chest. Arm bangles jangled as she waved her arms about. Constantly she interrupted herself.

"Wilder! We saw the most . . . oh, you're having coffee!" She raised her arms like a conjuror. The bangles clashed to her elbows, and Wilder went for more cups.

"I see we came just in time," said Pete. He stooped forward and began moving the coffee pot and china about, searching for something to eat.

Lena's eye fell on James. Clapping her hands together, she cried, "And James is home! You're celebrating!" She leaned toward the dog, who drew back, nervously licking his chops.

Rilly at once stretched her arm protectively across his back. "He's got three legs now," she said as if afraid her mother might make some abrupt move.

"Three!" exclaimed Lena.

"Three?" inquired Pete, turning around to look curiously at James.

"That's one more than we have," said Rilly quickly.

Focusing on her apparently for the first time, Lena smiled delightedly and exclaimed, "Amaryllis, you're here too! How nice! What would we do without Wilder!"

"The perfect, built-in baby-sitter," said Pete.

Wilder handed them each a cup of coffee, and Pete said, "Cookies?"

Wilder returned to the kitchen.

Pete, awaiting the cookies, took up a position in the middle of the room, standing with sandaled feet apart and knees sprung back. His great toes were inordinately large, needed perhaps to brace his tall, reedy frame. His thin shoulders curved forward, giving him a consumptive look, though Vivian suspected his chest would do well enough should he choose to stand erect. His outstanding feature was an untrimmed, reddish-brown beard that covered from ear to ear the entire lower half of his face. Thick and wiry, it apparently drew, like Spanish moss from the oak, the strength it needed from his hair, which had declined, exposing a high, shiny forehead.

"As you know," he announced portentously through an opening in his beard, "we have been concerned, very concerned." Stirring his coffee, he turned his small, brown eyes first on Wilder, then on Vivian, expecting they should immediately understand his dark meaning.

"Yes, very, very concerned!" exclaimed Lena, tossing back her hair with the flamboyant gesture of a model for shampoo. It failed of its mark, for her straggly brown hair hung as before, partially over her face, until she gave it a quick twist behind her ear. "Ever since Gibson gave us notice that. . . . Ah!" She paused to smile widely at Vivian. "You have a guest!"

"That's Mrs. Fox," said Rilly. Her father made Vivian a slight, careful bow, maintaining, however, his serious face.

"I'm so glad to see Wilder has company," said Lena, pulling up a chair close beside Vivian's. "He so . . . where do *you* live?"

"Just down the. . . ." began Vivian.

"Nowhere where she has to move out, I'll wager," said Pete heavily.

"Why no, we. . . ."

"And in a month too!" emphasized Lena. "That's just not enough time to . . . and poor Wilder!" Lena and Pete both looked sadly at Wilder, sitting with his knees pressed together, holding his saucer with both hands. From long practice, he bore their joint regard calmly, the rings of his lenses increasing his watchful attitude.

Vivian, amused, found in Pete and Lena a curious resemblance. Both had thin faces and prominent noses, Lena's long and sharp, Pete's large and lumpish. Their expressions were both eager and hungry-looking.

"It's just not fair!"

"It's a breach of the unspoken social contract!" They spoke together, vehemently.

"What he's doing to Wilder! After all these years!"

"A man invests his entire life, financial and emotional, in a home and then has it taken from him!" Pete, still staring at Wilder, shook his head. "For us it's different."

"Yes, it's different for us!" said Lena. "We've lived here only a year, but Wilder!"

"He was born here," declared Pete, ignoring Wilder's growing embarrassment and raised hand, intended to shush him.

"He was born right upstairs, in *our* bedroom," said Lena, marveling. "Do you know, he was one of thirteen!?"

"No," said Vivian, glancing at Wilder, trying to imagine him as a baby.

Wilder's face turned a deeper red. Lena struck off on a tangent. "Do you have children?" she asked Vivian.

"Just one. A daughter, Corinne."

"One is good," said Pete authoritatively. "That shows you have a fine sense of social responsibility. Of course," he added, not wanting to fault Wilder's parents, "in those days it was different."

"So different!" echoed Lena. "No food monopolies, no Vietnam war. . . ." She leaned close to Vivian and said in a hushed voice, "They wouldn't take Pete, you know, but I tell him he must not feel rejected. Society has definitely not rejected him. He will serve in other ways . . . . Why Corinne?" Vivian was caught off-guard by this abrupt switch, and Lena asked again, "Why that name?"

Vivian smiled and shrugged. "Just a name we both liked."

"We," said Lena proudly, "had a special reason for naming Amaryllis. That's a spring flower, you know, and it was at the height of its season when she was conceived!" She smiled down at Rilly, nibbling a vanilla wafer and pretending not to hear. "So *we* had a very special reason."

"Lee," said Pete, reminding her, "we came to tell Wilder about the house we found."

Speaking often at the same time and echoing each other, they described in detail a house, not too big, "just right for our family unit," on a street that dispensed with sidewalks and curbs and was, besides, close to the grammar school—though they weren't certain they wished Amaryllis to attend public school. For the bright child whose spirit has not been stifled, public schools were woefully lacking. Their flood of words temporarily stemmed by this problem, they paused to stare deeply into each other's eyes in a profound consideration.

Then Lena brightened. "But it has a fenced-in swimming pool! That will be so healthy for all of us! You must come and swim with us! And there's lots of room for a garden!"

"We will utilize the land," declared Pete. "There's no reason why vegetables have to be relegated to the backyard. That's an absurd middle-class convention. We can plant spinach, tomatoes, even squash in the front yard." He paused, hoping for a challenge to this innovative notion. But Vivian and Wilder were silent. Only Rilly said, "I don't like squash."

"If only," cried Lena, throwing out her arms with a clatter, "we can get a loan!"

"Yes, there is that matter of a loan," said Pete. He put down his cup and thrust another cookie inside his beard, saying rather awkwardly over it, "We must get back to the shop now."

"We must!" exclaimed Lena. She snatched up her bag and turned toward Vivian. "I hope you'll come again . . . er. . . ."

"Mrs. Fox," said Rilly.

"Fox," said Vivian, "Vivian Fox."

"Ah," said Lena. "Vivian. One rarely hears that name nowadays. Well, Vivian . . . I won't say Mrs. Fox. Last names are so unnecessary, so ridiculously formal. Drop in and see us at the shop. We sell books and paperbacks, new and used. And records . . . . Do you do ceramics?"

"No, I . . . ."

"We sell ceramics too. People bring their work in you know . . . . If we get a loan, you must come for a swim!"

"Yes, if," echoed Pete.

They swept out of the room, shutting the door on the end of Lena's shawl. There was an exclamation, the door opened again and Lena put her head back in long enough to say, "Don't be a bother to Wilder, Amaryllis," pulled her shawl clear and shut the door.

After an interval of blank silence, Vivian said, "I must go too. Thank you for the coffee." She paused beside James, leaning over to stroke his head. "I'm sure James will be just fine, Rilly." At the door she hesitated. Frowning, she turned to Wilder and asked, "Is Mr. Gibson forcing you to move?"

Uncomfortable with the word "forcing," Wilder admitted he had been given notice to vacate. "For James and me it doesn't matter. It's just that . . . ." He waved his hand at the room. "All these things, Mother's things. The whole house is filled with her furniture. I promised her I'd take care of it. But," Wilder, embarrassed, looked everywhere but at Vivian, "I'm sure that's of no interest to anyone." He could not bring himself to say "you" to Vivian. He swallowed and was able to say, "There's no fault to be found with Mr. Gibson. He owns the house. He has the right to sell it if he wants."

"But I don't want to move," said Rilly. "I want us to stay here with you and James."

"Rilly," said Wilder firmly, "we must not burden Mrs. Fox with our problems."

Rilly leaned against Wilder and, looking coyly at Vivian, asked, "Will you come to see James again?"

Vivian promised to do so.

Not since the occasion of his mother's funeral had Wilder undergone such emotional stress. After Vivian had gone, he sent Rilly out with a skip rope he had given her that had a painted face and little bells on each handle. Then he sat down in his chair and sighed audibly. James raised his head and paid attention. But Wilder didn't move; he gazed at the chair Vivian had sat in, at the cup and saucer she had held, all quite transformed. In all his life Wilder had never seen a woman he thought of as beautiful until Vivian. Above the buffet was an oval photograph of his mother wearing a large hat with a rose under the brim and smiling coquettishly. But she bore no resemblance to the strong, shapeless woman he had known whose face had grown to be neither feminine nor masculine but simply a face that had endured. As schoolgirls his sisters wore braids and had grubby knees. Grown older, they wore hair curlers and old bathrobes. When they dressed for a party he saw them still as flat and colorless, even at times getting their names mixed and confusing one with the other. Girls shunned him. He knew himself to be unattractive, except as an object of fun. He ceased looking at girls or in mirrors and fell naturally into the role assigned him by genes and by accident: that of the stable son who stayed home to care for an aging parent.

Now, unexpectedly, this woman had struck into his life like a shaft of sunlight, brilliant and warming. With the grace of a queen she had sat in his chair, and he was bedazzled. He saw her there still, and felt the room and himself touched by her visionary presence. Impulsively he moved the chair back, turning it toward the wall so no one would sit in it until she came again, as she had promised. He washed the cups, handling hers with special care and setting it apart from the others.

He looked at James and marveled that by his sudden, quixotic rushing into the street, a thing he had never shown the slightest inclination to do before, James should have been the means of bringing her into his life. With affection strongly mixed with gratitude, Wilder rubbed James' ears, then realized with a skip of his heart that James' coat was almost exactly the same pale, reddish-gold as Vivian's hair. James' fur was short, thick and of a coarse texture, but Wilder, laying his hand on James' head, might have been touching the most delicate, air-spun filaments. Then there flashed in his memory the sight of Vivian bending over to pat James goodbye. The neck of her thin, flowered dress had fallen forward, exposing the swell of her breast. Wilder, stung, had instantly averted his eyes. Now, unbidden, the image of her gracefully bending figure, her hair alive with light, hung vividly before him. That glimpse of tender, curving flesh enticed his eye, and made her, after all, not a queen but a warm, living woman. His hand, barely touching James' back, trembled.

James, sensing a mysterious disturbance in his master, thumped his stub of a tail, twisted his head around and gave Wilder's hand a sympathetic lick.

Wilder blinked and rested his hand gently on James' flank. A virgin at fifty-one, he had fallen absurdly in love.

FIVE

Horseplay

Vivian lay sunning on a terry towel, one arm bent across her face, a bikini her only shield against the blazing sun. Shining from a cloudless sky, its intense heat penetrated to her bones and drew from her skin a dry, scorched odor. Under the towel the deck boards were hard and ridged but not unpleasantly so. From the lake came the drone of an outboard motor and the sigh of water breathing softly against the pebbly edge of the lake. From inside the cottage came the muffled splintering of ice cubes. The canvas blinds at both ends of the deck hung slack in the still air; they gave privacy and, like horse blinders, focused the view lakeward.

Vivian rolled over onto her stomach and propped herself up on her elbows. Her fair skin burned easily, but she was confident she had not been too long in the sun. These days she was full of confidence and energy. The days were not long enough by half. The gray world of past months was once more fresh and brilliant. The colors of earth and sky and water struck her vividly. Her ears caught every sound with fresh clarity. She squinted into the sunlight flashing on the lake, at the massed trees on the far shore, at the miniature summer cottages lining the lake edge, each with its matchstick wharf. She followed the motorboat, veering about, cutting a crystal-edged furrow that curled outward in ever-expanding, diminishing waves. She could see the flash of red on the side of the boat and the sun-sparkled water flying up behind its careening course. Her new-found delight in the world was exhilarating. She found herself perpetually smiling.

The screen door behind her opened and closed, and Marvel said, "Here, this is just what you need."

The glass was shockingly cold against her warm hand. The ice cubes, shot with fracture lines, glittered in the sunlight. Vivian twirled the glass and smiled over her shoulder at Marvel. He was not as powerfully muscular as Harry, but he was lean and sinewy. Graceful, Vivian thought. Fondly she saw that his skin had lost its earlier sunburned pink and was turning to a smooth, even tan. She was amused that his hair, which he kept so carefully combed, was roughened, the ends slightly curled up.

"What are you smiling at?" asked Marvel.

"You," said Vivian.

Marvel's eyes narrowed thoughtfully. "You'd better be careful. And drink your drink. It's good for you. Besides, I went to the trouble of squeezing the lemons." As she obediently tipped back her head and drank, tiny red sparks glinted in her hair, blanched to pale gold in the sunlight. Watching her, Marvel was convinced she was the most attractive woman he had ever possessed. He wondered briefly about Harry, not without a twinge of envy. Inexpressibly drawn, he leaned forward and kissed the warm, silky skin of her shoulder.

"You're always telling me what I need," said Vivian in a playfully plaintive tone, "or what's good for me. You think you always know what's good for me?"

"Yes," said Marvel, firmly, "I do."

"Always?"

"Always."

"Then you know that I've got to go home now."

"Not just yet," said Marvel. Beginning at her ankle he traced with one finger the shape of the back of her leg, the inner hollow of her knee, her thigh, and on up to the deep curve between her shoulder blades. With one sure gesture he pulled loose the two back ties of her halter.

"What are you doing?" asked Vivian faintly, feeling all the blood in her body had followed his touch. "I have to leave now."

"You know perfectly well what I'm doing," said Marvel. "And I'll tell you when it's time to go." He believed he understood

Vivian perfectly. After his initial mistake, a month earlier, he had learned that if he was never abrupt but always deliberate and quite firm, all things were possible.

He fancied himself in complete control. A practical man, at home with facts which he manipulated skillfully to his own advantage, Marvel had no idea he was acting a part in another's dream. And doing so admirably. He would have been deeply displeased to discover that his success resulted from his conforming to an image; an image, moreover—and quite insultingly, he would have felt—whose precise features were vague, even adaptable, but whose character was unshakably fixed. His sleepy moral sense would have been awakened indignantly by what he would have considered outright duplicity.

The lake cottage was one of Marvel's rental properties, thirty-five miles north of Warrenville. Luckily, he had acquired it just before he met Vivian. He often bought and sold lake cottages, never keeping any one for too long. He had brought Vivian to this one for the first time after showing her the house which she and Harry ultimately bought.

Their new house, set on half an acre of treeless, sloping land, was only seven blocks west of their old one in what had been, ten years earlier, a new development. It lay just outside the town limits and was the first development to eschew curbs and sidewalks, thus enabling the builder to turn his thrift to profit by creating for each middle-class home buyer the highly marketable illusion that he was really acquiring a small landed estate. The house was a U-shaped one-story, brick from foundation to windowsills, white-painted clapboard from sills to roof. A box hedge trimmed ruler straight grew along the front of the house, and two young maple trees tacked down the corners of the sloping lawn.

The driveway, paved with sharp, gray stones, ran straight back past one wing of the house. There was no walk from the street to the front door, and from the driveway only stepping-stones sunk into the grass. They were laid out in an S curve intended to be as natural as a woodland path but at intervals requiring an awkward stretch of leg. The difficulties of approach, however, were offset by the grandness of the front entrance: wide, paneled, double doors, each with a massive brass fixture of the sort that pages might grasp and pull open for the passage of a royal procession. On either side of the door hung ornate black lanterns, each supported by an angle bar and chain. And all around the shallow recess, like a frame, were panels of rippled, opaque glass.

It was, Marvel pointed out, an entrance one could be proud of, and it opened onto a hallway whose floor was covered with imitation slate of different hues. He showed her the kitchen, assuming it to be the most crucial room in the house. Its windows faced the street, affording a sweeping view of any activity in the yard—more importantly, in the street and neighboring yards as well. Then he stepped down two steps into the large, sunken living room and flicked a switch. Dramatically, light flared out against the ceiling all the way around the room from behind long panels fastened high on the walls and slanted outward like feeding troughs.

"What did I tell you?" inquired Marvel. "This house has style. The owner was transferred out of state; otherwise he would never have sold it."

Vivian nodded thoughtfully. She stood in the middle of the sculptured carpeting and turned in a slow survey of the empty room. Through sliding doors set into one wall she could see the terrace paved with bricks and the extended wings of the house that enclosed it. Weeds had sprouted between the buckled bricks. Two large bowl-shaped pots stood at one side, one cracked and empty, the other holding a small, very dead ornamental cedar. The view beyond was of a continuing gentle slope of field grass, devoid of bush or tree.

But Vivian saw a different view. On her inner screen she saw the living room furnished with a sectional sofa, broad-armed and deeply cushioned, a true conversation center, arranged in a curve or, perhaps, cleverly repeating the shape of the house, in a U. There would be several large ottomans for putting one's feet up or for sitting on, gracefully, knees crossed at an angle, body braced on one arm, possibly a glass in the other hand and one's skirt spread out. In the middle would be a large coffee table of inlaid wood. Beyond the sliding doors were wrought iron furniture, painted white, with flowered seat cushions, a matching chaise lounge, a glass-topped table with fringed umbrella and low redwood boxes filled with geraniums. She saw herself with a yellow watering can watering the geraniums. Her purple angel-sleeved gown, its many fine pleats gathered at the neck, floated about her ankles. In a sudden shift of scene, snow was piled against the sliding doors, wind-sculptured into curving drifts aslant the terrace. The empty planters were marked by glistening mounds of snow. A fire burned in the family room just off the kitchen. And in the "full" basement, tiled, paneled and beamed, was a Ping-Pong table. Corinne had always wanted a Ping-Pong table.

"I knew you'd like it," said Marvel. "Wait til you see the garage."

The garage sat well back from the house and looked like an enlarged toy barn. It was red with white cross beams on the two central doors that opened outward. It had a mansard roof and a weather vane in the shape of a rooster. On both sides of the barn-garage was a shed-like addition, each with a lower, sloping roof and its own white door.

"This would sell the house," said Marvel. "Great for storage, or . . . ." With real curiosity he asked, "Does your husband have a hobby? Woodworking? Cars?" Recently, grown bored with consistently winning at poker, Marvel had toyed with the idea of buying himself a plane and taking flying lessons.

"No, no hobby," said Vivian absently. She was thinking of a horse for Corinne. The horse could be stabled nicely in the room on one side of the garage, and she could use the other as a potting shed. The horse would graze on the slope, and she, aproned and gloved, could see him through the side windows as she worked at a long raised bench. She was lifting seedlings from trays, being very careful of their pale stems and delicate roots. Their first leaves had just unfolded, and she was planting each one in its own pot. Around her work area were scattered mounds of peat and moist black soil. Clay pots were stacked in corners. Ivy and ferns hung by the windows, and suspended from the slanted, wooden ceiling were bunches of dried herbs, rosemary, kiss nicholas and thyme. Vivian could smell their dry, spicy fragrance overlaying that of the damp soil.

Observing her expression and seeing it, shrewdly, as that of a woman who had already moved in, Marvel, job done, was free to switch tracks. Wasting no time, he took her arm and said in a confiding manner that hinted surprise, "Now we'll take a little spin and I'll show you something entirely different."

"What?"

"You'll see," he said with a roguish grin that dimpled his cheek. "You'll like it, I guarantee."

On the way to the lake, he reached for her hand and held it firmly clasped on the seat between them, a tacit sign of proprietorship. Vivian, pleased by this show of masterfulness, observed that he drove expertly with one hand and attributed to native skill what was really the result of much practice.

Trees bordering the lake marked its location like an oasis for miles across the flat farmlands, the green, rounded tops of the willows all leaning to the east. Seen nearer to, their trunks, nourished by an abundant supply of water, were enormous, two or more growing from a single base, their gnarled and hardened roots surfacing above ground. A scattering of pines and some scraggly bushes had been planted in rows between the cottages to give a semblance of privacy. They also cast a certain gloom, and the earth beneath their drooping branches was damp and spongy with needles.

All the cottages were named. Marvel slowed down as he passed Whit's End and turned in at Kosy Korner, an A frame with a small, separate garage just off the road. When he unlocked and forced open the warped back door, Vivian smelled the faintly moldy odor of an unaired beach house. A minimal kitchen and a bath were at the back. The rest of the space under the steep beamed ceiling was given over to one room with a large triangle of glass panes at its end. Beyond was an open deck. From the doorway Vivian could see straight through the cottage and across the lake to the far shore.

"How do you like it," said Marvel, not putting it as a question since he was certain of the answer. "It's a great little place, quiet, private, comfortable. Just right for us. Make yourself at home. Kick off your shoes. I'll get us a drink." Bel always kicked off her shoes when she entered the house.

Vivian didn't answer. She crossed the bare floor and stood facing out, her nose almost touching the glass. Her eyes were open but unfocused. She was aware of the view without looking at it. She had not stopped breathing exactly, nor did she feel, in the tradition of heroines, that she was standing on a precipice. Rather she was waiting, in a kind of still expectancy, for the curtain to go up, for the moment when they two would magically become the lovers who lived in her dream. Then everything would be transformed. How, or in what ways, it never occurred to her to wonder. She heard a cork pop and the tinkle of glass. Recalling Marvel's words, she mused fondly on the phrase, "Just right for us." He had joined them in that one word, "us," and she felt warmly enclosed as if the room had drawn cosily around her. She kicked off one shoe, then the other.

Against this very day and others he never doubted would come, Marvel had laid in a small store of food and drink. For this signal occasion, champagne, pink. He came briskly out of the kitchen with a glass in either hand and on the point of making a remark. Seeing Vivian, he stopped and caught his breath. Marvel, not a fanciful man, was quite struck. In a flood of sunlight, Vivian stood with unconscious grace, one hand resting on the glass, her head raised as though she searched for something far out on the lake. Her hair shone a burnishd red-gold; the skin of her bare arms and legs had a translucent glow. Barefoot and with the arrested quality of a porcelain figure, she seemed thrown into another dimension. Forgetting the champagne, Marvel set down the glasses and went to her, stepping into the sunlight even as he unknowingly stepped into her dream. Resting his hands on her shoulders, he murmured her name and leaned his face against her hair.

His action was perfect. As if on cue, Vivian turned, put her arms around his neck and held up her face for the kiss that was both the culmination of her dream and the beginning of reality. As a lover, as in everything he did, Marvel was commanding, if not brusque. But Vivian's strong sense that something extraordinary was happening was contagious. Caught by her mood, Marvel tempered his usual forthright manner with an unusual tenderness. His sudden perception of her the moment before as fragile was soon dispelled. She met him with such an outpouring of emotion that for one brief, shaken moment he confused her with Belvedera. Vivian, eyes tight shut, clasped him she had longed for, who had finally emerged from her shadowy dream and become, as promised, a live, passionate man. Extravagantly happy that she could at last express her love, she did so with eager, spontaneous warmth and a large measure of gratitude.

When her vision cleared, Vivian, lying serenely within Marvel's embrace, saw the room clearly for the first time. On the opposite side of the ceiling, rain had leaked in and stained the wood; on the wall was a rectangle where a picture had been thumbtacked. A card table and three chairs stood in one corner. Floor pillows were stacked in another. The floor was bare except for a small braided rug before the door that opened onto the deck.

"The roof leaks," remarked Vivian complacently.

"Mmmhmm," said Marvel, his cheek pillowed on her breast. "That's why the bed's on this side." They both giggled, finding that deliciously amusing. Suddenly he remembered the champagne and sat up. No bubbles rose in the stemmed glasses.

Vivian pulled the thin Madras throw covering the divan up around herself and sat swinging her legs, watching as Marvel emptied and refilled the glasses.

"To us," said Marvel. They touched glasses and gazed at each other over the brims as they drank.

"We must leave now," said Vivian sadly.

"Here," said Marvel, pouring out what was left in the bottle. "We'll finish this first."

But when Vivian, glass empty, reached for her clothes, Marvel tossed them aside. "There's plenty of time," he said softly. Perfectly confident of his ascendancy, he drew her down, pushing aside the throw. Vivian, charmed by his purposeful manner and as reluctant as he to separate, let herself be taken.

Moving from one house to the other had been accomplished with less inconvenience than Harry had expected, chiefly because they took with them very little other than their clothes. When Harry, Vivian and Corinne together first inspected what was to be their next home, it became quite clear that new everything was in order. Furnishings from the old house would be entirely out of place in this new setting. Even the china was no longer suitable. "Besides," exclaimed Vivian, "I'm tired of all of it, of looking at it, dusting it, washing it! I want something different!" And certainly from the blood-red fixtures of the master bathroom to the massive stone wall that housed the fireplace in the family room, all called out for good "American" furnishings: low overstuffed furniture and four-way lamps for the living room, old English chairs and chintz for the family room, white French provincial for Corinne's bedroom and black furniture with a high glaze and brass trim in an oriental style for the dining room.

Harry followed Vivian from room to room, as he had years before. As before, he only half listened. Then he had been concentrating on Vivian herself. Now he was inattentive for several reasons—none having to do with Vivian. For one, this house appealed to him no more than the previous one had, but since he could not live in the house he wanted, he was indifferent. This house at least required no rebuilding. For another, he and Logan now owned the skating rink, and his mind was full of plans for the apartments that would rise in its place. But mostly he was preoccupied with thoughts of Jenny.

He had now driven her home a number of times. The first time his pleasure was somewhat dampened by her request that they stop off at the grocery store, as that would save her carrying a heavy sack. Another time they stopped at the cleaners. But he was pleased to have these brief times alone with her even though her manner confused him. She sat primly, hands clasping the top of her purse, knees close together, feet side by side, the way his mother used to sit when waiting in the doctor's office. When he pulled into the driveway of the large frame house in which she had an upstairs apartment, she never lingered but got out immediately, thanking him as she did so and walking away with a swing of her skirt but without a backward glance. Yet she spoke in a challenging, flirtatious way, as if they were equals in every respect, an attitude new to Harry. Nor was she the least bit reticent about asking favors. It struck Harry that her behavior stemmed from the difference in their ages, but that thought was distasteful. He put it resolutely out of mind.

With these matters engrossing him, Harry was more than willing to leave the details of moving to Vivian, whom he knew to be as efficient at clearing away difficulties as he had been at reaching the goal line.

Corinne, rushing ahead of them from one room to another, was delighted with the new house. She had her own bathroom, done in brilliant pink, and the promise of a Ping-Pong table in the basement. Vivian had not mentioned the possibility of a horse, wanting to discuss it first with Harry.

Marvel handled the sale of the old house. He took a personal interest in the transaction and got a very good price, to his own and Harry's satisfaction. He also directed the house sale, but, since the pricing and tagging of the furnishings were done in the house and in consultation with Vivian, he delegated this chore to Calloway Claude out of a fine sense of tact.

The day of the house sale, cars, vans and pickup trucks lined both sides of the street for several blocks. Nearly an hour before the front door was to open for business, a queue began forming, starting on the doorstep and extending out to the sidewalk and down to the corner. The woman jogger, finding her usual course obstructed, had to cross the street in midblock.

"This," said Calloway, peering out a side window, "will be a biggie." He spotted the familiar faces of antique dealers, who knew from years of dealing who owned what and who was waiting for a chance to buy it. Some had come ninety miles or more. They waited silently, sharp-eyed and a shade hostile, ready to elbow aside anyone foolish enough to lay an inquiring hand on an item they had come specifically to purchase. The rest were those who came out of curiosity to see the house, and chronic bargain hunters, who would carry off as a prize a single chair, a plant stand or a pin dish.

At exactly nine o'clock Calloway opened the doors and stepped quickly aside as the line swept by him. Within ten minutes they filled every room in the house from attic to cellar. Eager as a horde of antennae-waving ants on the move, they picked up, examined, discarded. What one put down another took up. All day long people filed in as others, carrying their purchases, filed out. Some hurried back a second time. By late afternoon the house was dismantled. Only items too large to carry remained, to be moved out later.

Within a week a couple with five children moved in. They made improvements at once. They painted over the wallpaper and the oak woodwork. They broke out two front windows and installed a large picture window. They covered the polished floors with wall-to-wall carpeting and vinyl tile. They attached a large board with a basketball hoop to the front of the barn. They cut down trees and dug up bushes. They planted petunias where there had been only grass and placed in the middle of the front yard a ceramic donkey pulling a cart.

Harry, Vivian and Corinne might never have lived there. Passing by, they soon ceased to look at the house with any interest. It was no longer familiar. Their home for eighteen years now existed only in snapshots and occasional memories. They had sloughed it off and thought no more about it than a snake its discarded skin.

For Corinne the move marked the end of adolescence. She had both left her old home and finished high school. Expecting now that life would begin in earnest, she had energetically rid herself of all childish ties, emptying out drawers and closets of old dolls, toys, games, even a prized sled. She had dusted off her doll house and given it to a neighbor's child. Her old crayon-scribbled books were now for sale on the Secondhand Childrens' shelf in Lena and Pete's bookstore.

Settling into her new home, she put up Remington prints, filled a shelf with horse figurines and books on the training of horses. Her closet was soon redolent of the stable, for in mid-summer she went to work for Mr. Farley, helping him clean the barn and care for the horses.

Each evening at the dinner table, Corinne gave her parents a detailed account of her day with the horses, how Masie was off her feed, Brownie had cut his fetlock, Star had chafed withers, Duke a beginning cataract, and how Dr. Leatherwood had dealt with all these fascinating problems. She also gave them the latest total of her savings, intended to help pay for her education as a trainer, beginning in the fall.

Vivian and Harry listened attentively, with polite but re-strained enthusiasm. They marveled at their daughter's growing vocabulary. Knowing her sensitivity, their occasional glance at each other was carefully noncommittal. But Vivian was thinking: She is now eighteen. She has one best friend, a girl, also obsessed with animals. But *she* at least was going to the state university in the fall to become a veterinarian. Did they always think of animals? Never of boys? And Harry, who did not think of his daughter in connection with boys, thought: She's still a child. God knows what she'd be getting into at some training stable. Anyone could take advantage of her.

They conferred in the privacy of their bedroom, after Corinne was presumably asleep. Nevertheless they were careful to keep their voices low. They spoke in phrases, in sentences left hanging, in silences, as they pursued a joint train of thought. As usual when discussing their daughter, they were in perfect agreement, and they worked out what they hoped would be a solution. They would fence in an area adjoining one side of the garage and buy her a horse with the proviso that in the fall she would enter the state university for at least one year. They would keep to themselves the hope that after one year she would want to continue in school of her own accord.

That settled, Vivian turned to another subject. "Harry, I wish you'd buy that house where Wilder Fulford lives. You know, that man with the dog. It'd be a good rental property."

For the first time in their conversation, Harry looked at her. "A rental property! Why would I do that? If I'd wanted a rental property I'd have kept our old house."

"That was different. This house is already cut into apartments. You wouldn't have to do a thing to it."

"Ha! I've heard that before! An old house! There'd be all kinds of maintenance—roof, wiring, plumbing! There'd be no end to it. Besides, what would I want with it?"

"It's in good shape," insisted Vivian. She plumped up her pillow and got into bed. "Could use a little paint, maybe. You'd get a steady income from it."

"Yeah. A little paint. I know what that means. There'd be property taxes, which are going up."

"Harry, don't be so stubborn! It's a sound house in a good location, and you *know* you'd get income from it!"

"Damn little! And since when am I stubborn? You got your Continental, didn't you? I sure lost on that deal! You sold that house and got this one, didn't you? Now it's a horse and a rental property!"

Vivian's mouth set. "You wanted to sell that house as much as I did. And you made money on it. You just don't want to admit it. The horse is an entirely different matter. As you well know."

Harry, in shorts and socks, leaned forward belligerently. "You still haven't said why! And don't hand me that income line."

Vivian raised her eyebrows. "Well, it *would* bring in an income. . . ." Hearing Harry's warning growl, she went on, "Marvel Gibson wants to get rid of it, and I'm sure he'd sell it to you at a good price."

"A good price is right! Good for him! He never turns a dime that isn't!" Harry's eyes narrowed. "Why?" he demanded.

Vivian made an exasperated noise. "If he sells it, they'll all have to move out, Wilder and Pete and Lena and Rilly. Well . . . Pete and Lena may move anyway. But Wilder! It's his home!

Harry, his father built that house. He was born there, and he has nowhere else to go."

Harry stared. "Wilder and Pete and Lena," he said softly. "My God, the people you get involved with! You want me to buy that house so this Wilder doesn't have to move! My father built *his* house, but you weren't interested in buying *it*!"

"That's different! It's out of town. This house is within walking distance of everything. It's a good investment. Besides," said Vivian defensively, "I could look after it for you."

Harry sat down heavily on the bed. He spread out his right hand and jabbed at its palm with his left forefinger. "I am trying to run an insurance business. I've just bought you a new car—at a loss! And a new house, just because you wanted it! I have also, as you should well know, invested in a major property that may become the largest apartment complex in town. Now . . ." he paused, to take a deep indignant breath, ". . as if that weren't enough, you want me to buy a broken-down house so that some knock-kneed jerk won't have to move! Well the answer is no, absolutely no!" He twisted around and threw himself back on the bed.

After a moment's silence, Vivian said in a tight voice, "He can't help being knock-kneed," and turned off the bedside lamp.

Light from the bathroom shone through the doorway.

"You forgot the bathroom light," said Vivian coldly.

Harry grunted, swung to his feet, padded across the room and swept his hand heavily downward over the switch. There was instant, solid darkness, unrelieved by any street lamp.

"Damn!" exclaimed Harry, stumbling across the still strange room where he and Vivian shared nothing, having fallen into a pattern of coexistence which neither cared, as yet, to openly acknowledge.

Mr. Farley had no trouble finding a horse. "You wait here," he said to Vivian and Corinne. "I'll bring her out."

It was only nine-thirty but already heat shimmered over the fields, the kind of heat that was said to make the corn grow so fast one could hear it rustle. It cast Vivian's and Corinne's shadows before them on the parched bare ground that held the dried, curved impress of countless horseshoes. From the barn they heard a hollow, echoing clip-clop. Corinne, eyes shining with anticipation, glanced at her mother and squeezed her arm.

Mr. Farley emerged into the sunlight leading a six-year-old strawberry roan. She stepped gracefully along beside him on slender legs, her plump, round body swaying with the rhythm of her walk. She arched her neck and playfully nuzzled his shoulder. When he halted before the women, she nibbled delicately at the brim of his hat.

"Like her?" asked Mr. Farley.

"She's beautiful!" exclaimed Corinne.

Mr. Farley looked faintly pleased. He leaned forward and said in a raspy whisper, "Ask her if her name's Molly."

Round-eyed, Corinne addressed the horse. "Is your name Molly?"

At once the mare bowed her head three times, then raised her right foreleg and held it out.

"Shake it," said Mr. Farley.

Delightedly, Corinne shook the mare's leg. "Mother! Did you see! She shakes hands! What's she want now?" Corinne asked, as the horse rather forcefully nudged Mr. Farley.

"Sugar. Here, you give it her."

Corinne held out a sugar lump and Molly picked it up daintily, her soft lips scarcely brushing Corinne's hand.

"Where did you get her, Mr. Farley?" asked Vivian.

To that, Mr. Farley looked wise, as if he could tell if he chose, but he said only, "She *is* an onusual horse." It was a considered statement. Corinne and Vivian waited, knowing from his meditative tone that he had more to reveal. Mr. Farley held back for a moment. He rarely had such a good audience. Sure of their amazement, he said, as proudly as if it were his own achievement, "She's a dancing horse. Let her hear music and she'll dance. Play a record for her and she'll waltz in a circle, keeping time pretty as you please."

Both Corinne and Vivian were properly astonished. Whatever horse Mr. Farley had led forth Corinne would have wanted. But a performing horse surpassed all her fancies. She glanced in silent but fervent appeal at her mother, who was trying to calculate how much a talent for dancing would increase the price. Molly, over whose reddish coat a marvelous glow had been cast, was a serenely confident horse. Her long-lashed brown eyes modestly lowered, she allowed Corinne to stroke her forehead while Vivian arranged with Mr. Farley for payment and delivery.

Harry was having dinner with Jenny in her apartment, a desired but once seemingly hopeless eventuality. He had carried bags of groceries up the steep outside steps and into the small kitchen, always in a state of flux, and held them while Jenny cleared a space. But he had got no further, for she immediately began "putting away." Finding himself secondary to the storing of a sack of potatoes or the prompt refrigeration of a pint of heavy cream, he had backed out the door onto the narrow landing and departed, apparently unnoticed.

Jenny was intimidatingly self-possessed, seemingly unsurprisable. Whatever came within her orbit, work or people, was immediately identified, docketed and dispensed with. In the office she had a habit of saying, "Oh, *that!*" which cut everything, large and small, down to a size so easily handled that it was scarcely worth mentioning. When asking that anything be retyped, whether for her error or his, Harry invariably apologized. He, who had been a marvel of athletic grace, felt in her presence increasingly awkward, a clumsy intruder in her life. He began to search for any means of breaking through her aplomb so he could approach her with the warmth her manner so often seemed to invite. Recalling her frequent references to meals in progress, he ventured one or two cautious questions.

On this occasion he had taken her not only to the grocery store but also to the liquor store. She looked at him over the tops of several bottles of wine which she had insisted on holding on her lap, trusting only herself to see them safely to the kitchen. "Cooking is my hobby," she said, as if he should have known. "I even thought of becoming a chef, but I decided that was too confining, spending all my time in a kitchen." She smiled archly. "I'd never find anybody that way, would I? Would you like to come to dinner? I'll make you a flaming juniper pork stew."

Harry, moving more slowly and caught with an unnecessary "no" to her first question, switched midway to a definite "yes."

He thought of bringing wine, then didn't, lest she find his choice unsophisticated. Candy she might think childish. He came, finally, with flowers. She would open the door. He would present them. Struck by their beauty, she would admire them, and when she expressed her gratitude, he would lean across their fragrant tops and kiss her. It would be a fine beginning.

Jenny had made great preparations, to the extent that she could in an apartment of one large living-dining room, a minis-cule bedroom and a kitchen that seemed to have been converted from a hallway. Its inadequacies, however, did not worry her. As soon as she found a proper husband, she would acquire a proper home. Meanwhile she rather enjoyed making do. She had raised both flaps of a small mahogany table and put crocheted place mats on it. She set out two candles whose twin flames reflected prettily in the window, as they had in a magazine ad she had seen in which the window overlooked the New York skyline. Here the window overlooked a driveway and the house next door; but no matter, they would scarcely be seen in the dark. As in the ad, her dress was simple black, with narrow straps and a straight skirt. But whereas the model's lacquered blonde hair was upswept, Jenny's long black hair was pulled smoothly around to one side and held there by a large barrette. She was entirely pleased with the effect, which seemed to her extremely French. She was certain Mr. Fox would admire it. She still thought of Harry as Mr. Fox, although she had tried saying Harry several times and listened for the effect. It was disappointingly unromantic. But she supposed she could get used to it in time.

She heard the slam of his car door and stood waiting for his knock, ready to open the door and step back so he could have the full effect of herself in the black dress against the room beyond with the charming little table and the candlelight.

Harry had barely knocked once when the door opened. His initial plan had to be scrapped because Jenny immediately stepped well back and he had to proffer the flowers at arm's length. As he did so, there was a loud ding from the kitchen.

Alerted, Jenny thrust the flowers back at him. "There's a vase in that bottom cupboard. Just stick them in that, will you?" She seized a pan on the stove, lifted its lid and peered critically inside, shaking it as she did so.

Harry leaned down and opened a cupboard. A five-pound sack of sugar fell out. He set it back, pushing to make room, whereupon several cans of consomme tumbled out, one rolling across the floor. Harry went down on one knee, replaced one can and reached for the other. He could see no vase.

"That's not the cupboard," said Jenny. "The next one." There was a door on either side. Harry hesitated. "On the right," said Jenny.

Feeling foolish, Harry opened the cupboard on the right. Nothing fell out, but the vase, he discovered by bending his head almost to the floor, was at the back, behind stacks of dishes. He laid the tissue-wrapped flowers on the floor, and by careful maneuvering was able to lift the vase out safely.

"Do get up!" said Jenny. She snatched up the flowers, took the vase and ran water into it. "Here, put it on a table somewhere."

Harry did so. Returning to the kitchen, redolent of roast pork, he tried to stand as close to Jenny as he could, which was difficult because she kept moving about, turning abruptly from stove to sink, tripping over him. Wherever he stood, what she needed was directly behind him. The evening was very warm, the kitchen, with one small window, very hot. Jenny's face was becomingly flushed, but under his sport jacket Harry's shirt was damp.

"Excuse me," said Jenny, elbowing past him to stir something on the stove. Seeing him run a finger under his collar, she said, "Wouldn't you be more comfortable in the other room?"

"I thought I could help," said Harry.

"Well, you could hand down the glasses." Jenny, on tiptoe, reached up to a cupboard awkwardly placed above the refrigerator. Seizing the opportunity, Harry put his hands on her waist, ostensibly to steady her, and impulsively kissed her bare shoulder.

"Mr. Fox!" exclaimed Jenny, "not now! The apples need stirring. Please, just get the glasses. No, not those. The ones with stems."

Vivian, at such a moment, would turn, put her arms about his neck and let burn what would. Jenny, he recognized, was more single-minded. But he drew hope from the implications of "not now." He handed down the glasses, and they smiled at each other with forebearance.

"Now, you sit at the table, and I'll bring the drinks," said Jenny.

"Let's sit on the couch."

"No, no, at the table," insisted Jenny, wanting the effect of the candles.

They lifted the long-stemmed glasses filled with a pale liquid and touched brims, the candle flames sparkling effectively on the crystal and in their eyes as, gazing speculatively at each other, they took a first sip.

"I had planned a clam juice cocktail," said Jenny, "but since there's gin on the meat, I thought a gin drink would be better. It's called Café de Paris. The recipe called for absinthe, but I couldn't get that, so I used sweet vermouth." Harry nodded and took another exploratory sip. "But the heavy cream goes very well with the gin, don't you think? Of course," she went on, "it's the egg white that pulls it all together."

Harry drew back slightly. He turned his glass about and pursed his mouth.

"I *knew* you'd like it," said Jenny.

Speechless, Harry forced a smile, then swallowed the substance in his mouth, trying to ignore its glutenous texture.

"Go ahead," urged Jenny. "I made enough for two. It said to stir gently. I hope I didn't overstir it. Did I?" she asked, filling up his glass a second time.

"It's. . . ." Harry swallowed again. "It's perfect." And looking at her, at her glossy head and the graceful fall of hair over one bare shoulder, he added, "Just perfect."

"I'm glad," said Jenny. "You can have most of my second." And to calm his somewhat garbled protests, she said coyly, "I'm sure a man like you can handle it, but all that cream is too much for me—it's very fattening."

"Call me . . ." said Harry, concentrating as he swallowed, on the enticing curve of her mouth, ". . . call me Harry."

"Harry," she said in sweet agreement, and on the strength of her submissive look, he downed the contents of his glass and tightened his chest muscles against the revolt of his stomach.

"You can come and watch, if you'd like to . . . Harry," invited Jenny, "while I flame the gin on the stew."

Harry rose at once, glad to move about and eager for dinner to be over so they could settle down to the "now" she had referred to. With a carelessness bred of three Café de Paris cocktails, he tossed his jacket at a chair and joined Jenny in the steamy kitchen where she was measuring out tablespoons of gin and pouring them over pork and apples. Pretending to observe, he put his arm cosily around her waist and leaned his head over her shoulder. He rubbed his face against her thick fall of hair, ready, should she turn her head, to kiss her. She gave him a roguish side glance. Encouraged, he tightened his embrace. Taking hold of her soft, rounded chin, he gently tilted her face toward him, his lips touching her cheek. He scarcely heard the strike of the match, but suddenly flames shot up before him.

"Good God!" exclaimed Harry, leaping back. His stomach lurched upward.

Jenny, smiling delightedly, shook the pan back and forth over the burner. "Isn't it dramatic? One of my favorites! Now I'll just add the whipping cream and get the lingonberry preserves and it'll be ready in a minute."

Harry was glad to sit down. He felt on safer ground out of the kitchen. Jenny carried in the pork stew, rich with sauteed apples and cream sauce. Its strong smoky aroma filled his nostrils and called up too clearly the mixture of cream and glassy egg white. "It's quite hot," remarked Harry. "Maybe we should sit on the couch for a while and give it a chance to cool."

"But it's *supposed* to be eaten hot," said Jenny. "It's not a bit good cold. It gets all thick and greasy and. . . ."

"Mmmmnn," said Harry, having heard enough. "Better now." Slowly, methodically, under Jenny's watchful eye, he ate, stew and salad and rolls and an unavoidable second helping of stew.

"Maybe," suggested Harry, "I should move my car?" Partly he wanted to see if he could stand up and partly he thought fresh air might help settle his stomach.

"Whatever for?" asked Jenny, carrying away their plates on which the remains of the sauce had already congealed.

"I saw the people downstairs looking out their window when I came. Don't they share the driveway?"

Jenny laughed. "They don't even have a car. No, it's just that when I make something special I give them most of it because I can't eat it all." She paused. "I hope you won't be disappointed, but I didn't make a dessert. We'll have a special coffee instead."

Harry swallowed hard several times and nodded. "That's . . . that's fine." He sat very erect, his shoulders well back to give his stomach all the room he could. When Jenny brought the coffee in pedestal mugs, he rolled his eyes at her and tried to smile.

"Are you quite comfortable on that chair?" asked Jenny, her head tilted prettily to one side. "Would you like to. . . ."

Harry raised one hand, carefully. "No. No, I'm fine. Thanks. I was just thinking . . . I'll have to leave soon."

"Oh!" said Jenny, in a falling tone of voice. "But not before you have your coffee! It's chocolate mint."

Harry grasped the mug handle firmly and raised it, keeping his eyes steadily on Jenny's face. The pungent aroma of mint cleared his sinuses, but the thick, sweet coffee wrought a cataclysmic change in his stomach. He felt a small upward ripple like the beginning of a flood that threatened, in its regularity and increasing strength, to get entirely beyond his control. Pressed for time, he stood up abruptly and involuntarily put out both hands toward her. "I must go," he said thickly.

Struck by his pained expression and the importunity of his gesture, Jenny also rose. She placed her hands in his. He was impetuous and romantic, a bit old-fashioned, but his action reminded her strongly of a perfume ad she had always been fond of.

Harry squeezed her hands until they hurt and stared at her wildly. "I must go," he muttered. He rushed out the door and stumbled headlong down the steps.

Downstairs a curtain moved sideways. A man and a woman, heads close together, peered out.

"Left early, didn't he?"

"Mmn. Seems to be in a fair hurry."

"Whatever she made this time it sure smells good. Wonder if there's any left."

Jenny heard the car roar into life and screech back onto the street and away. All her efforts had been worthwhile. Now she could clear away and get to bed in good time. Tomorrow, after all, was a work day. She discovered his coat, fallen beside a chair. She held it up and shook it, turning it about and giving it a brush or two as she would a prospective purchase. Yes, he was a possibility, a distinct possibility. She now had no difficulty at all in thinking of him as Harry.

Harry drove home almost blindly, pulling off to the side once and leaning out of the car to be violently sick. Reaching home, he slammed to a stop and rushed inside, passing Vivian and Corinne without a word in his haste to reach the bathroom.

Vivian followed and stood in the doorway. "What happened?" Harry, braced over the blood-red toilet, retched helplessly. Vivian shook her head. "You know the Kiwanis dinners aren't very good. You should have skipped the dinner and gone to the meeting. What did they have? Fried clams?"

Harry fumbled for the faucet and Vivian handed him a glass. "Harry, I did something today. I bought that house. I took the money Dad left me and bought it. Marvel Gibson gave me a good price."

Harry lifted his head and looked at her, bleary-eyed.

Vivian raised a defensive hand. "I know, don't say it. Just don't say it. It needn't concern you at all. I bought it with my money, and I'll deal with it."

Harry leaned over the sink, shut his eyes to its bloody color and doused his face with water.

"Think you could lie down now? Here," she steadied him across the room, where he fell sideways onto the bed. He experienced such unutterable relief, at least for the moment, that he never noticed Vivian's removing his shoes and lifting his legs onto the bed.

Vivian left the light on low and shut the door. Tomorrow, she thought, she would tell Wilder and Pete and Lena that they didn't have to move. She found buying a house of her own exciting, and she quite looked forward to tomorrow.

Lost and Found

When Vivian swung her Continental in to the curb in front of the house that Mr. Fulford, Sr., had built, Rilly was playing hopscotch. She had scratched the squares on the short stretch of pavement leading from the sidewalk to the front steps and was all but hidden by the woody, untrimmed hedge. James, a would-be participant, sat on the steps, alert and bright-eyed, his whole body jerking impulsively forward with each toss of the stone.

"A bad throw, Dottie!" exclaimed Rilly. She was teetering on one leg and bending over, trying to reach the stone, which lay in the far corner of a square, when Vivian's sudden appearance caused her to lose balance. Her raised foot came down, and she pitched forward with both hands on the pavement. She stayed for a moment, an inverted V, looking up sideways at Vivian.

"I knew she'd miss," said Rilly smugly. "Dottie's not as good as I am."

Vivian glanced around. "Where is she? Hiding?"

"Oh no," said Rilly, standing upright. "I'm Dottie." She held up a small, grimy palm. "These are my best stones. This one's mine. This one's Dottie's. See?"

"I see," said Vivian. "That's very clever of you."

"Mr. Fulford showed me how. And he helped me find the

stones. They have to be zackly the right shape. I keep them under the steps. So I don't lose them."

"Very wise," said Vivian. "Is Mr. Fulford home?"

"Not now. He went downtown. He walks a lot."

"I'll go on then," said Vivian. "Maybe I'll meet him. I have something to tell him."

"Is it a secret?"

"Not really," said Vivian, smiling. "I can tell you."

"And James," said Rilly. James cocked his head attentively.

"And James," agreed Vivian. "If I miss seeing him, you can tell him that he doesn't have to move. This is my house now, and he can live here for as long as he wants to."

"Your house?" asked Rilly, stretching out the words. "Then can we stay too?"

"Of course you can if your . . . if Pete and Lena want to. I'll stop by the store and speak to them."

Downtown Warrenville was dominated by two buildings, the courthouse and the post office. The courthouse, unlike so many others, was not domed or multi-gabled. It did not occupy the center square. Nor did it have four entrances to accommodate approach from any of four streets. It occupied a corner, and its brick walls, severe rather than majestic, abutted the sidewalks, allowing no space for grass, plots of cannas, or fountains to collect trash and beer cans. The architect had allowed himself two flights of fancy. One was the Florentine clock tower, tall and slender, with airy latticework at the top. The other was the main entrance, an extraordinarily wide arch that gaped like a huge mouth, inside of which a flight of steps rose to a shallow landing and a double set of doors. No matter how brilliant the sun or deep the snow, the upper steps and stone landing, hollowed by countless passing feet, were always gloomy, chilly and bare. It was an entrance that chastened many hearts and caused their owners to speak in subdued tones when they stepped onto the tesselated marble floor of the lobby.

Across the street was the U.S. Post Office, a gray stone building with just enough space between itself and the sidewalk for a thick, green hedge. Its entire front wall was a series of high windows with rounded tops. Inside, above the slots and cages, the entire length and two ends of the wall up to the ceiling were covered by one continuous mural depicting the settlement and growth of the Midwest and the Midwesterners, men, women and children. All were strongly muscular, resolute, square-shouldered. All were simply dressed in aprons and overalls. Their sleeves rolled up, they gazed steadily into the future as they plowed, reaped and struck glowing bars of steel. Solemn cattle and horses strained to help, and all was done by the light of a glorious sun, whose fanned rays served for both rising and setting. The post office had been built by the WPA. The mural had been painted by the WPA, and the downtown sidewalks were stamped WPA.

Vivian parked halfway between the post office and Pete and Lena's bookstore. They had begun with several small rooms in a block of old buildings, all five stories high. These buildings had been the subject of much controversy, dividing the town, like all of Gaul, into three parts: those who wanted to preserve and restore, those who wanted to tear down and erect glass and concrete, and those who didn't give a damn so long as taxes didn't go up and the streets were kept cleared for traffic. The first group won out by demanding respect for their hard-working forebears, a respect which none of the town's politicians dared being accused of lacking. The entire block was declared a treasure. Scaffolding was erected, and citizens who crossed the street could observe the refurbishing of the old brick fronts and the high, narrow windows, whose wooden, Gothic trim changed pattern from the first floor to the next all the way up to the ornate facades that fronted the flat roofs. The progress of the work was reported in the newspaper, along with stories about the original builders and the first businessmen to occupy the premises. Old photographs were resurrected and printed in the newspaper: cornerstone ceremonies with men in fitted coats and tall hats; the new horse-drawn fire wagon; jocular, straw-hatted men leaning in doorways, the rear end of a delivery wagon at one side. Sparks of pride were struck as older readers, remembering and marveling, made out the lettering on store signs and windows. Meanwhile, to satisfy the urge for progress, less cherished buildings were razed and replaced by structures of patterned concrete, or shining metal, with whole walls of blue-tinted glass or vertical rows of prison-like slits. There was general agreement that no building be erected that would be taller than the courthouse tower or in any way obscure its two clock faces. Even so there were those resolute, far-seeing citizens who said little but foresaw a time when the old clock tower would be a dwarfed relic, when Warrenville would raise a grand skyline of tall, gleaming buildings that would be their pride and make their town distinctive across the entire state.

Pete and Lena were happy in the old building. As their trade increased, they had added other space as it became available. The result was a labyrinth of small, oddly shaped rooms connected by inclines or rickety, homemade steps. There was a half-basement where one entered with bent head, to avoid the pipes, and read the titles by the light of one bare bulb. There were semi-lofts where one could look down on the heads of browsers. There were books new and used, hardbound and soft. There was a room for children's books and one for used records. Every bit of wall space was covered with shelving. Chairs were placed in out-of-the-way corners, and on one centrally located table were paper cups and an ancient but functional coffee urn that steamed all day long, blending the aroma of coffee with that of old bindings and yellowing pages. The worn floorboards sagged underfoot and a fine dust sifted down from the old beamed attic through successive floors to settle comfortably on books and shelves and begrime the hands of customers.

When Vivian entered, a bell attached to the screen door alerted Lena, who was arranging sets of ceramic earrings inside what had once been a candy counter. Sunlight, filtered through the hazy front window, fell like a yellow fog across the dusty floor and a corner of the glass showcase, lighting up an old brass cash register.

"Lillian!" exclaimed Lena, tossing back her hair. "Good of you to come by. Did you just drop in or can I help you find something?"

"Vivian," corrected Vivian, and seeing Lena's face go blank, added, "my name's Vivian."

"Oh. Of course. Vi-vi-an," Lena repeated, sounding the syllables to impress them on her memory.

"I just came by to tell you. . . ."

"Let me get you a cup of coffee!" Skirts and necklaces swinging, Lena started toward the coffee urn.

'No, thanks, I really haven't . . . ." But Lena was already filling a cup. When she heard Vivian's news, she called excitedly for Pete.

Their quiet broken, customers turned and stared. One

reader sitting on the balcony removed his glasses and looked down curiously. A boy came from the children's section and stood with his thumbs hooked in his pockets, observing the three of them with a skeptical expression.

"Peter! Guess who's our landlord now!" Lena grasped his arm and shook it for emphasis. "Just think! Lillian says we needn't move until we're ready!"

Heads tilted toward each other, they beamed at Vivian in unison. "Of course, you know," said Peter warningly, "we *do* want a house of our own, and as soon as we get a loan, we *will* be moving out." Having faced her honestly with this disappointing fact, their smiles faded. Anxiety wrinkled their foreheads and saddened their eyes.

Vivian hastened to reassure them. They could stay as long as need be, move whenever they wished. There was always a demand for apartments. She was sure she would have no trouble renting.

Convinced, Pete and Lena smiled once more. The balcony reader put on his glasses and resumed reading. The boy went back to the juvenile section and continued his search for an illustrated book on sea turtles.

Pete and Lena followed Vivian to the door, offering her another cup of coffee, a book, a record, anything at all. Vivian backed out the door, promising to come again.

She was on her way to the lake, to meet Marvel, and had just turned on the ignition when she remembered she had bills to mail and stamps to buy. Snatching out the key, she hurried back the half block to the post office. Not until she returned to the car did she discover that her key ring had unsnapped and the ignition key was missing. She looked around the floor of the car, ran her hand along the sides of the seat. No key. She got out, looked at the street alongside the car and then began slowly retracing her steps, eyes bent on the pavement.

"Lost something, lady?"

Vivian glanced up. A large stocky man confronted her, a tight-fitting T-shirt with the words Bourbon Bowlers stretched across his broad chest. His bulging muscles suggested he spent part of every day pumping iron.

"My ignition key. Somewhere between my car there and the post office."

He traced the route between car and post office with a

calculating eye. "Can't be *too* lost. We'll find it, never fear." And with that unexpectedly poetic admonition, he began to search, even going so far as to push back the hedge at intervals and peer under its branches.

Vivian was searching in front of the post office steps when a familiar voice spoke behind her.

"Er. . .excuse me, Mrs. Fox. . .have you lost something?"

Vivian straightened up. "Mr. Fulford! I was hoping to see you today!"

Wilder's swimming eyes took on a glazed look. She had *hoped* to see him! His roughened skin turned a deeper red. His ears, which were very sharp, heard what she was saying, but his brain, turned to jelly by this unexpected meeting, followed more slowly.

". . . weren't at home. I've just been to the bookstore to tell the Mitchells, and to the post office, and now I've stupidly lost my car key."

That she had lost a key he registered instantly. Anything touching her was important. But that she—*she*—had solved his own personal problem ricocheted inside his brain, leaving him tongue-tied. Eager to do her any possible service and grateful for any activity to end his standing before her gaping, he propped his shopping bag against the side of the steps and began searching back and forth across the sidewalk, giving close attention to the strip of worn grass between it and the curb. Vivian returned to searching along the base of the steps.

A red bug pulled up and a plump woman got out. On the point of dropping a penny in the meter, she paused, hand raised, at seeing three people absorbed in a close scrutiny of the sidewalk. She poked the penny in the slot and banged the meter. Then, the thickset man being nearest her, she tapped him on the shoulder.

"Did you lose something?"

"I didn't. The lady there lost her car key."

"Oh." She looked down on either side of herself as though she might have stepped on it. Involved, she leaned forward intently and began her own search.

"It has to be here," muttered Vivian, working her way down the steps as the woman was working her way up.

The post office door opened and a small woman carrying a large black handbag stepped out to find her way blocked. She addressed the plump woman.

"Why Dolphine! Have you lost something?"

Dolphine glanced up. "Oh, it's you, Jane. No, I haven't." She nodded toward Vivian, now moving slowly along the curbing. "She has, her car key."

"Where did you lose it?" inquired Jane, joining Vivian on the sidewalk.

"Somewhere between the post office and that cream-colored car there," answered Vivian.

"Well, it shouldn't be hard to find then," said the woman. Pressing her bag to her side, she leaned forward and began searching.

Backs bent, heads down, they went back and forth, passing and repassing each other until finally Vivian straightened up and sighed with exasperation. They all paused, glad to straighten their backs, except for Wilder, who had opened the car door and, kneeling on the street, thrust his arm in under the seat. When he stood up, they all were watching him. Smiling sheepishly, he held out the key.

"Oh, Wilder!" exclaimed Vivian, dispensing with formality, "what would I *ever* have done without you!"

Wilder blushed.

The bowler from Bourbon, satisfied that the lost had been found, went on his way without comment.

"See?" remarked Jane, smiling all around. "It's just a question of looking in the right place." Pleased with herself, she nodded and left.

"Wilder, you got your trousers dirty! I'm sorry!" Vivian moved as if to brush his knees. Wilder stepped back quickly.

"No, no. It's nothing." He slapped at his trousers. "It'll brush off."

"Wilder Fulford, that's it, of course," said Dolphine, who had been standing to one side watching. "I was trying to recall your name. I haven't seen you in years. Wilder and I went through school together," she said to Vivian, and put out her hand. "I'm Dolphine Humphrey. I direct the community theater. Perhaps you saw our production last spring."

"Vivian Fox," said Vivian, "and I'm afraid I didn't."

Even in a crowd they would have caught each other's attention. They shook hands, appraising one another as they spoke. Each was amused by the other's curiosity, and their smiles were spontaneous but sly.

Vivian wondered how she could have missed meeting Dolphine, who obviously set her own style. She was no taller than Vivian, but she had an hourglass figure clearly emphasized by a molding undergarment. Her dress fit over it like a taut skin. Her blonde hair was arranged in deep waves that set off her rounded face and plump neck and exposed her ears, adorned with faceted earrings that flashed multicolors in the sunlight. A matching, double-looped necklace lay rather than hung on her bosom, which could be seen to breathe like a swelling sea. Her smooth cheeks were delicately tinted, her large, light brown eyes artfully enhanced. Serenity sat fixed on her wide brow. She could be amused or disinterested, kind or disdainful, but never ruffled. Her consciousness of self was so strong that she escaped, although narrowly, being either old-fashioned or vulgar. She chose to be neither young nor old. Her wise and knowing look said she had always been, and would always remain, thirty-eight.

Dolphine instantly saw Vivian as grist for her mill. Such red-gold hair and radiant skin belonged on stage. She perceived that Vivian had a poise that could be built on, an energy that could be directed.

"You should come to one of our meetings," said Dolphine, with a slight but characteristic shift of her hips. "We have workshops between productions. Very informal. You might enjoy taking part."

"Not me," said Vivian, her smile widening. "I've no experience of that kind whatever."

"All the better. You would bring a freshness of interpretation to whatever you did." Then, trying a bit of bait, "A woman with your looks could command the stage."

Vivian laughed outright. "I can't even command my own daughter."

But Dolphine was too shrewd to believe that. Her knowing smile said as much. "Think about it. We meet Wednesdays, eight o'clock, in the old candy store near the high school. You would find it a most stimulating group."

As they spoke, Wilder stood awkwardly to one side, waiting to be released. He wanted to mop his forehead, but felt it would be unmannerly. As if by design both women turned and addressed him almost simultaneously.

"Nice to have seen you again, Wilder."

"Could I give you a lift home, Wilder?"

Wilder, eager to escape, stammered, "No . . . no, thank you. I . . . I have an errand or two. . . ." Unthinkingly he pulled out his handkerchief and scrubbed nervously at his forehead.

Dolphine smiled at him tolerantly. To Vivian she said, "I hope to see you some Wednesday. So glad you found your key," and walked away with perfect balance on four-inch heels and with a mesmerizing sashay of shoulder and hip that would have been instructive to Jenny.

Wilder picked up his brown paper bag and, holding it like a shield against his chest, hurried off flat-footedly in the other direction, his knees brushing past each other. His trousers, freshly washed and pressed, were several inches too short. They were now also soiled from kneeling in the street. But that was of no consequence. He was as intent on reaching home as a woodchuck on reaching its burrow. That she should have secured his home! He needed privacy and time to ponder this extraordinary event. It appeared to him that he owed her everything. At the corner of his block, he stepped aside to allow the woman jogger to pass undeterred. Her thin face was flushed. He could hear her shallow, panting breaths. Staring glassily ahead, she passed without a glance, oblivious to him and all around her.

James welcomed him ecstatically, bouncing on his three legs and making short, eager dashes between him and the kitchen. Wilder opened a can and filled James' dish. While the kettle heated, he surveyed the furniture and family portraits, the painted plates and fluted vases, his mother's treasured possessions. Now all could remain as they were, undisturbed. And he could remain in his father's house, which had come to be part of him, a living tissue. Had he been forced to move out, Wilder felt he would have shrunk inside, like a plant cut off at the root. He would be forever in her debt. Of that he was ashamed. "I am beholden to no man, nor will I ever be," his father had said. It was a principle deeply imprinted in his son. But conflicting with his sense of deep obligation, Wilder also felt a happy excitement, a warmth centered about his breastbone. As a man who never hid things from himself, he had to admit he was happily in her debt, for that was at least some sort of bond between them. His ears still glowed recalling her careless exaggeration, "What would I ever have done without you!" Perhaps some day he would find a way. . . .

Vivian and Marvel always came to the cottage separately but within a few minutes of each other. For the first time in three months, Vivian was late. Hurrying inside, she saw Marvel standing out on the deck. Though he must have heard her approach, he continued looking across the sun-shot lake. Vivian slipped her arms around his middle, laid her cheek against his back and hugged him.

"Sorry I'm late. Been waiting long?"

Pompously Marvel consulted his watch. "Exactly one hour, four and a half minutes."

"Oh dear, I am sorry," murmured Vivian contritely, and squeezed him again. "I stopped off to tell the Mitchells about the house, and then I lost my car key. Marvel, you should have seen. . . ."

Stiffly he turned to face her. "Why come at all? If you had to notify everyone, why didn't you go to the newspaper? Tell the whole town? If that's more important to you than I am, then that's what you should do."

Vivian looked at him in surprise. "Marvel! You *know* that's not so! If I hadn't lost my key . . . ." Her voice faded before the coldness of his gray eyes. His mouth was hard and unforgiving. Hurt, she averted her gaze, and giving a slight involuntary shrug, withdrew her arms and stepped away. "I said I was sorry, and I am. If you'd rather I'd go. . . ."

"Not much, you don't!" If he disliked waiting, he disliked her withdrawal even more. He seized her wrist and jerked her back. "I didn't drive all the way out here and stand around for nothing!"

"For nothing!" Affronted, Vivian tried to pull free, but he allowed her indignation no time to grow. His embrace was strong, and Vivian, feeling herself in the wrong and wanting to be forgiven, was at a disadvantage. He importuned her with angry but unmistakably pleading kisses, and her short-lived resistance quite melted.

Propped on one elbow, Vivian studied Marvel's face at close range. There were fine lines at the outer corner of his eye, a deeper line between cheek and mouth. Thoughtfully she stroked one finger down his cheek and across his lower lip. He made a mock snap at her finger and smiled lazily. Vivian reflected on how different he had looked when angry, how cold and arrogant. She had never imagined him so, or as short-tempered. But he had confessed to thinking—after an hour's wait—that she was not coming at all. Then she had understood. She saw that his anger, even crudely expressed, indicated the depth of his love for her. She had hastened to assure him as tenderly and lovingly as if he had suffered physical injury that not being with him was unthinkable, that her whole life revolved around her time with him. Incited by anger and insult, renewed pledges and forgiveness, their lovemaking recalled that of their first meeting.

As Marvel bent to tie his shoestrings, Vivian thought to ask, "How did you like the Kiwanis dinner? It made Harry sick."

Marvel shrugged. "It was okay, the usual. But Harry wasn't there. He didn't get sick from overdone beef and cold potatoes."

"Yes, he was. He always goes to the Kiwanis dinner."

"No, he wasn't," said Marvel, flipping his tie. "I wanted to speak to him about something, but I couldn't because he wasn't there."

"What did you want to speak to Harry about?" asked Vivian, sidetracked.

"A business matter."

"What business matter?"

Marvel, on the point of making a sharp answer, thought better of it and softened his reply. "Just business. You don't want to hear about it."

"Yes, I do," insisted Vivian.

"No, you don't," said Marvel and kissed her. They always paused at the door for a last embrace. "And don't pout."

"I'm not pouting."

"Yes, you are." He kissed her again and smiled ingratiatingly, showing his dimple. "Next Tuesday?"

"Tuesday," agreed Vivian.

Driving home, Marvel recalled that next Tuesday he had a luncheon meeting with an important client that was apt to run longer than usual. But if he were a little late getting to the cottage, it wouldn't matter. Might even be a good thing.

As Vivian drove home, she wondered briefly where Harry could have gone. Probably someplace with Logan. And what business could Marvel have with Harry? That they should be doing business seemed to her unfitting in the circumstances, and she was irritated that Marvel had put her off. He was forever ordering her, telling her what she did or didn't want, should or shouldn't do, a habit she at first had delighted in. Even when he had been mistaken, she had suffered it, happy to indulge him. Suddenly it struck her as surprising that he should think she wasn't coming. Why would either of them ever not come? What could be more important? The question made her uneasy. She knew—though at the moment she brushed them aside—that there were many circumstances that might easily keep her away. What she had dreamed of as everlasting appeared, all at once, vulnerable to chance and change. That he had assumed as true what had not yet occurred to her as possible suddenly made it not only possible but quite probable . . . that maybe . . . one day . . . she might not come.

As Logan strode down the street, his long legs striking out at a jaunty angle, he caught sight of Vivian talking to several people outside the post office. He quickened his step, but before he could reach them, they dispersed. With a wave of her hand at a man carrying a sack, Vivian got into her Continental and drove off. Logan grinned, remembering Harry's grumbling over the loss he took for that car. But Logan knew Harry hadn't really minded, that despite his grumbling he would do anything for Vivian. Logan liked Vivian. She was Harry's chosen, and she was everything that Harry's wife ought to be. Toward her—and Corinne, for whom he had stood as godfather—he had a protective, proprietory attitude. He would even, mock-seriously, defend them against Harry himself, against a pretended omission of duty or uncalled-for sternness. It was Logan's way of expressing his fondness for them all.

Recently Harry had been moody, preoccupied, impatient. Whenever Logan reminded him of this or that, Harry gave him what Logan thought of as Harry's "gimlet-cyed" stare. For himself, Logan didn't mind, but he was concerned about Harry's state of mind. And, as an extension of Harry, for Vivian and Corinne.

When Logan entered the office, Jenny was speaking on the telephone, and he could see through the glass partition that Harry was not at his desk. He sat on the corner of Jenny's desk, swung one loosely jointed leg and doodled on her note pad. Jenny, taking notes, made faces at him.

"I wish you wouldn't do that!" said Jenny, hanging up. She immediately recopied her notes and crumpled up the doodled sheet.

"Rather nice designs, I thought," said Logan.

"It's a waste of paper," declared Jenny, tilting her chin. "And time."

Logan had given up long ago expecting anything but a tart answer from Jenny. Invariably his mild attempts at friendliness or humor fell flat. She did not like him, that was clear. Why, he didn't know. He did well enough with other women. Had, as a matter of fact, on at least two occasions, to disentangle himself from what had threatened to become permanent relationships. Jenny went on working, ignoring him. No doubt she disliked his sitting on the corner of her desk. He stood up and noticed Harry's jacket, neatly folded.

"Where's the boss?"

"Harry? He called in. Said he didn't feel well. He'll be in later."

"But that's his coat?"

Jenny paused briefly. "Oh, yes. He forgot it when he left my apartment last night."

Logan retired at once to his own office. He tilted back in his chair, braced one foot against the edge of his desk and thought. Jenny's offhand answer had blurred the landscape, and he had to adjust his sights.

Harry! Trying to make Jenny! It was only natural that Harry should step out now and again. Women were strongly attracted to Harry. Logan remembered once in Harry's own living room when a married woman was so taken with Harry that in a fit of envy she had picked up a book and thrown it at Vivian. It would be hard for a man like that, aware of his power, not to use it occasionally. But with discretion and in a strictly nonserious way, so as not to hurt Vivian or a girl like Jenny, blinded by hero worship. Aside from Corinne, who was still a baby, he had never known a more untouchable girl. She was almost . . . he searched for a word and settled for "encased." She was almost encased in . . . he had thought, "prudery," but that wasn't very complimentary, and he switched to "primness." She was encased in primness. He thought that put it pretty well. If he were to reach out toward her and tap, there would be a ting as of his finger against an invisible, protective glass bell. With Miss Prim and Proper it was always "Mr. Fox" and "Mr. Gamble." Now, suddenly, it was "Harry"—whom Logan had missed at last night's Kiwanis dinner.

Logan brought both feet down hard on the floor. He would

interpose himself. He would not allow Jenny to be hurt, though he knew Harry would never intentionally hurt anyone. He would shield both Jenny and Vivian. And Harry from himself. A man like Harry, of greater strength and daring than that of lesser men, did sometimes fail to see the simplest things and needed the unobtrusive help of a tactful friend.

SEVEN

Triangle

Harry was accustomed to a Logan who followed his own bent, came and went at his own times without tiresome questions or explanations. He was good-humored and brisk. He had marvelous ideas which he pursued enthusiastically to the benefit of them both. He had a fine sense of proportion that allowed him to kick his golf ball from a poor to a better lie and then take a good swing. Women, including Vivian, Harry knew, had tried at various times to marry him off, but Logan had such buoyancy of spirit that he successfully eluded them by embracing all who came his way but holding on to no one. Above all, he and Logan were good friends, which was why, Harry believed, they were also good partners. There was nothing subtle or complicated between them. No temperament. No rivalry. Like brothers, they understood each other, and both understood that Harry was boss.

Suddenly, Logan's pattern of behavior changed. Whichever way Harry turned, he tripped over Logan. Logan, usually late arriving at the office because he had stopped off to do business on the way, now unlocked the front door and was there grinning when Harry arrived. When Harry buzzed for Jenny, Logan appeared right behind her. If Harry stopped at Jenny's desk, Logan was at his elbow. At lunch time when Harry tried to outwait him, Logan worked on and on, sometimes going without lunch altogether. And instead of whistling off in the late afternoon, Logan began taking a deep interest in after-work activities, proposing that he and Harry play a round of golf, look at a piece of property, or go out for a beer.

Worst of all, a nervous intensity radiated from him that made Harry uneasy. He grinned excessively. Harry at first said nothing, but observed Logan with the serious attention due an old and valued friend. He gave him opportunities to speak out and relieve them both of whatever burdened his mind, but Logan apparently had nothing to say. Harry was baffled. He was not used to analyzing other people's motives any more than he analyzed his own. Like Marvel, Harry was a proud facer-of-facts. At any given moment he knew what he wanted. The why was unimportant because, at bottom, all people, rich and poor, were everywhere the same: they scrambled for a living and wanted everything they could get; they ate when they were hungry and bled when they were hurt; and they loved family, home and country, in that order. It was an old, familiar litany that Harry had heard repeated many times by his father, whom it had comforted and sustained as now it comforted and sustained Harry.

But as Logan's aberrant behavior continued, Harry grew increasingly restive. He couldn't so much as say good morning to Jenny without Logan's hovering about. It occurred to Harry that Logan might be interested in Jenny, but when he discovered Logan checking on his whereabouts, he concluded that for some strange reason he himself was Logan's concern. Wherever he went, Logan dogged his footsteps. Secretaries greeted him by saying, "Mr. Gamble just called, asking for you. Didn't leave a message." Business associates joshed him. "Logan's keeping tabs on you, eh, Harry?" Once, backing out of Jenny's driveway, he saw Logan parked across the street. Before he could get out to speak to him, Logan waved and drove off. Harry began to doubt his own position. Could something be threatening him? Could he be running some unsuspected danger from which Logan was trying to protect him? Harry shook himself. There was nothing wrong with him. He was perfectly fit. If Logan had something on his mind, why the hell didn't he come out with it! Harry enjoyed puzzles only when he could face them squarely and solve them either by clear thinking or brute force. In this instance he had ceased to care which. If it took a good sock on the chin to set Logan straight, he would give it to him. Harry resolved to take this matter into his own control the very next time Logan interfered.

As it happened, the next time was at Jenny's. The candles romantically shed their overlapping circles of light, the wine scintillated in the Corning wine glasses, and Jenny leaned toward him beguilingly, her eyes gentle, her smile inviting.

"Harry, have some more lobster mousse."

Harry nodded, totally absorbed in gazing at Jenny and in planning the hoped-for end of the evening. But even as he concentrated wholly on her, he was guardedly practicing a technique he had evolved for dealing with her cooking. He began by taking very small amounts. He concentrated on identifying as well as he could the lethal contents at first bite. Jenny, always eager for his initial reaction, mistook analysis for relish. Gratified by this obvious appreciation of her efforts, she didn't notice the amount he took, only that when urged, he took more. When urged a third time, Harry smiled and nodded. If pressed, he would take firm hold of the server, whereupon Jenny, satisfied, happily shifted her attention to dessert and coffee. Prompted by some inner signal, she would briskly remove everything from the table, not noticing whether he had taken more or not. Later, after Harry had gone, she would be pleasantly surprised to find enough left over for her to take a dish down to her landlady, and where the recipe said Serving for Four she would cross out Four and substitute Six.

Harry had just successfully maneuvered his way through dinner (which Jenny proudly told him had been in the making for two days), and was confidently facing dessert when there was a tattoo on the screen door. In the dim light Harry could see only a man's silhouette, but the stance was familiar.

Logan entered with the breezy familiarity of one who had been expected. Jenny, though surprised, at once became the hostess adept at handling unexpected guests. She offered him a chair and got out an extra plate and cup. Logan thrust his long legs under the small table and grinned affably at Harry, who was staring at him in stony, unbelieving silence. Thinking they were to communicate wordlessly, Logan raised his eyebrows and rolled his eyes in clownish anticipation at the cake, a prodigy of whipped cream and chocolate which Jenny had just placed in the middle of the table.

Harry, his knee crowded by Logan's, moved sharply away. Otherwise he sat ominously still. His patience, exasperation, irritation and other weak-kneed emotions were gone. He burned with an anger that he contained for Jenny's sake. But he eyed Logan narrowly, wanting to smash him, to lift him, a thin bag of bones, straight off his chair and lay him out flat.

Jenny brought coffee and deftly cut the cake, two large pieces and one small.

"I sure got here at the right moment, didn't I," commented Logan, blissfully wolfing down the cake.

"Mmn, yes," said Jenny, impressed by the speed with which he ate.

Harry, cake untouched, stirred his coffee and continued to stare at Logan.

"Excellent, excellent," exclaimed Logan. Becoming uncomfortably aware of Harry's frozen scrutiny, he began meticulously cleaning all the cream from his plate.

"Have another piece," said Jenny, pleased.

Logan, uneasy, glanced at Harry.

With a twitch of his facial muscles that passed for a smile, Harry said, "Yes, have another."

So Logan consumed a second piece, almost as fast as he had the first. Harry watched grimly as Logan once more cleaned his plate. Then he said with insolent grace, "Here, have mine too." He placed his untouched plate in front of Logan.

Logan started to speak, then hesitated.

"Eat it," said Harry.

"But that's yours," protested Jenny. "Let me cut another ..."

Harry, his eyes on Logan, held up a commanding hand. "No. He can have mine." His voice was soft. "Eat it." He might have been saying, "Drop dead."

For Logan, seeing Harry explode on the football field or wither an opponent at a meeting of the town council was glorious. But never before had he felt Harry's wrath directed at himself or at such close quarters. He picked up his fork and ate, sadly, though the whipped cream was still seductively smooth on his palate and the chocolate deliciously dark and rich. He had never intended to anger Harry. That was the last thing he wanted. And physical coercion of Harry was out of the question. He could only continue—painfully but tactfully—on his present course and hope that Harry's anger at him would soon pass.

Jenny, seeing Harry's cup was empty, went to the kitchen for the coffeepot. As soon as her back was turned, Harry leaned forward. His eyes, close up, had a meaner look than Logan had ever thought possible. He scarcely moved his lips, but his words were sufficiently audible.

"Now you've had your dessert, get the hell out! And don't hang around outside or. . . ."

Jenny's return cut short his threat, but Logan felt its weight hanging over him. He pushed back his chair, thanked Jenny and left as abruptly as he had come. He drove off in such a hurry that at the corner he had to screech to a stop to avoid hitting the woman jogger.

Downstairs they watched Logan go and heard the squeal of his brakes.

"Two now it is," the man remarked. "And one a crazy driver."

"He didn't stay long, though. Bet he came at the wrong time."

"One's okay. Two I don't like. Not in *my* house."

"She's a nice girl. And a good cook."

"Cook or no cook, she's a hippie! All that hair and short skirts. Probably up there smoking pot. God knows what color we'll see going up there next!"

"She's a good tenant! Quiet and clean! You're glad enough to eat what she brings us."

"Yeah? Well, just let me see a black going up those steps and it's the end! You hear? The end!"

Pot in hand, Jenny looked after Logan. "What a funny man!"

"Has he been here before?"

"Never," said Jenny. Then, not wanting Harry to think Logan wouldn't have wanted to come, she added primly, "I've never invited him."

They sat together on the bumpy couch, ostensibly to drink their coffee, actually to embrace, as they had done on several previous occasions. That is, Harry embraced Jenny. She allowed him to hold her while she laid one hand tentatively on his shoulder. When he kissed her, she rested her head back and gazed at the ceiling.

The first time Harry kissed her, he had done so gently, not wanting to alarm her and because, held close, her frame was so slight, so slim, he could feel her ribs and backbone. He was awed by the knowledge that he could snap her in two. And, because of her youth and inexperience, he had not expected an immediately passionate response. However, he had hoped for a degree of warmth that would, rather quickly than otherwise, be transformed into passion. Instead she had accepted his caresses sweetly but coolly, like an invincible princess. When, driven to elicit some response, he pressed her too hard, she would suddenly turn her head, giving him a painful crack on the bridge of his nose. Or with a twist of her shoulders and a push she would stand up and remark that she still had to clean up the kitchen and tomorrow was a workday.

By now Harry had learned she wasn't easily startled or breakable. She was lithe but strong, and Harry yearned for her to direct her supple strength against him. Feeling strongly self-assertive after his anger at Logan, Harry embraced her not so gently, and he determined that tonight things would be different. He saw with surprise that as he kissed her, she gazed wide-eyed at the ceiling. All the girls he had ever kissed had closed their eyes. Certainly Vivian did. He drew back just a little and asked softly, "Jenny, why don't you close your eyes? What are you looking at?"

"I'm not *looking* at anything," said Jenny frankly. "I'm judging."

"Judging!" Harry stiffened. "What?" he asked before he could stop himself.

"My reaction, of course. I think that's important, don't you? A girl has to know before she can form a lasting relationship just how. . . ."

In the candlelight her eyes were large and shiny; their seriousness was somehow painful to him. Harry hugged her close, cutting off her words, and rubbed his cheek against hers. "Stop, Jenny!" he whispered. "Stop! It's not a thing you think about! Jenny, I love you! Do you hear? Just close your eyes and . . . ." A loose spring twanged and jabbed sharply into his elbow. "Let's get off this damn couch!"

"The bed *would* be more comfortable," said Jenny calmly, and prudently blew out the candles.

The bedroom was a back corner room. Though a window was centered in each outer wall, a large tree shaded the back of the house and made the room unusually dark. To catch any breeze, Jenny had pulled the bed from against the wall so it extended crosswise into the room. Harry walked right into it.

"Can't see a damn thing!" he exclaimed under his breath. "Can't we turn on a lamp?"

"Oh no!" said Jenny quickly. "You'll adjust in a minute. It's quite light, really."

Gradually the furniture emerged as dark, fixed shapes. Jenny was a lighter, fluid shape, raising her arms and bending. Wanting a unity of mood, of spirit, Harry tried to assist her with zipper and hooks. But in each effort she forestalled him with the same efficiency she showed in office and kitchen. When she was quite ready, she lay back, one arm, like a last defense, across her breast, her hand at the base of her throat.

"Jenny," asked Harry, his voice muffled against her hair, his hand caressing her soft, fragile shoulder, "is this the first time?"

Jenny shifted slightly. "That's not a very nice question." She sounded indignant.

Immediately contrite, he tightened his embrace. "Jenny, I only . . . ."

"That's nothing you need to know."

"No! No, of course not," whispered Harry, losing all interest in conversation. "Oh, Jenny . . . ."

Jenny lay quite straight. Not rigid, but still, like a patient undergoing an operation. Harry, forgetting all restraint, expressed the love that for weeks he had felt as a keen, persistent ache. But despite the intensity of his emotion, the lavish generosity of his love, Jenny continued to elude him. She was delicately beautiful, as he had known she would be. She was pliant and acquiescent. She was maddeningly unresponsive.

Spent and breathing hard, Harry rolled over onto his back. The night was oppressively still and humid. In the tree whose branches touched the eaves of the roof, a cicada whirred its prolonged, falling note, ended abruptly, then, rewound, started up again. From the depths of the house came the faint frenetic voice of a television. Beside him Jenny lay on the other side of an invisible barrier. The weight of the muggy night pressed on Harry's chest. He could think of nothing to say to her. For himself, he could not put into words his choking disappointment. He had thought that his dream was within his grasp, that he was about to experience a shared joy that would illumine and give new purpose to his life. Instead, he felt as if he had been washed up on a rocky beach. He hesitated to turn his head and look at her. She might be staring at the ceiling, judging again. That thought afforded him a sad but tender amusement, and he resolved to be patient. After all, he was older, stronger, the man. He was turning toward her when suddenly Jenny spoke, like the Sphinx, out of the dark. Her voice was low but quite distinct.

"He has a big appetite for such a thin man."

Harry was momentarily disoriented. "What?"

"Mr. Gamble!" said Jenny, as if expecting Harry should have followed her thought. "He ate three big pieces!" Moving quickly, she put on a long robe, went into the living room and flicked on the lights. From the doorway she said, "You know, I think you'd better go now. My landlady might not like your staying so late, and I've still got the dishes to do."

Harry forgot what he was going to say.

At the door he held her close, and searched her face for some sign, some recognition of a firm bond between them. But her clear brown eyes and friendly smile were secretively open. He left with her promise that she would come with him to see the site of the new apartments. In the car he saw with surprise that it was not a week later, but only 11:33 of the same evening.

Downstairs they heard the crunch of his tires backing out of the gravel drive. They glanced at the clock and raised their eyebrows in unspoken comment.

Upstairs Jenny cleaned up the kitchen and wondered about Logan. Why had he come? And why, after nearly finishing the Lincoln Log—there wasn't enough left to take downstairs—had he left so abruptly, without any explanation! Irritated by the very memory, she snapped the cupboard doors shut on the shiny clean dishes. He was *such* an exasperating man!

EIGHT

Disasters

For several weeks, morning and evening, the strains of *The Skaters Waltz* floated out over the neighborhood, entering every ear, indoors and out, penetrating every consciousness. Its tireless, gliding rhythm outdid the drone of sit-down mowers and the roars of Saturday TV baseball. Neighbors flipped their steaks on backyard grills to waltz time. Motorists, at a distance, concluded there must be a traveling carnival nearby.

Finally, one morning at breakfast Harry asked sharply, "Can't that horse do anything but waltz?"

"I don't know," said Vivian thoughtfully. Then suggested waggishly, "We might try her with a two-step or the fox-trot."

Harry's cup struck hard against the saucer. Vivian, glancing sideways, caught his unamused stare. She half smothered a giggle. "Well, she's an old-fashioned horse."

Harry stood up. "It was your idea. You'd better deal with it. I think the neighbors may be getting up a petition. I'll be late this evening. Don't bother with dinner for me."

Vivian remembered it as a joint idea, but it was not worth arguing about. She and Harry lived under the same roof, spoke together briefly, at breakfast and dinner, about household matters and occasionally conferred about Corinne. Otherwise they carried on their lives as independently as roomers in a boardinghouse. Their years together had fallen into limbo. Memories wiped clean, they might have been born the day before yesterday, so little did they have in common. Each was preoccupied with his vision of the future, elusive maybe and vaguely defined, but certain to be wonderful.

Vivian leaned on the fence and watched her daugher riding Molly bareback, round and round. The portable phonograph, volume turned well up, was on the ground near the fence. Though the day was just beginning, there was no morning freshness in the air, only a continuation of the heat and oppressive humidity of the night and the day before and the day before that. The temperature had been in the high nineties with no rain or even a cloudy day for over two weeks. Only in those yards where all day long sprays twirled or fanned or crept was the grass still green. Lines formed at the municipal pool, so crowded one could only jump in place. Attendance at the two movie houses soared, the back rows largely occupied by mothers whose babies, plagued with heat rash, could at last in a hermetic chill fall asleep. The third theater, not air-conditioned, closed its doors. Tempers grew short, and even the heat-loving corn began to look dusty and, like the trees all over town, a bit ragged and limp.

Only the insects throve. They chirred and leaped and sang dry, raspy songs. Their iridescent wings, faceted eyes and armored bodies flashed deep blue and green and gleaming black in the sunlight. But Vivian thought she detected a subtle change. The sun shone fiercely, bleaching the cloudless sky as it had for days past, to a misty, fathomless white, yet this morning its light had a veiled quality. The air was unnaturally still. By late afternoon there might be a thunderstorm.

Abruptly Molly broke her pace, stretched her neck forward and shook her head, pulling hard on the reins. Vivian turned the phonograph off. It occurred to her that *The Beautiful Blue Danube* might be a good change and that Lena Mitchell might have it among her used records. She waved at Corinne. "Time to go. Mr. Farley'll be waiting."

Every day Vivian drove Corinne to work in the morning and picked her up in the late afternoon.

"Will you be late again today?" asked Corinne as they drove along.

"I wasn't late yesterday," said Vivian.

"No, but this is Tuesday. You're always late on Tuesdays."

"Corinne!" Startled, Vivian glanced at her daughter. "Whatever do you mean, on Tuesdays?" laughing a bit at the silliness of it.

Corinne raised her eyebrows. "You're always late on Tuesdays," she repeated, a fact she had recorded in her diary followed by a series of question marks. What she did not record was her uneasy observation of her parents. She perceived a detachment about them, an impersonal quality that made them all three separate, like strangers. Sometimes, when they were together at dinner, she had felt almost invisible. It was nothing she could put into words. Nor would she have wanted to give it the reality of concrete expression. Still, she was curious.

"You go swimming?"

"Sometimes," said Vivian, her eyes on the road.

"I just wondered. I thought you were working on that old house you bought."

"I am, but not every single day." Vivian's tone implied that would be unreasonable.

"I just wondered. I tried to call you once. You weren't home. Then I got that Mr. Fulford, and he said you weren't there either. I just wondered."

"Why?" asked Vivian, frowning. "When was that? What did you want?"

"Oh, nothing. I don't remember. But I just thought I'd ask because if you're going to be late, I'll start walking home. Or maybe Mr. Farley will give me a lift in the truck."

Vivian pulled into Mr. Farley's drive, stopped the car and turned to face Corinne squarely. "There's no need for that," she said sternly. "It's too far and too hot for you to walk home, and I don't want you walking on these narrow roads. I said I will pick you up and I will! You hear?" Corinne glanced at her and nodded. "Okay?"

"Okay," said Corinne and got out.

Fulford, Sr., would have marveled at the work being done on his house, although he would have told Vivian that dark gray paint was more practical than white. The front and rear steps had been rebuilt and the rusty mailboxes replaced. The house painters, who had done the inside stairway and the halls, were nearly finished with the outside. Taciturn men, they wished to be left alone to scrape, prime and paint in silence. They remarked briefly on James' three legs and stoically observed the woman jogger, who passed every day at the same time, morning and afternoon, fully expecting to see her keel over from the heat; otherwise they kept to their ladders, coming down only when Wilder brought them cold beer.

James never relaxed while they were present. He gave up his midmorning and afternoon naps in order to monitor the banging in the hall or the activity outside the windows. In the evenings, when the painters had gone, he would sniff suspiciously at their ladders, laid lengthwise against the side of the house, and then lift his stump in comment.

But he regarded Vivian's painting the unoccupied rear apartment herself as an entirely different matter, as did Wilder and Rilly. For all of them, Vivian's arrival in paint-stained shirt and jeans, a scarf knotted around her head, became an eagerly anticipated social event. Besides a regular break for refreshments, there were consultations about color, cupboard handles and outlet plates to be unscrewed, furniture to be shifted, including a massive upright piano, stuck windows to be unstuck, drop cloths to be spread, and endless errands for Rilly and James to run. In comparison, weekends were flat and dull. Even James moped, as if there were nothing to do but doze until Monday, when he would resume his duties and they would again have a jolly iced-tea break and he would get an extra vanilla wafer to crunch.

For Wilder, weekends were both respite and warning: respite from the week-long strain of watching every word he spoke, of controlling his expression; warning of what it would be like when the work was finished and she no longer came. He must guard against growing accustomed to what would soon end. Staring in the mirror at the homely stranger that was undoubtedly himself, he imagined speaking to her, saying, "Good morning," or anything at all, and watched to see if that impossible face gave him away. It seemed not to, but then, could he rely on it? In a moment of impulse, would it remain so bland? Love was supposed to ennoble, to transform. For him it had not done so. He turned away with a bitterness that lingered until Rilly came knocking excitedly on his door.

"Mr. Fulford! Mrs. Fox needs you to help her move the chest!"

Then, forgetful of self and quite transformed, he hurried to help her, and neither she nor Rilly nor even James, who was sensitive to every nuance, noticed the difference.

This morning Rilly skipped down the sidewalk to meet Vivian. She held up a small cardboard box with holes punched in the lid. "Bet you don't know what I've got in this box!"

"A furry brown caterpillar," said Vivian, speaking out of her own childhood.

"Nope! You'll never guess, so I'll tell you. It's a grasshopper, a flying grasshopper! See?" She lifted the lid slightly. "Her name's Ethel and she spits."

"Spits!"

"Yes. They all do. Tobacco juice. I can make Ethel spit. Mr. Fulford showed me how. You hold her right behind the ear . . ." Rilly held up her thumb and index finger, the width of a grasshopper's head apart, ". . . and you say, 'Spit, spit, tobacco spit! George Washington, Shakespeare, spit!' Then you squeeze and she'll spit!" Vivian was amazed. "Not hard, though," said Rilly, shaking her head, "not to hurt her."

"No, you mustn't," agreed Vivian. "What do you feed her? Won't she die if you keep her in that box?"

Rilly tossed her head. "Oh . . . Mr. Fulford knows what to feed her. Besides," with a quick, sly grin, "there's lots and lots of Ethels!"

As they crossed the porch, Lena came down from upstairs. "Lillian!" she exclaimed, grasping Vivian's arm. "I was hoping to catch you. You're doing such a marvelous job with this house, you really are! Pete and I were talking about it just yesterday. It's so marvelous to have the drains work and the faucets not drip, I can't tell you!" She paused, suddenly abstracted. Her hair was pulled up into an Olive Oyl knot on top of her head. Bared, her neck looked unusually long and thin. Metal earrings with one ceramic bead at the ends dangled from her ears. Absently, she fiddled with a necklace. "Ah! I know what I wanted to tell you! We got a loan and it's all settled. We move next week! Imagine! Into our own home! We're going to have a housewarming party. You and your husband must come! To prove you're not angry at us for moving out just when you've made everything so nice!"

Vivian assured her she wasn't angry, that they would certainly come to her party.

Lena rummaged in her floppy leather bag. "Oh well," she said cheerfully, "can't find it."

"What?" asked Vivian.

"Doesn't matter!" said Lena airily. She waved and went down the steps. "Rilly, be good now, and don't bother Lillian."

That morning Vivian finished painting the bedroom, walls a warm cream, trim white. Rilly summoned Wilder, and together he and Vivian moved the massive bedstead back into place against the only wall where, in so small a room, it would fit.

"That's . . . quite a bed," said Vivian, catching her breath.

"It was Mother's," said Wilder. "It used to be upstairs."

Vivian regarded it with interest. "Looks very old. Had it been in her family?"

Wilder didn't know. Exertion had brought beads of sweat to his forehead and made his glasses slide down his nose. He removed them, turning the world into one huge blur, and took out his handkerchief. He didn't like thinking of his mother's bed, the place of origin and birth of all her brood. Or even looking at it, for it was impossible for him to do so without seeing her also, lying in it, her large, bony frame shaping skeletal ridges under the quilt, her sparse gray hair straggling on the pillow, her nose jutting out from her sunken face. Worst of all, he still saw her eyes, the eyes of a rebellious prisoner being hauled off to execution, who saw clearly that their positions should be reversed. He, unfit, should be leaving this world. She, able and strong, a producer of life, should be once more on the threshold. Feeling like a prisoner himself, Wilder had often been inclined to agree with her. But he had soon realized that life without her was a different matter. He discovered he was glad to be alive. Now he shied from thoughts of his mother as though from what she called the "great beyond" she had found him out and stamped "Unfilial" across his forehead.

Wilder dried his frames and mopped his head. Outside a ladder thumped against the house, reminding him of the painters, shirtless in the heat, their browned shoulders X'ed white from their overall straps, and thirsting for beer.

"I'll get the beer," he muttered, and asked Vivian, "Would you like some iced tea?"

He always offered and Vivian always accepted. They would

sit down where they could on the disarranged furniture. Rilly was the custodian of the vanilla wafers. James, off duty while the painters were quieted with beer, sat directly in front of her, his wistful gaze fixed on the plate of wafers. Sometimes, unable, like Wilder, to repress his desire, he pursed up his lips and gave a barely audible woof.

While Wilder fetched the tea, Vivian studied the carving on the headboard. The finish was very dark, almost black, with deep mahogany highlights. The entire top half of the high, square-cornered frame was carved with a profusion of leaves and fruit. In the middle, crowning all, was the double curve of the outspread wings of a bird in flight. Vivian traced what seemed to be its head, downbent, its feet thrust forward as if to land. Beyond that the carver's intention had wavered, his indecision hidden under vines and ambiguous shapes. Was it God's bird of morning or the night bird of death? Or, less solemnly, the dove of peace, carrying an olive branch? Or possibly, thought Vivian, smiling, the American eagle, clutching both olive branch and arrows, blessing the fecundity and the principles of honesty, practicality and good hard work for which Mr. Fulford, Sr., had so resolutely stood. Vivian decided, as she cleaned the paintbrushes, in favor of the eagle.

She drove to the lake a bit earlier than usual, wanting time for a swim before Marvel came. The moving car created a hot but welcome breeze. The rows of corn, whipping by, were tall enough now to hide a man. Their long, blade-like leaves that could clash metallically in a wind hung limp in the shimmering heat. Redwing blackbirds soared low over the fields, fanning down to light on fence posts. Vivian heard their whistles on the rushing air, the clear sweet notes seeming to trail behind her as she passed.

From a distance the lake appeared blue, but seen close up it was layered shades of brown. The surface layer was almost clear, only tinted by the lower, translucent layers of deepening brown. Vivian disliked the shallows, for the bottom hadn't the definite, clean texture of either rock or sand, but was soft and squishy. At every step she took the water was instantly muddied. She plunged forward into the water, submerging and rising far enough out to tread water without touching bottom. She swam back and forth, parallel with the shore, then turned over to float and keep watch on the deck for Marvel. He had stubbornly refused to swim, offering one excuse or another, until finally admitting he didn't know how. Vivian had been surprised. Harry was a fine swimmer. As if he sensed the comparison, Marvel took a dislike to her swimming. He would not respond to a call or wave, would instead turn his back and go inside. It was the one point of contention between them on which Vivian had not given in. But she always came out of the water as soon as she saw he had arrived.

Catching sight of him on the deck, she rolled over and swam in, scarcely disturbing the glassy surface. Before she reached the edge, he had gone inside. Hurrying out of the shallows, Vivian suddenly felt a sharp pain on the sole of her foot and saw the blue-green shine of broken glass. She hobbled to the deck stairs and sat down on the bottom step. Her foot was bleeding profusely from a deep, curved cut. She called to Marvel, but got no answer. She called again, but not until the third time, when the urgency in her voice was unmistakable, did he respond.

"I've cut myself."

Marvel raised his eyebrows, said nothing.

"Well, would you throw me a towel or something? I don't want to get blood all over the deck."

Marvel went away and returned with a towel, which he tossed down to her. With the towel wrapped around her foot, Vivian came up the steps one at a time under Marvel's condemning eye. He followed her in and leaned in the bathroom doorway, watching as she cleaned the cut and tried to stanch the bleeding.

"If you didn't insist on swimming, it wouldn't have happened," he remarked.

Vivian looked at him, eyes blazing. "What do you mean! If I didn't insist!" Furious, she picked up the wet, bloody towel and threw it at him. "Get out! Go and stand somewhere else! You're no help!"

Startled, Marvel caught the towel on his chest and threw it aside. "Now look here, I only meant. . . ."

"I know what you meant! You meant it was my fault! My fault that some fool is stupid enough to throw bottles into the lake!"

"Calm down, Vivian," said Marvel, coming closer and spreading his hands out placatingly. "Just calm down and . . . ."

"Don't tell me what to do! You're good at that, aren't you? Well go and tell someone else! I don't need your kind of help!" She smiled scornfully. "*Throwing* a towel at me! And how you helped me up the steps! What concern! What sympathy!" She paused, then added contemptuously, "A stranger would have been of more help!"

Marvel backed off, his face carefully blank, his eyes watchful.

Trembling with anger at him and at herself for being hurt, Vivian turned away and began impatiently opening and slamming drawers. "There must be some Band-Aids here somewhere!" Suddenly she held very still, then reached in and lifted out a pair of sheer dark blue stockings. Holding them up, she turned slowly to Marvel.

"Yours?"

He smiled slightly. "Yours, more likely."

Vivian held his gaze for a long moment, then said flatly, "I never wear blue stockings." She dropped them back in the drawer with a show of distaste and banged it shut. "Oh well, she can pick them up next time."

Marvel stiffened. "Now listen. You're drawing an entirely . . . ."

"I'm not drawing anything!" interrupted Vivian, fighting back tears. "I'm looking for a Band-Aid!"

"You know perfectly well . . . ."

"I don't know a thing!" exclaimed Vivian vehemently. Facing him with a look almost of wonder, she went on more slowly, ". . . not a thing . . . really . . . except that today I can't be late." It was a lame remark. Disgusted with herself, she turned away and, thinking aloud, said, "I should go right now. If I could just find something to put on this foot! It *would* be the right one!" Then, as if surprised he was still there, she glanced at him sharply. "Would you mind stepping out now? I'd like a little privacy!"

Finding the door shut in his face, Marvel shouted, "You needn't worry about being late. Harry won't care a damn!" He got no answer. Hands in his back pockets, he went to stand by the window, staring out and calling himself ten kinds of a fool for letting this happen. He should have been more careful of her. He hadn't realized she had such a temper. But when she came out, he would make her understand. Given half a chance, he was sure he could persuade her to stay, though those damned stockings would make it harder. Probably she would cry a little. He would comfort her and the whole incident would be smoothed over. It had to be, for he didn't want to lose her, not for some time yet.

When Vivian emerged, she had padded the cut and wrapped

it around with layers of cleansing tissues, all she find. She walked with a halt, setting her right foot down only on its heel. But by no means did she need support. The set of her head and shoulders was aggressive.

Marvel, solicitous, held out a drink he had hurried to prepare. "Here, this is just what you need."

"No, I don't," said Vivian shortly. "What did you mean, Harry won't care a damn?"

Marvel smiled, shamefaced but ingratiating. "Come on," he said coaxingly, "take one and let's sit down. I can't stand here with two glasses."

"Put them down then," said Vivian. "I want to know what you meant."

Marvel perceived this was more serious than he'd thought. She showed no sign of being sorry for all she had said. He put down the drinks and, coming close, took hold of her shoulders.

"Careful," said Vivian, glancing at her foot and stepping back.

"I hope it doesn't hurt," said Marvel. "You should sit down, or better yet, lie down and put your foot up." He took her arm to guide her to the couch, but she shrugged his hand off and stood like a rock where she was.

"It does hurt. And what I *should* do is get home and bandage it properly. But first I want to know what you meant."

Marvel was surprised by her persistence. He ventured to put an arm around her waist. She stood still but the fixity of her expression seemed to him unfriendly. He leaned closer, gazed at her meltingly. He spoke softly. He was confessing, confiding, begging for understanding all at the same time.

"Nothing. I meant nothing. I only wanted to hurt you." He made wanting to hurt her sound like a virtue. "I'm sorry."

"Why?" asked Vivian. "I was already hurt."

He smiled a sad, rueful smile. "You wouldn't even let me explain. You shut me out." He saw she was listening. "You *know* what you mean to me. You are everything I've ever wanted."

"Except for someone in blue stockings."

Marvel groaned, shut his eyes and shook his head. "All right, I admit it. It happened just once. But it meant nothing to me."

"It?"

"She. She meant nothing to me. She doesn't even live here."

(She did, in fact, live eighteen and three-quarter miles away by the back roads.) "She just happened to be there, and you weren't. It was really you I wanted. It isn't easy, living apart from you and . . ." inspired to show she was indirectly at fault, ". . . you know you said you wouldn't come oftener."

"Couldn't."

"But you *are* here now." He leaned his forehead against hers. His voice sank to a whisper. "I've missed you so." He bent to kiss her.

"I don't believe," said Vivian clearly, turning her head so his lips brushed her still damp hair, "that's all you meant about Harry."

Marvel couldn't quite cover his exasperation. They studied each other at close range. "All right," he admitted. The truth, after all, might make it easier. "He's been going about with his secretary a lot, to grocery stores and. . . ."

"Grocery stores!"

Marvel disliked her tone, which suggested he was slightly mad. His voice hardened. ". . . and his car's been seen parked in her driveway often and late."

"By whom?"

This was getting dangerous. Marvel encircled her with both arms and avoided her questioning look by rubbing his cheek against her hair. To that she had always succumbed. This time she stood straight as a stick. Persisting, he murmured, "Let's not waste time talking about that. What matters is us, just us. We're together now, and we won't be again for a whole week."

"What matters," Vivian said sharply, "is that my foot is still bleeding. You're leaning on me, and that makes it harder."

Stabbed, he drew back. He wouldn't have believed she could be so stubborn. Alarmed, he concentrated on securing the future. He held her elbows as if to brace her and smiled with sad understanding. "I know. You're punishing me. I deserve it. But you will come next Tuesday! Promise you will! You couldn't be that hard on me, not when you know how much I need you!"

Vivian hesitated, finding it suddenly difficult to speak. She had not thought ahead. "I can't . . . be sure. It depends, I guess, how my foot is."

He attempted to help her out to her car, but she evaded his hand and moved surprisingly swiftly, reaching the car ahead of him. Unaided, she slid under the wheel and slammed the door. It hurt to press the accelerator. The padding under her foot was showing bright red.

She forgot to wave.

Vivian amazed Corinne by arriving early.

"It's not time to quit yet," protested Corinne. Her face was sunburned, and wisps of hay stuck in her hair and to her T-shirt.

"I want you to come now," said Vivian firmly. "There's a tornado warning. So get in."

On her way back from the lake Vivian's attention had been lifted from personal matters by the awesome aspect of earth and sky. The stillness was judgmental. All life was hushed. No birds were in flight or moving clouds in the empty void. No puff of dust followed a farmer working his field. Cattle, closely grouped, stood like wooden toys with heads down and tails still. The bilious sun shed a glittering, veiled light across the countryside. The hood of Vivian's car, struck by its beam, gleamed a dull ominous orange. Hearing the warning over the car radio, Vivian had stopped at home only long enough to bandage her foot and had then gone for Corinne.

They put the car in the garage and returned Molly, who had been out grazing, to her stall. To the west the sky was greenish-yellow.

Corinne bemoaned leaving Molly. "I don't want to leave her out here alone!"

"Well, you can't stay with her. And you can hardly bring her into the house. She'll be all right. Come on."

"You're limping!" exclaimed Corinne.

"I cut my foot, that's all."

"How'd you do that? Is it bad?"

"On a piece of glass. It's all right now. I just don't want to start it bleeding again."

"How did you step on a piece of glass?"

Vivian made an unintelligible noise, then said, enunciating very clearly, "By not looking where I was going!"

Corinne was silenced. Inside she asked, "What about Dad?"

"He's probably at the office. I'll call him." Vivian expected that Jenny, whom she had seen once or twice and spoken to countless times on the phone, would answer. But she didn't. There was no answer at all.

That afternoon Harry took Jenny out to see the skating rink, which was in the process of being torn down, and the surrounding area, where excavation for the new apartments had already begun. The workmen were leaving, and Harry congratulated himself on his timing. It was harder and harder to avoid Logan, and he was hoping to have some time alone with Jenny.

Everywhere the ground was rutted and gouged by heavy digging equipment, now parked to one side, the tread of their immense tires caked with dried mud. Nearby were stacks of cement blocks, and near them pyramids of sand. Around the rink were piles of old boards and sections of roofing and sidewalls with torn tar paper still attached. Harry and Jenny, he holding her elbow, picked their way through to the open end that had once been the rink entrance. The office walls were still intact, but the huge roof was almost dismantled. Some of the beams were still in place, and they cast triangular shadows on what was left of the outer walls and the partially torn-up floor.

"I went to a skating rink once," said Jenny. "When I was small. It was scary. They had moving colored lights that made everybody look weird! It was dark in the corners, and the skaters went so fast and made so much noise! I didn't like it. Did you ever come here?"

Harry had. He and his sister Dolly used to come on Saturday nights. They had had moving colored lights here too, and he and Dolly had thought they were beautiful. Later he had come with Vivian. The other fellows had envied him because she was not only the prettiest but the best skater among the girls. They had skated side by side, hands clasped and arms crossed. Sometimes they boldly swung around to face each other, arms extended, and the carnival lights washed rapidly over them as they bobbed and slanted, whirling in circles down the length of the floor and back. Harry had a sudden vivid memory of Vivian at arm's length, hair flung out, eyes alight, the colors flashing across her face as they spun and glided. One night they won first prize.

Harry experienced a surge of undefined emotion. He turned toward Jenny, who was walking down the middle of the wide floor and looking curiously about. The hollow thud of her heels on the worn boards was the only sound in the heavy stillness. An eerie yellow light flooded down between the skeletal beams, a muted light that softened lines and washed out colors. It fell in hazy, dust-filled shafts, like a pale vapor, and made Jenny's diminished figure and the half-demolished building appear miragelike and insubstantial.

Harry called out. "Jenny, don't step on those boards! They're full of rusty nails." Beyond where she stood, the floorboards had been ripped up, revealing the dank crawl space underneath.

Jenny laughed. Balancing with arms out, she stepped up onto a haphazardly stacked pile of floorboards and stood teetering, looking about as if from a grand height. Harry came quickly around to the far side of the pile. Standing below her, he put up his arms around her hips.

"Come on down. I'll show you where the apartments are going up, and then we'll go somewhere for dinner. You'd like that?"

Teasingly, Jenny tilted her chin and pursed her mouth. "Mmmmnn . . . maybe."

"Then we could go back to your apartment."

"Mmmmnn . . . ." She fiddled with his shirt collar, pretending to smooth it. She was conscious of the effect of her hair, falling forward and shading her face. Playing a scene she had recently watched on television, she smiled demurely and slowly raised the level of her gaze to meet his.

Harry's arms tightened. "Kiss me," he begged in a whisper.

Enjoying her part, Jenny leaned down slowly. Eagerly Harry strained upward, and at that moment, her hair against his face, his lips almost touching hers, there was a yell.

"Hey, Harry!"

Harry started back. With the additional weight of Jenny leaning on his shoulders, the unsupported floor beneath him splintered and gave way. They crashed down together, amid falling boards and a cloud of dust.

Logan sprinted forward. Harry lay on his back, Jenny sprawled across him, struggling to rise from under several boards pinning her down. Logan pitched aside the boards and hauled Jenny up onto her feet.

"All right?" he asked, glancing over her swiftly.

Jenny nodded. "I . . . I think so." She brushed herself off and discovered a long tear in her dress.

Logan turned to Harry, partially raised on one elbow but grimacing with pain. Logan, ready to give him a hand up, hesitated. "What is it, Harry?"

"My leg. . . ." muttered Harry. "Hurts like hell." His right foot had gone through the floor. "Left leg's okay, but I think the other one's broken." Harry inched back, slowly withdrawing his right leg from the hole. Logan knelt and guided Harry's leg past the splintered wood. They both saw that his foot lay at a strange angle.

"We've got to get you out of here. There's a tornado coming. Didn't you see the sky?"

"I didn't notice," growled Harry. "Give me a hand up."

"You can't walk on it!"

Harry made an impatient sound. "Give me a hand, I said!" He drew his good foot back under himself and with a pull from Logan heaved himself up. "Now give me that stick! There! That one!" With the stick as crutch and an arm across Logan's shoulders, Harry swung himself to the entrance, not without considerable pain and effort. While Logan went for his car, Jenny stayed with Harry, her arm around his waist to help steady him.

"I'm glad," said Harry, breathing hard, "that you weren't hurt."

"Only a skinned arm and a rip in my skirt." They looked at each other solemnly.

"I guess we won't go out for dinner tonight. Or for some time." Because of the pain, his words had a bitten-off quality.

"I guess not," agreed Jenny.

They were very close, leaning together. Sadly, Harry studied her face as if to read in its serious but calm surface why this had happened to him—he, who had come through four years of high school football without so much as a sprained finger. He could see the flecks of color that made up the light brown of her eyes, each separate, curving eyelash, the delicate texture of her lip. It crossed his mind that now he could kiss her. But he didn't. It wasn't just that he was gritting his teeth with pain—worse, his impulse to do so had died. His every attempt to reach her had been fraught with disaster one way or another. He perceived that closeness could be deceptive. Failure was a concept Harry had never accepted. Nor did he now. But he was baffled. He felt under attack from some malign force. Since it was necessary to temporarily withdraw, he would put the time to good use. He would regroup and consider.

The hospital was a sprawling building evolved from a former residence surrounded by ancient maple trees to an imposing six-floor complex covering every inch of space from sidewalk to sidewalk. As Logan turned into the emergency drive, a sudden gust of wind hit the car broadside. It caught the swinging doors of the emergency entrance and whipped the nurse's starched skirt as she wheeled Harry inside.

"I'll tell Vivian!" yelled Logan and jumped back in the car. "I'll drop you off on the way," he said to Jenny, adding, "Vivian's his wife. He's married, you know."

"Of course I know," said Jenny crossly. "How could I not know!" Logan was such a silly man!

Turning the wheel to offset the now powerful steady push of the wind, Logan said, "Guess I thought if you knew you might not, uh . . . spend so much time with him."

Jenny tossed her head. "How I spend my time is none of your business! Besides," she added, not being able to resist expressing her ideas, "that concept of marriage is old-fashioned! It's not . . . not relevant any more!"

"Relevant!" exclaimed Logan. He braked for the woman jogger blindly crossing the intersection, her hair in her eyes, her shirt billowing, the wind at her back pushing her into a run. "Relevant to what?"

"To people's lives!" Jenny was impatient with his failure to understand. "You can't tie people together with a piece of paper! That's just silly! It's the relationship that counts! If one relationship has gone bad and another is good, then it's only fair to admit it." She looked at him belligerently, as if by saying nothing he had contradicted her. "Anything else," she said piously, looking straight ahead, "would be dishonest."

Logan skidded into her driveway. He was now more than ever convinced that Jenny needed looking after. She was as dangerous to herself and others as a child playing with a bear trap. But right now he had no time. He reached across in front of her and opened the door. "I've got to go. You get inside and stay there!"

Jenny slammed the door. Furious at his ordering her about, she turned to glare at him, but he was already backing out. The wind tore at her. Ducking her head to catch her breath, she ran up the stairs, her hair blowing wildly.

Black, towering clouds were moving swiftly eastward. Like the crest of a violent sea, they stretched out across the sky. Rapidly they enveloped the sun and, cutting off its sickly yellow light, brought early darkness. Rain began to fall, erratically at first, splatting on the pavement in nickel-sized drops, then in stinging gusts that increased in volume to a torrential downpour.

Logan had intended to drive to Vivian's and take her to pick up Harry's car. But the rain sluicing down the windshield so reduced visibility that he drove at a creeping pace and went straight home. Already the gutters were full of brown, rushing water. Spreading across the street, it fanned up on either side of his car as if parted by the prow of a boat. Not pausing to open the garage door, Logan left the car in the driveway and sprinted for the back door. The rain struck him with chilling force. As he reached the lattice-covered stoop and paused to fish out his key, a lightning bolt rent the air above him. Logan threw up his arm across his face, heard an ear-shattering, splitting sound and then a crash. Momentarily stunned, he lowered his arm and saw that the top of an old sycamore had come down across the hood of his car.

He called Vivian at once. The connection was noisy and faint. He heard himself yelling above the resounding thunder. Finally she understood and he hung up. Water trickled down the back of his neck. His shirt was a cold, clammy second skin, and his shoes were sodden. But before taking time to change, he brought the oil lamp into the kitchen that his mother, mistrustful of public utilities, had always kept on the hall table. He put it in the middle of the table and lit it. For good measure, he got a flashlight and laid it near the lamp. Then he got into dry clothes. And then he had a drink. Thinking of Harry's leg and his car smashed by the sycamore, he had another.

Vivian called the hospital. After several waits while the phone crackled and urgent voices broke in on other urgent voices, she was switched to another line and informed by an agitated voice that, yes, Mr. Fox *did* have a broken leg, but they were *very* busy. There had been a power failure. Mr. Fox would have to remain in the hospital. They would let . . . . Vivian jiggled the receiver, tried dialing the hospital back, tried dialing Logan back, but the phone was dead.

The center of the tornado passed north of Warrenville, but its path extended over the town and some miles beyond, north and south. Whirling winds uprooted trees, tore off roofs, brought down telephone and utility lines. People were trapped for the night in stores, theaters and taverns. Plate glass windows were whipped by the wind until they shattered. Signs were ripped off and blown away. Center stoplights tossed wildly about, and cars were stranded as streets and sidewalks turned into running streams.

At the hospital Harry, his leg in a cast, was given a sedative, rolled into an out-of-the-way corner and left to sleep until morning.

When the power failed, Jenny went to bed and fell asleep with the covers over her head to shut out the lightning. She was shocked awake by an apocalyptic blast of sound as lightning struck the tree outside her window, stripping off its bark from top to bottom. Brought bolt upright, she at first thought the house had been struck and rushed into the living room. No way could she turn from the lightning that cracked and spit in every direction, its eerie blue light illuminating the room in a series of overlapping flashes. Peals of thunder crashed together, shaking the house with their vibrations. Terrified, Jenny shrank down in a corner. Shielded behind the couch and an old easy chair, she doubled over and hid her face against her knees.

Corinne, learning that her father was in the hospital, was inclined to cry. She wanted to go at once to see him. But, as Vivian pointed out, the storm made going anywhere impossible. Even as she spoke, the lights flickered several times, went out, then came on again briefly—giving Vivian and Corinne time to scurry for candles—before they went out for what was ultimately almost twenty-four hours.

They had a cold supper in the downstairs rec room, where the effects of the storm were somewhat muted. Despite her worry over her father and Molly, who was alone in her stall, Corinne ate three sandwiches and, worn out from working at the farm, fell asleep on the couch.

Vivian was too· disturbed and restless to sleep. She went upstairs and stood in the dark, looking out into the violent, thunderous night. The storm was reaching its peak, its immense vortex whirling the wind and rain against the house from every quarter. Before such an onslaught, the house was no more than a shell, and Vivian was uneasily conscious of the thinness of the walls, the fragility of the windows. The room and the terrace beyond lit up in ghostly, surrealistic flashes; the glass doors between were glittering sheets of rain. It seemed impossible that it was only that morning that she had stood in the brassy sunlight watching Corinne and Molly. Disconnected and remote, the day's events, the words that had been spoken and those that hadn't, came back to her in snatches. Perhaps she had dreamed them all, the sad wistfulness in Wilder's eyes, the hurt and reproach in Corinne's voice. Logan's anxiety and reassurance crackling over the telephone were somehow comic, and that Harry had broken a leg and was in the hospital seemed wildly improbable. But the dull, steady pain in her foot—that was real enough. And it recalled Marvel, who stood at a distance, in the background of her thoughts, awaiting judgment. She did not want to remember his hostile indifference and duplicity; they were painful and shaming. She wondered fleetingly if she had seen it all correctly. Had she misunderstood, misinterpreted? At that moment, such questions were scarcely important, impossible even to hold onto. They slipped from her mind just as an echoing roll of thunder died away, leaving, for a moment, a strange quiet above the steady downpour of rain. Vivian shivered, her skin prickling in the breathless pause. Suddenly, with a high, splitting sound that swelled to a piercing volume and spread out upon the shattered air, the sky was illumined by a gigantic branched tree of lightning. Ice blue with a rose-tinged edging, it flared out against the black clouds, again and again, like the giant pulse of the universe. Vivian stumbled back, awestruck. As the thunder exploded, shaking the windows with its mighty vibrations, she turned and fled downstairs. Should Corinne have been frightened awake, she must be there.

By morning the rain had stopped. The sky was a chastened, washed-out gray, with no discernible break in the high-riding clouds. North of Warrenville the tornado had cut a swath, leveling crops and farm buildings and devastating one small town. Raw foundations in the ground marked where buildings had once been. Boards, bricks, roofs, windows, trees, all were gone, swept away without a trace. Along the sides of the tornado's path were blasted tree trunks and sections of houses, ripped apart and left with outer walls askew, their roofs gone or caved inward, their exposed insides a shambles. People caught out in the fields or on the highway were never found. Nor were those who had remained in their houses. The rest of the small population who had sheltered in a church basement emerged to begin resurrecting their town.

In Warrenville the river was running high. Sewers were clogged by debris and unable to carry off the sudden volume of water. Streets were flooded and impassable because of broken branches and fallen trees, which had dragged down telephone and utility wires. Antennas, signs, fences were blown away. Chimneys and church steeples were toppled. One of the clock faces on the courthouse tower had lost its hands.

Before daylight repair crews were out and busy, pumping water, repairing transformers and power lines. But it was several days before the streets were cleared of trees. Power saws whined from morning till night. City dump trucks and any others that could be pressed into service carried away tree trunks and branches.

Harry had to spend another day and night in the hospital before Vivian could get through to drive him home. By then he had become proficient with his crutches and was able, at home, to answer the telephone when it surprised them by ringing.

"It's some woman who wants Lillian!"

It was Lena, inviting them to a housewarming party.

NINE

Pool Party

Rilly sat sulking on the grass near the swimming pool. It was large, for a pool, almost as long as the house itself, which, for a house, was small. The water was smooth and shiny as blue glass in the sunlight. Rilly squinted at it from under her brows. She hated it. And the house. And her parents for moving away from Mr. Fulford and James, and for making her go into the water. She never would again. Not ever. When Lena called to her through the kitchen window, she pretended not to hear. Lena called again; when she still didn't answer, Pete stepped out of the back door and came toward her. Seeing him, Rilly jumped up and ran to the iron link fence that surrounded the backyard. She curled her fingers through it and hung on, looking back defiantly at her father.

Pete's beard opened and showed his teeth in a hairy laugh. "Come on, Rilly! You don't need to do that. I'm not going to throw you in!"

Rilly didn't answer, nor did she let go her hold on the fence. Earlier that day, after coaxing her into the shallow end of the pool, he had solemnly promised to hold her by the straps of her bathing suit while she splashed her arms and legs. Instead he had let go. She had gone under at once, her whole head submerged. Pete had pulled her out, laughing and thumping her on the back while she choked and coughed.

"If you'd just kept on splashing, you'd have been swimming! C'mon, let's try. . . ."

But Rilly had hit him with her fists and screamed. "Put me out! Put me out!"

Pete had hesitated, still amused.

"Better put her out," cautioned Lena.

Since then Rilly would not let Pete come near her.

"Lena wants you to help carry out the food. People will be coming soon."

With exaggerated caution, Rilly sidled toward the house, circling far out around her father, never taking her mistrustful gaze from him until she reached the door.

"Come on!" said Pete, feeling sorry but also a bit resentful. "It was just a little ducking!"

"You promised!" exclaimed Rilly accusingly. Her chin trembled at the memory. She went inside, letting the door slam behind her.

Pete sighed. He hoped she wouldn't make a point of it all evening in front of everyone. But for Pete, as well as for several others, the evening was fraught with mishaps, although its face was innocent enough.

The sun was calmly declining in the west, spreading its last, rosy light across the sky. In the east, a partial moon had risen, still so wan it was lost among the wispy, cottony clouds. The air was still and hot enough to make the pool inviting. A few chairs were scattered about the yard, some borrowed from a neighbor, but not too many. "Keep them on their feet," was Lena's motto for any party. There was a punch bowl inside on a table in the dining area, another one outside on a picnic table.

Pete was especially proud of the punch. It contained rum, whiskey, brandy, Benedictine, champagne and strong tea, plus assorted fruit juices and a dash of bitters. "It is," he declared each time he tested it, "a festive punch for a festive occasion." When guests began to arrive, he received them with exceptional warmth and a jarring clap on the shoulder. He immediately served each a glass of punch with the admonition that thereafter everyone was to help himself.

When Harry, Vivian and Corinne arrived there were already people in the pool, tossing about a large beach ball. Corinne, eager to get in the water, hurried inside and shed the shirt and blouse she had on over her bathing suit. Other guests, who had not come to swim, stood about out of splattering range, talking and drinking punch. Those who knew Harry and Vivian nodded and raised a hand in greeting. Lena, seeing them, dropped a sentence in midair. Arms outstretched and earbobs swinging, she rushed to welcome them.

"Gregory! So glad to meet you! Lillian told me about your unfortunate accident! How dreadful having to wear that heavy cast in such hot weather! Here, sit right here. I saved this lounge just for you!"

Harry was at once on familiar ground. Eager concern for his welfare was the attitude he had always encountered in women, and he responded quite naturally. He let the Gregory pass for the moment and smiled a lazy, ingratiating smile that crinkled his eyes and accented the clean, strong line of his chin and jaw.

"If you don't mind, I'd rather sit on a straight chair." He gave his crutches a little shake. "You know—easier to get up and down."

"Of course! I should have . . . ." With a sense of urgency suggesting impending disaster should Harry not sit down at once, Lena dragged up a sturdy redwood chair. She entirely forgot Vivian, who went off with Pete for a tour of the new house. Lena watched solicitously as Harry put the crutches aside and lowered himself into the chair. She brought him a glass of punch and a paper plate loaded with cheese and crackers. Then she plopped down on the grass and gazed at him, mesmerized, as she twisted her beads into knots.

"I must tell you how generous, how . . . humanitarian it was of you, Gregory, to buy that house on Green Street. Not on our account, of course, but for Wilder's sake. If only you knew . . . but then, you must, mustn't you! Wilder will want to thank you himself, I know. He should be here . . . somewhere." She waved vaguely to one side, unable to bring herself to look away from Harry.

"I'd sure like to meet *him*," said Harry. "But I can't take credit for buying that house. My wife bought it. And my name's Harry, not Gregory."

"Harry!" Lena looked stunned. "Harry? Oh, *that* doesn't sound right at all! You *look* like Gregory. Is Harry a nickname?"

"It's the name I was baptized with."

"Baptized! How quaint!" Lena beamed at him. "Old-fashioned, but nice, very nice!"

Rilly appeared before them, hands clasped behind her back. "Pete says we need more potato chips."

Lena got up. "This is our daughter, Amaryllis," adding, over her shoulder, "she wasn't baptized."

Rilly studied Harry, his cast, his crutches. She would have liked to touch the plaster. Instead she said, "Bet you don't know who Ethel is."

"No," agreed Harry genially. "Who is she?"

But Harry's penetrating blue eyes and affable grin overwhelmed Rilly, and, to save face, she blurted out, "I won't tell!" and ran off.

Explosive shouts came from the swimmers. The ball rose from a cascade of water, sailed out of the pool and bounced onto the grass near Harry. With a swipe of his crutch, he got the ball and tossed it back. A cheer rose from the pool.

"Good fielding, Harry. Remember me? M.T. Reardon, from the local rag? Just call me M.T. I did a piece a few months back on your project out at the skating rink. We talked once."

"Yeah," said Harry drily. "I remember. Over the phone. The connection must have been bad."

M.T. was a short, square man who appeared to have little forehead because he combed his hair sideways, across his round head, the foremost strands brushing the tops of his eyeglasses. His ears were noticeably large and set at right angles to his head. One of M.T.'s worst memories was of his mother, now deceased, clasping her hands and lamenting, upon hearing him called M.T. Jug, M.T. Jug, by nasty little boys, "If only I'd taped his ears back! If only I had!" But given his name and his ears, M.T. had learned the hard way to brazen out facts. What he couldn't change he would flaunt. He cocked his head as if to listen all the more sharply and held up a hand.

"Easy now! Don't get belligurrent! No belligurrence called for a-tall! I know you think we got a little fact wrong here and there, but it's easy to slip between pen and print."

"Yeah, well, your little slips sure created a hassle for me with the city council and the permit office."

A woman of modest appearance holding a clipboard with ruled paper stopped and smiled apologetically for her interruption. "I'm Hester Morris. I'm with the International League for

Peace. We're getting signatures for an anti-Vietnam War ad to be put in the New York *Times*. Would you care to sign?"

"Sure thing," said Harry. He added his signature to the list and was going to hand the board over to M.T., but M.T. was not one for swimming against the current. While Harry signed, M.T. walked away and began talking to someone else about the articles he had written.

"I've never gotten a rejection—not one." He flexed his shoulders proudly. "They know they can rely on me, that when they see the name M.T. Reardon, it'll be aimed right down the middle of the alley! Yessir, I've written for papers all over this country."

Dusk deepened into night. The summer moon shone with such a glow that it blanked out the immediate stars. But it went largely unnoticed, outshone by the glaring spotlights fastened to the back of the house which funneled light on the pool and its adjacent area. The swimmers made rippling shadows in the sparkling water, and people sitting on the edge dangling their legs in the water could be brilliantly seen. Those moving about the yard through the gnat-filled shafts of light were cut into kaleidoscopic slices of dark and light. Lena brought out citronella candles which flickered in orange-tinted holders.

Inside, candles, whose light had been lost in the waning daylight, now cast rings of light over the hand-woven tablecloth and highlighted the faces of those eating peanuts and guacamole and filling their glasses from the punch bowl, refilled for a third time.

Lena, fixing another plate to take to Harry, paused to make an introduction. "Lillian, I want you to meet Swanger Blynt. He works at our bookstore, and he's also a poet." She leaned close to Vivian and whispered, "His wife's psychic!"

With a dramatic flourish, Swanger grasped Vivian's hand and held it tight. He tilted back his head and narrowed his eyes to slits. "You," he said pontifically, "are a peach! A wood nymph in nile green! Join me in some dandelion wine, and we will go out together and twine vine leaves in our hair!" He held out a nearly empty wine bottle and tried to pour from it into Vivian's glass. "Your spirit has not been elevated till you've drunk of this wine, pressed by the hand of a poet! And I've more, right where I can lay my hand on it."

Vivian backed away. "Thanks, but I really prefer the punch."

"Pah!" said Swanger loudly, attracting curious glances from others around the table. "Just like all of them," waving his bottle, "your palate's been ruined. Or . . . perhaps not! Perhaps you're put off by my name, by the clipped, cold sound of Blynt! You must think of me only as Swanger! Try rolling that on your tongue! Stretch out the *s* and *w*, round out the *a* and *n*, and snap it together with the *g-e-r*. It's like playing crack-the-whip." He put his arm cosily around her shoulders. "I bet you were great at playing crack-the-whip."

"As a matter of fact, I was," said Vivian, shrugging off his arm. "Swanger *is* an unusual name."

"And I," said Swanger, pressing forward as she backed away, "am an unusual man. Did you notice my ears?"

"No, I can't say . . . ."

"Well look at them, woman! Look!" He bent his head sideways, close to her chest. Vivian, tilting back, looked and saw with amazement that instead of being rounded, the tops of his ears rose in little fleshy, pointed protuberances.

Swanger raised his head. He saw her amazement and his eyes glinted triumphantly. His hair was sparse, his figure slight, his complexion gray; but his ears were pointed! "It's the outward sign of my inborn calling, of my poetic heart! I see what others miss!" Vivian, backed into a corner, held her glass of punch between them. Swanger leaned close, peered at her intently. "And I see that your eyes are like deep, limpid pools! Come, let us go, while we are in our prime, and take the harmless folly of the time!"

"Pools!" exclaimed Vivian. "My daughter's in the pool! I must go and . . . and check on her!" Thrusting with shoulder and arm, she squeezed past him

Swanger raised his bottle and called after her, "Send home my long strayed eyes to me, which, oh, too long have dwelt on thee. . . ."

Vivian held open the back door for Pete, who was carrying two pitchers of punch to refill the outside bowl.

"Party's going well, isn't it?" he asked Vivian. "I saw you talking with Swanger. He always brings his own wine—deadly stuff!" He stumbled. "Oops! Oh, it's you, Allegra!" He giggled and raised one of the pitchers in salute, slurping out some punch. "Just refilling the jolly old bowl!"

Vivian stopped to speak with Allegra, who had rented Pete and Lena's old apartment. She caught sight of Marvel and Belvedera, who were standing in partial light near one end of the pool.

"She is a quite striking woman, is she not?" commented Allegra, perceiving Vivian's interest. Allegra always spoke distinctly. It was her character to do so. She was an interior decorator, and elegance was her forte—of manner, dress, and, as far as possible, surroundings. Her hair was always perfectly coiffed; her smart but conservative clothes always set off her black skin. Her strongly molded face was reserved, contemplative, and on one of her long, graceful hands she wore a large, square-cut amethyst.

As they both contemplated Belvedera, a man came and stood uncertainly beside them. A fringe of hair grew like a wreath around his head from ear to ear; otherwise his head was bald. But below his small and undistinguished nose grew a thick black mustache that completely overshadowed his upper lip. Seeing neither woman noticed him, he chewed nervously at the mustache, then cleared his throat and said bravely, "Did you know that the purse crab sometimes reaches a weight of twenty pounds?"

The women turned to him in surprise.

"Why no," said Allegra. "I didn't. A twenty-pound crab?"

Alarmed at having gained their attention, he said, "Yes, yes, all of twenty pounds. It's a matter of record. You see, they're fond of coconuts, and coconuts are very fattening."

"Yes," agreed Allegra, "indeed they are."

"I . . . I think my glass is empty," he said, boggled by their joint gaze. Downing his drink at one gulp, he backed away, knocking over a citronella candle.

The women turned again to observe Belvedera.

"Just recently I did her living room and solarium. Greens and white, with a touch of yellow. It's a color scheme quite complimentary to her. You choose not to swim?"

"Not tonight, no," said Vivian. She was going to offer as an excuse her still sore and bandaged foot but Allegra saved her any explanation by saying, "No doubt it is wiser not to with so many participating. Ah, here is Miss Rilly."

Rilly, gloomy-faced, stood beside them. With her was a little boy, plump and restless. Rilly sighed audibly. "This is Eddie. He lives next door. I'm supposed to show him my room."

At that moment Pete, dressed in swimming trunks, went by,

gesturing and laughing and bumping into people, like the Pied Piper inviting them all to follow him. He went to the deep end of the pool and paused on the brink, a stripped scarecrow. His trunks hung loosely on his thin, bony frame, and in the glaring light his skin was as white as if it had never been exposed to the light of day. He raised his arms above his head, bent his knees, yelled, "Look out below!" and leaped. Water rose around him like a great crown. There was a general laugh and clapping of hands.

Swanger, pursuing his muse, stumbled outside. He threw back his head and opened his arms to the moon. "Ah, on such a night as this, on such a night. . . ."

"What a sensitive man!" exclaimed Lena, passing.

Hester came up and tapped him on the shoulder. "Would you give your signature for an anti-Vietnam War ad?"

"My signature? Why, my name is writ large in the heavens, and if that be so, why not in your ad! Here," he took her pen and with a tipsy flourish inscribed his name in two-inch-high letters. "Let that give pause to all who look upon it, for the brief night goes in babble and revel and wine!" Peering about, he saw a small woman sitting alone on a bench set against the back of the house. Her feet were tucked back out of sight and she had no glass of punch, only a woebegone expression. She sat sideways, one hand clasping her other arm as if she were cold or frightened.

"A wee, tim'rous beastie," he muttered and half fell onto the bench beside her. "Reveal your name and strike me to the heart!" he exclaimed, thumping himself on the chest.

She shied away, but managed a slight, uncertain smile. "I'm Pauline Reardon. You may know my husband. He's right over there talking to. . . ."

"Fie on your husband! The dull-eyed night has not as yet begun, and my bottle is empty! I must fortify myself and thee! Come, you will be my guide!"

"Oh, I don't think I should go any.   ."

"Radiant sister of the day, awake, arise, and come away!" Swanger seized her hand. "Yes, yes, you must! I need you to help me negotiate the four corners of the earth!"

Eddie, following Rilly through the house, looked about scornfully. "This isn't near as big as our house. How many telephones you got?"

"One," said Rilly.

"We got two. One's red. How many bathrooms?"

"One and a half." Rilly saw from his expression that that wasn't nearly enough.

"Huh! We got two and a half. This your room? Sure ain't much in it." He scuffed his heel in the rug. "Not much of a rug either."

"It's new!" said Rilly indignantly.

"Yeah? Doesn't look it. This all you got to show? We might as well go back out. I want some of those crackers."

Feeling herself challenged, Rilly looked at him with dislike and said, "I got a spitting grasshopper!"

"A what?"

"You heard! I got her right here in this box. Her name's Ethel."

"I don't believe you." Rilly tossed her head. "Show her then!" Rilly opened the box slightly and Eddie peered in. "She spits? I don't believe it." But he didn't sound too sure this time.

" 'Course you have to know the right words," said Rilly smugly. "Then you give her a little squeeze and she spits!"

Eddie grabbed the box, lifted out a disspirited grasshopper and, holding it between his stubby fingers, squeezed. There was a distinct scrunch. "See? She didn't spit. I knew she wouldn't."

Rilly drew in a long breath and screamed, "You squashed her! You did it on purpose!" Furious, Rilly kicked at Eddie's shins. "You go home!" she cried. "I hate you!" and hit at him with her fists.

Eddie, not in his own territory, backed off, yelling, "You hit me first! You kicked me first! I'm going to tell!" He turned and ran for the back door, dodging the people in the dining area and in the kitchen, who turned amused looks as Rilly, crying, chased after him. Everyone except those in the pool heard their cries and were looking toward the door as Eddie and Rilly came tearing outside. Lena and another woman hurried forward. Eddie grabbed at his mother.

"She hit me first! She kicked me! Twice! For no reason at all!"

Lena caught Rilly under the arms and pulled her, kicking and screaming, off Eddie's back. The mothers conferred briefly. Then Eddie's mother escorted him home to bed.

"Rilly," said Lena, "I *am* surprised at you. You should never hit anyone! Especially a guest!"

"But he squashed Ethel! And he said . . . he said our house isn't as good as his! We haven't got enough bathrooms! I hate him!"

"Hush, Rilly! You mustn't say that! Hating is wrong! He's really a nice little boy."

"He isn't! He's mean! And I hate him!"

"Rilly, what would your father say if he heard you talk like that? And all these nice people here listening!"

"I don't care! Pete's mean too!"

"Ohhh," said Lena, shocked.

Rilly began to sob. "He let go of me! After he promised to hold me! He let go!" Her voice trailed off into a wail, and she ran inside to her own room and slammed the door.

All evening Marvel had studiously avoided encountering Vivian. Sharp-eyed, he had picked her out at once and thereafter, because of Belvedera, had looked in every direction save hers. He strolled about, cautiously sipping punch and speaking casually to the men. In no time at all he knew who, among the men present, was of any consequence and, among the women, he had singled out those meriting attention. Circling about, he arrived by indirection at Beanna Blynt, who was recounting a past experience.

"I saw him as clearly as I see you. He was a cavalier, with a fitted coat and lots of buttons. He had a lace frill and a plumed hat."

"Where was this?" asked a woman, joining the group.

"In France, in an old chateau where we stopped overnight. I was just coming out of the bathroom—you should have *seen* that bathroom—anyway, there he was, coming along the hall. He stopped, almost in front of me, and took out a snuffbox. It was gold, with jewels on top. He sniffed a bit in each nostril, then took out a large handkerchief and held it to his nose. He looked straight at me. Then he turned and walked right through the wall."

"Did he sneeze?"

"I heard nothing," said Beanna, rather shortly. "I only *saw* him."

"Do you often see ghosts walking around like that?"

"Yes, frequently. Just the other day, I was on my knees, weeding the garden. I looked up and there was this man in old work clothes and a straw hat. He was carrying a scythe and mopping his forehead. He walked right past me."

There were assorted exclamations and eager requests to hear more. Beanna smiled benignly and obligingly recalled other manifestations she had witnessed. Beanna had a generous nature and was inclined to be lavish in all she did. Her hair, sleeked back from her forehead and held by an amber band, sprang out around her head and ears in a thick, dense mass. She wore a long, African print gown which made it difficult to discern exactly how full her full figure was. But a V neckline gave indication of an ample breast. Around her neck hung a heavy chain with a large medallion made of nuts and bolts and cotter pins.

Marvel stood at her elbow. He said nothing, not believing a word she said. But he paid her the compliment of his undivided attention. He even gallantly refilled her glass. Beanna, who was quite at home carrying on two dialogues at once, accepted his attentions graciously but distantly. Her eyes, as sharp as his, were attracted elsewhere.

Pete, whose arms were getting tired from playing water polo, heaved himself out over the side of the pool. He wanted more punch. He wanted also to speak to his wife, to tell her he had lost his contact lenses. He had known his loss as soon as he surfaced and opened his eyes on a blurred but beautiful scene. The water, spotlights, people, candles, stars, all were multiplied; every line was tripled and quadrupled. Every shape was softened and enhanced; every color was luminous and dazzling. Ordinarily losing his lenses made Pete very tense. But seeing the world through a lovely haze of myopia and punch, he thought it hilarious. Beard and body dripping, he moved forward and, seeing a female form he took to be Lena, threw his arms joyfully about it in a wet, bear-like hug.

Allegra stood stock-still. Then she turned her head and said politely, "You are getting me quite wet."

Pete, still able to recognize that he held a much sturdier body than that of his wife, let go instantly and began trying to apologize and brush off the wetness at the same time.

"Please," said Allegra, stepping away, "please, don't bother. It is quite warm. I will be dry in no time."

"Allegra," said Hester, coming up with her clipboard, "would you sign our anti-war ad?"

Having failed to find Lena, Pete went off at once, aiming himself in the general direction of the punch bowl, where a blurred but kindly person filled his glass. He drank down the lovely liquid and, being drawn irresistibly to the flashing blue water, leaped back in and joined the game, not knowing on which side he played.

Belvedera prowled about like a cat surveying new territory. Her dress, an ankle-length sundress with straps, was a geometric print of deep shades of red and cerise. It fit her lithe figure snugly, then flared out to flow gracefully as she walked. Her black hair curled against her bare shoulders. Had she not been his wife, Marvel would have singled her out instantly. Watching Marvel as he strolled about, she observed that the one attractive woman he never glanced at was the one with red-gold hair wearing a pale green dress. That was the one Belvedera wanted to meet.

Beanna, on the pretext of speaking to Lena, disengaged herself from her audience and circled around to the other side of the yard. She struck up a conversation with Vivian, and as they talked she gazed at Harry, lounging comfortably with his cast propped up on a chair. He was speaking with a bald man with a bushy mustache who had just told him that the moloch, though it has many sharp spines, is an entirely harmless lizard.

"Who," asked Beanna, sipping her punch, "is that gorgeous man over there?"

"Which do you mean?" asked Vivian, turning to see where Beanna was looking.

"That one, with the cast!" Beanna glanced at Vivian with amuscd surprise that she should have to ask. "He's the only handsome one here!"

Vivian raised her eyebrows innocently. "Oh. Him. His name's Harry Fox." She looked at Beanna round-eyed. "He sells insurance."

"I see," said Beanna. "You *will* excuse me, won't you?" She moved off in Harry's direction, approaching him slowly and swinging her medallion. She paused in front of him and was about to speak when suddenly she was grabbed from behind in an enthusiastic embrace that almost lifted her off her feet. She flung up her arms and the medallion, thrown back over her shoulder, struck Pete sharply on the cheekbone. He let go so fast Beanna would have fallen had she not caught hold of Harry's cast.

Pete, bent over in pain, clapped a hand to his cheek. "Lena, Lena, I think I'm bleeding!"

"Lena is in the kitchen," said Beanna, shaking herself.

"I know you'll give us your signature, won't you, Pete?" asked Hester, tapping him on the shoulder. "I didn't have a chance to ask you before, you went off so fast."

Dazed, Pete reached automatically for the pen, which Hester had to place in his hand. He scrawled his signature and left a wet patch on the paper. Not trusting himself to make it safely between the candles and chairs and people to the back steps, he headed for the pool, where the water sparkled under the spotlights.

"And you?" asked Hester of Beanna. Beanna signed, and Hester went off, checking to see if there was anyone she had missed.

"May I sit down here, beside your cast?" asked Beanna. "One gets so tired standing."

Harry grinned. "Sure thing. Move it over. It doesn't have to take up a whole chair." Beanna shifted the cast slightly and sat. She leaned against it and draped her arms gracefully over it. She stretched out her neck toward him and said, "You know, we were bound to meet! Would you like to hear some of my psychic experiences?"

Corinne, dripping wet, her hair pasted to her skull, came rushing up, calling out, "Dad! Dad! You've got to come and see me dive! I've learned to go off the board! Really I have!" Shivering with excitement, and half turned to race back to the pool, she gave his shirt sleeve a tug. "Come on!"

Beanna murmured, "Oh, do you think you should?"

Corinne flashed an indignant look at this nobody who presumed to speak to her father. Harry, who would have walked on crutches from coast to coast should his daughter have required it, easily swung his leg from under Beanna's arms and stood up.

"Here, let me help you," said Beanna, reaching for the crutches, but Corinne snatched them up first and handed them to her father.

With Corinne going ahead and Beanna trailing, Harry swung himself across the yard toward the pool, past Lena, who was saying, "But are you absolutely sure?" to the man with the mustache. Seeing Harry, she nodded and waggled her fingers. Stubbornly refusing to be sidetracked, the man said insistently, "Yes, it is absolutely a fact that the remains of the Glyptodon extend as far north as Mexico and even Texas."

Corinne stepped out on the springboard. Sobered by the

consciousness of her father's critical eye upon her, she paused, then with one graceful motion raised her arms, bowed her head between them, and after a fraction's hesitation, dove smoothly and perfectly into the water.

For Harry it was a moment of revelation, a scene he was to hold in his memory for as long as he lived, a set piece, like a movie still with no sound: a lit pool with seal-like, bobbing heads, dim figures grouped in the background, and in the center, poised in the brilliant light, his daughter, transformed, no longer thin and awkward but gracefully slender, with the clean, strong lines of an aimed arrow. With a vibrant concentration that he felt in his own bones, she paused for a breathless moment before plunging into the flashing water.

Surfacing, Corinne swam to where her father stood and looked up at him, her eyes shining, eager for his praise.

Harry smiled down at her. "That was fine, baby, just fine!" His smile deepened. Covering the sadness that had swept over him, he grinned and said, judicially, "It wasn't perfect . . . but almost."

Corinne laughed and splashed water at him. But she had glimpsed his pride in her and was satisfied.

Marvel, his usual caution blunted by punch, was unaware that Belvedera and Vivian had met. They had no need to introduce themselves because Lena had done that for them, remarking on how well they complemented each other. Vivian, curious about how Beanna would fare with Harry, had seen and understood what was going on when Harry got up and followed Corinne to the pool. Chatting with Belvedera, Vivian moved across the yard to watch her daughter dive. Then, both women observing Marvel down on one knee talking to a girl in the water, they naturally gravitated to that end of the pool. They were, in fact, standing behind him and could hear the cajoling tones of his voice and see the girl's flirtatious response as she scissored her legs in the water.

"I'm so glad I caught you all together!" exclaimed Hester. "I do believe, if I've counted correctly, that you three are the last ones I must ask to sign our anti-war ad. That will make an even thirty. I would have had thirty-seven, but seven wouldn't sign."

"We'd be glad to sign, wouldn't we," said Vivian to Belvedera, as if a kind of sisterhood existed between them.

"Certainly," said Belvedera. She printed her name in large,

forceful letters. Leaning over, she tapped Marvel on the shoulder. "Sorry to interrupt, but could you look here a minute?"

Annoyed, Marvel stood up, not expecting to see Vivian standing beside his wife. Seeing the flicker of shock in his eyes, Belvedera handed him the clipboard. "Hester's collecting signatures for an anti-war ad. She needs yours. Do you need any money, Hester? I'm sure Marvel would be glad to help pay for it."

Marvel frowned. He was angry at his wife for putting him in this false position, at Vivian for standing there, blandly innocent, and at Hester for doing what she was doing. "You know I won't sign that! Or give them one cent!" He thrust the clipboard at Hester. "You're not doing a damn bit of good! What you ought to be doing is getting signatures to go in there and bomb hell out of them!"

The silence was broken by a laugh from the girl in the pool. "C'mon in," she called. Marvel half turned. As he did so, Belvedera gave a quick thrust with her elbow against his back. For a moment Marvel hung on the edge, tilted forward at an impossible angle. Then, arms beating the air, he fell with a great splash into the deep end. Alarmed, the girl swam to the far side of the pool. Belvedera and Vivian exchanged glances.

"My, my," said Vivian.

"And with all his clothes on too!" said Belvedera.

Marvel, who had gone down and come up again, was splashing frantically, gasping for air and yelling for help.

"He doesn't seem to know how to swim," said Vivian mildly.

"No," said Belvedera, "I don't think he does. I guess I'll have to save him." With a swift gesture, she unzipped her dress and stepped out of it wearing a black bikini. There were exclamations and cries of dismay. Harry muttered, "Damn this cast!" Lena cried, "Oh, save him, somebody! Save him!" She waved her arms to catch the attention of those playing water polo.

As some, realizing there was a crisis, came swimming, Belvedera dove in. Grabbing the back of Marvel's clothes at the neck, she hauled him over to the steps at the corner of the pool, where several people reached down and helped pull him up. They peeled off his coat and slapped him on the back.

"Are you all right?" asked Lena, anxiously. "Are you sure you're all right?"

Marvel heaved and coughed, unable to answer. He was quite

a different Marvel than Vivian had ever seen. His clothes stuck to him; water ran down his face and out of his shoes. Immersion seemed to have shrunk him. His head, with hair clinging wetly to it, was revealed to be round as a billiard ball and small for his frame. Even his features had lost their distinction. Eyes bulging, mouth open, his cheeks working like a bellows as he gasped for breath, he reminded Vivian of a beached blowfish. Visibly shaken, he was not merely ordinary but comical, a man dunked and rescued by his wife.

Vivian tried hard not to laugh, but the corners of her mouth twitched uncontrollably. As Belvedera stooped to pick up her dress, their eyes met in a quick glance of shared amusement.

"Are you really all right?" asked Lena, for the twentieth time. Marvel, still gulping air, nodded dumbly. "I wouldn't have had this happen for the world! Come inside! You must get dried off! I'll make you a cup of strong, hot coffee!"

Belvedera took Marvel's arm. "Don't worry, Lena. He'll be fine. He's a marvel, he is."

As they all went toward the house, M.T. came to meet them. Utterly oblivious of Marvel's condition, he demanded crossly, "Where is my wife? I can't find her anywhere. She's not out here, and she's not in the house. Where is she?"

"Perhaps she's . . . I mean," said Lena, "did you knock on the bathroom door?"

"I did that," said M.T. impatiently. "There's no one in there. I looked in every room in the house!"

"Oh dear," said Lena. "Would somebody please call Pete?"

"I'll get him," said the man with the mustache, eager to be of service.

Belvedera and Marvel went inside. They decided to go home without waiting for coffee, and Lena loaned Marvel some of Pete's clothes. The others searched every corner in the yard, thinking Pauline might have fainted or gone to sleep. Pete was summoned from the pool, but it was apparent that he could not see well enough to find anybody.

"Perhaps," suggested Allegra, "she went home."

"She wouldn't do that," snapped M.T., "not without telling me. Besides, it's too far to walk."

"Beanna, you're psychic! Tell us where she is!"

Beanna had, in fact, already made some observations, concrete rather than spiritual. Searching for Pauline, she realized that Swanger also was missing. She noticed, besides, one of his empty wine bottles abandoned on the bench. "I suggest," she said cleverly, "that you look in our car."

There was an immediate rush, led by M.T., to the street where the cars of the guests, parked on one side only, were strung out for some distance. As they approached the Blynt car, they could hear a voice chanting:

> *Go fetch to me a pint o' wine,*
> *An' fill it in a silver tassie,*
> *That I may drink before I go. . . .*

"My God!" exclaimed M.T., wrenching open the door, "he's got my wife!"

Unperturbed by all the faces looking in at her, Pauline was slumped comfortably against Swanger, who had one arm about her shoulders. Her hair was tousled, her clothes rumpled, and she was listening with obvious pleasure to Swanger's song, keeping time to the beat with one raised finger. She smiled serenely at them all as he took another swig from his nearly empty bottle and continued to sing.

> *The trumpets sound, the banners fly,*
> *The glittering spears are rankèd ready.*

M.T. gritted his teeth. "What have you done to her, you drunken moron! Pauline! Come out of there!"

But Pauline made no effort to move, and M.T. went around to her side of the car and hauled her out, ignoring her mild protests.

Once out and on her legs, which seemed disposed to buckle, Pauline confided to M.T., "I had some wine! Some daaaandy lion wine!" Her knees bent and she sagged down. M.T. pulled her up. "He . . . he spoke po'try to me!" She sagged again as she leaned forward to gain M.T.'s full attention. "Bee-yoo-tee-ful po'try! You should have heard it! Yes," bobbing her head, "you should have!"

M.T. stuffed Pauline in the front seat of his VW with some difficulty because her legs kept sliding out, and left at once, neglecting to thank his hostess. Beanna drove away with Swanger undisturbed in the back seat. The others, returning to the house, could hear him still singing,

> . . . *we'll go no more a-roving*
> *By the light of the moon, the moon, the moon.*

Thinking all problems now resolved, and the punch bowls empty, most of the guests scattered to their cars and left.

Lena was insisting that those remaining must come inside and have some strong coffee when Pete met her at the door. Vivian was beside him, saying, "Now, Pete, don't frighten her! Try to be calm! She's probably gone next door, to Eddie's."

But Pete blurted out instantly, "She's gone, Lena! Rilly's gone!" He was wearing an old pair of glasses he had kept for emergencies, and their lenses magnified his fright to alarming proportions.

Lena stared at him. "What do you mean Rilly's gone!"

Pete laid his hands on her shoulders. "She's gone! She's not in her bed. She's gone!"

Lena shook off his hands and rushed down the hall to Rilly's room. Vivian followed, trying to reassure her. Finding Rilly's bed empty, the pink and white quilt not even folded back, Lena began to cry.

And then the telephone rang.

TEN

Law and Disorder

The Warrenville police station, a block south of the post office, was a one-story, L-shaped brick building. As the bastion of law and order, it was, both inside and out, the cleanest, most scrupulously kept building in town with the possible exception of the hospital. At the front was a flagpole, with geraniums planted around its base and encircling a stone memorial in the shape of an open book with the names of policemen whose lives had been lost in World War II and the Korean War incised on its pages. The area enclosed by the L was black-topped, with spaces carefully marked for patrol cars and visitors. At night the light poles shed a glaring light on the parking lot and building, bringing into prominence the bars on the rear windows. It caused Rilly to blink and turn her face against Officer Travis' shoulder when he carried her from the car inside.

Being carried was nice. Her legs were tired. She had almost reached Mr. Fulford's house when Travis had pulled up alongside and asked her where she was going. At first she had been intimidated into silence by being spoken to by a policeman in a police car. But when Travis got out of the car, hunkered down beside her and, looking at her with round, worried eyes, tried to coax her into telling him her name and where she lived, she hadn't been scared any more. Still she wouldn't answer because he kept telling her he would take her home, and Rilly was determined not to go home. Not ever. At least not for a long time.

The station room was divided by a high counter. The far side, where right always prevailed, had several large desks, type-writers, chairs and file cabinets. The near side, where right was always in question, was completely empty save for a faint antiseptic odor of pine. The barred rooms at the end of the building had two occupants, brought in at noon on a charge of disturbing the peace at an anti-war demonstration outside the courthouse. One had been carrying a sign saying: Vietnam, Love It or Leave It. The other, passing by and seeing the sign, had been so enraged that he had leaped from his car—leaving it to dam up traffic for several blocks—and attacked the sign carrier. Ever since, they had had bouts of yelling accusations at each other, jangling Desk Sergeant Sidney Kemp's nerves and causing him to consider discharging one and detaining the other. The question was which should be detained. The sign carrier had had a permit and had been attacked. But Sid's sympathies were with the attacker. It was a dilemma, for Sid had two passions. One was for peace. He could not abide altercation. He had become a policeman so he might promote the peace of the community. He had always believed that too much talk was a bad thing. Sid's way was to size up a situation, then act, keeping words to a minimum. He and his wife always spoke in monosyllables or sentences of five to six words, and they had been happily married for over thirty years. Sid's other passion was fishing. For miles in any direction, across state lines and even into Canada, Sid knew the best rivers and streams for fishing. With uncanny prescience he found the deep, quiet pools where the biggest fish mooned in the depths until, goggle-eyed with surprise, they snapped at Sid's hand-tied fly.

Sid had just "settled the hash" of the prisoners and in the interval of quiet was typing out a memo reminding the staff to clean out their lockers when Travis came in carrying a child which Sid saw at once was small, female, and either frightened or asleep, since her head was bowed against Travis' uniform.

Travis was too earnest a young man to have a sense of humor. Nor did he have ambition of cosmic scope. He wished, simply and modestly, to do his duty as Sid—the man he most admired and tried to emulate—would have him do it. In his effort to honor his uniform and the principles it represented, he looked for duty everywhere. All too often he found it. Sid, his patience worn by Travis' constant proving himself, would, on such occasions, become more taciturn than ever, unwittingly making himself all the more impressive in Travis' eyes.

Gently Travis sat Rilly down on the counter. His fair, smooth-cheeked face was a mixture of concern and hitherto untapped paternalism.

"Not on the counter," said Sid.

Travis immediately scooped her up. Sid brought a straight chair from behind the counter and placed it with a thud in the middle of the floor. Travis eased Rilly down onto it. She sat slumped down, not looking at them, her hands in her lap and legs dangling.

"She's lost," said Travis. "I found her wandering along North Green."

Rilly pursed her lip. She had not been lost. She had known exactly where she was. Out of pride she was almost tempted to speak, then didn't because they would take her home and she didn't want to go home.

"Name?" asked Sid.

"She won't talk," said Travis. "Maybe she's forgotten her name."

At that silly notion Rilly raised her head slightly and from under her brows looked at Travis with withering scorn. Feeling herself observed, she glanced quickly at Sidney. But it was too late. He had seen her rebellious spirit. Caught out, she dropped her eyes and pouted.

Sid turned quietly on his rubber heels and went behind the counter. Ignoring Rilly altogether, he gave Travis some paper work to do and resumed his own typing. The sporadic clack of their typewriters was, for a time, the only sound. Rilly was inclined to slip down on the smooth straight chair. She braced both hands against the seat and leaned her head against her raised shoulder. She thought of getting off the chair and leaving, or at least walking around. But she didn't quite dare. If only Travis had been there, she would have gone around the counter and pushed the typewriter keys. But there was a sternness in Sid's face and iron gray hair, a look in his dark eyes that said, "I know you, young lady, inside and out," that kept her pinned where she was. Restlessly she began kicking her heels against the chair legs.

Sidney ignored her. Travis was distracted. Having found Rilly, he felt a personal responsibility for her. He trusted Sid's methods implicitly; otherwise he could never let her sit there like that. He envied Sid his steady, unshakable manner. Travis always thought of Sidney as Sid but would never address him as anything but "Sir." Once when Sid, in a rare burst of conviviality, had invited him along on a fishing trip, Travis had called him Sidney. But that had been out in the countryside and they weren't wearing their uniforms. Sid hadn't even noticed.

Suddenly there was a banging from the rear of the building and a furious voice yelled, "Wake up, you bastard! If you think you're gonna sleep, you've another think coming! It's god-damned hippies like you who'll sleep anywhere who're taking this country to hell in a hand basket!"

Travis raised instantly from his chair, looking in alarm at Rilly. Calmly Sidney rose. As he went down the hall he said, "Ask her again."

Travis did. He coaxed and cajoled, but Rilly just kicked her heels. Sid returned, having spoken sharply to the prisoner about language fit for a child's ears. Travis, conscious of Sid's eye on him, tried reasoning, pointing out how worried her parents must be and that he knew she wouldn't want to worry them.

Rilly studied Travis, down on one knee beside her, then Sid, shuffling papers behind the counter, pretending not to listen when all the time she could see he was. Staring at Sid, she said, "Hannah Maria."

Travis beamed. "There! You see? You *can* tell us your name! Hannah Maria. That's very pretty. Now, what comes after Maria?"

Rilly squinted, still looking at Sid. "Kaziah Kasander."

Travis, mouth open, on the verge of triumph, said "Ka . . what was that?"

Rilly rolled her eyes at the ceiling. "Kaziah Kasander."

Helplessly Travis turned to Sid, who was already flipping through the telephone book.

"There is no Kaziah. Or Kasander."

"Hannah," said Travis gently, "there must be another name. What comes after Ka. . . ."

"Kasander," said Sid sternly.

"Isabel," said Rilly promptly. "Isabel Klinglesmith."

"Oh ho!" said Travis, thinking to enter into her game. "So *that's* your name, Isabel Klinglesmith."

Sid found no Klinglesmith. "There's a Klingle*n*smith," he said.

"That's probably the one," said Travis, still full of confidence. "It's a long name for a little girl to say." He smiled kindly at Rilly as Sid dialed.

But the Klinglensmith's little girl was married and had two children, boys.

Sidney regarded Rilly thoughtfully. Her eyes were almost almond-shaped and the slight tilt of her head emphasized their slyness. She would be harder to catch than any trout. Observing the baffled look on Travis' face as he appealed earnestly to Rilly for what Sid could see she had no intention of giving them, he thought, not for the first time, that Travis would never make sergeant.

". . . not the right name. That isn't very nice. You *must* tell us your last name."

"Comfort Fry," said Rilly.

Sid checked the book, though he suspected what he would find. There was no Comfort listed, or Fry, but there were two Freys.

"It's worth a try," said Travis.

"You call," said Sidney, giving the phone a push. He and Rilly watched as Travis dialed. One Frey didn't answer. The other was irate at being awakened by the police asking fool questions. Travis apologized, explained, and apologized again in a flood of confused words. Sidney shook his head at such waste, and the faintest suggestion of a smile appeared on Rilly's face.

When he put down the phone, Travis was as nearly angry as he could be. He had been tricked and now abused. "What you need is a spanking!" he exclaimed, seeing Rilly now in quite a different light. "You'd just better tell us your right name!"

Thus threatened, Rilly said pugnaciously, "MacGregor!"

"No," said Sid quietly, and moved so as to cut off her view of Travis. "No, that's not it." In a calm, matter-of-fact voice he asked, "Do you want to sit there all night?"

Rilly didn't. The chair was hard and uncomfortable, and she

was tired. The contentiousness faded from her face. She dropped her eyes and said as though the words were squeezed out of her, "Fulford, 419 Green Street."

That had the ring of truth, and this time Sid dialed.

"No, I am not her father," said Wilder.

"But she gave us your name and address," protested Travis, for the third or fourth time.

Wilder was first surprised then rather pleased to think anyone would take him for Rilly's father. Sidney never had, not from the moment Wilder appeared, out of breath and mopping his forehead. Had he been, he would have rushed to his child at once. Instead, after an anxious, searching glance at her, he came straight to the counter and, unasked, gave the name, address and phone number of her parents. As Sid waited for the ring, he contemplated Rilly's bowed head, not bowed in submission but in resistance. Sid could feel it the way he could feel a fish at the end of his line, stubbornly resisting. In this case, resisting what? As a tearful, frightened voice spoke in his ear, he began to suspect that Rilly's head was merely the tip of the trouble.

Pete and Lena arrived with a screech of brakes and a slamming of doors. They burst into the room and rushed at Rilly, both exclaiming and talking at once.

"Rilly! We were so frightened! Why? Why? Where were you going? Oh, my dearest child! You should never, never . . . ." Lena, kneeling, tried to embrace Rilly, but she pulled away and regarded her parents with a frown and a pout. Distraught, Lena looked to Pete, and Pete turned to Wilder and the policemen.

Sidney had recognized Pete and Lena when they came in as the owners of the bookstore. He considered them to be a little strange, as people are who spend all their time indoors with books, but basically they were hard-working businesspeople, a stable part of the community. Sid saw their hippie appearance as a move with the times, a kind of living window dressing, good for sales.

"Officer Travis," he said, "found your daughter walking down Green Street."

Pete and Lena looked at each other in sudden understanding, then turned to Wilder. "She was going to your house! But why, Rilly? Why didn't you tell us?! Oh, Wilder, if only you'd come to our party, this wouldn't have happened!"

Unexpectedly the focus of attention, Wilder turned a dull red. He couldn't possibly tell them why he hadn't come, concerning as it did his passion for Vivian. He hunched his shoulders nervously and the bright overhead lights reflected in his thick lenses, giving him the hopeless look of a hooked fish.

"You folks can go now," said Sidney, impatient with all useless talk and wanting to clear the station before the other patrols checked in.

"Yes, let's go home," said Lena. "It's been such a difficult evening! Wilder, we can drop you off." Pete bent to pick up Rilly.

"No!" said Rilly, shying away and hanging onto both sides of the chair seat. "I don't want you!"

Lena was shocked. "Rilly! He's your father!"

"I don't care! He dropped me! I could have drownded!"

"What's this?" asked Sid.

"Nothing, Officer, really nothing," said Pete, embarrassed. "Lena, you . . . ."

Sidney held up a hand and Pete was silenced. "Dropped?" he asked Rilly. "From where?"

"In that old pool! He promised to hold me, but he let go! And I went down!" Her face began to crumple.

"Really, Officer," said Pete, "it was just a ducking! Her head barely went under." In the face of Sid's stern, judging eye, his explanation sounded lame. "I pulled her right out, didn't I, Lena?"

"Of course you did. Shame, Rilly. Come on, you should be in bed."

"No! I won't go back there!" declared Rilly. "I hate it!" She collapsed like a rag doll, her knees hanging, her petulant chin resting on her chest.

Lena made a despairing sound, and Wilder stooped down by Rilly. She looked at him from under her brows.

"I'm sorry I didn't come, Rilly, but I couldn't."

Rilly nodded once. "That's all right. It was a bad party anyhow. Do you know what? Lena didn't want me to tell, but that awful Eddie came over from next door and he killed Ethel!"

Travis snapped to attention. Sidney turned sharply around.

Here, perhaps, was the real trouble, revealed by a child.

"What did you say?" He addressed Rilly, but Pete and Lena both began speaking hurriedly. Sidney waved them to silence. He stood in front of Rilly, regarding her sternly.

"What," he asked, with a severe glance at Lena, "didn't your mother want you to tell?"

"That Eddie killed Ethel!" exclaimed Rilly. "He took her and squashed her, just like that!" Dramatically she squeezed one hand into a fist.

Slowly Sidney stepped back, his alert gaze encompassing them all. He was about to speak when Wilder, who had temporarily lost his voice, said quickly, "It's not what you think! Ethel's a grasshopper!"

Sidney stopped dead.

"She's a *flying* grasshopper," said Rilly, with an urge for precision. "Eddie took her right out of her box and squashed her! I kicked him! Anyway, he's too fat! He ate up one whole bowl of potato chips!"

Sidney went behind the counter. He might have been alone so calm was he. He straightened the log book. He picked up a couple of pens lying carelessly about and put them back in the holder. When he looked up, everyone was watching him. Travis held his breath.

"Take your daughter and go home. Now. All of you. And in future, take better care of her."

They turned to go, but when Pete reached again for Rilly, she began to sob and kick her heels.

There was a banging as of a shoe on metal, and a voice yelled, "What are you doing to that kid, torturing her?"

"Travis," said Sidney, and jerked his head toward the back hall.

Pete caught Rilly's hands and held them tight. "Please, Rilly, you're very tired. Come home with Daddy and Mother. I'm sorry I dropped you. You know I wouldn't want to hurt you. We need you."

Rilly choked back her sobs, and after a moment, all teary-eyed, said, "I'll come if."

"If what?"

"If you shave off your beard. It's ugly!"

Pete was stunned. "My beard? Shave it off?"

Rilly sniffled and nodded. "I can't see your face. It's scary!"

"You can do that, Pete," said Lena, trying to speed their departure, "tomorrow morning when we're all home and. . . ."

"Now," insisted Rilly. "Now. I can see Mr. Fulford's face!"

Pete turned helplessly to Lena, who turned to Sidney. "Do you have a pair of scissors we could borrow?"

"This is a police station," said Sidney, "not a barbershop."

Lena tossed back her hair. "And this police station is run on taxpayers' money. I am a taxpayer, and I need a pair of scissors. Do you want us to go home or not?"

It was, Sidney recognized, an admirably clear-cut summary of the situation. "Travis," he said, "get the scissors. And a wastebasket."

When they left, Pete was carrying Rilly; one thin little arm hung loosely about his neck, her head lay against his shoulder, just below his stubbly chin that in the morning would be shaved to a final smoothness and would, to the gratification of all concerned, prove to be exceptionally strong. Rilly was asleep by the time the screen door closed behind them.

A sprinkling of reddish-brown hairs lay on the floor around the wastebasket. Sidney carried the chair back behind the counter. That child, he thought, had she been a boy, could have grown up to be a remarkable policeman.

"Travis," he said, "fetch the broom."

ELEVEN

Halloween

The late October morning was still gray and the air had a cutting edge when the jogger emerged and began her morning run. A thin mist hung over the river and moved among the trees along its banks. In the east a faint stain of color promised another crisp, sunny day. The chill struck against the jogger's bare, muscular legs where the once firm padding of flesh had fallen away, but as she fell rhythmically into pace, her mouth open and lungs working like a bellows, her blood sped through her veins, warming her body and bringing a flush to her face.

The streets were still empty, but lights were on in kitchens, and here and there clouds of exhaust billowed out of open garages where car engines were warming up. A dog of mixed parentage, who later in the day would strain at the limit of his chain to loudly protest the jogger's passing, was still curled inside his house, his snout tucked under his shaggy tail.

Her route now took her beyond the old neighborhood into the newer, where the earth sloped up gently west of the river, and she had to run in the street for lack of sidewalks. Elbows swinging, knees lifting mechanically, she might have been jogging in place while time and landscape spun past, for her concentration was inward, blind to all save self. Vivian, drinking her morning cup of coffee, saw her pass and was reminded of a Halloween cut-out she

146

had seen pasted on the window of a house, its round eyeholes staring, its mouth agape.

All over town jack o'lanterns sat on doorsteps, sometimes two or three together in graduated sizes, each with a different expression, grinning or crying, exposing their cog-like teeth. Others sat in windows or hid under bushes, their eyes peaked and mouths rounded in frightened O's. Scarecrows, wearing old hats, faded plaid shirts, torn pants and half-laced boots, sprawled lumpishly on porch roofs or hung limply over railings, staring maliciously through painted eyes at passers-by. One, caught out before his time, dangled by his broken neck from a rope tied to a branch, his body turning lifelessly in the wind.

Today, for the first time since Corinne had gone to the state university, some two hundred miles south of Warrenville, Vivian did not have to feed and water Molly. Yesterday Mr. Farley had taken her back to his farm to be boarded until next summer, when Corinne would be home again. Vivian missed Corinne. At first whenever Vivian had occasion to go into her room, she half expected, against all reason, to find Corinne there. But the closet door was shut, the bedspread smooth, the dresser top bare of all essentials. Sensing, for perhaps the hundredth time, the emptiness of the room, which impressed on her the fact of separation of flesh from flesh, she would turn and go out and find some practical or unnecessary chore to fill her time.

Surprisingly, Vivian missed Molly as well. Harry scarcely spoke in the morning. Nor did she. Until he left for breakfast in town, they moved silently past and around each other, letting the familiarity of their routine speak for them, adding only an occasional word or nod. There was no anger or even much interest between them, aside from their joint deep concern for Corinne; it was as if in a magnetic field they had entered a dead spot where their impulses toward one another altogether ceased to operate. Molly, however, was solid and lively and welcomed attention. When Vivian opened the door of her stall she stamped her feet and nickered. Playfully, she would nudge Vivian's shoulder, pull at her sleeve and blow out soft, warm breaths.

Now she, too, was gone. Vivian rinsed out her cup and turned it upside down in the drainer. There weren't even any dishes to wash. Maybe, seeing the jogger disappear down the street, she should take up jogging, but she laughed to herself even as the thought crossed her mind. She made the beds, collected damp towels to be laundered, considered replacing some curtains, but replacing curtains was pointless. Everything seemed pointless since Marvel.

Vivian had never returned to the cottage, though she had debated briefly doing so. But after the party at Lena's she never so much as considered it. She wondered, in fact, how she could ever have been so foolish as to have gone the first time. How could she have so mistaken Marvel for the man she thought he was? He was not handsome or spirited. He did not have that fortitude and understanding that had so drawn her. Nor was he truly loving. She must have been mad to have seen him so. Worst of all, she knew now they had never shared that singleness of heart and mind for which she had longed. The curved, white scar on the sole of her foot was a constant reminder of what had been for her a sudden awakening, when she first saw him as crass, selfish and devious. Then, as he had stood by the pool, water running down his face, she had seen him as comic. Never again could she regard him seriously, and she wondered that a woman like Belvedera, with whom she had felt an immediate rapport, could care for him as she evidently did. They might never have met, so completely had he dropped out of Vivian's consciousness. Whenever he came to mind, and that was rarely, she had to laugh. He had shrunk with a marvelous rapidity from heroic size to the everyday stature of a comical man.

But her awakening cost her ten pounds and a lingering depression. Days and weeks sped by while she stood still. Whatever animating spark lit other lives was, for her, missing. She cleverly gave the illusion of life by being attentive to details. Her hair shone, her clothes were smart, but she cared for herself, as she did everything else, mechanically. Today would be filled by running errands and going in the afternoon to the bookstore. Lena had asked her particularly to come, to help them welcome a friend of theirs, a writer, for whom they were having a small gathering in the bookstore.

"You must come, Lillian," Lena had said, "he's such an exciting man! He has so much of worth to say! He's only stopping over for a week or two. He has some family or other still living here. I do want him to feel that he's appreciated, especially here, in his place of origin!"

Vivian parked in the public lot behind the courthouse and walked to the bookstore, past glass fronts decorated with orange pumpkins, corn shocks and goblins. The bookstore window was elaborately decorated, inspired, Lena confided later, by a wish of Rilly's for a giant spider web. Spanning out from a lower corner of the large glass pane was a web made of cord with a realistic droop to the cross strands and a large fuzzy black spider crouched near the center. In the opposite, upper corner hovered a pair of spooks, looking suspiciously down at the spider. Inside the store, a cardboard witch on a broomstick flew above the cash register, where a man wearing a fake flesh-colored nose and black plastic spectacles was ringing up a sale.

"You're just in time," he said, addressing Vivian, who stared for a moment before recognizing Peter. She hadn't seen him since he had shaved off his beard, and she was unprepared for his aggressive jaw and large teeth.

He grinned. "Fooled you, didn't I?" he asked, pleased by her surprise. With the hooked nose above his curving jaw, he made a perfect Punch. "They're in the middle room. Go right on back."

The middle room was the only one in the store graced by a rug, an old grass mat that tended to ripple underfoot. Now it was held down by an odd assortment of chairs which Lena had picked up at auctions and house sales. Placed roughly in a semicircle, they were almost all occupied by women, except for several elderly men, whose afternoons were apparently as empty as Vivian's. They all faced a man who was sitting crossed-legged on the floor, his extended arms draped over his knees, his hands hanging limp. His shirt was open, revealing a heavy chain necklace and a bare stretch of chest. His turned-back cuffs flared out from his wrists. His tan trousers were creased and baggy. Though the late October temperatures were in the low forties, he wore only studded leather sandals on his bare feet.

Lena was just settling a plump woman on an old kitchen chair with a split seat when she saw Vivian.

"So glad you came," she whispered. She wore no Halloween mask but a scarf tied gypsy fashion over her head and large gold ear hoops; her cheeks were rouged in two red circles and her eyes were heavily outlined in black. "Here, sit here." She pulled up a folding slat chair. "He prefers to speak very informally. You can ask questions any time. Jerry enjoys a give and take."

As a late-comer, Vivian sat a little behind the others, a group of about twenty-five. There was no one directly in front of her, and after she had ascertained by a quick glance around that Dolphine Humphrey was the only person there whom she knew, Vivian gave her attention to the speaker.

". . . no, no!" he was saying in response to a question. At the second "no" his sharp eye paused on Vivian, then moved on. "Reading is work! Reading is demanding! You don't read for entertainment or as a pastime. Any writer worth his salt requires not only your attention but your energy! You must be fully involved. You must work to get at his meaning."

Vivian began wondering how she could tactfully compliment him after his talk since she had never read any of his books. All she knew about him she had gained from an article in the newspaper. His name was Jerry Nickle, he was now working on his fifth novel, and the critical acclaim, which he had received in abundance, redounded to the credit of Warrenville, whose fertile soil had nourished the growth of his extraordinary talent.

Seeing his eye on her again, Vivian assumed an attentive expression. His sitting position made her think of oriental statues, all the more so when, without moving his arm from where it rested on his bent knee, he suddenly raised his hand and pointed one finger stiffly upward.

"You think fiction should tell a story, but that's not so. That notion died over a generation ago. The novel that tells a story is dead. Fiction is *not* about people or places or ideas. All that is trivia, incidental. Writers have pushed the frontiers of literature beyond that, for we now understand what fiction is all about!"

His audience listened, totally absorbed and eager to have the true nature of fiction revealed by this man, one of their own but at the same time part of the vanguard of culture. As he spoke, finger pontifically raised, a small man came wandering in from a back room. He wore baggy pants, patched coat, a frazzled rope wig and a conical, small-brimmed hat. He hunched forward and averted his face as if all he wished was to go about his work, shelving books, unnoticed and without disturbing the speaker. But from the moment he appeared, shuffling close to the wall, the furtive quality of his movements caught everyone's attention. All eyes were drawn to him, flickered back to the speaker, then irresistibly strayed again; for he would pull a book half off the shelf, hesitate, shake his head, then push it back, or he would scan the upper shelves, tilting backward so far that everyone was transfixed, expecting him to topple over.

Seeing the attention of his disappointingly small audience fastened on a point behind him, Jerry Nickle paused in midspeech to glance over his shoulder. He saw only the back of a seedy character with an armload of books. Turning back, he continued speaking, a dour look on his wide, flabby-cheeked face. Vivian saw then that the deep lines around his mouth and eyes had not been etched by smiles of pleasure or goodwill. They fell readily into an expression of truculence and ill humor. Nor did his eyes, aimed frequently at her, track properly. One appeared to be cocked.

"Fiction," he continued in a louder, more aggressive tone, "is about words, thousands and thousands of words, like pieces of a gigantic jigsaw puzzle."

Surprise and wonder showed on the faces of the audience, and behind Jerry Nickle, like an exclamation point, a book fell with a thud to the floor. Ducking his head, the shabby man quickly picked it up and restored it to the shelf. Though Vivian could not see his face, something about him struck her as familiar.

"Every writer," said Jerry, his eyes like gimlets, "every writer of any importance, that is, is playing a game of words. He creates his own language, which develops, becomes more deeply mean-ingful, as he goes on from book to book." His tone of voice demanded attention, and the audience, intimidated, listened fixedly. "The words are merely guidelines, a map for the un-chartered country of the writer's mind and soul. That is why you must read *all* of an author's works. He requires, he *deserves,* your devotion! Like a disciple, you must follow him faithfully, for his game is to create his own private world, all intertwined, one book with another, piece by piece. Then it's up to you, the readers, to discover that world! You must intuit!"

At that there was a tremendous crash as the man behind him, presumably making shelf space, with one grand gesture swept to the floor a whole row of books plus a ceramic statue of a child reading, which exploded into pieces. The audience, who had seen it happen, cried out and threw up their hands. Slowly the culprit turned to face them, and someone gave a faint, involuntary gasp, for his face was a chalk white mask with a frightening, meaningless grin. Within the deep eyeholes, outlined in black, his eyes seemed to glitter. He drew up his shoulders in an exaggerated shrug and raised his chin in a parody of pride, both defiant and menacing. The momentary hush was broken by a soft, appreciative laugh from Dolphine, who rose and, going over to him, laid her hand on his arm.

The books were quickly reshelved, the broken figurine swept up. Several in the audience urged Jerry to resume his talk, but he firmly declined, declaring modestly that he had said all he had to say. Receiving compliments and shaking hands, he moved, surrounded by admirers, back to the front room.

"Perhaps I should apologize," said Lena, aside to Vivian. "But I don't think I will. After all, it wasn't deliberate, was it!"

Dolphine Humphrey, seeing Vivian, separated herself from the group around Jerry Nickle and extended her hand. It was a plump, rounded hand, with smooth, tapered fingers and long, oval nails, lacquered in Seville Rose. Her index and little finger were embellished by ornate rings. She offered her hand not as a functional part of her body but as a valued ornament. She allowed it to rest gently for a moment in Vivian's. The keenness of her honey brown eyes seemed at variance with the softness of her smile, her hand, her whole cushiony body.

"I'm so glad we have met again," said Dolphine. "Weren't Mr. Nickle's remarks . . . stimulating! He *must* come to our Halloween production. Come, help me persuade him."

Vivian hesitated to do so and stood back as Dolphine, with an ingratiating sidewise shift of her hips, spoke to Jerry Nickle. Watching them, Vivian was unaware that the man in the mask had approached her until she felt someone press against her side. She turned and was startled to find the white, grinning face almost touching her shoulder. She drew back, and as he turned slightly to see if they were being observed, she saw between the strands of rope hair a pointed ear! Swanger Blynt! Even as Vivian recognized him, he spoke in a whispery voice.

"I see by your eyes that you know me, those unforgettable eyes that are like deep patches of trilby blue!"

Vivian was saved having to respond by Dolphine, who turned to her, saying, "I've been telling Mr. Nickle that he must come to our Halloween production next week. He would give the morale of our group such a boost!"

"Is *she* going?" asked Jerry, with a curt nod at Vivian.

Vivian saw now that what she had thought was a cocked eye was an illusion. It was merely that Jerry's left eyebrow was white, as if the stroke of a finger had wiped off its color. His other eyebrow was a faded brown, like his hair, which was straight and combed crosswise rather than back, which emphasized the width of his face. A tenseness around his eyes suggested he constantly made severe judgments. Like a man long used to sharp exchanges, he showed not the least friendliness. The stress he placed on "she" had a derogatory ring.

"I don't know," said Dolphine. Amused, she glanced at Vivian.

"She should. She's native here. If she comes, I'll come."

Swanger, who had bent forward, turned up his grinning face toward one, then the other, in an exaggerated show of interest. He slipped his arm through Vivian's and declared hoarsely, "No! She is coming with me to trip the light fantastic from tombstone to tombstone . . ." he tilted back his head and made a sweeping gesture, ". . . as the wild, tattered clouds blow across the frighted face of the moon!" His white grinning face uplifted, he paused dramatically, arm arrested in mid-air.

"Mmmn," murmured Dolphine, "you really should join our group."

Jerry Nickle said nothing, but the animosity in his wide, flat face deepened.

Vivian was suddenly out of patience. She had come only to please Lena. She had no interest in the speaker, an exceptionally disagreeable man, and she resented being spoken of as if she were an object. She pulled her arm from Swanger's grasp and with a brief, perfunctory nod, started for the door.

"Lillian!" Lena cried out, rushing up with a swirl of skirts and beads. "I must ask you! Could I bring Rilly to your house trick or treating? It's dreadful, I know, but after what happened last year, we're taking her around in the car, only to people she knows."

"Yes, of course." Vivian knew what she meant. The year before children collecting money for the UN had had their fingers burned picking up red hot coins thrown out to them on porches. Others had their mouths badly cut eating candy bars stuffed with broken pieces of razor blades and several had been rushed to the hospital from eating candy injected with rat poison.

"On Thursday, then!" The bell jangled behind her as she stepped outside. She had nearly reached the courthouse corner when she heard swift footsteps behind her and a voice said, "I know I was rude."

Jerry Nickle placed himself in front of her, unsmiling. His eyes were almost colorless, and daylight washed out his white eyebrow altogether, leaving his face strangely unbalanced. "I won't beg your pardon. Regrets are a waste of time. But you were right to walk off."

Vivian smiled slightly and started to pass him.

Jerry held up both hands, palms out. "Peace?"

"Peace," she agreed, but her indifference showed.

Indifference galled Jerry Nickle. He had been fighting it all his life. As a child, he had been passed by and overlooked by adults who saw nothing to give them pause in his flat child's face and cool, unappealing eyes. Early on he had begun testing methods for making his will felt, for forcing recognition of his superior talents. Convinced that people did not see because they did not look, he quickly learned that the best attention-getter was a frontal attack. After that, if one were clever and very positive, people could be brought to swallow anything, from a new religion to a theory of fiction. He had long since perfected his method, which had brought him to his present elevation as writer-theorist, and he had become, unwittingly, his own best subject.

As Vivian again started to walk past him, Jerry once more stepped in front of her. "Prove it," he challenged. "Prove you don't hate me!"

"Hate you!" Vivian laughed. "I don't even know you."

"That's right! You don't. But you're sure you don't like me. I can see it even in the way you stand. Look at you! Stiff. Just waiting to get away. Is that fair?"

Accused correctly, Vivian made a wry face, shrugged her shoulders.

"See? You know it's not. So why don't you prove you can be a fair-minded woman by having a drink with me, now." Vivian looked at him but didn't answer. "What a look!" he exclaimed. "Like a basilisk! A cup of coffee then, that's harmless enough," he added sourly. When she still said nothing, he flipped his hands open at his sides as if confessing and said, "Okay. I'm lonesome. I'm bored."

At what she took to be, finally, an honest remark, and one that struck a sympathetic cord, Vivian said, "All right. A cup of coffee."

The cafe set Jerry's teeth on edge. Its name, in gilt-edged black letters, arched like a rainbow across the wide front window-pane. Inside was one long, narrow, high-ceilinged room. Nothing obstructed the view from front to back. One could see at a glance anyone who happened to be there, drinking coffee or eating a hot roast beef sandwich. Near the entrance was a curved, glass-topped counter, with open cigar boxes and cigarettes on display inside, on top a toothpick dispenser and a dish of penny mints placed beside the cash register. The square tables, covered with white tablecloths and set at angles for easy serving, were laid with flatware, cups upside down in their saucers, and water glasses, each holding a paper napkin folded with two points sticking up. At the far end of the room were two black swinging doors, the one on the right with a metal plate across its bottom and its opening edge worn pale from the pushing of waitresses' hands. The ceiling was covered with white squares impressed with an ornate design. One, near the back, was stained with brown and patched with what looked like a metal pie pan, sealing the hole where a stovepipe had once been. Now the room was heated by a large metal box that stood in a back corner and periodically blew warm air through slits in its side.

Jerry sat hunched forward, elbows on the table, holding with both hands the thick, white cup, into which he had dumped four heaping spoonsful of sugar. "I suppose," he threw at her, "you're sitting there finding fault with my using too much sugar."

"Not at all," said Vivian coolly. "I was thinking you need every bit of it—you look so sour." She surprised herself by speak-ing so. Only when treated rudely by a salesperson was Vivian ever openly rude. In any exchange of goods and money she was quick to assert herself, but not otherwise. Like all those she knew, including her family, she rarely articulated her true thoughts or feelings, or even recognized them for what they were, for she was to herself an unknown country. Jerry Nickle's blunt, boorish manner had released an inner tension that had oppressed her for weeks. Vivian answered him in kind to maintain her self-respect but discovered, to her own amazement, that she enjoyed doing so.

Jerry's flat gaze speculated on the wall decoration, panels

depicting idyllic scenes: lakes, willowy trees, lavender mountains and pastel castles, painted, frame and all, in pale, romantic colors directly onto the pebbly walls.

"Native art," he sneered.

"You're native here too, remember. Why do you come back if you don't like it? You don't have to, any more than you have to look at the walls. The coffee's good."

He had a lizardlike habit of moving his eyes without moving his head. Doing so gave a deeply thoughtful appearance to what was mere calculation. "Why not? I check in here on my trips from coast to coast. I'm restless. I drop in on odds and ends of family."

"Odds and ends?"

"Well . . ." the corners of his mouth pulled down wryly, ". . . my mother and a sister or two. And believe me, they *are* odd."

"But your mother must be glad to. . . ."

"Don't give me that sentimental hash about mother!" he interrupted roughly, warming to the creation of the picture he wanted her to have. "Dear old Mom has never forgiven me for leaving home, for getting married, for having three kids instead of six—though," he added as an aside, his lids drooping, "there may be some uncounted,'—or for my profession. 'Scribbling away one's life is not work,' " he mimicked in a higher tone, then shifted down to a growl. "Or for my life style in general. So I check in, but don't ask me to enjoy it!"

He paused, giving her a chance to say something, but Vivian drank her coffee and looked at him coolly, obviously expecting more. She was curious, he could see, even slightly amused, but not yet involved.

"You're so damned complacent!" he said coldly, determined to draw her in. "Sitting there, complacent as hell in that coordinated blue outfit, every shining hair in place! At a time when a mindless war is splitting families and tearing this country apart, you can sit there like that! Are you so insulated by these miles of corn you don't know what's going on?" Seeing her eyes widen and chin lift, he leaned forward angrily. "This is fertile ground for the Ku Klux Klan and the Minutemen! It is not all fat pigs and soybean oil!"

"Nobody ever thought it was!" said Vivian, setting her cup down hard.

"But I suppose," he went on, "here in the good old Bible belt you and your husband . . ." having noted her ring, ". . . and your children go to church every Sunday and listen to a bland sermon delivered by a bland preacher and come out edified, washed clean as the driven snow. Except now the snow is polluted!"

Vivian had listened with increasing anger. "How dare you 'check in here,' as you say, and presume to criticize what you don't know anything about! Your mother may well be right about you! *You* are the one who is insulated! On your trips from coast to coast you are obviously flying too high! For one thing, my husband and I and one child do not go to church or listen to any sermon, bland or otherwise! That happens to be our choice! But if we did choose to go, that would be all right too! For another, we certainly know what's going on as well as you do, probably better, and I don't need to explain to *you* all the things that people here are doing about it. As for appearances, that is a matter of personal taste, for those of us who *have* any taste, that is. Personally, I find necklaces and open shirts, intended no doubt, to show off what passes for a manly chest, in very poor taste. A writer must be shallow indeed to take dress as an indication of one's state of mind. I've never read any of *your* books, but I thought that sort of thing was true only in dime novels."

For the first time Jerry Nickle smiled, broadly enough to reveal his left incisor. Crowded forward, its sharp, overlapping point gave his smile a certain devilishness. "Well, you're flesh and blood after all!"

Vivian sat back, annoyed. "You were baiting me!"

He pursed his lip. "Maybe, just a little. But I meant what I said and so did you. Exhilarating, wasn't it, to speak your mind? It always is. Don't be mad. Admit it. Before, you were bored. Now you're not. When I saw you come in and sit down, I said to myself, there is a lovely but bored woman. And I was right, wasn't I?" He knew by her oblique glance that he was. Seeing her still hesitating between amusement and pique, he remarked, "The cure for boredom is intellectual stimulation. So we should get along just fine—I'll talk and you can listen. Clearly you have a perceptive intellect or you wouldn't have noticed my chest."

At that, a bit reluctantly, she smiled.

"Come on," he said, standing up. "I've got to get out of here. This place makes me feel I'm in a 1920's western."

Using a combination of memory and instinct, Jerry found a

congenial tavern, the Lucky Horseshoe. For authenticity there was a Percheron-sized horseshoe nailed above the massive metal-studded door. Inside and beyond the short, screened entrance-way, the atmosphere was as enveloping as a return to the womb. The light was dim, and there were no angles or corners anywhere. Candles flickered in small cups studded with variegated glass beads. The low stuccoed ceiling curved down like the smoky top of a cave. Black plastic padding lined the curved booths, arranged in labyrinthine fashion and topped by Moorish latticework. The round wooden tables were of such dark finish that they shone like wet, glistening pools. The bar, in a central position, was shaped like a narrow horseshoe; globules of color from lights embedded in the ceiling swam on its glossy surface and sparkled on the bottles and glassware ranged in tiers behind the barman.

"This," exclaimed Jerry Nickle, "is my kind of place!"

Vivian shrugged. "They could use more light."

"It's just that here in the Midwest you're not accustomed to a modern bar," said Jerry.

Vivian slid around the table and settled herself comfortably. "A rash remark, Mr. Nickle, that reveals your ignorance. This is not the backwoods. We have bars here that are in just as poor taste as any in the big cities. Besides, you mustn't think we don't get around. Midwesterners are notorious travelers. Sometimes we go even further than from coast to coast." She rested her chin on her crossed hands. "I'd have thought you'd know that, having grown up here."

Jerry Nickle studied her as if she were one of his word problems. "Good," he murmured, "so good . . ." edging closer and throwing an arm behind her, ". . . that I'll even let you touch my white eyebrow. All women want to. Go ahead." He leaned his head forward.

"Thanks, but I really don't care to." She glanced behind her with mild curiosity. "I'm waiting for that intellectual stimulation you mentioned."

Jerry withdrew his eyebrow and his arm. "After we have a drink."

"You have a drink. I'll just listen. That was to be my part, remember."

A sleepy-eyed waitress eased over to their table, took Jerry's order and, with a glint of reproach at Vivian, went off without a word.

Words were Jerry Nickle's game, and he played it for an hour and a half. The ambience of the Lucky Horseshoe suited him perfectly. Its shadowy light gave his lined face profundity. His sharp incisor was wryly humorous when he let fall personal details—just in passing—such as that people, even his family, were more interested in his fame and income than in his work, or his wife cared only for her Japanese flower arrangements. His manner was aggressive, as if he faced a committee of critics instead of one silent woman. It was easy for Vivian to listen. His words were often, to her, amusing. And she bore with composure his agate-hard gaze, directed, for the most part, at her, although he did ponder his glass, the moist rings on the tabletop, and the waitress' retreating backside when she brought him a refill. The intensity of his gaze was designed to make clear that he obviously saw nothing but his inward vision of, "words, like a multitude of fingers that play delicately upon the harp of the soul, words not to be understood but felt, and being felt bring illumination and meaning to life." As he spoke, totally absorbed in laying out for her the pattern of his current work, his energy, too vehement to be confined, burst out in sudden, abrupt movements. Rising up slightly from his seat to stress a point, then throwing himself back, he pressed his thigh tightly against hers. His hand shot out and grasped her shoulder, his finger ends painfully emphasizing his words. His foot, in an impulsive move, trod forcibly on hers. Vivian winced, but listened, following his thought. It seemed simple enough in principle, but she couldn't help wondering how it would work when applied.

When she left, Jerry demanded she come again the very next day because she listened so beautifully. He could feel the depth of her understanding, and it animated his imagination as never before.

But Vivian found his creative energy too strong for every day. Her shoulder was bruised and her toes sore. She needed, she said, time to mull over his ideas. She did promise to come on Friday to Dolphine's production.

During the intervening days, Vivian did think, not so much of the theory as of the man. In her thoughts his image gradually underwent a metamorphosis. His face grew less truculent, became, instead, careworn from striving, essentially unsupported, to set forth his ideas and make himself heard, as he said, "in the marketplace." His eyes were not cold but inward-looking; his white eyebrow not merely a lack of pigment but an amusing, perhaps even endearing, flaw that made him human after all. And it was only natural that such a man, always in the public eye, should have become blunt and direct in his speech. It was refreshing. It cut through layers of hypocrisy, did away with so many of what Jerry termed "less vital" words.

Vivian intended to be prepared when they next met, and to that end got from the public library several books Jerry had mentioned, including one of his own. She settled down on the sectional sofa, willing enough to see theory put into practice, but after some twenty pages in which abstruse characters and portentous events made no sense unless one had read a previous book, she gave it up and fell into a reverie of her own.

Vivian knew without thinking twice that she could never find Jerry's ideas important. They seemed to her, if anything, a little silly. She smiled, in sympathy with Swanger, remembering how fast Jerry had leaped to his feet. But he did have drive and force of mind. Vivian imagined them sitting once again in the Lucky Horseshoe, at some vague, future time. They would sit in the same booth, for which they would have an attachment. She could feel again its padded comfort and see the sparkle of glass bottles under the soft, colored lights. Jerry, his ghostly eyebrow lending a touch of glamor to his harsh expression, would throw out ideas, sometimes with such energy that heads would turn at the bar and the waitress glance at him suspiciously. There would be no end to his flow of words, and she would listen—not always agreeing. She already had questions and objections. But she knew how he would take them, she was sure, appreciatively and thoughtfully, for he seemed to thrive on challenge. That would be the nature of their friendship, an intellectual give and take, as Lena had said, a clash of minds that was exciting and far beyond anything merely physical. It was even possible that in time she might become a kind of touchstone, one on whom he could test his ideas. Contemplating such a future, Vivian became pensive and absentminded.

That evening Harry came home and unrolled on the dining room table drawings showing sectional views of the foundations for the apartments. Vivian paused to glance at them and at Harry, head bent over sheets of calculations. But she was too caught up in her new dream to take any interest in blueprints. They were, after all, intensely practical. She was concerned with the more elusive matters of thought and emotion. She brewed a fresh pot of coffee for Harry and went serenely to bed.

Harry was glad Vivian had asked no questions. He had no wish to speak to her of the disaster that threatened his building enterprise, his insurance business and their entire future. Grim-faced, he studied the specifications and his own figures, and what he found was more effective than coffee in keeping him awake.

The next day Harry and Logan went to the building site and examined the poured foundations. They discovered a bone-chilling truth: the building inspectors were correct in finding the concrete footings short of the required depth by a good four inches and the steel reinforcements insufficient. When Harry and Logan had made quite sure of this, they had a conference. They sat silently on either side of Harry's desk, glumly contemplating the fact that their contractor had cheated them.

"Damn him to hell!" exclaimed Harry through his teeth. "I didn't like him from the start, glad-handing all over town!" He hunched forward over the desk, his narrowed eyes intense with anger. He socked his fist into his cupped hand. "If I could get hold of him I'd pound him into a pulp!"

"No way we can?" asked Logan. He slouched in his chair, long legs crossed at the ankles, his chin on his chest.

"Hell no! The bastard's always on the move! Never at home, never at work, always in between. Last time they said he was at some site out of state. He knows, all right!"

"There's no way he's liable? You're sure?"

"Sure?" Harry glared at him, and Logan knew then how frightening it must have been to have faced Harry on the playing field. "Sure I'm sure! There's no way we can hold him! *We're* liable! Those footings have to be ripped out and repoured and we haven't the funds to do it. We're overextended as it is. And if we don't do it . . . either way we're ruined!"

Harry contemplated the fuzzy surface of his blotter. He had finally said aloud the word that had been ringing in his head for several days, days in which he had eaten little and slept less. In the midst of his checking specifications or toting up their assets, a quiet, inner voice would remark, "There goes the horse," or "We'll have to sell the house and be worse off than when we started," or, worst of all, "Guess that ends Corinne's college." How could he explain to her! He felt tired. As a money-making machine he was wearing out. But too soon, much too soon. His father had never worn out. Until the day he died he was as clever and crafty at turning a profit as he had been when he handed Harry an insurance business like a big present wrapped in tissue and tied with a bow. In the same way he had, years earlier, handed him a football and said, his eyes alight in his shrewd, lively face, "Run with it, boy!" He had expected everything of Harry, and thank God, Harry hadn't failed him, at least not while he was living. Now a sense of shame was beginning to seep into Harry's bones.

"Well," said Logan cheerfully, hauling himself upright in his chair, "you can have all I've got. It's not much, but it's yours. Interest free," he added with a grin.

Harry raised his head. He had memories of Logan when his lean face was a little fuller, his tightly curled hair a little longer, offering him his notes before a test, an extra quarter for lunch, his car for a date, offering, in any way he could, his allegiance. Harry remembered, as he raced down the field, slipping in the mud and glimpsing Logan, arm raised and mouth open in a yell, expressing the same eager confidence then as now. Looking at Logan, Harry's whole face softened into a smile. "You're some joker," said Harry.

Pleased but embarrassed, Logan began talking rapidly.

Harry only half listened. Logan had broken his despondency, given him the sense that this too was just another game. When a frontal attack wouldn't work, devious tactics would. He had many friends, old classmates and boosters, all of them business or professional men, all fellow Kiwanians. Within that brotherhood they accommodated each other whenever possible. It struck Harry that he had done his share of favors and gladly. Thus far he had needed none in return. Now was the time. Now he would draw on what could be for any man a lethal pressure.

At lunch he would speak to this one and that. In no time the word would be out. It would be seen that what had happened to Harry and Logan could happen to others. Trouble for one was potentially trouble for all. Some projects might have to be scrapped, others delayed, but such inconveniences were acceptable when it was a matter of protecting the common good. A united front was the only way.

Logan saw Harry's thoughtfulness harden into resolve, the

light of shrewd calculation make his eyes sparkle like glass chips. He was ready when Harry slapped his hand flat on the desk, pushed back and said, "Let's go to lunch."

Antrum Puckett, the contractor, was a man of average size, with straight, white hair combed back from his forehead and a face whose blandness was probably attributable to the puffy contour of his forehead and cheeks, which seemed to overlie not bones but cotton. He was fond of hooking one thumb in his natty striped belt and tapping with the forefinger of his right hand a blueprint, a page of specifications, a contract, and saying, "That will do the job. Yessir, I think that will certainly do the job."

That afternoon his several phones rang frequently, each time with bad news. Jobs were cancelled, indefinitely. Materials on order were found to be out of stock. No telling when shipments could be made. Substitutions were out of the question. Bills, heretofore comfortably let slide, suddenly demanded payment. And the banks, regretfully but firmly, found themselves unable to extend credit or grant a loan. By the end of the next day the phones didn't ring at all.

The air was decidedly chilly, and Antrum began to see specters of doom everywhere he turned. He decided to put himself forward, confidently. He began by making phone calls but his cheery affability made no impression on switchboards or clerks in outer offices. The messages he left fell into a void. Then he presented himself in person, but was stopped by secretaries who were sweetly uninformative and adamant about not opening doors. When he did gain reluctant admission to an inner office, the man behind the desk, one-time drinking pal or golf partner, looked at him as if he had a spot on his lapel. The hands he had shaken were no longer extended. All over town he had become invisible.

He went out to the Fox-Gamble apartment site and found it deserted. He mooned about, one thumb hooked in his belt and stared morosely at the footings. Then he began estimating how long it would take to rip them out. And what it would cost. And what it would cost if he didn't.

After a week in which nothing changed for the better and his secretary began to look at him strangely, he went to see Harry.

Harry tilted back in his swivel chair and said, "Have a seat."

The words were cordial enough but his eyes were dead cold. Logan came, leaned in the doorway—it not being worth his while to come any further—and dusted off one knee as if a cloud of dirt had just blown in.

Puckett had to turn his head around to see one, then back to see the other. He couldn't keep an eye on them both at the same time or catch any signals. Being at a distinct disadvantage, he smiled jovially.

"Took a look at your apartment site the other day. Not a soul around. How come? Thought you boys wanted a roof on before bad weather."

"I'm surprised," said Harry, "that you had the time to drop by. You've been so busy."

"That's true, I have been, but. . . ."

"Yeah," drawled Logan. "Thought you were all tied up in some out-of-state deal."

Puckett spread his hands. "Well, I am, but I've got to keep tabs on. . . ."

"That interests me," said Logan. "What're you working on, out of state? A really big project?"

"It *is* big," conceded Puckett, "but not. . . ."

"Maybe," cut in Harry, "you're thinking of folding up here altogether, of moving out?"

"Why no," said Puckett, squinting, "nothing like. . . ."

"We would hate to see you do that," said Logan. "It would be such a loss for Warrenville, a good, reliable contractor like you!"

"And think," said Harry, "of the loss it would represent to you!" He made a little deprecating click out of the side of his mouth.

Puckett glanced over his shoulder at Logan, who shook his head and said, "Yeah, what a loss!"

Puckett grinned, grasping at the positive. "Boys, one doesn't often encounter this kind of concern. It does me good to know you care."

Harry swung forward and leaned on his desk. "So you checked out our project, did you? How'd the foundations look to you?"

Puckett raised his eyebrows in mild surprise. "Why fine, fine. My men did a good job."

"As far as they went," said Harry.

"Only," said Logan from behind, "they didn't go far enough to meet the specs and satisfy the building code."

Puckett's smooth, oval face grew longer and his mouth pursed into an indignant O. Like a god-damned shell-shocked egg, thought Harry.

"That can't be," said Puckett. "There's a misunderstanding somewhere."

"That's right," said Harry forcefully, "there is. About four inches' worth. But we knew if we mentioned it to you, you'd make it good."

"Well, now. . . ." Puckett hesitated. "That's one hell of an expense you're dumping on me! Think of the work hours!"

"We have," said Harry. Puckett, meeting his unyielding gaze, knew that Harry had thought of that and a good deal more. "We know," went on Harry, "how busy you are on all those other jobs, in and out of state. But we're sure you can spare the men for this. Shouldn't take too long if they get right on it."

"Besides," said Logan suddenly, causing Puckett to flinch inwardly, "think of your reputation. Everybody knows you for an honest man. You've got to protect yourself, haven't you."

Puckett rose. Harry did not. But even standing Puckett was intimidated by Harry, who watched him like a large, disgruntled cat eyeing its supper. No telling what a man like that might not do. Puckett, not a native of Warrenville, had miscalculated Harry's position in the community. Well, he would know better next time. Meanwhile he didn't extend his hand—too soon for that—but he summoned up his old joviality. A smile slid over his face, his voice grew hearty and, leaning against the desk to show how at ease he was, he tapped its surface with his index finger and said as if promising a special favor, "Tomorrow morning, tomorrow morning on the dot my men will be there! You'll see! The fur will fly! When Puckett Contractors does a job, we do it right!"

That noon Harry drove out to the deserted apartment site, on the edge of town, just off the main highway. There were a few old maples, which had shaded the rink in summers past, still standing, leafless and isolated amid piles of excavated dirt and stacks of building materials. Harry had insisted on saving them, visualizing them as one day shading the apartments and a well-kept lawn. The area beyond was all farmland, now gone to stubble or ribbed with rows of corn shocks. Breaking the horizon were wooded areas, some more remote than others, their very small-ness enlarging the sense of space and distance. Harry was glad no one was about. He had thought of taking Jenny to lunch, but she had already left, and so had Logan, which was just as well. He preferred now to be alone. He zipped up his jacket, turned up his collar and hunched his shoulders against the cold wind. Below the gray vault of sky, rows of ragged cotton clouds moved before the wind. In the metallic light, the distant bare trees shaded from black to lavender, the dried and brittle fields to soft chamois and brown. A flock of birds, feeding on their way south, rose up from the ground and like one elastic body soared out on the wind, swung around and slid back down to earth. It was the kind of cold, blustery day that made Harry want to run, to stretch his legs, to feel the blood pound in his veins and draw the sharp, exhiliarat-ing air deep into his lungs. He scooped up a stone and flung it hard with a twist that sent it spinning through the air to land with a thud in a pile of damp sand. He threw another and another until the sandbank was pitted with holes.

Flexing his shoulders, he sat down on a stack of cement block and thrust his hands into his pockets. The old rink was now entirely gone, and from where he sat he could see, fanning out, the partial foundations for the five separate buildings that would make up the complex, the foundations that tomorrow Puckett's crew would begin ripping out and repouring. For days Harry had been skirting the edge of bankruptcy. He had thought of little else. Now that the danger was past and his fierce anger at Puckett subsided, he would have turned to Jenny, but sitting there in the cold, gusty wind, he faced the fact that between him and Jenny there was a breach. He hardly knew how it had come about. First there had been his broken leg and the clumsy, unromantic busi-ness of cast and crutches. Then had come the trouble with Puck-ett. During those weeks, while he was preoccupied, time and events had moved past him. Jenny was changed. She was no longer approachable. She dropped copy on his desk without pausing for a word or look. Rather than bring a message person-ally, she spoke to him over the intercom. When he passed her desk, she was too busy typing to glance up. Inexplicably she had shut him out, and he was baffled. Always, from the very begin-ning, circumstances had contrived to separate them. Even when he had held her close she eluded him. When he spoke, she missed his meaning; when he tried to demonstrate his feeling for her, her attention was elsewhere. He had not even been able to arouse her jealousy. Beanna Blynt had come into the office several times, once to inquire about his leg, once to suggest she might be interested in a new insurance policy. She had made her interest in him quite plain. He had responded gallantly, hoping Jenny would react. But Jenny, observing Beanna, had smiled sweetly and gone on, undisturbed, with her work.

Harry stood up. Tomorrow he would push to make as much progress as possible before winter set in. More than a dozen of the apartments were already signed for. The project would be a success, an attractive and needed addition to the city. He and Logan would make a fine profit on their investment. His father would have been proud of him. But as he drove back into town, Harry felt no lift of the spirit. His sense of achievement was blighted. He was beginning to suspect that no matter what he did, for some inscrutable reason Jenny would always be for him unattainable. Unaware of the seed of discontent she had sowed or of the size to which it would grow, Jenny had given Harry, for the first time in his life, a sense of failure.

According to his custom, Marvel had given Belvedera a present. He had brought it home in a carton, confident, as always, that Bel would be delighted. This time she didn't have to pretend. She was glad it wasn't purple, and named the white kitten Louie, after an uncle who had a cast in one eye and was considered by the entire family to be quite strange. The kitten, who clung like a cocklebur to Belvedera, was walleyed, with one blue eye and one pale amber. His two eyes, being at cross-purposes, gave him a clownish expression that suited his insistent and very vocal disposition.

Belvedera appreciated his lively company, for Marvel, having lost Vivian, was living through a painful adjustment. After a good dinner and an indifferent perusal of the evening paper, he usually fell asleep. It was a familiar pattern to Belvedera, and for some evenings she amused herself by rolling crumpled paper balls for Louie to chase or watching him tumble inside a paper bag. He especially enjoyed hiding behind the newel post and flashing out a paw at a wooden spool hanging from a string. The string Belvedera had tied to a metal figurine on top of the post, a nymph in diaphanous dress. She was poised on one foot, running, the other extended behind her, and she looked back over her shoulder in fear—or hope—of being pursued. One raised arm supported a small ornate lamp that at night cast a dull yellow gleam. It had been a wedding present which Marvel had insisted be placed in its present position. Neither as lamp or decoration was it one of Belvedera's favorites. Tying a string to the nymph's raised back foot for Louie's entertainment was the first real use she had found for it. Louie, goggle-eyed, made assaults on the spool, rising up like a boxer and swiping at it as it swung past him. Once, by slowly pulling a string, Belvedera lured Louie into leaping with claws extended onto Marvel's midsection. But Marvel only grunted, mumbled something unintelligible and turned over.

Belvedera sighed. She began to think, as she sometimes had in the past, that life was livelier for them both when Marvel was having what he fancied to be a clandestine affair. At least it kept him alert. She even began considering whom among her acquaintances she might put in his way as a kind of morale builder until he found someone himself or—and though this she devoutly wished, she was coming to despair of its ever happening—he came to be content with her.

For Halloween Belvedera had baked dozens of cookies and polished half a bushel of Jonathan apples. Before dusk came the preschool children, small groups shepherded by a mother, children so young that the bags they clutched were almost as large as they were. They stared up at Belvedera through masks wider than their faces and had to be prompted to hold open their sacks. During supper the next group began coming. They too were herded along by mothers, armed against the dark with flashlights. But they were experienced and needed no prompting. Giggling in anticipation they had their bags open and ready when Belvedera came to the door.

As the evening grew later, the children grew larger. There were fewer bunny rabbits and ghosts and more Frankensteins, Draculas and walking TV sets. Marvel, totally uninterested, fell asleep on the couch. Louie, wrought to a state of high excitement by the constant ringing of the door chimes, the commotion of Belvedera handing out cookies and admiring the costumes, the strange voices and laughter, streaked madly back and forth to the door and around Belvedera's feet, hissing and dancing sideways when any of the tricksters leaned too close.

When, for twenty minutes or so no one came to the door, Belvedera began to pace restlessly about, Louie leaping at her ankles. She picked up one of her own cookies and stood gazing down at Marvel, sleeping, while she munched on it.

It was a quarter of eleven. No one else would come now. She might as well turn off the porch light and wake Marvel so he could go upstairs and back to sleep. Belvedera dusted the crumbs off her fingers and went to the door. She reached toward the switch, then paused and glanced back into the living room at Marvel, soundly sleeping, one arm hanging over the edge of the couch.

Abruptly, leaving the porch light on, she turned and went upstairs. In the bedroom she kicked off her shoes, pulled off her sweater and slacks, took off her bra and underpants. She turned and for a moment regarded her naked self in the mirror. She really had nothing to be ashamed of. And it was all going to waste. Quickly she put on a fur coat—another of Marvel's gifts—and pink slippers. She went down the back stairs and out the back door, closing it softly behind her. In the dark she went around the house, through the patches of light shining through the living room windows and up the porch steps. Putting her finger on the doorbell, she held it there firmly while inside the chimes sounded again and again. She was beginning to think he would never wake when suddenly Marvel jerked open the door.

Belvedera struck a pose and with one theatrical gesture threw open her coat and exclaimed, "Trick or treat!"

Stunned, Marvel stepped back. There was a high, splitting screech, Belvedera cried out, "You stepped on Louie!" and Marvel, stumbling, trod on the screaming cat once again, lost his balance and fell backwards, striking his head on the nymph's outstretched foot. Marvel, nymph and lamp crashed to the floor; Louie, his tail a bottle brush, arched his back and hissed, his blue and amber eyes staring wildly.

With a cry, Belvedera rushed to Marvel. Going down on her bare knees, she tried to embrace him, exclaiming, "Did you hurt yourself! Are you all right!"

Slowly Marvel sat up. In a daze, he said, "My neck feels wet." He put one hand to the back of his neck, then they both looked with horror at his bloody fingers.

"My God!" he said in a hushed voice, "I've split my head!"

That same evening Vivian, as she had promised, went to see the Warrenville Community Theater's production of *The Restless Corpse*. All over town entrance and porch lights were on and large orange plastic pumpkins placed over post lamps glowed warmly in the dark. Pulling up for a stop sign, Vivian was startled by tappings on the sides of the car. Grotesque heads appeared at the windows, grinning, leering, weeping. They peered in at her, waggling their fingers, and began hooting and howling. They wrenched at the door handles, and finding them locked, began rocking the car, jumping wildly up and down. One, in a black mask with red and white streaks and wearing a poncho, flung itself across the hood, stuck out its tongue and clawed at the glass. Frightened, Vivian began to accelerate, slowly at first, then faster. Those at the sides kept pace, hanging onto the door handles, but the one on the hood slid off sideways. Thinking it safe then, Vivian increased her speed. The others let go and fell behind. In the mirror she saw them prancing in the street, arms raised, shaking their fists at her.

The WC Theater was housed in a small frame building in the same block with the larger of Warrenville's two high schools. It had once been a candy and novelty shop, the delight of students, who for years filled it every noonday, pouring over the sloping counters to figure out which candies—licorice sticks, buttons, jawbreakers, or wax babydolls filled with sweet liquid—would give them the most for their money. When the candyman died, the building stood empty until the WCT group took it over. Long and relatively narrow, it could seat about seventy people. The two large front windows, once filled with boxes of peanuts, pencils, erasers and balloons, had been painted over. The slightly recessed center door opened directly onto the aisle that separated the rows of folding chairs. At the far end was the stage, about three feet above floor level, and off to one side a small room for the actors to dress in.

Jerry Nickle was waiting impatiently, stomping about on the sidewalk and flexing his cold fingers. There was no moon and no wind, but the air was chill and penetrating. Seeing Vivian, he went to meet her and took her arm in a chummy manner.

"Where've you been?" he demanded. "You're late."

"Play hasn't started, has it?"

"It's about to," he said sourly. "I've been waiting."

"Then I'm not late," said Vivian. She decided not to mention the fright she had had on the way.

"Stubborn woman. Another two minutes and you wouldn't have found me. I'd be somewhere nice and cosy with a drink in my hand."

"Please don't stay on my account. If you'd rather be somewhere else, go."

"You come with me?"

"Not now, certainly," said Vivian. "I came to see the play."

"Of course you did. Later, then."

His flat tone, like his flat, watchful expression, made judging his meaning difficult. He held open the door and they were greeted by two skeletons, one gravely selling tickets, the other solemnly handing out Xeroxed programs. Vivian would have gone to a front row, but Jerry pulled her into a back one.

"Never pays to go too far front. Harder to make a fast getaway." He spoke in an undertone but not so low as not to be heard. Heads turned, but at that moment the one bare bulb at the back was turned off and a ghoulish laugh from the stage opened the play.

In keeping with the occasion, the play was full of creaking doors that opened and closed by themselves, a corpse that moved from closet to closet and a trapdoor that raised slightly to emit a sulphurous gleam and a puff of smoke. The audience willingly let themselves be startled, frightened and amused, all except Jerry, who sighed, made gurgling noises in his throat and crossed and uncrossed his knees. He leaned heavily against Vivian and said hoarsely, "Let's go."

Vivian shrugged him off and kept her attention fixed on the stage. He grumbled but subsided.

When the curtain was pulled and the back light went on, indicating intermission, Jerry seized her wrist and was on his feet in an instant. He didn't stop moving until they were outside.

"Where's your car?" he asked, starting off in the direction she had come from.

Vivian pulled back. "What do you mean? The play's not over!"

"It is for us! We've put in our time. If that latter-day Mae

West asks you about it, you can lie beautifully about the first half. Don't look at me like that. She'll expect you to lie. Everybody lies. People lie to themselves and each other. Lies are what make the world go round."

Vivian stopped. In the bluish light of the street lamp his face looked weird. He tugged on her arm but she didn't move.

"Land o'mercy!" he exclaimed in a falsetto voice. "Don't go prim and proper on me again! I thought we were past all that." He paused and studied her. "Okay, okay. You and I—we're honest. And I can honestly say that I'm bored with all that back there and I'm cold and where the hell is your car? Are we to stand forever under this damn street lamp?"

Vivian shook her head. "You're impossible."

"I know. That's my greatest asset. Give me the keys." Vivian hesitated. "C'mon! When I go out with a lady, I do the driving." Once in the car, Vivian regretted having given him the keys, for he swung out from the curb and accelerated much too fast.

"Where are we going?" asked Vivian, seeing him take an unexpected turn. She had thought they would go back to the Lucky Horseshoe. Instead he headed north, along the river.

"Someplace out along here, where we can talk about words." He glanced at her sideways. "I'll give you an illustrated lecture." Vivian, already unnerved from her earlier experience, felt increasingly uneasy. She was quite silent, and her apprehension made it impossible for her to respond to his occasional smile.

When he reached an area where there were few houses and those well up on the bluff, he pulled off onto a dirt turnaround that was sheltered in summer by a willow grove. Now the willows' thick trunks and bare branches were silhouetted against the living, moving presence of the river, whose surface had a cold, pewterlike gleam.

"There's nothing," commented Jerry with satisfaction, "like a big, roomy car, just right for rich Arabs and affluent Americans." Sliding over, he swiftly put an arm around her shoulders, holding her firmly in place, and began unbuttoning her suit jacket.

"Stop that!" exclaimed Vivian, pushing at him and trying to twist away. "What are you. . . ."

"Ah, ah, no questions! I talk, you listen, remember? 'Soft' is a good word to begin with. Your lips are 'soft!' " He grabbed her jaw, his fingers pressing painfully into her cheek, and tried to pull her face around, but Vivian, struggling, jerked her head away. "So are your breasts 'soft.' They are also 'round.'" Repelled, Vivian strove to push him off, to twist free of the arm that held her. Jerry went on speaking in an intense, breathy monotone. "You are a construct of 'soft' and 'round.'" He slid his hand under her skirt and clasped her thigh. "Your legs are 'round,' also 'smooth.'"

"Stop!" exclaimed Vivian, "stop it! Take your hands off me!" Grabbing his ear, Vivian twisted hard, then, in an upwelling of violent anger, much harder, her nails cutting into the gristly flesh. With a cry of pain he let go and jerked back. His shadowed face, its deep creases like dark strokes on an ugly mask, was menacing, the one pale eyebrow a touch of evil. He held one hand to the side of his head.

"We will go back now," said Vivian. Shaken but furious, she pressed against the door, her hand on the handle.

"Oh no," he laughed, "not yet. Who do you think you're kidding? We both know why you're here." As he grabbed for her again, she pressed the handle, swinging her legs out as the door opened. He caught her arm and the back of her jacket. There was a tearing sound as she wrenched herself forward. Breaking free, she slammed the door shut with both hands and had started off at a run when she heard him howl.

She stopped and turned. The car door remained shut. Slowly, cautiously, she went back. Peering in she saw Jerry leaning sideways across the seat, hanging by one arm from the door that had slammed shut on his fingers. Quickly Vivian opened it. With a long-drawn groan Jerry cupped his hand against his chest and leaned forward over it, breathing audibly through his clenched teeth.

Vivian got behind the wheel. She pushed at his feet and legs. "Move over and sit up. I'll drive you to the hospital."

After a bit Jerry straightened up, ran his left hand through his hair. He stared at his right hand. "Hurts like hell," he said. "You think they're all broken?"

"I doubt it," said Vivian shortly.

He tried, ever so little, moving his fingers and found he could. "No thanks to you if they're not! My right hand, too! My writing hand!"

"Don't worry," said Vivian caustically. "All this should give you lots of words for your next book, like 'gross' and 'crude' and 'repulsive.' " She swung the wheel smartly and turned into the lighted driveway that curved between the two new brick wings of the hospital and came to a stop outside the emergency door.

"Don't wait for me," said Jerry. "I'd rather call a cab."

Vivian had no intention of waiting, but she did pause for a couple who were crossing in front of her on their way to the parking lot. As Jerry went in, they had come out. It was Marvel and Belvedera. Oddly, Belvedera had on pink satin scuffs and a fur coat, and she held tightly to Marvel's arm. They scarcely noticed the car, for they were engrossed with each other. As they passed, Vivian could plainly see a white bandage about five inches long across the back of Marvel's head.

TWELVE

Winter Thaw

The winter was hard. A new record was set for a sustained low temperature: sixteen degrees below was the highest point reached for three straight weeks. There was, in addition, a great deal of snow. But work on the apartments continued, for Puckett, as good as his second word, had "done the job right" and, spurred on by a press of bills and no income, had done it in record time. Knowing that bad things can always be put to good use, he bragged at Kiwanis— where once again hands shook his—of the fine job he had done for Harry and how glad he had been to do it, and he acquired, within a relatively short time, an enhanced reputation as "a damned good contractor."

Harry, however, now wary of such remarks as, "Sure, don't you worry. We'll take care of everything," haunted the site, checking every pipe, wire, stud and block. He spent little time in the office, relying entirely on Logan, who, in fifteen minutes every morning, kept him informed of business matters.

And every day he would bid Jenny a soulful "Good morning." She always answered politely, even looked at him kindly but with a distant eye and a limited warmth of expression that unmistakably warned him off. It pained and depressed him. He felt better out in the open air. Not good, but better.

Harry's being occupied away from the office brought about

the kind of physical separation between him and Jenny that eased Logan's mind about them both. He tried, in a gentlemanly way, to do the same helpful things for Jenny that Harry had done. Logan was attracted to Jenny and amused by her saucy, independent manner; but he persisted, despite strong impulses to the contrary, in holding to his paternal role. He was fourteen years older than she. He had checked to make sure, and those fourteen years were to Logan a barrier. He would never push himself on a girl so much younger, especially one who clearly didn't like him. They were also a shield which kept him safe, and safe was what Logan thought he wanted to be.

He had had, in the past, several girl friends; then, emulating Harry, he had settled on one, a girl named Debbie, a name then much in vogue. There were over twenty Debbies in school. His was pretty, with dark hair much like Jenny's. *Her* disposition, however, was perfect. She had a slow, sweet smile and no set ideas of her own. For six years they were a pair, and Logan assumed that some day they would marry, as had Harry and Vivian, but he was in no hurry. One Thursday Debbie told him she was indeed getting married—on the coming Wednesday to a trucker she had met three weeks before. It had to be Wednesday because he had a stopover in Warrenville that day on his way back from Toledo, where he had to pick up a shipment of steel rods.

If his shadow had detached itself and walked off, Logan couldn't have been more shocked. All his assumptions knocked galley-west, he retreated into the safety of established bachelorhood. The building of his and Harry's joint business was his future; Harry, Vivian and Corinne his family. Therefore, when Ned Tully, who worked at the bank, began appearing frequently in the office, chatting with Jenny and taking her out to lunch, Logan looked upon him benignly, and for some weeks regarded Ned as a possible solution.

Jenny was ready to give Ned the same serious consideration she had given Harry, through whose name there was now a straight black line. She had drawn it out of a strong conviction that with Harry nothing would work out right. Having made that decision, she thought she might suffer, lose her appetitie, be unable to sleep. But nothing of the sort happened. She was, as a matter of fact, full of bounce and eager to get to the office, where Logan, carrying Harry's share of the work as well as his own, was laboring under paper work. He didn't sit on her desk or scribble on her notepad but he did gather up his files and withdraw the minute Ned appeared.

"I'll speak to you later about this," Logan would say, nodding affably at Ned. "You can go now, Jenny."

"But it's not twelve yet," Jenny would protest.

"Never mind, never mind." With a wave of his hand he would retire to his own office.

Jenny had to grant he was considerate. But after several such occasions, she thought him altogether too considerate and frowned as he strode jauntily away and sat at his desk behind the glass partition, face averted as if nothing could induce him to glance up. Ned, the intruder, whose coat hung on him as limply as on a hanger, was even more irritating. He made a point of his waiting, even five minutes, by constantly consulting his watch. Jenny took her time. She disliked being pushed by either one, especially when she hadn't chosen the direction.

By mid-January the snow was a foot and a half deep in Warrenville and surrounding territory. Mounds of snow like dirty, porous cement lined the scraped streets and sidewalks. The cold morning sun, rising above a diminishing bank of clouds, bathed the trees in a ruddy light. It shone between the houses in long shafts, tinting the undisturbed snow a soft pink. It dazzled on icicles. Great lumps of opaque ice, built up by repeated thaws and freezings, hung from corner gutter spouts like frozen water- falls. Tires backing out of plowed driveways made a soft crunch, but a snapped branch or a dog's bark resounded sharply on the frigid air.

The jogger, bundled in layers of cotton knit and a yard-long, red and white striped knitted cap pulled down to her eyebrows, was forced to run in the street to avoid breaking her pace on unshoveled sidewalks. Oblivious to cars that slowed or braked trying to pass her, she kept to her route, her eyes and nose moist, her cheeks red, her breath hanging visibly in the air before her.

It was Saturday morning, but Jenny was up and dressed, in dark blue ski pants and a sky blue pullover. Her jacket and mittens lay ready on a chair near the door. She had filled a thermos with hot coffee and was just handing a cup of what remained to Ned, standing in the middle of the room. He also wore a ski suit and every few seconds struggled with his several cuffs to get a look at his watch.

"Have to get started soon," he said. "We want to get a number of runs in today." He had not wanted to waste time removing his jacket or his knitted cap, the top of which rose up like a crown in two peaks, each adorned with a pom-pom.

As he spoke there was a knock on the door. Jenny, through the thinly curtained glass pane, saw Logan on the landing. His coat collar was turned up around his ears. He wore no hat, and his brown curly hair was very crisp. He was blowing on his bare, cupped hands and doing a little tap dance as he waited. Jenny, her hand on the doorknob, was so wonder-struck that she never forgot that moment.

Ned, wondering at her not opening the door, asked impatiently, "Who is it?"

Jenny didn't answer, but she did open the door. Logan came in swiftly, his face alight. "Jenny, sorry to bother you, but . . . oh, you're going out." His glance fell on Ned, on his suit and cockaded hat.

"We're just leaving," said Ned. "Driving up to Kelley's Point for a little skiing. Should have left half an hour ago."

Logan agreed, with no noticeable enthusiasm. "That's a long drive."

"One hundred sixty-four and three quarters miles. I've clocked it," declared Ned, always proud to back up his figures. Then he grinned. "It's a great place to spend a cosy weekend."

"A week. . . ." Logan's voice failed. It struck him, like suddenly being doused with cold water, that as a solution Ned would be hard to take. Sobered, he turned to Jenny. "I mustn't keep you then." His lips felt unexpectedly stiff.

"There's no rush whatever," said Jenny, irritated with Ned's fidgeting, with his silly cap, with his being there at all. Ignoring him, she asked Logan why he had come.

Remembering, Logan was embarrassed. "Nothing important, nothing that can't wait. Thought I'd get caught up with some work at the office. But the files are locked and the keys are in your desk and it's locked, so . . . Saturday's a good day . . . no phones ringing . . . no interruptions. . . ." He glanced at Ned. "But it's a better day for skiing."

"Yeah," said Ned, grinning again.

It was the most repulsive grin Jenny had ever seen. "There's no way that I'll go skiing"—her slighting tone made it a worthless if not disgusting occupation—"if there's work that needs doing. Just give me a moment to change. .   ."

"Hey!" exclaimed Ned, thinking she must be joking, "come on now!"

Logan hastened to apologize. "Jenny, I never intended. . . ."

"Is there work or isn't there?" Jenny asked sharply.

Logan had to admit there was, but rashly added, "Please don't let that interfere. . . ."

"Hey!" said Ned. "We have a date, remember?"

"Hay," said Jenny angrily, "is for horses!"

Ned frowned like a baby getting ready to cry. "You can't break it off at the last minute!"

Jenny stabbed him with a look. "I can *do* anything I *want* to do!"

"But I've got reservations!"

Logan opened his mouth, but at Jenny's fierce look, shut it.

"Reservations," she said, speaking very precisely, "can be canceled. Or, better yet, you can take someone else!"

"Yeah," said Ned, nodding so the cockade on his cap bobbled, "yeah, I should have done that to begin with. Now I'll be over an hour late."

"Then you'd better hurry," said Jenny tartly.

When the door had shut behind him, there was an awkward silence. Jenny, for something to do, carried Ned's cup to the kitchen.

Logan stood with his fists in his overcoat pockets. Though he felt one part guilt to ten parts relief, he believed he should apologize. "I'm sorry, Jenny. I shouldn't have come. I've ruined your weekend." Now that Ned was gone, he found he could say it.

"You haven't," said Jenny coolly, lifting her chin. "You haven't ruined anything."

"But I thought you liked Ned."

"Do *you*?"

On the surface a reasonable question. But a certain challenge in her tone puzzled him, and Logan answered cautiously. "Seems a nice guy to me."

"Does he!"

Now definitely uncertain of his footing, Logan asked, "Don't *you* like him?"

"No!" said Jenny vehemently. "I don't!"

"Why not?" asked Logan, really wanting to know.

For a moment Jenny found herself hopelessly at cross-purposes. "Because," she finally flung out, "he's got limp hair, that's why!"

Logan was nonplussed. In one last effort to be reasonable, he said, "But he's . . . not much older than you. And he's got a good job."

Jenny stared at him, outraged. "Why, you're trying to marry me off! Well just let me tell you that when I *do* decide to get married, I won't need any help from you! Now why don't you go!"

Logan hesitated.

Jenny stamped her foot. "Go! Just go!"

After he had gone, shutting the door quietly behind him, Jenny paced back and forth. Finally she went into the kitchen and began baking gingersnaps.

Downstairs, they had observed Ned go up, then Logan.

"Coming pretty early, seems to me."

"Well, they're going out! Didn't you see what he had on?"

"I saw. Looked like a rooster. He works at the bank, that one. He'd be a good catch."

"What makes you think she's trying to catch anybody?"

"Women always have their hooks out. You caught me, didn't you?"

"Some catch! Listen, sounds like an argument."

"They'd better watch it. Fighting I won't tolerate. Not in my house!"

"Oh oh! There he goes, by himself. See, I knew she wasn't after him!"

"Sure, you know everything that goes on in her head. Look at that! *He's* leaving too. She's not after him either, eh?"

After a time a faint but pungent gingery odor filtered down. They raised their eyebrows appreciatively and waited eagerly for a knock on the back door.

But a whiff was all they ever got, for Jenny had experienced a revelation. Her sight of Logan waiting outside the door had shocked her. She had never seen him in just that way before. She knew in that moment it was Logan she loved, Logan she wanted. She was now convinced, as she measured and mixed, that this had always been true. Everything in the past had pointed to it. In a blissful flight of fancy she saw herself in *his* house—which she knew only from the outside—baking in *his* kitchen. It was inexpressibly cosy.

Logan, answering a prolonged ring of the doorbell, found Jenny on his doorstep. Her face was red with cold, but as serene as if she had never sent him off in a fit of temper a mere three hours earlier. Smiling at his surprise, she held out a brown paper bag and said, "Hold this, will you, till I take off my boots."

Logan recovered quickly but continued to adhere firmly to his big-brother approach. He took the bag and her elbow. "Not out there! Come inside."

"But the rug!"

"Never mind the rug."

One glance around the hall, which led straight back to the kitchen, and Jenny felt at home. Stairs went up at one side and had a lower and an upper landing, each lighted by a window with a decorative leaded top section that shed colored bars across the steps and bannister. There was a long runner on the floor, a table with twisted legs and a scalloped front standing against the wall, its dark top covered with an embroidered doily. On it were an oil lamp and an old silver tray. A mirror hung above it and just beyond, sliding double doors opened into the living room. Balanced on one foot, Jenny glanced up at him. "You don't mind my coming in? You're not expecting anyone?"

"No. No one. What's in the bag? It smells good."

"Gingersnaps. I made them. I thought you might make some coffee. But . . . if you'd rather go to the office, I brought the keys."

In her stocking feet she was shorter than Logan had thought. He gave the bag a little shake. "Couldn't go off and leave these, not fresh baked. Come on back; I'll fix the coffee."

But Jenny padded into the living room, curious to see what she was already disposed to like. The fireplace was of smooth, purplish, almost iridescent bricks, and on the heavy oak mantle were two photographs, an elderly man and a woman, in matching gold frames. Jenny smiled at them and tapped one with her fingernail. "These your father and mother?" She didn't need his answer to know. He had his father's face, his mother's hair and lively expression. So that was the woman who had hung the lace curtains, crocheted the covers on the chair arms, put away the dishes in the massive china cupboard in the paneled dining room.

And he who had hollowed the easy chair and rested his feet on the heavy, worn ottoman, where now Logan rested his. Jenny riffled through the magazine rack, sat on a straight chair with a needlepoint seat. It was bumpy and buckled in and out as she sat on it. She tried the padded rocker and saw that one of the ties was pulled loose. She would have to replace that. She was looking through the glass doors of the bookcases that flanked the fireplace when Logan carried in a tray with mugs and the cookies on a plate.

Jenny at once settled down on the sofa with her feet tucked up. Logan considered another chair, then sat beside her.

"You should build us a fire," said Jenny brightly, glad for the hot coffee. She forgot to hold it with fingers flared and gaze at him over the rim as she had done with others on other occasions. She even forgot about the state of her hair and the run that had started up the heel of one stocking.

"I haven't made a fire since . . . not in a long time," said Logan. "But there's wood in the garage. I could. . . ."

"Not now," said Jenny, stopping him. "We'll bring some in later."

This was Jenny with a difference. She wasn't flip or prickly. Logan marveled that she was there at all, curled up on his sofa with the contentedness of a cat who has made itself at home. So natural was her presence there and so beguiled was he by her easy use of "we" that without intending to do so, he stretched out his arm behind her and without realizing that he was going to speak aloud what was only a half-formulated thought, he said, "I'd like to kiss you, but I'm afraid."

Jenny's reaction was immediate. She froze. Then, setting down her mug and putting both feet on the floor, she turned to face him squarely. "Afraid!" she exclaimed, unable to believe she had heard correctly. "Afraid of what!" Indignant, incredulous, she leaned slightly toward him. "What do you think would happen!? Afraid I'd slap you? Or run screaming into the snow yelling 'Rape!'" She looked at him scathingly. "Afraid! Of what, for Pete's sake!" She jumped up and stood facing the fireplace.

Stunned, Logan started to speak, but Jenny suddenly turned around.

"Why do you think I even came here! Just for that key? Just

so we could go to the office and work? I couldn't care less!" Her face puckered and she turned away. "Oh, you're impossible! I should never have come at all!"

Logan touched her shoulder. "Jenny, I'm glad you came. I wish you never had to leave. But . . . I'm fourteen years older than you are."

Jenny spun around. "What's *that* supposed to mean! You think I'm a child, not *mature* enough for you!" Her eyes brimmed with tears. "Well! Just let me tell you. . . ."

"No, no!" interrupted Logan, not wanting to hear. "It's *not* that! It's that *I* am too old for *you!*"

"That's a stupid thing to say! That's just a mean excuse! If you *really* cared for. . . ."

Unable to resist any longer, Logan put his arms around her. Stiff with anger, Jenny tried to pull away, but he held her close. "You've been warned once," he said, "and that's all the warning you're going to get." This time her eyes shut of their own accord and there was no need to judge anything at all.

Logan's room was upstairs at the back of the house. A corner room, it had a slanted ceiling on two sides and one window overlooking the backyard. As a boy he used to study the figured wallpaper above him, and in the shadows of the ceiling, grotesque faces would emerge from its pattern. Now, with Jenny's head on his chest, he saw the pattern as just a pattern, for the late afternoon sun, reflecting on the snow, lit up the ceiling with a pale watery light. Eventually they would occupy the large front bedroom, unused since his mother died three years before. She would be pleased that the family home would be his and Jenny's home, that it would come alive once again.

Logan rubbed his chin against the top of Jenny's head. "Think I'll get dressed and bring in some wood. We can have a fire."

Jenny raised to look at him but kept her arm tight around him. "You can't go yet. You haven't asked me to marry you."

"Marry?" Logan's eyes opened innocently wide. "You don't need me for that! You told me so only this morning. Besides, you said marriage was just a piece of paper."

"I never said such things!"

Logan laughed. "You did! I remember everything you've

ever said to me, and . . . owh! No biting!" They tussled until he pinned her down. Leaning over her, he said softly, "I thought this was to be just a glorious weekend."

She met his gaze for a moment, then shut her eyes, put her arms around his neck and held him tight.

"All right," he murmured, his face against her tangled hair, "we'll get married whenever you say."

Not until later when he was bringing in the wood did Logan, with a sudden pang of apprehension, remember Harry.

THIRTEEN

Change of Cast

"You didn't tell me Logan was getting married," remarked Vivian. Harry, shielded by the evening newspaper, grunted. "Harry?"

Harry cleared his throat. "Didn't know myself til yesterday."

"They stopped in at our bazaar. She bought a pot and he got her a pair of earrings, those that Doris makes, a piece of metal with a bead at the end. She's a very pretty girl. I'm glad for Logan. It's time he had a family of his own. I think they'll be very happy together. They seem perfectly suited, don't you think?"

Harry took a deep breath. "Yeah."

Vivian looked up from her work, pen raised. As treasurer for the International League for Peace, she was toting up sales and expenses for their three-day bazaar. "Is that all you can say? Logan! Our oldest, closest friend! He's family!"

Harry slammed down his newspaper. "What do you want me to say! Sure, it's great! Just great! Now, can I read?"

Vivian was struck by his vehemence. He stared at the newspaper, but she could see he wasn't reading. His face was tense, his eyes fixed. She had been going to suggest they have a party for Logan and Jenny, maybe on a weekend when Corinne could come home for it, but now she didn't. Quietly, and with a new awareness, she resumed her figuring. The silence between them was

185

full of private, unshared thoughts, like the silence between strangers. After thirty minutes or so, Vivian arrived at her totals.

"Well," she said in a light, conversational tone, "after expenses, we made almost eight hundred dollars. That's quite good, more than we expected."

With an effort Harry summoned up his voice. "Mmmn, that's . . ." he had been going to say 'great.' ". . . that's fine." Not much of a response, but more than he had been able to manage when Logan had first told him. Then he had been speechless.

On his way out of the office after the usual morning rundown of business, Logan had hesitated, turned and said, "Harry?"

Logan was not usually solemn. Harry, about to put on his coat, stopped and waited.

"Harry, I. . . ."

Harry smiled. "Say it! Can't be any worse than Puckett."

Encouraged, Logan thought perhaps he had an exaggerated view of what it would mean to Harry. Might not be a blow after all. "Jenny and I are getting married. Week after next. I hope we'll have your good wishes." He made a partial gesture, wanting the assurance of a handshake.

For what seemed an endless stretch of time, Harry didn't move at all. His face tightened as if he had been struck. He studied Logan, taking inventory of all his features, one by one, and of his whole body. Then without a word he threw his muffler around his neck, hauled on his coat and walked out.

Several hours later he returned and strode into Logan's office. He came around the desk and thrust out his arm. Logan flinched, thinking Harry was going to hit him. But Harry grasped his hand forcefully and, though his voice sounded unnatural in his own ears, he wished Logan well. He wished them both well. He insisted, over Logan's protests, that they take two weeks off for a honeymoon. Having finally responded to Logan and acknowledged their close friendship, Harry was less displeased with himself, but he was no happier. It was difficult for him to believe that he could ever regard Logan in quite the same way again.

Beanna Blynt, drawing, perhaps, on her intuitive powers, called Harry at precisely the right psychological time. She had a matter to discuss and preferred to do so in the privacy of her own home.

The Blynt residence, like the Blynts themselves, was more complex than appeared on the outside. It was one in a row of houses, all versions of Midwestern Victorian, on an old residential tree-lined street that ran along the river bluff. The paint around its long narrow windows was flaking, a few shingles had blown off the porch roof and the front steps, halfheartedly cleared of snow, were worn and sagging. A milk box stood at one side of the door, a snow shovel leaned against the wall on the other side and beside it lay an old pair of boots.

Beanna, wearing a flowing gown of geometric blues and greens, opened the door and invited him in. Inside, the house showed what was to Harry an exotic face. The floor was laid with ceramic tile of Moorish pattern. The kitchen, on the right, was merely an extension of the entrance. Stainless steel counters and dark wooden cabinets were lighted by a row of large bulbs with visible filaments attached to a bar suspended from the ceiling. On the left, curving up beside a ceiling-high window, was a wide, free-standing staircase of gleaming wooden steps with no risers. Everywhere were plants, large plants with split leaves, fan-shaped leaves and unfurling leaves, and plants with outward-reaching roots. They stood in pots and tubs in the curve of the stairs, under the stairs, and before the huge window. Pots of trailing vines and succulents like strings of beads or tiny gray-green hearts hung from the ceiling in an ascending row that followed the curve of the stairs.

"Come this way," said Beanna, smiling. Gathering up her gown at one side, she preceded him up the stairs. "We live up here," she explained. "Give me your coat. And your brief case," she added, putting them both down on an out-of-the-way chair.

Whatever partitions had once existed had been removed so the upper floor was one spacious room. Its ceiling beams had been exposed and the end wall knocked out and replaced with glass panes from floor to ceiling, providing a view of treetops and, beyond them, the river. Near the window were some low-slung chairs and floor pillows; near the stairs were a round butcher block table and chairs of Swedish design. Against a side wall was a huge platform bed, covered with an Indian throw and heaped with pillows.

"It's unstructured," commented Beanna, "but we find it comfortable. Sit here, at the table. I'll bring the tea." She went downstairs and returned carrying a tray with a pot and cups. She moved her chair close to Harry's, and her gown, deeply slit, fell away, exposing her bare, crossed knees. "This tea I made myself, a blend of home-grown herbs. I think you'll like it."

Harry raised his cup and sniffed.

Beanna laughed. "You needn't be afraid of it."

Harry took a cautious sip, then another. He raised his eyebrows and smiled. "It's good. Different but good. What," he asked, looking straight at her, "did you want to talk about?"

Beanna was in no hurry to answer. She tilted her head and studied him with a frank, searching gaze. "I don't think . . . you should talk at all. I sense in you a deep sadness. Your aura is dim." She put out her hand in an entirely natural way and touched his hair lightly, tracing its wave with her fingertips. "And that is uncharacteristic. Normally your aura glows." Her hand rested on his shoulder. "You are a strong, vigorous man, a man of action. But just now . . ." she looked at him through half-closed eyes, ". . . just now your spirit flags. I will talk. You must relax, be comfortable. Here," she rose and bent over him, and he breathed a faint scent as of woods in the rain, "give me your coat. And loosen your tie. Ties are horrible, strangling things. Swanger refuses to wear them. Now," she sat again and leaned her knee against his, "drink your tea."

Harry did so. The tea was warm and aromatic, like Beanna herself. She was a striking woman, and he enjoyed looking at her, which she was pleased to have him do. Her high forehead was perhaps her best feature, set off by her hair being smoothed back and held by a narrow band, as when he had first seen her, then fluffed out to frame her head and face like a soft headdress. Her cheeks were high and round, her mouth very full. He had an impulse to touch her hair, curious as to its texture.

"You're wondering about my hair," she remarked, having observed his glance. She bent her head toward him. "It's real." The fluffed ends were softer than he would have imagined. "I used to wear it differently, but Swanger likes it this way."

She poured Harry another cup of tea. "He's a very talented man. He remodeled this entire house himself. He's a fine carpenter, though he prefers to think of himself as a poet. That's because he's a romantic. You have much in common. You are a practical man of business, and you set great store on physical prowess." She smiled cunningly. "Both very important. But underneath all that you are a romantic. That is why, like Swanger, your spirit sometimes suffers. You must learn to care for it. Here," she waved her hand gracefully, "you are free to be yourself, as Swanger and I are free. We are deeply attached to one another, but we allow each other perfect freedom." She paused and Harry waited. They smiled into each other's eyes.

"We were, as I told you months ago, fated to meet," she said.

Harry smiled broadly. Fate would have been helpless without Beanna.

Seeing the glint in his eye, Beanna chided, "Ah, ah, mustn't think sharp thoughts! You'll ruin the ambience. Come, we'll be more comfortable over here."

Harry, amused and willing enough, let himself be led. It was all so easy and natural. No coyness, no misunderstanding of motive. Just simple, uncomplicated desire and, it seemed to Harry, of consequence to no one.

"Just lie back, I'll take off your shoes." She also took off his loosened tie and his shirt. He managed his trousers himself. Her gown opened conveniently down the front, and Beanna, smiling like the Mona Lisa, drew him down to her swelling breast.

Making love with Beanna was like riding a billowy wave. He was cushioned and caressed and finally thrown up on the beach, spent and breathless.

"You see," said Beanna, after a quiet interval, "I was right. All the psychic influences were in perfect conjunction."

He kissed her goodbye at the foot of the stairs, standing beneath a Cissus antarctica. So gracious were her lips and so yielding her body that he was tempted to go back upstairs, but Beanna drew back and placed one finger across his lips.

"No more today. If you wish to, come back the day after tomorrow. At two." She smiled. "I'll make you a pot of tea."

At first Vivian had gone to Mr. Farley's only so she could report to Corinne, whose every letter concluded with questions about Molly. Then she began going oftener. The barn was cold, its dust-filled air swirled by sudden chill drafts whenever the large doors opened and banged shut. Mr. Farley, bundled to twice his size in several old plaid shirts and a lumber jacket, was always busy but never hurried. He went from one chore to the next without pause, following an apparently endless routine, and though she was not directly a part of it, Vivian was drawn by this steady, repetitive round. It was to her simple, purposeful and satisfying. Mr. Farley appreciated the work she did. He also thought her presence brightened up the stables considerably. He anticipated her visits with as much pleasure as Molly. Eyes watering slightly from the cold, he would pause for a brief greeting and take the opportunity to blow his sharp, reddened nose. Molly, eager for the apple Vivian always brought her, would stomp impatiently and bend her graceful neck to look around.

Vivian filled her feed bin, swept out the stall, and then, with as much care as if Molly were going to a fair, she curried and combed, brushing her rippled mane all smoothly to one side. From the top of stacked bales of hay in an adjoining stall, two curled-up cats watched her, their coats fluffed out. Vivian spoke to them as she worked, trying to tease a response, but they stared, unmoving, as smug as two odalisques.

Once, as she was leaving, Mr. Farley asked, "Why don't you take her out? On a sunny day. She could use the exercise."

But Vivian wasn't ready to do that. Sometime, maybe, she told him. She wasn't certain of anything these days except of a generalized discontent. Her days were filled; still she had an old, familiar sense of aimlessness, that what she spent her time doing could be done just as well by someone else or, possibly, not done at all and with no loss to anyone. Only Corinne's occasional letters and caring for Molly gave her any satisfaction. Because she was indifferent, Dolphine was able, finally, to persuade her to come to an evening workshop.

Vivian arrived late and had to park at the end of a line of cars. She made an effort to hurry, wondering why she bothered since it didn't matter in the least. When she entered, Dolphine was standing on the small stage, addressing fourteen or so people scattered about on folding chairs in the unlighted area. Vivian slid into one near the back.

Dolphine was wearing a pink knitted dress that fit her rounded figure like a pillowcase a pillow. The unshaded light above her sparkled on a large brooch with a red stone and entwined gold leaves that was pinned to one shoulder. "The secret," Dolphine was saying, "is relaxation, total relaxation." She let her raised hand fall back, palm upward, and moved the upper part of her body slightly to one side as she surveyed her audience. "Now I want you all to stand up, and if you're wearing anything terribly bulky, remove it."

Chairs scraped on the bare floor and several people removed their sweaters.

"You should keep yours on," said a low voice near Vivian. "It's cold in here."

Surprised at being so ordered, Vivian turned her head. Two chairs away stood a tall young man in dark clothes. In the dim light he appeared to be Scandinavian, with longish, blond hair. He faced front as if he had not spoken, and for an eerie moment Vivian thought she might have imagined it.

"Now," said Dolphine, "I want you to fall forward over the chair in front of you. Come on, everybody! Bend! That's right, hang forward. Let your arms flop. Think of yourselves as rag dolls. Let all the tension drain away. Let yourselves go limp."

Vivian, her cheek against the metal chairback, her arms hanging on either side, wished she hadn't come. Her hair fell partially over her face; through it she could see the young man's face, also upside down.

"Now your body is relaxed, you must empty your mind." Dolphine spoke with the serenity of a prophet ordering the future. "Cast out all thoughts. Your mind must be blank, like an empty slate."

"She doesn't realize," whispered the young man, "that's most people's normal state."

Vivian discerned a faint smile on his face and turned her head in the other direction, feeling his remark somehow reflected on Dolphine. Her chin against the back of the chair, she heard Dolphine say:

"Now you're relaxed. Empty. Your own concerns have vanished. They no longer matter. You are ready now to receive a new and different life! To express another character and other emotions. You will move and speak as a different person. You will think differently. Your voice will be that of the character who takes over your body. Now slowly straighten up, slowly, to preserve your receptivity, and I will tell you the situation we will work with.

"The scene is the Alps, in winter. There has been a bad storm, and a small plane has been downed. The passengers have scattered, by twos, to look for help. At one side of the stage is a chalet, an inn. Now . . ." Dolphine paused, looked out over the waiting group and pointed. "You, Stan, will be the innkeeper, and you, Jean, his wife. Come on, step up here. Mmmmn . . . you, Vivian, and you, August, will be the first ones to reach the inn. Come along, let's not waste time."

Vivian hung back; she suggested someone else take the part. But the young man, who turned out to be August, moved forward, forcing her out of the row, and Dolphine shut off all protest by commanding, "No speaking out of your parts! You two stand over on this side. You have tied yourselves together with a rope for safety—just hold hands, that will do—and you are climbing up a steep slope. You are cold, hungry, exhausted! We will add other characters as we come to them. Now . . ." Dolphine stepped down from the stage, executing, to keep her balance, several little dancelike steps that gave her body a buoyant swing, ". . . begin!"

The four on stage stood woodenly, staring out at the audience, recruits hoping for direction.

"Well, come on! You have your characters! Let them flow out of you! What would an innkeeper be doing? What would an innkeeper's wife be doing?"

Stan pondered a moment, then began filling imaginery tankards and wiping his hands on what must have been a long apron. Jean, looking worried, made a few dusting motions; then, inspired, began enthusiastically making a bed.

"And you two, climb!"

August grabbed Vivian's hand and lifted his feet in exaggeratedly high, sideways steps.

"Wait!" cautioned Dolphine, sashaying forward, "you're tied together! If one moves, the other must move!"

Vivian would have turned and walked off, but August jerked her hand, and, thinking that the best way out would be to get it over with as quickly as possible, Vivian began stepping in time with August.

"But you're climbing!" protested Dolphine. Turning to those sitting around her, she asked, "What is missing from their realization of this scene? They're climbing a slope, remember."

"They'd be bent over!"

"They'd be out of breath!"

"Of course!" said Dolphine. She turned expectantly to Vivian and August, who glanced at each other, then quickly away, both suddenly overcome with an impulse to laugh. Leaning forward and heaving long, audible breaths, they moved toward the middle of the stage.

"Good, good!" exclaimed Dolphine. "But now you see the inn! How do you let us know that you see it? That you *know* you are saved?"

Instantly August straightened. Tall and lean, he shielded his eyes with his hand Indian fashion and stared into the distance across the four feet separating them from Stan and Jean, still busy filling tankards and making beds.

"I see an inn! A light! Two lights! If we hurry, maybe . . ." his voice choked with laughter, ". . . we can get a Scotch and soda!" He grinned. Vivian began to laugh. Stan and Jean and all the others laughed, everyone except Dolphine. She closed her blue-tinted lids and shook her carefully coiffed head and plump shoulders with such pained disapproval that everyone laughed all the harder.

"Come down, come down from there," said Dolphine, waving all four off the stage. "You are all very naughty. I see there is not a shred of seriousness in you tonight. Very well. We will try another time. Now for the business half of our meeting. Someone turn on the lights."

Their joint experience gave Vivian and August a sense of companionship. They sat down together and as they listened would catch each other's eye in shared amusement.

Vivian thought him an unusual young man, judging his age as twenty-seven. He was actually twenty-five. In profile he suggested a Viking. His facial bones were prominent; his streaked blond hair swept back from his forehead with the faintest suggestion of a wave. She saw him on a boat, his long-lashed ice-blue eyes staring out over a cold gray sea. His long, bony fingers would be at home with ropes and sails. His name, August Larsson, was Swedish, and facing each other on his boat-necked sweater were two reindeer between bands of snowflakes.

"I'll drive you home," said August, when the meeting broke up.

"Thank you," said Vivian, "but I have a car."

"Then let's go someplace, get that Scotch and soda. My treat."

Vivian smiled. "I must get home. Thanks anyway. Another time maybe."

One brilliant, sunny day following a heavy snowfall, Vivian came home from Farley's and found an old Buick Skylark parked in front of the barn and a set of tracks leading toward the terrace at the back of the house. Following them, she found the intervals were too wide for her step and she foundered through windblown drifts up to her knees, well above her boots. Rounding one wing of the house, she was startled to see a man standing at the terrace door, his hands cupped against the glass, staring in.

"Hello there! What do . . . oh, it's you, August!"

He turned, waved and came toward her, striding through the snow as if it were his element. "Yes, it's me. Only it's Ah-goost. But *you* can call me Gus."

"I prefer August," said Vivian. "If you were coming out, you should have called."

"I like to be unexpected. That way I find people as they are. If you'd known I was coming, you'd have gotten all fixed up."

"Not necessarily," said Vivian dryly.

"Oh yes you would. As it is, you're in work clothes. There's even some hay sticking to your coat. You must have been in a barn somewhere." He removed the hay and took her arm. "Come on, let's go inside. I'd like a cup of coffee, wouldn't you?" He started off, pulling her along at his pace.

"I can manage," said Vivian, trying to free her arm. But he refused to let go, saying, "We'll go in the back door. It's quicker."

"I see you know where everything is."

"Sure. Nothing to it. This is a very conventional house. You left the door unlocked too. You shouldn't do that, you know. And you should have shoveled the walk."

Vivian made an exasperated sound. "I always leave the back door unlocked. As for the walk, neither my husband nor I had time this morning. But then, you like to find things as they are."

"In the future, you must lock it," said August calmly, holding the door open. "It's unsafe not to. I'll shovel the walk before I leave." Seeing the snow had got inside her boots, he said, "Go on, don't mind me. Get your slippers. I'll look around. And take that scarf off your head."

Vivian changed her damp slacks and socks. The scarf, which completely hid her hair, she always wore when she went to the stables. About to pull it off as she normally would, she changed her mind and left it on. He was much too young to think he could boss her about.

As she made the coffee she heard him downstairs. "How did you know," she asked when he came back up, "where I lived?"

"I asked. Got any cookies? I like something with my coffee."

"Sorry, no cookies. Bread, if you'd like that."

"That'll be fine. With some jam, please."

Vivian got the jam, then poured herself a cup of coffee and waited. In some ways he reminded her strongly of Corinne, and she was certain he would have more to say. He did.

"I'm a C.O. I just got back from doing two years in an Army hospital. Got any sugar?"

"Here. How was it, working in the hospital?"

"Okay," he said thoughtfully, stirring in three large spoonsful. "It was really okay. Saw a lot. Learned a lot. I'm glad I did it, you know. And in my time off I did some studying. I'm going into architecture next fall. I don't usually talk about myself but I'm telling you because I think you have a right to know."

Vivian raised her eyebrows. "I see." She didn't see, really, but on second thought suggested, "That's why you're so interested in the house."

"Partly. Only partly." He looked at her steadily, intently. "Aren't you going to ask me why else?"

"Well. . . ." He really was childish. Vivian had never liked guessing games. "Why else?"

"Because of you, because of our strong mutual attraction for each other. You wouldn't come out with me the other evening, so I had to come here. Besides, I wanted to see the environment you live in."

"Now just a minute. . . ." began Vivian, but August held up his hand and patted the air.

"Don't spoil it by pretending you didn't know. When I first saw you I knew instantly. You shouldn't fight it. It's a fact, and one thing I learned in the hospital is to face facts because there's no way to change them. . . . You needn't be afraid."

Vivian, amazed and uncertain whether to be amused or indignant, said, "I certainly am not afraid."

August smiled teasingly. "I'm bigger than you. And much stronger."

"And I," said Vivian, "am much older than you and I have a

husband and a daughter nineteen. Those are facts too, and ones you should keep in mind."

"Age," said August, unperturbed, "can't be counted in years. Some people are grown up at twenty; others, never. Sometime I'd like to meet your family, but not until you have more confidence in our relationship."

Vivian laughed and shook her head. "August. . . ."

"Gus."

"August," repeated Vivian firmly, "we can be friends, but only friends. Is that clear? You can think of me as. . . ." she hesitated.

"As an aunt?"

"Yes," agreed Vivian, relieved, "as your aunt."

August said nothing. His naturally stern features took on a sober cast. He stood up. "I want to see the rest of the house."

"Of course," said Vivian, assuming the problem settled and ready to humor him. But August stepped close to her and pulled off her scarf.

"You have," he said softly, "the most beautiful hair I've ever seen. And you smell of horses." The reindeers were at her eye level and for one moment Vivian thought he was going to embrace her. Instead he laid his hand lightly on top of her head, stroking it in a paternal manner. "Don't," he cautioned, "make the mistake of treating me like a boy. I'm not." He turned away. "This kitchen is straight out of an ad for linoleum. It doesn't suit you at all."

"What do you mean?" asked Vivian, glad for the abrupt switch of subjects. "It's convenient to work in, and that suits me."

"It has no individual character, no personality. It reflects suburbia, not *you*." He explained patiently, secretly pleased by the opportunity to express aloud a theory he had recently read that had struck him as utterly true. "Your home is an extension of yourself. That doesn't mean it can't be convenient and comfortable. It must be that, but it should express your taste, your interests, your activities. Look at this living room! That lighting went out years ago. You know what it reminds me of? A funeral parlor! That soft, indirect light all the way around. Nothing harsh for the mourners. You can almost hear the organ. The corpse would be laid out in the middle."

"What an unpleasant thing to say!" exclaimed Vivian. "This is a charming . . . ."

"You think about it," said August, "just think about it. You'll see I'm right. What's this, master bedroom? Mmn, double bed," he mumbled, displeased. "Dressing table and a ruffled skirt! Possibly, when you were ten, but not now." His tone was professional and positive. He touched the dressing table with outstretched fingers as if he might be going to say, "Pitch it out." "You're fond of perfume, but I see no comb or brush. You," he said, his eyes narrowing as he projected her into different surroundings, "should live with smooth, uncluttered lines and shining surfaces. And bold patterns, not spriggy, like that blouse you're wearing. Little flowers are for schoolgirls."

Vivian shrugged. "This is just an old. . . ."

But August had stepped into the bathroom. "My God, look at this!" He stood gaping at the blood red porcelain, "Slaughterhouse red! You could knife someone to death here and it would never show!" He shook his head at Vivian. "How have you lived with it!" He didn't wait for an answer but strode down the hall. He stopped in the doorway of Corinne's room.

"Your daughter's room, I see. A typical girl!"

Stung by his smug categorizing of Corinne, Vivian exclaimed, "She's no more typical than you are! She's charming and *quite* individual!"

August smiled at her tenderly. "Mother defending her young."

Vivian immediately felt foolish and clicked her tongue.

"I apologize," said August. "I should have said, a typical girl's room. White French provincial. Ruffled curtains." He groaned. "Photographs in the mirror frame!" He took a closer look. "All of horses. The *same* horse." He glanced at Vivian questioningly.

"That's Molly, Corinne's horse."

He raised his eyebrows. "You keep horses?"

"Just one. We board her while Corinne's away at school." There was no reason, she told herself, why she should feel apologetic or offer explanations. She moved impatiently, wanting him to go. August, with the tolerant smile of an understanding parent, went on to the last room.

"This, no doubt, is the inevitable spare room. Everything's so predictable in these houses." He paused, drew his brows together. "But this room's used." He noted a quilt, thrown across the foot of the bed rather than folded, a pair of shoes lying beside a chair, women's clothes hanging in the partially opened closet, the dresser top. "Here," he said, with a triumphant smile, "is the comb. And brush." He reached out and grasped Vivian's shoulder. "*This* is your room!" He nodded toward the back window but without taking his eyes off her face. "With a view of the slope." His smile deepened. "A room by herself!"

Vivian shrugged her shoulder, but he did not let go. His expression was altogether too wise, and she resented being put on the defensive. "You asked to see the house and I have shown it to you," she said tartly. "You should confine your remarks to architectural matters. That, you said, was your interest. Anything else is none of your business."

But instead of being put in his place, August beamed at her as at a child who has just gotten something wrong and is immediately all the more endearing. "No," he corrected gently, "I said I was *going* into architecture. My *interest* is *you*."

With another of his abrupt switches he let her go and left the room, where she had indeed been sleeping by herself for some months, and headed for the back door. Vivian followed, exasperated beyond measure that the harder she tried to assert herself as a mature woman the more immature he made her feel.

Putting on his coat, he told her she would have to move. "You can't be happy when your personality and the place you live are in conflict. Only when you and your environment are in harmony are you truly at home." He remembered the page where he had read that sentence and smiled, pleased by how well it sounded, spoken aloud. "I'll see you at the theater next week. I won't kiss you yet. I don't think you're ready." Vivian refused even to respond to that, and he smiled roguishly at the severity of her expression. "You'll just have to wait awhile."

As he closed the door, he said, "Thanks for the coffee. And the bread. And the jam." Then he opened it again and leaned back in. "Did you make it?"

"The bread," said Vivian, eyeing him sternly. "Not the jam."

"That's what I thought," he answered and shut the door.

Through the window she saw him shoveling the walk clear of snow. With easy swings of the shovel he scooped up great chunks and pitched them away. The sun glinted on the fall of powdery snow that followed the shovel and shone warmly on August's pale yellow hair. When he finished, he propped the shovel by the back door and strode off toward his car. Not once had he glanced toward the window, but halfway to the car, without turning and as though he had known all along that she was watching, he raised his gloved hand and waved goodbye.

Vivian smiled in spite of herself.

One morning Allegra Smith called to say that the roof was leaking. Vivian went at once to inspect the damage and found two leaks, one in the living room, one in the kitchen. Allegra had placed a plastic pail under each, into which drops fell in contrapuntal and syncopated rhythms. Vivian promised to send someone to do what could be done in the attic as a temporary measure until spring, when she intended to have a new roof put on. Meanwhile she smelled a delectable odor coming from a pot on the stove.

"What are you cooking?" she asked Allegra. "It smells marvelous!"

"Let us hope," said Allegra, "that Mr. Fulford thinks so. I've been trying to entice him to eat. He has been quite ill with the flu and has not had proper care. He is so alone. After I leave in the morning there is no one here to help him."

"I didn't know," said Vivian, concerned. "I wish you had called me. I can come easily, every day. What about James?"

"Rilly comes and walks him in the afternoons. Well, I must hurry." Being careful not to splash her elegant suit, Allegra began ladling the soup into a container.

"Here," said Vivian, reaching for the ladle, "let me do that. I'll take it down. You go on." Allegra hesitated. "Really, I want to; I promise to see he eats it."

The moment Vivian touched Wilder's door there was a sharp, muffled bark; as she pushed it open with her foot, there was another, much closer, followed by a low, warning growl as James appeared, his fur bristling. Seeing Vivian, he was overcome with embarrassment. He waggled and whimpered and bounced ahead of her on his three legs, doing his best to trip her up.

Vivian called out Wilder's name, not wanting to startle him. But he was startled all the same. He had expected it would be Allegra, that she would put down her soup and go and he wouldn't have to move his throbbing head. Hearing Vivian's voice, he felt a dim panic. He would not have her see him like this. His first impulse, childish, he knew, was to hide his face against the pillow, his second was to turn his back and feign sleep. But the effort to turn was too great and, in any case, it was too late. She was already in the room, scolding him for not having let her know he was ill.

Vivian put the tray down on a small table and stood by his bedside, looking down at him. His pillow was so old and flat that his head was scarcely elevated at all. His hair had that peculiar limp texture and dullness consequent to running a high temperature. His pocked face was quite gray except for an area around his eyes corresponding to the shape of his glasses. There the skin was bluish white and seemingly paper thin. As helpless and exposed as an overturned turtle, Wilder clutched the bedclothes against his chest, unable to raise his eyes.

"Wilder! You *have* been ill! You're so pale and you've lost weight!"

Hearing the commiseration in her voice, he dared to look up. Her face was not quite distinct, but the tilt of her head and her concern were evident.

"Allegra has sent you some soup and crackers. Here, we must prop you up." She leaned over and grasped his pillow. "Oh, this won't be enough. Wait, I'll get those on the sofa." She came back with two pillows, embroidered in crewel by his mother. Vivian slid her arm under his head and lifted him slightly while she stuffed the pillows behind him at an angle. "Now, can you slide up a bit?" He made a weak effort to do so, suddenly conscious of his worn pajama top and its frayed buttonholes. But Vivian seemed not to notice. She spread a napkin over his chest and placed the tray across his lap. "Can you feed yourself? Are you strong enough?"

Wilder, a bit faint, nodded, still gazing at her.

"Here," said Vivian, smiling at him, "is your spoon." His fingers closed around it but he continued to stare at her as if he had forgotten what he was to do with it. Vivian waited, then, thinking he was embarrassed to eat when she did not, said, "It's not a bit pleasant to eat alone. I'll put on the kettle and have a cup of tea with you. But you begin, while the soup's still warm."

Vivian brought her tea and sat in a chair beyond the foot of the bed. At that distance her face was a pale blur, her hair a radiant nimbus. Wilder would have been content to lie back and gaze at it, but, to please her, he tried to eat. The soup was good, but swallowing was painful. His hand shook and the distance from bowl to mouth was too far. Soup dribbled on the napkin. Moisture broke out on his forehead. He grew dizzy and his head, too heavy for his neck, fell back against the pillow. His hand went slack; the spoon dropped onto the tray with a small clink.

Dimly he heard her calling him and felt a cool dampness against his head and face. His eyelids were too heavy to lift, but he seemed to be ascending through a gradually clearing darkness to the surface of consciousness. Vivian was bending over him, her face anxious and worried. He wanted to tell her it was all right, but he couldn't speak.

". . . was all my fault! I had no idea you were so weak!"

When he was once more fully conscious, she sat on the bed beside him, gazed at him earnestly and smiled as if welcoming him back from a far place. "You frightened me; you should have told me you were too weak." Her words seemd a reprimand but her tone was warmly solicitous.

"Now, we'll try again. This time I'll spoon it out. All you have to do is swallow." She dipped the spoon and held it out, but Wilder, mortified that of all people Vivian should feed him, turned his head aside. "But you must eat," Vivian insisted, "to regain your strength. Think, Allegra made this just for you. You must try, if not for your own sake, then for hers, for Rilly's, for James', for me."

Because of his weakness, moisture threatened to fill his eyes. He blinked several times, then obediently opened his mouth.

Thereafter Vivian came twice a day, every day. She brought him a plump new pillow and restored the sofa pillows to their place. She brought him a warm blanket, saying he needed an extra one since his room was a converted porch and not as warm as it should be. She brought him custards and puddings and using his kitchen sometimes made him scrambled eggs and toast. All these things he meekly accepted, unable to refuse her.

Rilly came to take James out and stayed to chat and share James' vanilla wafers. Allegra dropped in after work, and Lena and Pete brought stacks of books.

For Wilder his convalescence was a kind of heaven. Admonished to do nothing but sleep, eat and grow strong, he was freed of worry over his own clumsiness and lack of grace. He was free to lie back and gaze at Vivian, to watch her making herself at home in his home, to listen to her voice and be ordered by her. He shut away all thoughts of what it would be like when he was well and there would be no reason for her to come again. He refused to contemplate how barren his life would then be. When such thoughts threatened his present happiness, he fell back for comfort on one of his mother's favorite, if ominous, quotations, "Sufficient unto the day is the evil thereof."

Vivian did continue to go to the little theater meetings, and she struck a bargain with Dolphine. She would work on sets, ferret out props, apply makeup, but she would *not* take a part. Dolphine was disappointed but agreed, needing all the help she could get, and with the private hope that she might, sometime, persuade her otherwise. The play for spring was to be *Charley's Aunt,* a sure hit.

At the first meeting after August had come to Vivian's house, he was waiting for her outside. Vivian saw him as she approached, the small entrance light casting his long shadow across the scraped sidewalk. She had not been able to dismiss him merely as a young man who enjoyed shocking his elders. There was more to him than that. Besides, she wasn't *that* much older than he.

She thought a simple "Hello" would do, but August reached out and took both her hands, holding them as he carefully scrutinized her face. Just so did Vivian search Corinne's face, on her brief visits home.

Apparently satisfied, he let her go. "I've missed you."

Trying to establish a light, jolly tone, Vivian said, "And I've missed you. There's been no one to tell me how dreadful my house is."

"Don't joke," he reproached her. "I mean it."

She regretted the pained look in his eyes. Wanting to comfort but not encourage him, she smiled as she would have at Corinne. "August, don't be so serious. Let's go in."

From then on at all the weekly meetings, they worked together, building, painting, running lights; it was accepted as natural by the entire group that they were a team. August did have a part in the play, but even then, it was Vivian who coached him in his lines. And wherever they were, there the fun centered. They worked hard; at the same time they laughed a great deal. August was full of jokes and crazy antics that made everyone laugh. But always he looked to Vivian. It was she he played to and no matter how amused they all were, there was an undercurrent between them that the others were never able to enter into. Sometimes, when rehearsing, Dolphine had to quiet the entire group. She never raised her voice but struck her pencil sharply on the back of a chair. When there was a shamefaced silence, she would take a few deliberate steps and with a swing of her plump shoulders and a sideways swish of her smoothly molded hips, would say, addressing August, "I do wish you would bring some of your verve for a comic line to bear on the comedy at hand. Now, let's begin that scene again." As those on stage began to speak, her glance would rest speculatively on Vivian. A shrewd observer, sensitive to the tides of emotion in those around her, Dolphine was more aware of the developing tension between Vivian and August than was Vivian herself.

Vivian's mood was much too light to be disturbed by Dolphine, her self-assurance much too strong. She was inclined to laugh, whatever Dolphine's conclusions, certain they would be wrong, because Vivian believed herself in command of the situation. And why should she not be? She was older than August, more experienced, more levelheaded; her judgment would more than balance his youthful impulsiveness. Of course, it was only natural that she should be flattered by a younger man's attention. Time enough when she was old—a state sufficiently remote for her to contemplate it with complacency—to give up all sense of being attractive, especially when she could indulge herself a little now and no harm done. For she was determined August should not be hurt. Beneath his brash arrogance and playfulness she thought him to be as vulnerable in his youth as Corinne. She was sure that he meant what he said to her, and, modestly, that it was not because of any fatal attraction of hers but because a kind of youthful madness had seized him. Just as suddenly as it had come she was certain it would pass.

Vivian did not, however, want to think that he would forget her. She began to see herself as he would see her when he was fifty or sixty. It was a charming, appealing role, inevitably tinged with sadness for what might have been were it not for those fourteen years. But that gave the part depth and contrast of mood. Vivian entered into it naturally, responding on cue with just the right tone and gesture. Dolphine, had she been able to see the full performance, would have applauded.

August, at sixty, was still handsome, tall and lean, with the craggy face of an elder sea lord. His hair, more gray than blond, swept back off his forehead as though blown by a northern wind. Women still looked at him, soft-eyed. But within his memory lived one woman, younger, now, than he, for whom he had an especial tenderness, a special kind of love.

Vivian, as that woman, would understand him. She would be gay and laugh with him as an indulgent mother with her son. She would listen to his dreams of the future, encourage him, possibly even inspire him. Wisely, she would allow him to love her only as an unattainable ideal. And when he found someone his own age, as she knew he would, she would gracefully withdraw, having kept her love for him hidden. But she would know with an absolute surety that no one would ever be to him what she had been.

As a result of her new dream, Vivian once more met each day with a sense of anticipation. Even Mr. Farley noted a change in her. Her face was animated, her step brisk. Molly's coat was brushed with such vigor that she pranced in her stall and wanted to run.

August didn't come again to her house, but they were together at rehearsals at least once a week, and, as the date of performance drew nearer, much oftener. Working together as they did, it seemed only natural that August should, in a companionable way, catch Vivian around the waist, or while listening to directions from Dolphine, stand with his arm across her shoulders, or rest his chin on the top of her head.

The evening of dress rehearsal was remarkable in two respects: it was the occasion of the worst ice storm in decades and Vivian was shocked into a revision of her dream.

In the small, crowded dressing room, everyone was in a flurry, changing clothes and putting on makeup. Vivian outlined eyes, applied little red dots, darkened eyebrows, heightened color, adjusted wigs. August had to be aged. When it was his turn, he sat down and held up his face.

Vivian had not touched him before. Now, as she smoothed face paint over his forehead, cheeks and chin, her fingertips fell of themselves into a tender motion, as though she were touching the face of a loved child. Tracing lines across his brow, she stroked back his hair. It was of sleek texture but heavy like strands of silk. Her hand lingered over it, and for a second she forgot what she was about. Encountering his gaze fixed on her face, she flushed and lightly brushed her hand down over his eyes, as if to shut them. But August continued to look at her with a faint knowing smile.

Disconcerted, Vivian scolded. "How can I put on wrinkles when you stare like that! Look over that way and crinkle your eyes for a minute." Carefully she drew wrinkles fanning out from the corners, aware as she did so of his unwavering look. Nervously, she caught her underlip between her teeth. She deepened the laugh lines on either side of his mouth and added several smaller ones. Conscious of the strongly modeled curve of his lips beneath her fingers, she was suddenly swept with the desire to bend down and press them with her own.

Abruptly Vivian drew back, turned aside and began cleaning her fingers on a rag.

"Finished?" asked August. His tone was teasing.

But Vivian had regained her composure. "Yes, I think so. No, wait! Your hair has to be dusted." A small cloud arose about his head as she brushed gray into his hair. "There, now *you're* ready," she said as if he were nothing special, and turned at once to the next actor, who had been waiting impatiently, putting his glasses on and off and clearing his throat.

"I hope we get through early," he said, sitting down and tucking a towel under his chin. "It was raining earlier, but now it's turned to sleet. The road'll be slippery going home."

The dress rehearsal went off well. There was only one mishap. A cue was mistakenly picked up which resulted in their skipping two entire pages of dialogue, but that was felt to be minor. Dolphine announced that she was pleased, in general. However, she had made copious notes and after they had changed and cleaned up, she would give each one final directions.

Stanley went out for pizzas and hot coffee and reported that the storm had stopped but that everything was covered with a sheet of ice. "I barely made it," he said. "The car slipped all over the road."

There was an immediate stir, expressions of dismay and doubts about getting home safely, suggestions that they leave at once. But Dolphine took them firmly in hand.

"You will please sit down and listen. This is your last chance before opening night. If the storm has stopped, another hour will make no difference. I want you to take notes. You can have your pizza and coffee at the same time. Now. . . ." Thoughtfully she patted her hair, loosely waved yet always perfectly in place, adjusted her upper torso and began. She went over her notes with individual members of cast and crew; those she finished with were dismissed and left, two or three at a time. When she finished with August, he whispered to Vivian, "Let's go."

They stepped outside into a world made of crystal. With the passing of the storm the wind had died, leaving a brittle stillness and an air that vibrated with cold. High overhead the moon, one eighth gone, flooded the sky with a blue-white light. Far out from the moon glowed an immense luminous ring. So brilliant was the light that it obscured the stars. Every surface glittered. Telephone poles were made of glass, the wires of bright silver. Tree trunks glistened and branches drooped, every limb and twig coated with ice. Hedges, weighted down, split apart. Evergreens bent like hairpins, embalmed in ice, their tops almost touching the ground. The moonlight swam in the glassy streets and sparkled on the iced surfaces of sidewalks and yards, on the glazed sides of houses and on roofs that glittered as if coated with diamond dust.

August, apparently struck with moon madness, uttered a gleeful whoop, grabbed Vivian's arm and started off at a run.

"Wait! Stop!" cried Vivian, having to run to keep her balance. But August laughed and ran on, pulling her along. Slipping and sliding, they careened across the school grounds, their boots splintering the ice with sharp, crackling sounds.

"Where," gasped Vivian, out of breath, "are we going?"

"There's a slope here, somewhere! We used to. . . ." Even as he spoke they reached the top of an incline that slanted down to the playing field. Too late they tried to stop. Like clowns they teetered, then went down in a swirl of arms and legs, August first, Vivian after. They slid all the way to the bottom and lay for a moment panting and helpless with laughter.

August raised himself on one elbow and leaned toward her. "Hurt?" he asked, smiling.

Vivian shook her head. "We could have broken our necks."

"But we didn't. Want to try it again?"

Vivian laughed. "No thank you. Once was enough." She started to sit up. "We may have to go the long way around to get back."

"Before we go anywhere. . . ." said August, leaning closer. His voice trailed off, but his expression was purposeful. Holding her head firmly, he bent down and kissed her.

Vivian felt she was falling down another, steeper hill, and when he kissed her again, she surrendered to her earlier impulse. She stroked his hair, delighting in touching it as she had so wanted to do, and responded with a warmth that broke through the maternal role she had envisioned for herself.

Officer Travis had been on patrol duty for two and a half hours. In that time he had rescued a motorist whose car had gone off the highway into a ditch, given a ticket for speeding, answered a burglar alarm that had been mistakenly tripped, and picked up a drunk in the middle of the bridge who had fallen down and been unable to regain his feet on the ice. Because of the slick conditions, Travis was being especially sharp-eyed and vigilant, eager to do his duty.

Driving down the street behind the school, past the playing field, he was alarmed to see two figures lying at the base of the slope. Probably fallen! Probably broken their legs, or, worse, their backs. He pulled over and switched on his outside light, though its swinging beam was largely wasted in the brilliant moonlight. He started across the field at a brisk trot. He would check first. An ambulance might not be necessary.

"Hi there! Anyone hurt? I'm coming!"

Startled by a ringing voice and the crunch of boots on ice, Vivian and August parted hastily and turned to face Officer Travis.

He looked down at them anxiously. "Either of you hurt?" he asked urgently. "I can have an ambulance here in. . . ."

"No, no," said August, getting up and giving Vivian a hand. "We're fine, Officer, just fine. We slid down the slope here, that's all."

"Slid. . . ." Travis frowned. "You been drinking?"

They both protested at once. "Not a drop. On my honor," said August, grinning and holding up one hand.

"Nothing like that at all," said Vivian emphatically, flashing August a look that said don't be foolish. "We've been working at the community theater. We took a walk before going home and fell down this slope. Slipped down. Our cars are parked back there."

Travis eyed the slope and them suspiciously. "You hadn't ought to be out here on a night like this," he said sternly. "Come with me. I'll drive you to your cars." He put Vivian in the front, August in the back and drove cautiously around the block. So odd did they both seem to Travis that he wished Sid could see them. He had an uneasy feeling that they weren't telling him the truth. Sid would know in a minute if they were lying. Travis half expected there would be no cars, but there were—a rusty Skylark and an imposing Continental, parked down the street from the old candy store.

"That one's hers," said August, pointing at the Continental.

Travis was surprised. She was a strange lady to be driving around in a Continental. A car like that commanded a certain respect. "I'll scrape your windows while you warm it up," he said. "You can't drive it like that."

"I'll do it," said August.

But Travis was still suspicious, especially of August. "You clean your own windows," he ordered sharply. "I want to see you both on your way."

For one glittering night the world was beautifully, eerily unreal. The declining moon was mirrored on every surface, fragmented into thousands upon thousands of shining moons, reflecting themselves endlessly back and forth.

With the coming of a gray dawn the destruction began, for though it was early March, the cold temperature held and there was no melting. Unable to sustain the weight of the ice, trees split apart, sometimes falling across already drooping wires and pulling them down. Some, their roots too near the surface, were completely uprooted and came crashing down, showering broken branches and ice as they fell. Gutterings came loose and hung like rigid festoons of metal and ice from the edges of roofs.

The hedge in front of Vivian and Harry's house—like all the other hedges—lay spread out as if it had been parted down the middle. The two limber young maples were bent over like whips. Using the metal handle of a long kitchen fork, Vivian tapped the ice encasing the trees, starting at their tops, breaking it off in short sections that slid off the small branches like pieces of piping. Gradually, as the ice was removed, the maples lifted. Still, they were not upright as they had been.

Surveying her house from the outside, Vivian began to have serious doubts as to its suitability. The lanterns were heavy and pretentious, the door handles awkward and impossible to grasp. Otherwise, it was, as August had said, conventional.

Inside was worse. Seeing it now through August's eyes, she found its defects so obvious that she wondered how she had failed to see them for herself. The furnishings were a hopeless hodgepodge. As August had pointed out, there was no unity, no single, clear perspective. She couldn't enter the kitchen without seeing herself in an ad for floor wax or wooden cabinets. She shuddered at the red porcelain, and at the fake girlishness of white furniture with painted flowers.

Inside and out, the house was all wrong. It filled her with distaste. August was right: it did not express her—or Harry, for that matter. But what would? Vivian pondered that, looking at her own reflection, at the enigma of her own face. If only she could decipher what lay behind it. August seemed to know, and certainly what he saw could not be a confused, middle-aged— hateful term!—woman with a grown daughter. She tilted her head and strained for a side view. Her chin and jawline were trim. She scanned her forehead, pulled at the skin around her eyes. No major wrinkles, not many fine ones. Her lids were firm and her lashes still long. She remembered being shocked as a child at noticing that her mother's eyelashes were sparse and stubby, worn down like the fine bristles in a hairbrush, and a little frightened when she had seen blood vessels like bluish knots on her mother's legs. She had seemed so vulnerable, her life's blood protected only by thin whitish skin. Vivian had pretended not to notice, secure in her belief that no such transformation would ever strike her.

She thrust her fingers through her hair and watched pensively as it fell back into place. Did fourteen years after all make that much difference? Certainly they had not last night. She closed her eyes and relived those few moments before the policeman found them. She had gone to sleep reliving them and had awakened to their memory. And in her memory August had matured. He was no boy, after all, but a man. Moreover, by some strange alchemy, August had made her younger. Her qualms and misgivings rendered her, she thought, younger, forgetting that certainty is the realm of the young.

Perhaps, as August said, he did know her better than she

knew herself. She wanted to believe he did. She saw him as strong and manly, humorous and straightforward, wise beyond his years. Gradually the old, familiar figure of her dreams emerged, this time with August's face.

One evening a week or so later, Harry was reclining on the sectional sofa, reading the paper. Vivian was pacing back and forth, pausing to look out at the terrace and the redwood tubs which soon she would have to refill with soil and plants. But now she had no interest in those tubs or the terrace or the barn, which, after all, she never had made into a potting shed. Harry, reclining because the sofa, a conversation center, was so deep and so soft that it was impossible to sit upright on it, was, nevertheless, not at ease.

"Why don't you settle down somewhere," he asked, giving the newspaper a shake as if that would put Vivian to rest.

She stopped and surveyed the room. Frowning thoughtfully, she said, "This house has never been right, not from the very beginning. I can't think why we ever bought it!"

Astonished, Harry lowered his paper and stared at her.

"Just look at this room!" she exclaimed. "It's like a 1920's funeral parlor!"

FOURTEEN

House~ warming

The new house, Harry and Vivian's third house, had not been hard to find, especially when Vivian had gone looking for it in a new Thunderbird. The "old" Continental—which had outlasted the MG by months—had been the first thing to be scrapped. Its size, once its greatest asset, had become laughable.

"It's a boat!" August had exclaimed. "How can you ride around in a thing like that! You should be fifty pounds overweight, wear one-inch heels and a hat like the queen mother. What you need is a convertible, like a red T-bird."

Harry had not been surprised by Vivian's complaints that the Continental was too long, too wide, too pretentious. He had privately thought so all along and was happy to trade it. Besides, it was always better to trade for a new car than pay maintenance. He suggested a Camaro. Vivian looked meditative and said she would rather have a Thunderbird convertible, red with white interior.

When Harry handed Vivian the keys and she smelled the new-car odor, redolent of rubber and sealants, and felt the surge of its V-8 engine, Vivian knew the Thunderbird suited her perfectly. There was nothing staid about it. It was flashy, sporty, a car for those who knew what they wanted, who brimmed with a youthful zest for life. Vivian, sliding behind the wheel, experienced at once a sense of liberation. Turning on the ignition and roaring out of the driveway, stones spurting from under wide wheels, was the start of an adventure. All her senses were alert, ready to react, her hands dramatic in their skillful control of power. She was impatient of speed limits and stop signs, at which she barely paused. She longed for the open road and a sunny day when she could put the top down and feel the sun and wind in her hair. A panorama unrolled before her: the countryside, fresh in spring green, leaves beginning to unfurl, plowed fields a rich brown; in the distance a curving highway, and coming over a slight rise a sleek red car, its top down. The bright sun flashed on the chrome and gleamed on the red-gold hair of the driver as she sped past, her loosely tied scarf whipping behind her like a banner.

In such a car one can find almost anything, and Vivian did. Rather, she recognized it, for it fitted exactly August's description of the sort of house which would best express her personality. It was one of a number of recently completed homes in a new development northwest of Warrenville that boasted an acre per house and no two houses alike. Each would be individual, distinctive, and would fit into its natural setting as if it were an extension of rock and earth. That the area involved was everywhere the same—perfectly level, with a healthy stand of hickories, maples and ash—made no difference. The lots were laid out in a simple grid, camouflaged for the natural look by curving blacktop roads. Individuality began with the placement of the houses, each on its acre. Front doors were not necessarily in the front or even on the side. Garages, all double and occasionally triple, were sometimes hidden underground at the end of a steep incline, ridged to counter the iciness of winter, or faced the street head-on, their wide, gaping doors and broad expanses of cement obscuring the houses, reduced to mere adjuncts. Much of the distinctiveness of each house was achieved at one stroke by its roof. One, a bastardization of the mansard, sloped down steeply to within a foot of the ground, necessitating deep cuts into it to allow for windows. Another, patterned after a native hut, fit like a round straw hat on a square head, its curves extending beyond panels of windows except at the corners, where roof and house met. In the center it rose up in a kind of topknot, containing a complication of chains and louvers designed to facilitate ventilation. One strikingly modern house was notable for very little roof, being a close grouping of coffinlike boxes of varying length stood on end and connected at various levels by slanting wooden passages.

The builder had been at some pains to retain as many trees as possible, in some cases building around the trees so they became part of an enclosed porch or a passageway. For that area, they were unusually tall and sufficiently dense to inhibit the growing of grass. Occasionally the sun pierced between the lacy branches, and on the day Vivian found her house, it had done so, shining down like a pointing finger.

It created a fine effect, sparkling on the roof, which was made up of five swelling domes, coated with a glittery, white substance, and finished off at the top center with a little nub. The basic structure was that of the wheel—a hub with radiating spokes, with the unusual feature of a smaller hub at the end of each spoke—or, more impressively, molecular—a center unit with four connected units. The center and four outer units all were rounded, with large panels of glass from roof to foundation. The four radiating hallways were also glass walled, so it was possible to see straight through them. The trees, sky and passing clouds were all reflected in the glass, in changing, airy patterns of dark and light.

Vivian lost no time in contacting Mr. Lamb, of Lamb Realty, and he showed Vivian and Harry the interior, which offered the utmost in both openness and privacy. From the large center living room one could turn to each of the cardinal points, look down a hallway and glimpse a section of the kitchen-dining room, or, if the doors were open, the master bedroom or the two smaller bedrooms. Only the hall leading into the garage had a door that was kept permanently closed. The floors throughout were laid with oyster-white ceramic tile. Supremely easy to care for, said Mr. Lamb. The hallways had low, flat ceilings of acoustical tile; but the four living units gave a great sense of spaciousness, for their domes were open to the top except for major cross beams, given a dark finish to resemble that found in old barns. Above them, the inner curves were lined with successively shorter sections of wood as the dome drew to its center point.

Harry, referring to the beams and the woodwork, was immediately corrected by Mr. Lamb. They were definitely not wood but plastic, much, much better than wood. More easily cleaned, more easily replaced, and much, much cheaper. But more important than cost—he could see that for Harry quality, not cost, was the major factor—was the fact that wood was outmoded. The emphasis now was on man-made products, so much more serviceable, as well as flexible.

Harry wondered about the difficulty and expense of heating such a . . . he hesitated, not wanting to say outright, "birdcage of a house."

Decentralized? Suggested Mr. Lamb politely, and Harry went along with that. None whatever, Mr. Lamb assured him. The glass was Thermopane throughout. And should there ever be a cold snap, one could always draw the curtains. Seeing Harry's private smile, he thought twice and added that one *did* have to bear in mind that the overall cost of such a home would be somewhat more than that of a conventional house. The difference was what one paid for distinctiveness and originality. Mr. Lamb's dignity was almost affronted at having to point this out. One could not expect to pay for a home that was, after all, unique, what one would pay for . . . . Mr. Lamb waved his hand and curled his lip, loathe to say anything ungenerous. . . . well, let us say, a merely ordinary house.

There was never any serious doubt about their buying the house. Mr. Lamb felt that from the start, observing how Vivian preceded them, not listening at all or asking any questions, but going ahead from room to room as if she were alone.

Essentially, Vivian was alone, totally absorbed in her dream of the furnished house. It unfolded before her, spacious and uncluttered, the walls of glass reflecting and enlarging the inside, allowing trees and sky to be a part of each room. Spread out though the house was, it was unified by color, materials and texture. Everything was in shades of white and cream, with here and there a vivid splash of color. White shag throw rugs softened the large areas of gleaming tile. Other rugs, with a more formal, raised design, also white but with, perhaps, a contrasting thread of brown, covered the larger areas under the furniture, which was throughout of the same style. There was one thinly padded chair with two cushions, narrow arms and a firm, straight back. Otherwise the chairs were of shining tubular chrome frames with white fabric seats and backs. The coffee table top was thick greenish glass set in a ring of chrome. On it was a cobalt blue bowl holding two hawthorne branches. Suspended from one of the beams was a mobile of little silver ships. The draperies were double hung, the outer ones filmy and white, the inner, heavy tapestry of a shimmering blue-green. The four halls were curtainless, but in each at midpoint were several large plants in colorful pots to create the effect of stepping outdoors when going from one room to another. The beds were on raised platforms, the dressers of shiny white plastic with metal corners. In the kitchen pots of ivy hung before the glass wall. The white tile counters were bare, smooth and gleaming. No toaster, cannister set, bread box with an American eagle or a cunning set of spice jars marred their stark geometric lines. On the large, central butcher block was a ceramic bowl with three blue bands, filled with grapefruit, oranges and a spiky-topped pineapple.

In these instantly furnished rooms Vivian saw herself in flashes of the future, moving about the house as if it were inhabited by a ghostly crew of Vivians, all serenely occupied: paring apples, their red skins spiraling onto the white tile counter; serving coffee in the living room, the fine Swedish cups with their stylized leaf design reflecting in the glass tabletop; closing the draperies against the stinging sleet of a winter's night; watering the plants and hanging ivy, herself with watering can reflected in the glass; keeping accounts at the chrome and glass desk with its three suspended drawers and red telephone; tying up her hair before bathing in the molded, high-impact, one-piece combination tub and shower. All these Vivians wore long gowns, white or peacock blue or Nile green. Their gestures were graceful, their step buoyant and free. They moved lightly across the tile floors and soft white rugs because here, at last, in this shining house, they were at home.

Harry was willing to move for several reasons. He had never cared for the second house and nursed a deep-seated aversion for red porcelain. Each morning, by the time he had finished shaving, his teeth were on edge—a bad beginning for any day, but especially so when he was in a generally disspirited frame of mind.

But more than such surface dissatisfactions made Harry welcome a change. The truth was that he no longer had any zest for life. He was in good health. His business flourished. The apartment complex was progressing well and almost on schedule. He had every reason to be satisfied. Instead he was plagued by a sense of pointlessness, of futility. He had never been troubled so before and wondered if it were a natural consequence of turning forty. It coincided with his failure with Jenny, whom he tried never to think of. Her place in the office had been filled by a pleasant woman who needed an occupation now that her children were in high school. Logan frequently mentioned Jenny, but to Harry that Jenny was an altogether different person than *his* Jenny, who was beauty and youth itself. Impossible she could be anyone's wife. Since she had gone, Harry had suffered a death of the spirit. Of course he had Beanna, but that was entirely different. She gave him a moment's peace. With her sly humor she made him smile and had restored in considerable measure his damaged self-esteem. He had grown very fond of Beanna. They were at home together. But he knew when he looked into her eyes that one day without making any conscious decision about it, he wouldn't come again. That foreknowledge only deepened Harry's melancholy. At lunch his Kiwanis friends slapped him on the shoulder, chafed him about being a sobersides, encouraged him to get out on the field and toss a few balls. A spring tonic was what he needed, what they all needed.

Harry agreed he needed something. He longed for a change, any change that would stir up his life, bring him out of the depression that had settled over him like a persistent fog. Change would do it.

He dreamed of getting in the car and driving, no matter where, just on, to another state, another city, where everything would be new and different. As the miles clicked by, all his problems, boredoms, disappointments would fall behind, lost in the constantly changing landscape. And when he chose to stop, he would step out reawakened, eager for any challenge. Indeed, the very strangeness of the air swelling his lungs would imbue him with new-found strength and hope.

Such an escape was impossible, but a change of any sort took up one's time, filled one's mind with a hundred details that had to be taken care of, during which whole weeks could fly by unnoticed. And then there was the getting used to new surroundings: where the light would hit his face in the morning, where he would find his socks, which was the best chair to settle down in to read the paper. It also meant a change in routine, in the time he had to allow for getting places, and in driving patterns, the best route going to and from the office or the favored grocery store. It meant, in addition, new neighbors, new faces, even new neighborhood dogs.

So Harry welcomed moving to a new house. It was not a house he would have chosen, but he recognized its unusual features. Owning such a house was a clear indication of his status in the community, and he was willing to give it a try.

For the week following Corinne's return home from her first year at college, Vivian planned an open house, a multi-purpose party. It would celebrate Corinne's homecoming and be an opportunity to invite Logan and Jenny, also August, when there would be the cushioning effect of others present. It would, besides, be fun, or so Vivian hoped, at least for the others. For herself she needed most to be constantly occupied. A full schedule, with constant demands on her time had come to be her only means of holding August off. He had grown increasingly insistent that she come away with him for a weekend, or even a day, and refused to understand why she hesitated. She was, after all, free to come and go as she wished; he could see that. When she protested she was not free, he only laughed. Even to herself, Vivian could not, or would not, explain her hesitation.

One evening, when leaving the little theater, he had insisted on kissing her goodnight, there on the step.

"August, no! Somebody will. . . ." But he had roughly embraced and kissed her, not stopping even when the door behind them opened. Angered, Vivian pushed at him.

Dolphine, stopping beside them, said pleasantly, "I don't think we'll have any rain tonight after all, do you?"

Vivian agreed. August, sulky and resentful, walked off without a word.

The two women walked together toward their cars, Dolphine chatting as they went about their next play, *The Voice of the Turtle*. Vivian was grateful for the dark. Dolphine's voice was gently persuasive in tone as it always was, but Vivian, newly sensitive, heard behind the softness a subtle disapproval, as if Dolphine had swished her hips and said, "My dear, think a moment! He is a mere boy, and you are old enough. . . ." Vivian shuddered, said goodnight in as normal a voice as she could and hastened to her car.

Vivian had not been able to forget Dolphine's expression. That she had been so completely unruffled, had spoken so matter-of-factly, ignoring the scene she had come upon, trivialized it, made it not scandalous in any way but simply gauche, something any mature person would politely overlook. Hardly a pleasing reaction to reflect on. Vivian was at first embarrassed, even ashamed, then resentful and rebellious. After all, what did a difference in age matter if they cared for one another? Older men married younger women every day. Look at Logan and Jenny. No one faulted them. Besides, she, Vivian, was not old. Men found her attractive. Why could she not choose as well as they? And what of August? Should he be hurt because of a difference in age that obviously meant nothing to him? But no matter how Vivian put the case or slanted the argument in her own favor, she could not make up her mind. Vivian hated indecision. She wearied quickly of tiresome inner debate. If only August had left matters as they were! Her lovely dream had been so satisfying, a fulfillment in itself.

She decided what to do while out riding Molly. She had gone as usual to Mr. Farley's. The day was breezy and threatened rain, but the air smelled of spring. Even the cats were astir outside, sharp-eyed, lifting their neat noses in quick little sniffs. Molly was eager to run, and Vivian let her go at a canter. The ground was still hard but the trees were wrapped in a pink haze, and the saffron yellow of distant willows following a stream stood out brilliantly against the brown landscape. Rocking along on Molly's broad, comfortable back, Vivian experienced a refreshing clarity of mind. The breeze blew back her hair and cleared away all contrary arguments. She suddenly knew exactly what she would do. She would put the entire matter out of mind. She would think no more about it, one way or the other. She would concentrate on what had to be done in the next few weeks: move from one house to another, dispose of old furnishings and acquire new, all before Corinne came home, and once they were nicely settled, have an open house. She refused to be rushed into anything. That August wanted her she didn't doubt, but she was certain that once she had explained to him what she must do, he would understand and be patient.

Corinne's homecoming was not altogether a happy event. Moving from one house to another when she was there to take part was one thing. Returning after an absence to a totally strange house and finding that all her possessions had been moved from where she had confidently left them was an entirely different matter. It was a violation of trust. And that one's own mother had done it was even worse. She stood in the middle of the strange room designated hers and looked about. Her things, handled and arranged by another, seemed no longers hers. No doubt she would find things missing, high-handedly thrown out as junk. It was much too late to retrieve them. Any protest would be received with hurt surprise, and she would appear ungrateful. After a year at college, Corinne was too sophisticated to cry, but there was a tight knot of anger in her middle that made it difficult for her to look at either her mother or father. She made a thorough inspection of the house inside, responding only with nods and mmn's to Vivian's enthusiastic comments. She made two complete tours around the outside, her progress watched anxiously from inside by both Harry and Vivian.

"I don't think she likes it," said Vivian, swallowing hard. "I don't understand her. I thought she'd be so pleased." Her eyes stung with an impulse to tears at this rift in their understanding, especially at her homecoming. Her disappointment was half indignation at what struck her as a singular lack of appreciation.

Harry, thumbs hooked in his belt, watched his daughter, who at the moment had paused by an ash tree, rested a hand on its trunk and tipped back her head to survey its top. Then her glance came down to the domes of the house and then to the walls of glass. "Well," growled Harry, "it's new to her. You know kids don't like change. Give her a chance." He stepped back. "Don't let her see us watching. That'll only make it harder."

Eyeing the house, Corinne thought it freaky, just plain freaky. And there were her parents, watching her, as if she were a baby! They didn't seem to understand that she was a grown-up person.

To Vivian's surprise Corinne evinced little interest in Molly. Or in anything else. At dinner Harry and Vivian questioned her politely and delicately, as if she were an unpredictable stranger whom the smallest wrong word might affront. She *did* plan to go back next fall. And yes, she was happy there, though she made that admission grudgingly and with a shrug. Harry and Vivian exchanged a doubtful glance and took another tack. She was, they discovered, somewhat interested in psychology, slightly interested in political science, also, though again only slightly, in chemistry. When Harry raised the question—very cautiously—of veterinary science, Corinne stared at him as if he had lost all reason and laughed. As to friends, she had a few. Yes, she knew some boys, but at that question her expression and tone became so belligerent that they abandoned all further attempts to discover what she had done or hoped to do. She retired very early, like a haughty guest, and shut her door firmly. Harry and Vivian, puzzled by this new manifestation of their daughter's character, told each other that once she adjusted to being home she would become her normal self.

Corinne's true interest in college was twofold: men and the anti-war effort. Men had burst upon her consciousness like the sun onto the firmament. Her preference for psychology and political science was for the teachers themselves, rather than for their subjects. To her teachers she appeared backward and dull. When everyone else wore an Afro or hair to the waist, she wore hers in two short, stiff braids. She was morosely attentive, stolidly unresponsive. They thought her lacking in perception and comprehension. Had they but known she understood their range in ties and had taken inventory of their socks. She noted when an elbow patch was coming unsewed, a shirt was fraying at the collar or a button was missing. More, she had learned and could anticipate their every mannerism, tic and eccentricity. They were, in fact, her best subjects, even though their age was against them. They were over thirty and thus responsible for the mess the country was in. Had either one, however, shown the faintest interest in her—she knew several girls who met regularly with their teachers—she would have forgiven him instantly. The chemistry lab instructor was not too old. He was quite straight, and that counted against him. But his straightness was understandable, expecting as he did to get a high-paying job with a big chemical company. His presence alone made the tedious experiments, broken tubes and horrible odors bearable. Depressingly, his girl was always waiting for him outside the door. No one waited for Corinne, although she was aggressively active in large anti-war groups. She regularly took her turn manning a table displaying literature calling for a boycott of chemical companies producing napalm and defoliants, opposing escalation, bombing, free-fire zones and use of mother-bombs. She attended rallies and handed out literature outside campus buildings. To the young men she knew, she was a good worker, dependable even if it rained. As a girl, she didn't exist. None of this was Corinne inclined to share with her parents, but she did agree to go with Vivian to a little theater meeting.

She came out of her room, where she had spent hours rearranging everything, dressed in baggy blue jeans and an old plaid shirt, her hair parted in the middle, skinned back and braided in two thick, fuzzy braids that didn't quite reach her shoulders.

Vivian looked at her and hesitated. "Couldn't you, mmmnh, comb out your hair? Just for a change, you know."

"What's wrong with it the way it is? I like it this way!"

"Well, nothing, really," said Vivian, smiling. "Braids *are* very nice. Maybe you could tuck in your shirt?"

Corinne looked down at herself, then at her mother and frowned. "Why? What's wrong with it out? I like it out. It's comfortable. I'm not always stuffing it in. Well, if you'd rather I didn't go at all, then. . ." She turned petulantly away, but Vivian caught her around the waist.

"Oh, don't be silly! I *want* you to come."

August, who had been watching for Vivian's Thunderbird, came to meet her. He started to embrace her before he was aware of another person behind her.

Vivian laid a hand on his chest and turned toward Corinne. "August, this is my daughter, Corinne."

Corinne nodded, said, "Hi." August gripped her hand and shook it vigorously. Then he linked arms with Vivian and they went off, leaving Corinne to trail behind them.

Of all the people her mother introduced her to that evening, Corinne liked Dolphine best. Dolphine was sincere, really sincere, and showed an interest in her as a person. But she was captivated by August. She watched him constantly, and when, during the first part of the meeting, everyone sat down, she, sitting at the back, was shocked to see August place his hand on her mother's knee and her mother respond by laying her hand on his and stroking it. Then August whispered in her mother's ear and when she whispered back, Corinne distinctly saw her kiss him, a quick, tiny kiss, but a kiss nevertheless.

Corinne was stunned, then overwhelmed by disgust for her mother. How could she lead him on in that way! How could she, an older, married woman, do such a thing! Jaw set and her eyes, even her chest, hot with anger, she moved forward and sat as a deterrent on Vivian's other side. All that evening she watched and saw how her mother looked at him and smiled, and laughed at what he said. The tone of her voice when she spoke to him made Corinne burn with shame.

Riding home she slumped down in the seat against the door, as far from her mother as she could get. Vivian wanted to hear what she had thought of the meeting and of the people she had met, but Corinne mumbled and refused to talk. Vivian gave her an understanding pat. She was tired, of course, and they could talk about it tomorrow.

Corinne's flesh tightened away from her mother's touch. She was remembering how, when they left, August, recalling her presence, had seized her hand again. Corinne was still dazzled by his large, quick grin and the piercing blue of his eyes, a much lighter blue than her father's. Her hand still felt the clasp of his. . . . Dolphine had noticed her mother's outrageous behavior. Corinne was certain she had and that she didn't like it either. Corinne had felt that strongly in the way Dolphine had put an arm lightly about her shoulders and said smoothly that she hoped Corinne would come to the next meeting. She had meant it, too! And she *would*! She *would* go again!

At the next meeting several scenes occurred that had nothing to do with the play. They were impromptu, unrehearsed and unexpected, not only by Dolphine but by the participants as well.

August arrived a bit late. The set crew, of which Corinne was now one, was hammering boards together. Dolphine and the others were blocking out a scene. Vivian and Corinne, both with an eye on the door, knew the moment August entered, and Vivian saw at once that he had something exciting to tell her. As always, direct and outspoken, he drew her urgently aside, careless of who was watching or listening. He told her—eyes alight and eager for her response—that his uncle, who had a farm a few miles out of town, had gone away for two weeks, taken the whole family, and had asked him to keep an eye on the premises.

"Think of it! A whole two weeks! We can go tomorrow, every day, or for the weekend, have it all to ourselves!"

Faced with an immediate need for such a decision, Vivian was dismayed. "August, please," she said, speaking barely above a whisper and glancing nervously past him at the others, all studiously ignoring them. "Not now, not here. They'll hear us!"

"Then where? *Here* is the only place I ever see you! When I come to your house, you're never home. Or . . ." with a sudden resentful suspicion, ". . . at least you never come to the door."

Pained, Vivian protested. "You *know* that's not true!"

"We're forever saying hello and goodbye! I'm tired of it!" His voice was angry and reproachful. "I thought you'd be glad! Why don't you stop worrying about what other people think! They all know anyway. Look, we could go tomorrow! I could pick you up or meet. . . ."

"I can't go anywhere tomorrow! You forget! That's our open house! You're coming, remember? I *want* you to come! And everybody *needn't* know! Not if you behave yourself. Look, they think we're having an argument."

"We are!"

Vivian chided him with a look. "Please. We'll talk later."

All evening Vivian was ill at ease, troubled at not being free to respond to August as she would have liked. She was as conscious of his every change of expression and his underlying discontent as if he had been her child. She hovered near him, caught his eye or touched him whenever she could, hoping to reassure him.

And all evening Corinne watched her mother with a smoldering jealousy. She caught every smile they exchanged, prompted, of course, by her mother, and found it sickening. She noted each time her mother paused beside him, touched his shoulder or the back of his head, and was fired with angry resentment. How dared she! She had no right! She had made her choice years ago and should touch only her father like that!

When the meeting broke up, August left promptly, scarcely waiting to speak to Vivian, giving her an offhand, unconvincing excuse of having to meet an old buddy downtown. They stood to one side, near the door, as the others left. Unobtrusively, Vivian twined her fingers through his, beseeching him with her eyes to understand.

"Promise you'll come tomorrow! It's really on your account—and Corinne's." He smiled slightly, studying her face, but his eyes did not smile. Vivian discerned a reserve, a distance in his expression that frightened her. She had been too abrupt with him, pushed his patience too far. Out of fright, she capitulated and said, "When the party's over, the very next day, we'll . . . we'll go out to your uncle's farm. Just we two. I promise!"

August sucked in his lower lip and nodded, without conviction. There was no sudden animation in his face, no responsive glow in his eye or pressure of his hand. He disengaged his fingers and left without a word more.

Helping Dolphine straighten chairs and put things away, Vivian tried to compose her face. She smoothed her brow and fixed on a bland, pleasant expression. Her inner dismay was unlike any she had previously experienced—rather more fear than dismay, the kind of fear she had had in dreams when she was striving to run but her legs were weighted and some amorphous menace was about to engulf her. Her control of their relationship had slipped, and he had taken it up. Suddenly she was suppliant, and he . . . he in the strength and absoluteness of youth might find her lacking, had, perhaps, already. . . . She shut off that thought and looked up to find her daughter confronting her, her face tense, her mouth trembling. Vivian put out her hand.

"Corinne, what's wrong?"

Corinne jerked back from her touch. "Why don't you leave him alone! Everybody was watching you!"

"Corinne, whatever . . . ."

"Don't pretend! Everybody saw you! Smiling and touching him! You couldn't keep away from him!" Her lip curled with disgust. "How he must have hated it, being pawed like that!"

For a second Vivian was stunned. Her eyes widened with shock and then, without thinking, she swung her hand up and slapped Corinne across the face. Corinne's head jerked to one side; her cheek flamed with the red imprint of Vivian's fingers. She drew her chin down and stared from under contracted brows at her mother. A visible tremor passed over her hunched shoulders.

Vivian breathed shakily, momentarily dazed by her own action. Then, realizing what she had done, her face crumpled. "Oh, Corinne!" she exclaimed, on the verge of tears, "Corinne!" She reached out both arms to clasp her daughter, but Corinne shrank back. Stricken by the sight of her own fingers crimson on Corinne's cheek, Vivian stretched out her hand as if to wipe them away, but didn't quite dare to touch her face. "Corinne, baby, I'm sorry, so sorry! Please! Let's go home!"

"No!" exclaimed Corinne vehemently. "I won't! I'm no baby and I won't go anywhere with you! I hate you! That's not my home! That's a stupid, stupid house!"

Dolphine, a quiet onlooker, calmly took them both in hand before they backed themselves into corners from which there would be no graceful way out. She touched Vivian's arm soothingly. "You go on home. It's late, and we're all a bit tired. Don't worry about Corinne." She put an arm about Corinne's shoulders. "She'll be just fine. I'll bring her home myself a little later."

Vivian hesitated. Quite unable to speak, she looked from Dolphine to Corinne, who stood with downcast eyes, leaning against Dolphine's motherly side.

"Go on," urged Dolphine, seeing her painful indecision. "Everything will be all right. We'll finish up here together, and I'll drive her home. You'll see! Tomorrow, after a good night's sleep, everything will be different."

Vivian left. She drove home, numb to the smooth power of the Thunderbird, insensible even to the spring night and the luminous half moon whose light was dimmed now and then by passing wisps of cloud. Pulling into the garage, she barely noticed the glistening domes of the house or the moon-cast shadows drifting across the glass walls. Harry's door was shut. In bed, Vivian lay quite still, listening. Even when, after an undetermined period of time, she heard the door quietly open and shut, she had difficulty falling asleep.

After her mother left, Corinne would have enjoyed a good cry, but Dolphine gave her a shake and joshed her out of tears into a rather shamefaced laugh. Shifting her shoulders sideways, a motion that always preceded a statement of principle, Dolphine declared that highly emotional scenes should be reserved for the stage and not otherwise wasted. Besides, Corinne had had something to say and had said it—always preferable to keeping it bottled up. However, having once expressed herself, she should remember to behave toward everyone, including her parents, with manners becoming a young woman.

"Well, *she* thinks I'm a baby! You heard her."

Dolphine considered that, tilting her head and surveying Corinne with a shrewd eye. Dolphine deplored wasted human potential, of knowledge, appearance or ability, and she saw it being wasted on all sides by people who were blind to it, timid and unadventurous or altogether lacking in drive. She spent her time, whenever she could, realizing inherent possibilities. Nothing gave her deeper satisfaction. She was certain, for instance, that Vivian could be a compelling actress if she could once get her on stage and bring her to a state of self-forgetfulness. Swanger was another with great, unrealized possibilities. Corinne, she was equally certain could be strikingly lovely, and her fingers itched to refashion her. After the scene she had just witnessed, Dolphine knew that Corinne was not timid. Whatever improvements Dolphine could effect, Corinne would put to good use. Dolphine decided to deal with her frankly.

"I can't say I blame her," she said coolly. "And before you get indignant, examine yourself. You look like a sloppy scarecrow. God knows what's under those baggy pants and that flap-tailed shirt. Hanging shirttails are an abomination. Those frizzy braids are worse."

Corinne looked as if she might cry after all. She hadn't expected criticism from this woman with whom she had instinctively felt at home. "So I'm homely!" she exclaimed belligerently. "I can't do anything about that!"

"I think you are spoiled but hardly homely," said Dolphine. "I see you have to be instructed. We'll begin at the top, with your hair. Sit."

The next morning was overcast, but toward midday the clouds drifted away to the east and the sun warmed the red buds and flowering crab trees and teased open the bulbous magnolia buds. Everything—from the windows to the chrome to the glasses marshalled on the kitchen counter according to size—shone, glittered, sparkled, gleamed, reflected, in harmony with their various surfaces, just as August had said Vivian's home should. The front door stood ajar. Restless and uneasy, each for his own private reasons, Vivian and Harry awaited first arrivals. They rechecked the liquor supply, cut more rye bread, put out extra ashtrays, and spoke occasionally in shorthand phrases that each understood and to which no vocal response was necessary. Neither saw the other. Harry could not have told the color of

Vivian's dress, and Vivian could not have said if Harry wore a tie. Corinne did not appear at all.

"Why not?" asked Harry. "She hasn't even had breakfast and it's nearly four." He was tense. Logan and Jenny were coming. The thought of seeing Jenny had caused his hand to jerk when he was shaving, and he had cut the skin over the hollow below his jawbone. In the other bathroom he would scarcely have noticed. Here, red drops splattered dramatically on the dead white porcelain and tile and spread rapidly like a pink dye on the water, leading him to believe for a moment that he had damn near cut his throat. Beanna was coming too. With her husband. Harry wished the day were over, or that he could walk out and not come back until after dark. It irritated him that Corinne was not yet up.

Vivian could not explain. Like Harry, she had paused several times at Corinne's door and listened. Vivian had dressed with great care expressly for August in a soft champagne-colored dress, the color he said most suited the reddish gold of her hair. Her earrings were square-cut stones, ice blue, like his eyes. She was tempted to open Corinne's door, go in and turn about on her heel for Corinne's inspection, as she always used to do. She wanted to tell her that it wasn't at all the way she thought. She wanted—needed—to touch her, to look into her face and see there the open, loving warmth of her daughter. But she hesitated, finally rapped a knuckle once on the door and asked, "Corinne? You up?" There was a muffled "Yes." "Aren't you coming out? People will be here soon." "When I'm ready." After a pause, Vivian asked, "What are you going to wear?" hoping to be invited in for a consultation. "Something." And with that indifferent reply Vivian had to be satisfied.

Everyone came at once. The house was suddenly full of people, and soon Harry and Vivian were too busy to dwell any longer on their various apprehensions. Their guests, whether touched by spring or the excitement of exploring what all agreed was a novel house, were unusually exuberant. They trod carelessly on the white rugs, went unabashedly into bedrooms and baths, waved at each other through the glass walls of the hallways and to those gathered in the middle room. Rilly had to be lifted up to touch the little ships, bobbing steadily in circular but contrary directions in the stirred-up atmosphere.

"I do hope you don't mind our bringing Rilly," said Lena, "but I waited too long to call for a sitter and then couldn't find one. Besides, she wanted so much to see your new house." Lena, wearing her usual long skirts, had twisted her hair across the top of her head like a coronet, with an ornate rhinestone comb holding it in place, and put on high-heeled silver sandals in honor of the occasion. "Your house," she whispered breathily to Vivian, as if whispering lent greater weight, "is just beautiful! So unusual! I love the halls, going off in all directions!" Then, struck by doubt, she leaned closer. "But do you ever get mixed up? Go down the wrong one and have to come . . . . oh, cheese puffs!"

Vivian, catching sight of Logan's curly head, left the puffs with Lena and went to welcome him. Logan had his arm around a young woman—not Jenny—whom he had just kissed on the cheek. Vivian didn't immediately recognize her, and when Logan said, grinning, "Say, Viv, you should have warned me! A year away from home and she comes back a heartbreaker. All the boys in town will be knocking at your door."

As he spoke, Vivian, with a shock, recognized Corinne, a totally new Corinne. Her hair had no part. A soft mass of tiny corkscrew curls framed her face and shaded her wing-shaped eyebrows. Her eyes were darkly outlined to accent their slant above her wide cheekbones. Her wide mouth and full lower lip were a soft natural rose. She wore gold hoops in her ears and a snug-fitting dark blue dress with a short, pleated skirt. The very simplicity of its lines drew the eye irresistibly to her slender figure. Her changed appearance had wrought a corresponding change in her manner, as if she had put on a mask or assumed a part. She accepted Logan's compliment not with a girlish giggle but with perfect poise, a faint smile that barely showed her teeth and a slow sideways glance.

Vivian was amazed, but gratified and very proud. "You look lovely," she told Corinne, "just perfect. That's the dress we got last fall, isn't it?"

"This is the first time I've worn it," said Corinne, thawing a bit toward her mother. She had faced her somewhat defiantly, not knowing what to expect. "The earrings are Dolphine's. She gave them to me." In view of her triumphant metamorphosis, she was ready to call a truce. Also she was trying to practice Dolphine's dictum that manner and personality were at least as important as appearance, and could be, if sufficiently striking, even more important.

"Vivian, have you any tomato juice?" It was Allegra, speaking to Vivian. "Not for me, for that lady over there. She says she's on a diet."

"Later," said Vivian to Logan and Corinne. So far she had not seen August and had begun to worry that he would not come. She was carrying the tomato juice but looking for August when a woman said, "That must be for me. Thank you so much." Vivian scarcely knew her; her husband was a friend of Harry's in Kiwanis. Just then she caught sight of August, speaking with some people who were looking upward and gesticulating at the curved inner side of the dome. She tried to catch his eye, but the tomato juice woman took her arm and turned her away, saying, "I'm a Bahai, you know, and I find your house deeply fascinating. We must talk about it because I'm certain it's highly symbolic."

Harry had not yet seen Jenny. He was speaking to Marvel and kept his gaze fixed on him as if by strictly limiting the periphery of his vision he might be spared the sight of her.

"Some house you have here," remarked Marvel.

"Think so?"

"Oh sure. Resale value will be excellent." He was on the point of telling Harry that the folks living in his father's house were thinking of moving if they could get their price when into his line of vision came a girl in a dark blue dress. Her figure he saw in one swift glance was superb, especially her long slim legs. He immediately saw a challenge in her slightly bored, pouty expression. An experienced hunter, he recognized at once the hunter in her. A beginner, but nevertheless . . . . Contemplating her, his eye softened and his cheek dimpled ever so slightly.

". . . those people on the farm? Heard anything recently? . . . . Marvel?" Seeing he had lost Marvel's attention, Harry followed his gaze and saw Corinne! He almost couldn't believe it. He felt a surge of pride and smiled for the first time that day, thinking no wonder she hadn't come out of her room until after four! Then, understanding the nature of Marvel's expression, he said, still smiling but with an unmistakable hard warning in his eye, "That's my daughter, Corinne. Just back from college a couple of weeks ago."

Marvel blinked. Harry's meaning was clear, his menace as

palpable as the bristling fur on a dog's back. "A very pretty girl," said Marvel politely, and pivoted smoothly to face the other direction. "Incidentally, Ed Hacker is thinking of selling out and going to Florida. Might be worth your making an offer if you're still interested."

Harry was interested and was about to suggest that Marvel speak to Hacker on his behalf when he thought he saw Jenny. "I'll get back to you," he told Marvel.

Marvel, seeing a man from National Bank and Trust with whom he had some business standing just beyond Harry's daughter, moved toward him. In the crowded room it was natural that he brush her arm as he passed and pause to say softly, "Pardon me." She slanted a cool, undisturbed glance at him, then away, apparently absorbed in her conversation. Marvel was pleased. He had brought himself to her notice and he always liked combining business with pleasure.

Harry approached Jenny from an angle. He had been uncertain of her at first because she had cut her hair. He knew he must face her sooner or later and steeled himself to do so now. She was standing by the table speaking with a woman whose hair was combed into a huge French roll that curved up over the back of her head like a Grecian helmet. Together they were examining one of the hors d'oeuvres, a twist of pastry with a dark filling.

". . . ground fine, an egg and flavoring. That's all, very simple. There *is* the pastry, of course. That's a different matter."

"Jenny," said Harry. He was moved by this meeting, their first since her marriage. His voice was husky. He extended his hand as if to bridge the gap of a lifetime.

Jenny turned, arched her eyebrows in pleased surprise. "Harry!" she exclaimed. Seeing his outstretched hand, she laughed and held up her fingers. "I'm all sticky. I should have picked up a napkin." She looked about for one, but Harry grasped her hand and held it.

"It doesn't matter," he said.

The woman with the French roll, intrigued by his solemnity, took an active interest in them both. She looked expectantly from one to the other, holding, meanwhile, a bite-sized stuffed cream puff in abeyance.

"It has been a long time," said Harry, searching her face for any sign, however slight, that she had missed him, that she remembered their times together.

Jenny laughed. Her eyes were shiny and clear of all memories. "Oh, not so long as all that! How are things at the office? Logan says your new secretary is very efficient. I hope she doesn't find any misplaced files."

Harry, still tightly holding her hand, was unready for commonplace exchanges. Jenny saw he was even more preoccupied than usual and thought to rescue him. She nodded at the woman holding the cream puff and said, "Dotty Reeves, Harry Fox."

"Oh, we've met before," said Dotty, "but it's Jim you *really* know." Her husband was a lawyer and Harry's fellow Kiwanian. She put out her hand and Harry, forced to relinquish Jenny's, gave it a brief, dutiful shake. "I'm so glad though to have the opportunity to congratulate you on your house! It's truly remarkable. It just proves again that we don't need to look to the east or west coasts for innovative ideas. We have all the talent we need, right here in the Midwest! And such good food!" She popped the puff into her mouth. "Mmmn, crab!"

"Is it?" inquired Jenny, immediately picking one up. "I love crab! Your wife," she said, smiling at Harry, "is such a good cook. Here, wouldn't you like one?" Head to one side, she held it out to him as if she were trying to put at ease someone socially inept.

Harry had no desire for food. He was oppressed to the point of speechlessness. Perhaps this was another of those enervating dreams where he strove to speak to people who would not see or hear, whose faces changed like quicksilver as they looked slyly at him and maliciously chattered nonsense. There she stood, ostensibly Jenny! But his Jenny had a delicacy of figure; she moved with quick grace. Her temperament was mercurial, her moods readily apparent in the open innocence of her lovely face. Her eyes, shadowy in candlelight or veiled by her long hair, were eloquent and deep. Harry knew because their enigmatic quality used to make him groan inwardly.

Now he could have groaned aloud. He wanted to demand of this impostor: Where is she? What have you done with her? For this Jenny was perfectly ordinary. There was nothing willowy about her. She stood squarely with no particular grace. Her face had the usual unremarkable features of fifty million other young women. Worst of all, she had greeted him with no more special recognition than if they had met five minutes before. He might never have touched her at all.

Harry turned away, unnoticed by the two women who, like a pair of chemists, were analyzing by taste test the contents of the crab filling. Wanting to be alone and perhaps take an aspirin, Harry started toward his bedroom, realized he had taken the hall to the garage, came back and took the right one. Entering his room, which was also the study, he passed a group coming out who had been admiring the room, Beanna among them. She hung back, letting them go on without her.

"This is your room, isn't it, Harry? It radiates you. The effluence is particularly strong." She paused, arrested by his expression. "Something is wrong. You look . . . gray. Come," she touched his wrist, "over here, by the desk. You can seem to be showing me your work. Don't speak but give me your hand." She pressed it firmly against her heart. "There. Now you are absorbing sympathetic, healing vibrations. Concentrate." Lightly she touched his hair, his face. "Your trouble is diminishing. You must come tomorrow, and then it will fade away altogether." Her smile was a marvelous blend of seductiveness and friendship.

Harry managed to smile back. Out of gratitude he bent down and kissed her.

Corinne was delighted by her mother's reaction. Pretending a sophisticated coolness she in no way felt, she looked for Dolphine, to report her success, and found her trying to persuade Howard Tibbs, owner of Warrenville's largest hardware store, to join the WCT. Howard was short, rotund and bald except for a fringe above his ears. Dolphine was appealing to his sense of drama; Howard had no sense of drama. Being unaware of his Pickwickian appearance, he was at a loss to understand Dolphine's interest. He was excusing himself on the basis that being on the city council left him no time. He and Dolphine both welcomed Corinne's interruption. Delivered, Howard went at once to refill his glass.

Biting her lip to keep back a giggle, Corinne told Dolphine that her mother had scarcely known her. "And that real estate man . . . you should have seen him!" Her eyes sparkled with triumph. What, now, would be August's reaction? If only he would come!

"What's this that strikes my sight!" exclaimed a voice. Dolphine and Corinne turned to see Swanger staring at Corinne, the back of one hand pressed to his forehead, the other dangerously tilting his glass. "A living houri! I thought I should have had to travel back in time to ancient Persia, but there she stands, compounded of beauty, like the night, wrapped in spices and mystery! Only an orient pearl pendant in the middle of her alabaster forehead is missing! Oh, come with me, and I will ope the shell of every oyster. . . ."

"*You* come with *me*," said Dolphine firmly, taking his arm and turning him in the other direction. "Drink that before you spill it all over this white rug, and I'll tell you what I've planned for you in our next production."

At that moment Corinne saw August. He was talking to some people she didn't know and pointing at the ceiling. Then he separated from them and started toward one end of the table. Corinne approached from the other end, examining the food as if none of it were satisfactory.

August had come a little late. On purpose. He had seen Vivian trying to catch his eye but had pretended not to. He was not as angry at her as he had been and he saw that she had dressed to please him. Still, he felt a strong wish to punish her. She had put him off just once too often. What rankled most was her patronizing manner.

Reaching for a black olive, he hesitated, seeing several feet from him a girl he had not seen before. She had stunning legs and sexy hair. He could see only a bit of her profile, a small, neat nose and an appealing lower lip.

"Would you like an olive?" he asked, extending the dish.

"Thank you, nooo," said Corinne, continuing to survey the table for anything at all she might conceivably want.

"A piece of cheese maybe?" August speared a yellow cube and offered it.

"Perhaps. Yes," she decided, and took it from him carefully. "Thank you." She turned her head then and looked straight at him.

It was, to August, a piercing look, although in no way sharp. It professed indifference yet it challenged. August said, with a degree of uncertainty because there was something vaguely familiar about her, "I don't think . . . we've met. I'm August Larsson."

Corinne permitted herself a faint smile and said, "I'm Corinne Fox." Seeing his shock of surprise, she took a neat, satisfied bite out of the cheese cube.

"You were hiding yourself!" he accused, preferring always the offensive position.

"You . . ." commented Corinne, in no hurry and daintily selecting another, larger, cheese cube—she had, after all, had no breakfast—". . . weren't looking."

"I'm looking now," said August, and he had every intention of making up for lost time. Her cool, unperturbed manner indicated she had no interest in whether he looked or not. August knew better and was, besides, fascinated by her level, inscrutable gaze and deliberate manner. "Show me around, will you?"

Corinne shrugged a shoulder. "If you want. Of course, it's not *my* kind of house at all."

Vivian, busy being hostess, assumed August would find her. She caught sight of him once. Corinne seemed to be showing him the house, and Vivian felt a little stab of disappointment. She had wanted to do that herself and hear his comments. But it was just as well. They could talk about it at leisure tomorrow. Having finally committed herself, she could hardly wait for tomorrow to come. Her hidden excitement lent a sparkle to her eye and a vivaciousness to her manner. Briskly she offered platters of stuffed mushrooms and pinwheels just out of the oven to ravenous guests, received gracefully compliments on the house, paused to chat with this one and that. She was amused thinking how surprised they would all be if they knew how much she wished them gone, the day finished and tomorrow come! Tomorrow, when there would be just August and herself, alone.

She encountered Marvel, who, on seeing her, immediately stiffened. She offered to refill his glass.

"Water, not soda," he said pompously.

Vivian's smile widened. "I *know*."

Swanger, arm in arm with Dolphine, accosted Vivian with an expansive wave of his free arm. "This," he proclaimed, "is a housewarming not for a house but for a poem in plastic and glass to the female form divine!" Raising his glass, he exclaimed, "A toast to the only five-breasted house in captivity!"

All within earshot paused in their conversation and stared.

Heads turned. Behind him, Pete stopped short in midsentence. "What did you say? A five-breasted what?"

Swanger rolled his eyes, then winked broadly. Pete rapidly surveyed the women in the immediate vicinity, then eyed Dolphine suspiciously.

"No, no," said Swanger. "The roof, the roof!"

"Swanger," said Dolphine mildly, with a sideways shift of her bosom, "you are incorrigible, but," drawing him away, "I know just the part. . . ."

"Mrs. Fox, could I please have some ginger ale?"

Vivian went to the kitchen, Rilly skipping beside her, enchanted by the white tile floor.

"I like your house, Mrs. Fox. I'm playing hopscotch in the hall. Oh, thank you." She took the glass and ran off. "Come and see!"

But Vivian had been struck, rather unpleasantly, by Swanger's toast. Standing by the hanging pots of ivy, she pondered the garage roof, seeing it revealed through Swanger's eyes. She was diverted from that train of thought by seeing two people come around the garage. To her surprise, they were Corinne and August, strolling together. Impulsively, she raised her hand to rap on the glass, then hesitated, as their manner excluded interruption. They walked close together, with heads bent, looking at the ground. August was talking and as they veered slightly Vivian saw that he held her hand. They stopped and faced each other. Corinne tilted back her head and seemed to be contemplating the trees. Then she looked at August and said something that caused him to grin. Giving her arm a swing, he spun her around and started off at a lope toward the row of cars parked along the street. Corinne stumbled on her high heels. With scarcely a pause August dropped her hand and caught her up around her waist. She flung her arm around his. Together they disappeared beyond the cars. In a moment Vivian heard the loud revving of an engine and then saw the old Skylark zoom down the street out of sight. She heard it screech to a stop at the stop sign where the street turned out onto the main road and then heard its fading roar as it took off again.

"Don't worry!"

Vivian started. Belvedera, standing behind her, had come

into the kitchen in time to see Corinne and August run off. "Sorry, didn't mean to startle you. I was watching too, and I can understand how you must feel, expecially these days when they insist on going their own way." Struck by Vivian's expression, she said sympathetically, "Really, I don't think you need worry. I was talking to your daughter earlier. She's charming, very levelheaded, and seems to know exactly what she wants." Belvedera smiled, remembering her own first sight of Marvel. "And I would say she wants him. They would make a lovely couple." She raised her eyebrows. "My mother always says, 'Marry young and grow up with your children. That's the best way.' I was eighteen when I married Marvel and I've never regretted it." She shrugged and a momentary wistfulness shadowed her good humor. "So far, all *I've* got is a cat." Then she grinned. "But I'm still trying! Come on, the party's not in the kitchen." She linked her arm through Vivian's and drew her along. "You know, this house is absolutely wild! Like a movie set! It must be fun once you get the directions straight. I was looking for the bathroom and found myself in the garage!"

Vivian, needing, like Harry, a few minutes alone, worked her way across the living room and, finding an opportunity, went down the hall toward her own room. But she had taken the wrong hall and found herself at Corinne's door. As she was turning back, the sight of a couple in Harry's room standing close together caused her to stop and stare. Harry and Beanna! He with his hand against her breast. Vivian's first impulse was to look away, to turn and run, but an appalling inertia held her, and even as she watched Beanna caressed Harry's head and he bent and kissed her.

Swiftly and quietly, Vivian rejoined the others. She resolutely closed her mind to all thoughts of Corinne and August, Harry and Beanna. She geared herself to deal with the friends and semi-strangers filling her house until the last one had gone, until the remains of the party had been cleared away, until she could retreat to her own room and shut the door behind her. Smiling but numb she moved among her guests, automatically making appropriate remarks.

Harry didn't have an opportunity to speak to Marvel again, but he spoke to many others, refilled glasses with "just a touch," and took good-naturedly a lot of joshing about living in a glass house. He was looking for Bill Wheeler of National Bank and Trust to let him know he wanted to come in and discuss a loan, when his glance fell on Jim Reeves, standing off to one side. He was a big man who wore his custom-tailored suits with the same comfortable ease as an actor his costume. He softened his conservatism by wearing long sideburns, an easy concession since they flattered him. They were becomingly gray, in contrast to his dark brown hair, and their tendency to curl gave him a slightly roguish look, increased by an attractive glint in his eye, which, however, was deceptive, for it reflected not devilment but a constant cagey sifting of pros and cons. He was smiling down at Beanna, who held his hand and was tracing with her finger the lines in his open palm, glancing up at him now and then to judge the effect of her words. Finally she gave a playfully despairing shake of her head and a shrug. Reeves quickly closed his hand, trapping her fingers, and spoke rapidly in his polished, confidential style. Beanna smiled archly and drooped her head to one side. He said something further, brief but persuasive, for she inclined her head and lowered her lids in acquiescence. He released her hand and they turned in opposite directions.

Harry felt sick. He went to the kitchen, got a glass and filled it. After several gulps that hit his stomach like hot lead, he felt even worse.

Then, as if at some mysterious signal, triggered, perhaps, by one departure, everyone left, sweeping out, like lemmings, with one accord. Their going created a void, a heavy stillness filled with stale smoke, gray-black smudges of ash on the white rugs, crumbs on the white tiles, a smear of mustard on the tablecloth, and scattered everywhere paper plates and plastic glasses, some with soaked cigarette butts and olive pits.

Silently Vivian began stacking glasses and collecting the dried-out leftovers.

"What a mess," muttered Harry. "I'll get a trash bag and. . . ."

"I wish you wouldn't," said Vivian sharply, her back turned to him. She felt him hesitate "I prefer to do it myself." Her voice was cold and flat.

Harry shrugged. If she wanted it, she could have it. He would take a shower. Leaving the room he suddenly remembered Corinne. "Where's Corinne?"

"She went out, with . . . that young man." Vivian could not speak his name, nor could she look at Harry.

"Oh. That blond fellow."

"Yes."

Harry had spoken to him about architecture. "He's going into architecture. Said this was his kind of house. Seemed like a good kid though."

"Yes," said Vivian. Picking up the stacked tray, she went to the kitchen.

In the shower, the shower head dialed to massage, high, Harry stood with the water hiccuping against his chest. With a slap of his hand he turned it to normal, and the water beat steadily, coursing in rivulets down his body. Slowly, arms at his sides, he tilted forward until his head was directly under the water. Like a jogger, he breathed through his gaping mouth as the water pounded on his skull, poured around his ears and down his neck and ran together into one stream off the end of his nose. It made a pleasant wavering blur around his eyes and a drumming in his head that shut off all noxious thoughts.

Vivian steadily and methodically cleared away the remains of the party and washed up everything in the kitchen. When she was quite done, she turned off all the lights except one outside the front door and one small light in the living room. She reached her own room calmly enough, but once inside with the door shut behind her, her reserves broke down and she began to shake. In the dark she kicked off her shoes and with cold, quivering fingers wrapped herself in a quilt. She sat curled up against the head of the bed and after a bit she stopped shaking. She had not pulled the curtains, and beyond the grayish glass panes was an almost solid dark. The white plastic dresser was a ghostly gray block; the mirror above it had the dull sheen of gray water. There was no sound. She settled further down in the folds of the quilt. Her eyes burned and she shut them but she did not sleep. She heard a bird cry several times. She heard a car at a distance. Later she heard another car, the drone of its engine growing increasingly loud as it came closer, so close she could hear the sing of its tires on the road. Then she sat up and raised her head to listen. But it went on past, its headlights cutting a swath through the dark as it rounded the curve.

FIFTEEN

Shock Treatment

With little thought of what she would need and none of what "went together," Vivian threw some clothes into the suitcase open on the bed. For several days following the party she had been unable to work at anything, though she kept telling herself she must be reasonable. She couldn't eat or sleep; all she could do was remember, over and over, August running off with Corinne and Harry with Beanna. Maddeningly, she felt herself reduced to a mindless collection of nerve ends. In the mornings she stayed in her room until Harry left. Then she moved through the house like a prisoner, arms folded, hands clasping her upper arms, loathe to touch any part of a house that so reminded her of August, *was* August. He had created it for her imaginatively, and like a fool she had gone out and found it in actuality.

When Harry told her that Corinne had gone off to spend several days with a girl friend, she almost laughed, but had said, "Yes, of course," and gone back to her room. One thing became clear; she had to get out of the house. She had effectively isolated herself from everyone. She had to withdraw, be alone, in surroundings that were impersonal. The one possibility was the house she always thought of as Wilder Fulford's father's house, and the small unoccupied apartment at the back.

James was the first to detect her presence. He was lapping

water from his bowl in the kitchen when he heard sounds through the wall. He barked and growled, urging that attention be paid. Wilder, seeing the direction of his concern, concluded that someone had moved in. He was not one to notice cars, but Allegra was. She recognized at once Vivian's Thunderbird parked alongside the house, and, thinking that some work was being done in the house, went to inquire.

The door to the apartment was shut. Allegra, about to knock, stopped with hand raised. She heard voices arguing vehemently. Not wanting to intrude, she was turning away when it struck her, curiously, that the voices sounded much the same. She hesitated, then, certain that one, at least, was Vivian's voice, she knocked. Instantly there was silence on the other side. Allegra waited briefly, then knocked again, insistently.

After another silence, Vivian's voice, very near the door, asked, "Who is it?"

"Allegra Smith. Is that you, Vivian?" Another silence. Allegra began to be alarmed. "Please, Vivian, open the door!"

Slowly it opened, and Vivian looked out at her. A more hangdog look Allegra had not seen in a long time. Vivian's hair hung uncombed, her eyes were dull and smudged, her expression woebegone. Allegra did not hesitate. She walked in as if she had been invited and saw at once the suitcase standing unopened by the bedroom door.

"With whom were you speaking?"

Vivian looked at the floor. "Nobody."

"Vivian, I distinctly heard you arguing with someone."

Even here, thought Vivian, I can't be left alone. She made an impatient sound and said, "Myself! I was talking to myself." Then, resentfully, "Don't you ever do that?"

"Oh, all the time, but *not* like *that*!"

"Well . . . ." Vivian turned away. "I had a lot to say, and it wasn't very pleasant."

"What one says to oneself often is not. You are planning to stay here?" Vivian barely nodded. "Then come up and have dinner with me. I have a stew cooking and I would appreciate company."

"No! I couldn't. Really, Allegra, I couldn't eat anything. Thank you anyway."

Allegra stepped closer. She took Vivian's hand, which was

clenched into a fist, and held it. "Vivian," she said firmly, "look at me."

Hesitantly Vivian raised her eyes. Allegra showed no trace of curiosity, reproach or surprise. So far Vivian had not been able to cry, but Allegra's large dark eyes held such a depth of sympathy and her fingers such warm strength, that combined they touched off a wellspring of tears. Vivian leaned her forehead against Allegra's shoulder and cried.

When she had recovered, Vivian washed her face, cupping the water to her swollen eyes. Emerging from the bathroom, she laughed shakily, stroking the water off her face. "No towels. No sheets, no blankets."

"My, you did come unprepared. But never mind. I have extra towels and bedding you can use. Come on, we'll have dinner now. A little wine would do you. . . ."

Vivian shook her head. "Please, Allegra, I can't eat."

Allegra studied her. "At least tea and toast. Otherwise, no sheets or towels."

Thus bribed, Vivian, who was light-headed from sheer emptiness, managed to swallow the tea and toast. Later Allegra knocked at Wilder's door. He might, she suggested, knowing it would please him to do so, give Vivian breakfast.

Wilder was dumfounded that Vivian should be staying in the apartment behind him and hearing she was not well, wanted to go at once for a doctor.

"No, no," said Allegra, "she is not physically ill. She is suffering from a virus of the spirit." Allegra would have added, had she not some time ago perceived Wilder's devotion to Vivian, that she also suffered from a bad case of self-pity. She tapped Wilder's arm. "Don't worry, Mr. Fulford. Once she starts eating, she will be fine."

All that evening Wilder hovered near the kitchen wall adjoining the rear apartment. James, mystified but expectant, looked up at Wilder, down at his bowl, then up at Wilder. But Wilder failed to notice, so intently was he listening for any untoward sounds that might indicate immediate help was required. He thought he heard crying, as, indeed, he did, for Vivian, having once begun, would wipe her eyes and blow her nose only to be overtaken ten minutes later by another paroxysm of tears.

Wilder planned breakfast like a general laying out an offensive. Short of cracking the eggs, he had deployed everything before he went to bed. But all his efforts and those of Allegra were of little avail. Vivian would eat almost nothing. She didn't comb her hair or bother to dress but sat in a corner of an old overstuffed couch, her feet tucked under her housecoat. She cried much less but slept more and more, dozing off throughout the day so that she lost all sense of time. Wilder was troubled by her continued malaise, her utter lack of interest in anything. Her behavior was alarmingly like that of a cat his mother had once had that went into a similar mysterious decline and refused to eat. It had moped, as Vivian was doing. Its eyes had glazed, its fur had lost its sheen. Its head would droop forward until its warm, dry nose rested flat against the cushion. One morning it was dead, and Wilder had had to put it in a shoe box and bury it. Now Vivian looked at him in the same vacant way.

"There must be *something* we can do," insisted Wilder, haunted by his memory of the cat.

"She will not let me call her family," said Allegra, "but I agree, something must be done soon. Let us give her one more day, and if she does not improve, I'll ask my doctor to come and see her. What she really needs is a good hard jolt!"

Antrum Puckett was the man who provided it.

The note that Vivian left behind on the kitchen counter affected Harry strangely. At first it had little or no impact. It was simple and brief, saying only where she had gone and that she wanted to see no one, not much different in tone from pick up a quart of milk on your way home or don't forget to put out the trash. Nursing his own disillusionments, he had wanted to be left alone. Now he was. Entirely alone.

The house was uncomfortably quiet, emptily quiet, as if it had been abandoned. Harry was drawn to Vivian's room. A quilt lay on the floor where it had fallen. Harry picked it up and tossed it back onto the bed. Unlike Vivian to have left it there. The mirrored closet door was shut, the white box of a dresser bare. The entire room was as impersonal as a display room in a furniture store. It was then that Harry's memory stirred. He recalled how silent and withdrawn she had been, and he returned to the kitchen and reread her note. There was no explanation between the lines, just two statements of fact with no hint of why—or for how long. Those questions bore thinking about, and Harry would have liked to settle down in a comfortable chair, put his feet up and ponder them. But there was no comfortable chair in the house. He did not care to sit on a floor pillow like some damn Yogi. Or in a canvas sling. The straight thin back and high ends of the two-seated couch straitjacketed his arms and in no way accommodated his spine. Like living in a god-damned bird cage, thought Harry angrily, sitting on one of the glorified camp chairs. She wanted to see no one—that meant even Corinne! Then it struck him. She didn't want to see him either! He grasped the chrome arms of the chair, thrust it back and stood up in one violent motion. Why? Why? Indignantly he took several quick turns around the room, setting the little silver ships to bobbing. Could she have found out . . . or suspected. . . . No. How could she? He returned to the kitchen and stared hard at the offending note. He opened a can of soup for dinner and ate it standing up. He left the note lying untouched on the counter.

It was still lying there several days later. It lay also in the back of his mind, wherever he was or whatever he was doing, a piece of white notepaper with a bent corner and a center crease, as if she had folded it, then after all left it lying open. He had half expected she would have called by now, but she hadn't. That made it all the easier for him to decide what *he* would do. If she could act independently, then so could he. Today at Kiwanis he would tell Marvel to make an offer for the farm and sell this joke of a house. That prospect made his morning shave in a bathroom with the antiseptic look of an operating room just bearable.

He was leaving the hotel dining room when Antrum Puckett fell in beside him.

"So you're going to sell that fancy house you just moved into, eh?" Puckett chuckled. "Couldn't help but hear you talking to Gibson back there."

Harry said nothing. He paid his bill plus two cents and picked up a mint.

"Good idea, though," went on Puckett. "Cut down your overhead when a family breaks up."

Harry carefully unwrapped the mint. "What the hell are you talking about?"

Antrum pursed his lips. "Oh well . . . it's the sensible thing to do. When your wife goes off with a younger man you don't want to rattle around in a big house like that." He watched Harry's face to see how it hurt.

Harry stopped dead in the lobby. He put the wrapper in an

ashtray standing by one of the four large pillars that upheld the ornate plaster ceiling. As he popped the mint into his mouth, he seemed to be contemplating the mosaic of the state seal set in the middle of the marble floor. When he looked up, his eyes were almost black with anger.

Puckett drew a long face. "Maybe I spoke out of turn. I figured you knew. That young blond fella, name of Larsson. Hangs out with the little theater crowd your wife's mixed up with. Understand it's been going on for quite a spell." He paused to wave two fingers at another man coming out of the dining room—a bit of insurance against Harry's possibly socking him, as he seemed to be on the verge of doing. Prudently, Puckett stepped back two steps. "Have to speak to Medaris over there, a big job out by the steel plant. But don't you worry. It'll go no further. You can rely on me."

Wilder was adept at making omelettes. He mixed in a little farmers cheese, some cut-up pepperoni and, if on hand, some chopped green pepper. He turned it onto a plate and slid it back into the pan with one smooth motion. This particular omelette he had made with special care, hoping to tempt Vivian's palate. It represented Vivian's last chance: if she didn't respond to it, Allegra was going to call the doctor.

But though the omelette threw off a most enticing odor, and though Wilder said he had made it expressly for her, and though Allegra, who believed no meal would properly digest without wine, poured her a glass of white wine, Vivian refused to stir from the couch. James, joining in, jumped up beside her, laid his head on her side and rolled his eyes at her in a parody of mournfulness. Wilder was flummoxed. Allegra was about to speak sternly when there was a knock on the door and a voice said, "Mother?" All were startled. James sat up, thrust out his chest and barked sharply.

Hearing a bark, Corinne opened the door slightly and peered around it. She stared at her mother a moment, then opened the door wide and came in, followed closely by August.

"Mother! *What* are you *doing* here? This is crazy!" She glanced at Allegra and Wilder, standing together by the table. "Hi. Say," turning back to Vivian, "you don't look so good. Are you sick?" Her jeans fit without a wrinkle or a quarter of an inch to spare, and over her blouse she wore a striped sweater that fit so snugly it barely met the top of her jeans.

Vivian, who had frozen at seeing the two of them, found her voice and sat up straight. "I am not sick and I don't think much of the way you look either. Now please go."

Allegra and Wilder moved instantly. "No, I don't mean you . . . you stay. I want *you* two . . ." speaking directly to Corinne, ". . . to go."

Corinne curled her lips in against her teeth, then said resentfully, "I don't understand *why*! After all, I *am* your daughter! And neither does Daddy! I didn't even know where you were, and you're my own mother! Daddy had to tell me. We only came because Gus has something to tell you."

"I *don't* want to hear it," declared Vivian. It was her most positive statement in two weeks.

Corinne nudged August with a glance. "I'll go in the bathroom for a minute" (as they had prearranged), "while you tell her. Then we'll go."

"No!" exclaimed Vivian belligerently. "You stay out of my bathroom! Go somewhere else!"

Corinne hesitated. James curled back his lip and snarled at Corinne.

"Well . . . Mrs. Fox . . ." began August, but as Vivian looked squarely at him, his voice died. Gus had been dreading this moment. He had planned to appeal in a flattering way to Vivian's older and therefore greater wisdom, as well as to her motherly instincts. He had counted on doing so in private. He would have sat down beside her, taken her hand in his. There would even have been a bittersweet sadness between them that would have lingered ever after. But to speak in front of Corinne and a couple of weird strangers! It meant loss of face whatever he said, and he had half a mind to chuck the whole thing.

"Go on!" said Corinne impatiently.

"Yes. Well, Mrs. Fox. . ."

"Why don't you call me Vivian?" asked Vivian, her face stony hard.

"Of course," muttered Corinne disgustedly. Going over to the old upright piano, she swung around a couple of times on the stool and then began picking out "Three Blind Mice" with one finger.

August's face reddened. He swallowed visibly. "What I . . . we . . . want to say is that . . . it was very sudden . . unexpected. We didn't plan it, it just happened."

Vivian raised her eyebrows. "What did?"

Corinne spun around on the piano stool. "What he's trying to say is that we fell in love!"

"Ohhh, *that*!" said Vivian, nodding. "And why did you bother to come and tell *me*?"

"Bother!" exclaimed Corinne, jumping up. August thrust out a warning hand at her. James laid back his ears and growled.

"We *bothered*," said August hotly, relieved to be aggressive, "because we thought as a mother you would be interested to know about your own daughter and that we're living on my uncle's farm!"

"And in the fall we're going to go to school together!"

"We might even get married!"

At that moment the door was thrown open. Startled they all turned and saw Harry, seething with anger, holding back the door as if he had just uncovered a conspiracy. His fierce glance touched every one of them, then bore down on August. He strode forward, shoulders bunched. "There you are! Right where I thought I'd find you, you young bastard!" As they stared amazed, Harry fastened his hands in the front of August's clothes and shook him so violently that his head whipped back and forth.

Corinne cried out. She rushed forward and grabbed at Harry's arm, trying to pull his hands away. James leaped to the floor and made short dashes at Harry, barking furiously.

"I'll make you sorry you were ever born!" said Harry, grinding out his words. And amid exclamations of alarm, Harry drew back one powerful fist and smashed August on the chin, laying him out like a felled tree on the floor.

Corinne screamed, the others gasped. James, transported, dashed in and fastened his teeth in Harry's leg.

"Ouwh!" yelled Harry, spinning around, ready to kick.

Vivian, galvanized into action, grabbed up James, twisting and snarling. "Don't you dare!" she cried.

"He bit me!" yelled Harry.

"No wonder!" exclaimed Vivian.

Corinne pounded Harry's back with her fists, her eyes brimming with tears. "You beast! You hit him! The only man I've ever wanted in my whole life! The man I may marry! And you hit him! Oh!" she wailed, "I hate you!" Sobbing, she went down on her knees beside August and cradled his head in her arms.

"I'll get the ammonia," said Allegra, but as she started toward the door, August opened his eyes and groaned.

"Marry *you!*" Dumfounded, Harry turned to Vivian, who was still clutching James.

"Ohhh!" cried Vivian, fit to burst with exasperation. "Ohhh!" she cried again, and stamped her foot. "Get out! All of you! Get out!" James hid his head under her arm.

"But I thought. . . ." Harry stared at her, unable to say what he thought.

"I don't care what you thought!"

Harry felt blood running down his leg. "But I'll have to go to the hospital!"

"Then go!" exclaimed Vivian.

Silenced, Harry put a hand under August's arm and hauled him up onto his feet. Corinne clung to August's other arm. Moving carefully, the three of them left, Harry casting one look back at Vivian before he quietly shut the door.

"We should go too," said Allegra aside to Wilder.

"No, don't go," said Vivian. She took a deep, reviving breath. Her eyes were wide and alert. Her whole stance radiated energy and purpose. "I think you should pour us all a little wine. It will go beautifully with the omelette."

The Farm

Harry sat on the front porch steps and watched the empty moving van bounce down the dirt lane and turn onto the highway. He had sat there years before when the house had been emptied from attic to cellar, when all the accumulated goods of a lifetime and more had been carted off to storage and the door locked on the empty house. Then he had been in a hurry to get on with his life, to carve out for himself a position of respect and importance in the community as his father, Harley M. Fox, had done, a position that would have made his father proud. Now he was back and in no hurry at all.

The steps needed repainting. The swing hauled up against the porch ceiling needed to be let down and revarnished. Inside, furniture, old trunks and countless cartons, dirty and musty from years in storage, waited to be unpacked and put in place. Energy was needed, and drive. Harry had neither.

When the van was out of sight he got up and went inside. The screening on the lower half of the door bulged outward from the pressure of knees. One corner had sprung loose from the frame and curled upward. Flies could get in. His mother had never tolerated flies. At the first frenzied buzzing against window or ceiling she would whip out the long-handled swatter with the fuzzy bias edging. "There's a fly!" she would exclaim and thrust the swatter into his hand.

248

In the front and back parlors to the left of the center hall, furniture was crowded together, grimy and needing polish. Floor lamps, one of wrought iron, without bulbs or shades, stood by cartons of dishes and yellowed linen. The bricks above the fireplace opening were blackened and needed scrubbing. Above the mantle was a large circular mark where the wallpaper was a lighter shade. A picture in a wide, cream-colored frame had once hung there, a painting of flowers against a delicate blue background that his mother had been particularly fond of. Harry remembered it had sprays of larkspur and red poppies. In several places the wallpaper had split; the plaster underneath needed repairing.

In the dining room to the right of the hall the high-backed straight chairs were paired, seat to seat, one set of legs in the air. Harry lifted them off and stood them on their feet. Their hollowed seats needed reupholstering. The long table that could, when extended, comfortably seat twelve and had done so on Sundays and holidays, was gray with dust from the padding that had covered it. His mother used to cover it with a cloth crocheted by one of her sisters, its lacy pattern standing out against the dark wood. In the center she had put a ruby red glass bowl and matching candlesticks that glowed like fire when the sun struck them.

The hallway wallpaper, originally of a cream background, had aged to a burnt orange, deeper in the upper corners near the ceiling. Around the switch plates it was soiled to a dirty gray. But unchanged, needing only a good polishing, was the triangular base of the staircase, handsomely finished in oak paneling. Harry and his sister Dolly had heard many times how their father had ordered it done when the house was built. "For the de-lec-ta-tion of your mother," his father would say, enjoying rolling the syllables on his tongue. "Remember, son," he would add, fending off his daughter, who, knowing what he was going to say, would begin to pummel him, "it doesn't take much to keep a woman happy, a bit of wood, a gewgaw here and there. . . ." Then he would wink at Harry and rumple Dolly's hair. His mother would bridle, pretending indignation, and say that though they all knew what his theories on the subject of women's happiness were worth, no one could deny that theirs was the finest staircase in the county.

The yellow sun of late afternoon shone through the curtainless parlor windows, across the hall and into the dining room. Harry, standing knee-deep in memories, saw in its warm light dust motes revolving endlessly above the bare, dusty floors. Around him the house was still, not empty but drowsing.

His glance was drawn upstairs, and he laid his hand on the smooth, narrow bannister. The stairs' runner was threadbare and slippery. Must be replaced before someone slips and falls, he thought. Someone. That's a laugh. Who, besides himself? His daughter, furious at him, had gone off without a word with a boy he didn't even know. His wife . . . lived in her own house. Without thinking he went to his old room at the back, where the rear window overlooked the kitchen roof. He pushed the oak dresser with its tiltable oval mirror back against one wall and put together the white-painted, knobby iron bedstead. He maneuvered the springs and mattress from where they had been propped down onto the frame. When the mattress flopped onto the springs, a cloud of dust rose and made him sneeze. The mattress, faded and with tufts missing, sagged in the middle like a swaybacked horse and had a musty odor. Harry opened the window, then stretched out on the bed. The springs twanged under him, and because of the hollow and the shortness of the bed frame, he lay at an angle with his feet hanging over one side. Harry crossed his hands under his head and let his thoughts roam, not altogether without direction.

Marvel had sold the other house—a quick turnover at a good profit, the kind of deal that would have delighted his father. And he would have grinned over the picture and write-up in the paper of the apartment complex: Warrenville's Newest Apartments for Easy, Fashionable Living, Where Your Key Opens the Door to Taste and Distinction. He would have slapped the paper across his thigh and said, "There, boy, you laid it to them!" To him everything had been a game, and he had always been one jump ahead. Harry narrowed his eyes, thinking back, trying to remember more subtle signs and signals. Had his father ever been disheartened? There had been times certainly when he had been sober, preoccupied, and had kept to himself, working alone in the barns and the fields or had rattled off to town in the truck on unexplained errands. Had he ever faced an emptiness of the spirit that made all his clever deals pointless and stale? Hard to believe he ever had made such a fool of himself as he, Harry, had done, not once but several times. He would not have been so witless as to see, as Harry had in Jenny, what wasn't there or so foolish as to try to recapture his own youth. And what if he had known Beanna! Harry smiled faintly, thinking of them face to face. Fox and vixen, they would have amused and delighted each other. But his father would never have seen her as being exclusively for him. Shrewdly, he would have seen the game for what it was: each for himself.

Had he ever—and for Harry this was the most vital question—even briefly, been estranged from his wife? Had she ever merged into his days' routine to such an extent that he no longer distinguished her as an individual but only as a set of familiar responses? And if so, what had he done about it? Harry could not remember when he and Vivian had become strangers, so imperceptibly had it happened. Now the persistent, nagging fear at the heart of his discontent was that *he* had ceased to exist for *her*, that someone else filled her consciousness as Jenny had filled his. Perhaps that, rather than Beanna, was why she moved out. There may have been truth, though apparently wrongly applied, in Puckett's nasty tongue. If so, something must have gone wrong for her—as it had for him. Only once before, when Corinne was young and seriously ill, had he seen Vivian as worn and harried as when he had burst in on her. Remembering how he had hit August, Harry was ashamed. He might have broken the kid's jaw. What rankled was that he had meekly left when she ordered them out. He should have insisted on staying. He should have made the others leave and stayed with her. He saw that now as an opportunity missed, and he ached with regret. But by God, she had sent him packing! Hollow-eyed or not, that was his Vivian! Only . . . she wasn't his any more.

He sat up and swung his feet to the floor, sitting sideways on the bed to look out over the roof. He could see part of the barn and the long shed that housed the car and farm machinery. Beyond was a gentle slope down to the pond, not deep, but sufficient to splash in on a humid day. He had once had an old leaky row boat that he used to push out and float around in. Dolly had bailed with an old coffee can. Once, when he was older and full of devilment, he had coaxed Vivian into it and their combined weight, as he had expected, had swamped it. As the water rose about their ankles, Vivian had cried out in pretended alarm. The boat had sunk beneath them, and they had splashed their way out, slipping and sliding in the mud. He had taken the opportunity to put his arm around her. She, dripping wet and mud-splattered, had laughed.

Now the setting sun, a blood red orange, could be seen through a grove of trees, not yet fully in leaf. The sky was suffused with a glow that dyed the pond's mirror-smooth surface a deep rose. Though it was not yet dusk, Harry could hear the peepers, their voices rising in chorus from the damp, springing earth, and the sweet, high chitter of the martins. Leaning forward, arms on knees, fingers interlaced, he sat on, gazing out at the day's fading loveliness.

Around him, with whispers and sighs, the house settled. For Harry, senses newly tuned, it was alive with the scenes and voices of the past: his mother's hands lining up jars of freshly made strawberry jam, his father's chuckle, the chink of coins and the slap of cards, the rhythmic metallic rasp of the porch swing on a summer's evening, a bright, backward glance, and a man's voice calling in the dusk.

SEVENTEEN

Revelations

"Molly's pregnant!"

"What?"

"It's true. She's going to have a colt. Soon, Mr. Farley said. He said he doesn't know how it happened, but it did."

Vivian filled Corinne's cup and pushed it across the old porcelain-topped kitchen table. They sat on stools in Vivian's apartment kitchen. "You finally went out to see Molly, did you? I thought you'd lost all interest in horses."

Corinne made a face at her mother's jibe. Why did she have to hark back to things as they were ten months ago! "Why do you say it like that! You and Dad, you knew my wanting to be a trainer was just a phase. That's exactly what you said! Why be mad at me when it turns out you're right?"

Vivian shrugged. "I'm not mad." And she wasn't. She regarded her daughter with detachment, marveling at the easy changeability of youth to matters that cause parents—on their behalf—to vibrate for weeks.

"I just wanted to show her to Gus, that's all. But Dad had already taken her out to the farm. Mr. Farley called him because you hadn't been coming." She paused, hoping her mother might explain.

Vivian declined to explain anything. "Did you go to see her there?"

"Yes, we did. And Dad was very nice. He apologized to Gus. Well, why do you look like that? He should have apologized. . . . Don't you think he should have? Barging in and hitting him like that!"

Vivian raised her eyebrows and considered, smiling a little. "Oh I don't know. I rather enjoyed it." And in retrospect she did.

Corinne's eyes opened wide. "Enjoyed it! He could have really hurt him!" she exclaimed huffily. "Just because he misunderstood! Gus wasn't taking advantage of me! He has no *right* to jump to conclusions like that! I don't care if he *is* my father! What if every time. . . ."

"Yes, yes," said Vivian. "Of course. It was a bad thing to do. What else did he say?"

"We–e–e–ll." She swished her cup. "Is there more coffee? He said that if we got married he'd pay for the rest of my college and . . . well, maybe a little bit more. That is, if you will agree too." She leaned forward, expectantly.

Vivian leaned back. "Oh. I see. *That's* why you came."

Corinne's face was a study. "*Not* the *only* reason." Her tone was peevish. "He said I *had* to ask you. That *you* had to agree *too*." She dropped her eyes. "I was coming anyway."

"Why?"

"What kind of a question is that! Because! You're my mother, aren't you?" She looked up, and Vivian saw she was on the point of tears. Her lip twisted slightly. "I . . . I care about you, that's why, and I want . . . I want you to go home! I want you and Daddy to be together, like always! I don't *want* you here! What are you *doing* here, anyway!" Tears brimmed in her eyes and she gave a little sniffle.

"Here," said Vivian, extending a box of tissues.

Corinne blew her nose. Relieved of the pressure of tears, she asked again, "What *are* you doing here? Daddy's lonesome. He misses you. Don't smile! He does. I could tell. He talked about you a lot. . . . I didn't know you were such a good roller skater. He said you were the best in seven counties, and that you won all the prizes."

Vivian studied her cup, turned it this way and that. "I don't know about *seven* counties. Actually, we won them together."

A silence settled over them, an easy companionable silence during which Corinne ate three tollhouse cookies.

"I'm glad you sold that house," she said shyly, not knowing how her mother would react. "I didn't like it. Gus did, but I didn't. If *we* ever get a house, it won't be like that." She spoke very positively, and Vivian was amused, picturing Corinne being peremptory with August.

"What are you smiling at?"

Vivian shook her head. "Nothing."

Corinne, though she didn't understand why her mother smiled, recognized, nevertheless, the love in her eyes. "Well . . ." she asked, pensively, feeling as she used to when asking for something she knew she didn't deserve but would probably be given anyway, ". . . will you?"

Vivian reached out and stroked the back of her hand. "You can tell your father I said yes. Whether you get married or not. It makes no difference."

"No difference! Don't you care what happens to me?"

"Of course I care. That's why I said yes. You should finish your education. But you're already living together, and you didn't ask permission, did you? If you want to marry, you will. If you want to separate, you will. Isn't that so?"

Corinne, abashed at having it expressed aloud and so bluntly, conceded it was. "But won't you tell Daddy yourself?"

Vivian frowned. "Perhaps. Sometime. But for now, you tell him." She saw that Corinne, hoping for more, was disappointed. "You remember how you did what you felt you had to do? How you lied and didn't care what anyone thought?" Corinne's eyes darkened and she nodded reluctantly. "Well, I left because I had to. No matter what anyone thought." She added gently, "I don't know how long I'll stay here. I don't know what I'll do."

After Corinne left, Vivian went outside and sat on the back stoop, her arms folded across her knees, her chin resting on her arms. The yard was not much wider than the house but was quite deep. In summer five large trees cast a dense shade over the yard; under them grass was sparse and gnarled tree roots twisted above ground like the coils of huge dark snakes. A flimsy wire fence ineffectually separated the yard from its neighbors. On one side it had been bent to the ground and trodden on by so many people and dogs taking a shortcut that it had rusted permanently in that position. Any effort at replacement would disrupt well-established traffic patterns. Mr. Fulford, Senior, would not have recognized the yard where he had raised a bountiful garden in an open flood of sunlight, well protected by a stout board fence from all trespassers, including marauding rabbits. Now the trees and lilac and spirea bushes made a setting conducive to reflection.

Vivian had spoken truthfully when she told Corinne she didn't know what she would do. Time for her had slowed almost to a stop. She floated through days that were indistinguishable, one from the other. She saw Wilder and Allegra often, Lena and Rilly occasionally. She took short, leisurely walks, accompanied sometimes by James. She spent hours sitting on the back steps. Though she appeared idle, she was busy examining with a sharp and critical eye her own past behavior. As James single-mindedly pursued and routed out ground squirrels, Vivian tracked down every past action, every motive, and held it up, dangling, to be weighed and judged. She saw clearly that she had been a fool. She had trapped herself, as so many times before, in her own dream. She was even able to perceive—in her newly awakened state—that she had mistaken a dream for reality. That had to be guarded against. Reality had to be hung onto. She remembered her father, trying to instill in her a factual turn of mind, raising his finger like one of the old prophets and pinning her with his eye to the back of her chair. "Always face the facts! Meet 'em head on! That is the only way you will ever set your house in order!" Vivian had always liked that phrase: set your house in order. It had the ring of majestic simplicity. Even as a child she had understood he intended "house" not in the narrow sense of an ordinary four-walled roofed building but in a large and grand sense. And even as she had listened, solemnly returning his solemn stare, she saw herself, like a princess, moving effortlessly through a splendid home whose rooms and curving staircases stretched endlessly ahead into a dawn-like future, and as she glided forward, with a nod of her head or a wave of her hand she conferred on everything a sublime order. Had he been able to view the effect of his words, her father would have thrown up his hands. But she could, when necessary, face facts as well as he and deal with them as summarily as ever he could, be they dull or worrisome or, as in this instance, unpalatable. Her involvement with August fell into the latter category, and she had not just faced it but collided with it when he and Corinne had confronted her. She had been shocked by August's transformation. Before her had stood no spirited, self-confident young man, impetuous perhaps but nevertheless sure of what he wanted and capable of constancy. Instead he had been tongue-tied and as fearful of what she might say in front of Corinne as a schoolboy afraid of being caught out. He had fidgeted with his hands, and Vivian had seen they were not mature and capable but boyish and untried. His neck was still so slender that his Adam's apple showed quite plainly at every nervous swallow. She had seen instantly the enormity of her error and had been filled with self-disgust, followed rather quickly, as evidenced by the omelette and the number of Wilder's biscuits she ate, by an enormous relief. No more anxious scanning for wrinkles; no more dire figuring, such as, when he's thirty-eight, I'll be. . . . In fact, having clearly perceived August's excessive youth, she had felt proportionately younger herself. That night she had slept soundly for the first time in weeks.

Her recovery had been rapid, but Wilder, who at first had spent hours with her out of a deep concern, continued to come because, knowing she was there, he couldn't stay away. One day he came with coffee and a date loaf that James was fond of, even though it stuck to his teeth.

Vivian had been examining the piano, an old, massive upright with bulbous front legs and an ornately carved front. With one finger she struck a series of keys. Accompanying each note was an audible click.

"Wilder, whatever happened to this piano? How come it clicks and all the edges of the keys are chipped out? Did someone in your family play?" It never occurred to her that that someone could be Wilder. And had she realized where her question would lead, Vivian would never have asked; nor, had he realized, would Wilder have answered as readily as he did.

The piano had been the focal point of Wilder's boyhood and youth. In its huge case, its dark finish crazed and roughened to the touch, were buried his one great ambition and his deepest disappointment. He had never spoken of either to anyone. But to Vivian, the only person in whom he had perfect trust, he suddenly wanted to tell everything. So happy was he to share with her the most crucial experience of his life that once started he grew freer and more candid. For once that small monitoring voice that invariably urged restraint was stilled.

"My mother played," said Wilder. "She played by ear. On

Sunday afternoons she'd play and sing for us." Wilder could still hear her voice, its intonations and throaty emotion as she sang, "Fly Away Kentucky Babe," or "Mighty Lak a Rose." "She thought every well-brought-up girl should know how to play the piano. She didn't care if they sang or not. They could sing at Sunday School. Every Saturday morning my four older sisters went for a lesson."

"Four," said Vivian, impressed. She handed down a bite of cake to James, waiting patiently beside her.

"Four, at seventy-five cents each. That was a lot then for Mother to put aside. My father thought it was a waste of his money. So they didn't lose it on the way, Mother always tied it in the corners of their handkerchiefs."

Vivian laughed. "Your mother must have listened to a lot of scales!"

"She did when she could get them to practice."

"They didn't want to?"

"They didn't want to learn at all!" Wilder spoke with more vigor than Vivian had ever heard from him. His voice was edged with scorn, unexpected in so mild-mannered a man. "They hid in closets, behind the clothes, and outside, behind the bushes. She had to drag them to it. And then they'd kick the piano and hit the keys with their fists so the whole piano vibrated. My father always said it was worse than two cats with their tails tied together." Wilder paused and stirred his coffee. Then he looked at Vivian, his eyes behind his thick lenses serious but eager for her reaction to what he was about to say. His words came in a rush and had the quality of a revelation. "But *I* took lessons too. I went every week. And when I began I was ahead of them because I had taught myself everything that was in their books."

"My!" said Vivian. Wilder had leaned slightly forward, and she was struck by his intensity. "You must have been very smart to do that. Your mother must have been very proud of you."

Wilder said modestly, "I wasn't smart. I just *had*. . ." he held out his hands, palms up, fingers curved, and shook them, ". . . *had* to play. Mother wasn't proud. She wouldn't spend anything for me to take lessons. She said the piano was for young ladies." Unable to resist appealing to Vivian, he smiled wryly and said, "She sent me out to pick potato bugs!"

"Oh, Wilder," said Vivian softly. She felt a rush of sympathy for him, for the boy he had once been and the hurt he had suffered and, as she could see, still felt.

Vivian's commiseration was like balm to Wilder. "But I took lessons anyway." A trace of his old determination lingered in his voice. "I spoke to Mrs. Patterson, the teacher. . . ." He interrupted himself. "Her first name was Vigue. My sisters called her Ague." He and Vivian laughed together. "She was a widow, and I offered to do odd jobs—cut grass, wash windows, scrub floors—in exchange for lessons. She was glad for the help. Sometimes I stayed with her little boy. He was asthmatic. Mrs. Patterson was very good to me. She often gave me lessons when I hadn't done any work at all. And when Mother wouldn't let me practice at home, she let me use her piano."

"You must have been talented, Wilder, or she wouldn't have done so much," said Vivian.

Wilder's eyes swam with gratitude that Vivian understood so quickly, without his having to say it first. "That's what *she* said. She told me I should go away to music school, that . . ." he hesitated, then, bathed in Vivian's warm regard, said what he had never said aloud before, ". . . I might even become a concert pianist." His whole face was illuminated, and through Vivian's astonishment he saw again his old dream of a bare stage, just himself and a grand piano, its top raised like a dark wing, and beyond the lights an unseen audience like a great expectant heart waiting to be thrilled.

"Didn't you ever go?" asked Vivian. Like Dolphine, she deplored wasted talent.

Wilder smiled as if amused at himself. "No. Mrs. Patterson moved away. Her son got worse and she had to take him to a different climate. And Mother was annoyed by my playing." He didn't say that two of his sisters had already left home, and that whenever he touched the piano his mother, angered by the perversity of her children, would cock her head and with fingers curved like claws, pound imaginary keys and sing mimicking tra-la-la's. Or that whenever she heard Eddie Duchin or Fats Waller on the radio, she would remark, with a malicious smile, "There, why don't you play like that? Then maybe you'd get somewhere."

"Oh, Wilder, that's a shame! You should have found some way. . . ."

"I couldn't blame her. She had eleven children and was having another. There was no money and someone had to stay and help here at home. Luther, my youngest brother, used the keys to teethe on."

"Teethe on!" Vivian was incredulous.

"That was the family joke. He just bit out pieces. Started at the top and worked his way down the keyboard. And the felts are moth-eaten. That's why they click. One winter a field mouse made a nest inside the case. But I don't think it matters. Mrs. Patterson was a kind woman. She didn't have many students, and she probably thought I was better than I really was." Wilder didn't want pity. He had come to agree with his father, who was fond of remarking that "Life was just one pipe dream after another." What he wanted—and he realized the ridiculousness of it—was Vivian's assurance that his teacher had indeed judged him correctly. He wanted her, only her, to see him as possessing an unrealized talent, to believe that he had the sensitivity, the capacity for feeling . . . to see that he was not altogether without distinction even though it was based on a mere possibility that had long ceased to exist.

"Oh, I'm *sure* she was right!" exclaimed Vivian. "You shouldn't think that! After all, she should know better than anyone. I'm sure she wouldn't have misled you. Don't you play any more at all?"

Her ready belief in him and her solicitude were sweet, so sweet that Wilder quite forgot himself. "No, I don't. I can't." She smiled and shook her head as if to gently admonish him. "I've never told anyone this before." For days, living so close to her, he had felt a compulsion to declare his feelings for her. He was afraid he would just blurt it out. He had several times started awake in the night, thinking he had done so, and breathed with relief to find it only a dream. Now her sympathy pushed him, and he fell precipitously, unable to stop. He heard himself speaking words that came of themselves. "I never wanted anyone to know until you . . . only you. . . . Ever since you came in my house and sat in my chair, I have thought only of you. . . . There is no one, anywhere, like you . . . no one so lovely, with such hair. . . . When I was sick and you came, it was like heaven. I longed to touch you, but I didn't dare . . . you fill my whole life. . . ."

He had spoken softly, as if spellbound. Vivian at first

thought she misunderstood, then knew she hadn't. She was, for the moment, too nonplussed to speak.

Seeing her surprise, and then a pained searching for words, Wilder knew this was no dream. He got up and went to stand at the window. Silently he cursed himself for a fool, twice, three times a fool, for saying aloud what could never be unsaid, what would be forever an embarrassment between them.

At length Vivian found her voice. "Wilder, I'm sorry, I should never. . . ."

"No, don't be sorry," said Wilder, surprised he could speak at all rationally. He turned briskly from the window and began gathering the cups and dishes onto a tray, not looking at her. "*I* am sorry. *I* should apologize and I do. I had no right to say what I did, and I can only hope you'll forget it." He started for the door. James, who had been asleep on the couch, woke up and yawned.

"Please, Wilder." Vivian followed him to the door, hesitantly put out a hand. "Don't go like this. I value your . . . regard." He stopped then and looked at her. "I do! Please believe me. I want us to be friends. Can't we go on being friends?"

Behind his thick glasses, Wilder's large eyes considered that. He was surprised to find that it was possible, after all, to face her. His feet were firmly under him. The house still stood. Nothing had really changed. Only *he* had suffered a lapse . . . and said what she probably already knew. He nodded at her. "Yes, we'll always be friends."

But they both took care to see less of each other. Vivian went out more often, and one day she drove to the farm to see Molly. As she turned into the lane she saw that Molly was outside, grazing in a fenced-in area adjacent to the barn. Confident that Harry would be at work for the afternoon, Vivian parked the car in the wide turnaround between barn and shed. It was immediately apparent to Vivian that Ed Hacker had been a slovenly and improvident householder. All the buildings needed painting. Old crates and pieces of lumber were piled haphazardly in the shed, next to a broken-down tractor. Rusted pieces of machinery, metal piping and sections of old hose lay scattered about as if once they were dismantled there was no hope of their ever being reassembled. A thick growth of weeds completely filled what had been the pig-pen, built out from one end of the barn. Higher than the fence, the weeds encroached on the lane and grew in a strip down the middle, their stems bent and grease-marked from the underside of Harry's car.

The top half of the barn door was fastened back. Vivian swung open the lower half and entered, brushing away floating strands of cobweb that caught against her face. The bright sun that outside had so mercilessly shown up rust and weed and peeling paint was filtered softly into the barn. It shone in luminous, dusty rays through cracks in the roof and the walls and through the small grimy windows hung with old cobwebs and dead moths. At one end of the barn were two rows of stalls. Harley Fox had put horses on one side, cows on the other, facing each other across their feed bins. The main part of the barn had a wide center area where one could look straight up at the high roof beams where the swallows nested. Large double doors opened onto it so that a wagon or a tractor could be brought inside. On either side were lofts, reached by ladders nailed to upright beams. Now the lofts were empty, old pieces of straw dangling down between the boards. A rusted rake with a broken handle was propped against the wall. An old rope with a frayed and greasy end hung from a nail. Several pails lay in a corner, one with its bottom broken out. By one stall some bales of hay were piled, and a broom leaned against them. The barn was musty. It smelled of dust and decay. Vivian missed the sweetish, nose-tickling odor it had once had, compounded of fresh hay, feed grain, and the warm breaths and bodies of animals.

She opened a door on the far side of the barn, stepped out into the sunlight and called Molly. The horse raised her head and at a second call came forward, sedately but with a swinging, rhythmic stride that reminded Vivian of Dolphine. Molly bobbed her head and pulled at Vivian's sleeve. She rolled the sugar lumps in her mouth and chomped up an apple. Wanting more, she pushed hard against Vivian, who finally offered her a handful of grass which she blew at, then accepted. Vivian stroked her head and swollen sides. Harry had cleaned out her stall but had not brushed her coat, which was dusty and dull.

Vivian could find no currycomb in the barn. She would have to bring one the next time she came. With her hand on the car door handle, she paused to study the back of the house. Not since Harry's mother, Leonia, died, had she been inside. She felt a strong desire to see it again, and to see what Harry had done. She glanced at her watch. There still was time before Harry should be returning, if only the back door were unlocked. It was, and she stepped into the kitchen.

When Leonia had first come to live in the house Harley Fox had built, the kitchen was a large, almost square room with a slanted wooden ceiling, a black coal stove, wooden cupboards attached to the walls and a small porcelain sink with a ridged, porcelain drainboard. The sink was possible only because Harley had laid a piping system and brought water into the house, for both kitchen and upstairs bathroom. In the shed attached to the kitchen there was, for good measure, a pump. Breakfasts and weekday dinners, she and Harley had eaten at a large round table in the middle of the bare wooden floor, a table which served her also as work counter. Harley had made it of a size to accommodate besides themselves the five or six children he anticipated. When Harry was five, Harley, to express his enthusiasm over his second-born, had modernized the kitchen. He installed a new and larger sink and counters on either side with cupboards above and below. He even fitted in little open shelves on either side of the window such as he had seen pictured in a magazine to hold the gewgaws of which Leonia was so fond. He replaced the coal stove with an electric stove on legs, which had the remarkable features of a dial temperature indicator beside the oven door and one burner that could convert from a surface unit to a deep well for soup or frying.

That modern stove had, through the years, been followed by several others, each more modern than the last, although Leonia always said that none of them baked as well as the first one. But the ceiling, sink and cupboards were unchanged. The Hackers had put down a square of linoleum. Its corners were chipped and broken; long worn ridges revealed the contour of the floor-boards.

Vivian had not expected so many barrels and cartons. The room was filled with them, hers and Harry's household goods as well as Leonia's and Harley's, many opened but none unpacked. She could see the paths Harry had cleared, to stove and refrigerator, table and sink, to back door and hall. She leaned against the counter and listened to the quiet house, sensing it around her, renewing her acquaintance with it. She touched the chipped corner inside the sink where the black iron showed through, and rubbed at the orange stain, telltale of a drip never properly fixed, both familiar. She had often washed dishes for Leonia, who invariably came with a flowered apron, slipped it over her head and tied it in back so she wouldn't "soil her clothes." No one could work in Leonia's kitchen without an apron. Even when she was bedridden, she would call out when Vivian went downstairs, "Don't forget your apron." Several dishes and a frying pan were in the drainer, at hand to be used again. Vivian opened one of the cupboards. Rings showed where dishes had been stacked.

The table needed scrubbing. The very first time Vivian had visited, on a fall afternoon, Leonia had served her and Harry a large piece of lemon pie, still warm and with a meringue two inches high. Then she had been "Mrs. Fox," and Vivian, in awe of her, had desperately wanted her good opinion because she was Harry's mother. She had been awkward and overly polite and had praised the pie so that Leonia, with a smile, had given them both another piece, but only a sliver because she had to save the rest for Mr. Fox. Then there had been a cloth on the table and in the middle salt and pepper shakers, a jar of mustard, a bottle of catsup, a cut glass tumbler holding a collection of teaspoons, and a little stack of "sauce" dishes.

Vivian had soon learned not to fear Leonia, who, after a few weeks of thoughtful scrutiny, accepted her as her own daughter. Vivian had never feared Mr. Fox. Harley's eyes had lit up at sight of her. There had been an immediate liking between them. He sometimes rested his hand on her shoulder, a mark of signal approval. Occasionally he had jokingly called her "Red." "Red, come over here," he would say, with a jerk of his head, "something I want to show you." At such moments the twinkle in his eye was of a different character. She always came promptly when he spoke, and as he showed her whatever he had found for her delight or wonder, she knew that if she had been other than his son's wife, he would have favored her as more than a daughter-in-law. Always he had called her, "my girl."

Vivian wandered into the dining room. The buffet and china cupboard had been moved out of the way into their former positions, but the rug still lay rolled up; the table, stacked with cartons, and the chairs were pushed to one side. Harry had made no effort to unpack anything. In the parlor he had not even put bulbs in the lamps. Upstairs she saw at once that he had been using his old room. He hadn't bothered to hang up his clothes. Suits were thrown carelessly across a chair; an open suitcase on the floor held a jumble of shirts, underclothes and socks. The bedding of the iron bedstead had been pulled up over the pillow in an indifferent attempt at "making the bed." The alarm clock sat on the bare floor. There were no curtains. The Hackers had taken the rods. But the blinds had not been pulled down even to midpoint. Unlike Harry. He disliked being wakened early by the full light of an unshaded window in his face. His shaving things were in the bathroom cabinet. A bath towel hung on a rack, bunched together and still damp. Automatically Vivian shook it out and hung it straight.

The other small bedroom, Dolly's room, was jammed with furniture and boxes. Her bed, an iron frame painted pink, leaned unassembled against the wall. Before Vivian and Harry were married, Vivian had occasionally "slept over" and shared that bed with Dolly, who was thrilled by the prospect of being a bridesmaid. Where there had been pennants and trophies in Harry's room, there had been dolls, ribbons and fancy pillows in Dolly's. One long-legged cloth doll always sat on the bed, its arms twisted around its bent knees. It was purple and its head rose up and curved forward to a point which had a little bell fastened to it. Vivian pushed at a carton with her foot, wondering what had happened to that doll. Dolly, living in California, had not been home since her mother died.

The large front bedroom, Harley and Leonia's room, took up two thirds of the width of the house and two of the three upstairs front windows. They faced east and looked out over the front porch roof, giving a view of the long front yard, the lane at the side, the highway, and the field beyond where Harley used to plant corn. Vivian entered hesitantly, uncertain of her own reaction, for the last time she had been in that room was after Leonia's funeral, to help Dolly pack everything for storage. Sorting through Harley's and Leonia's clothes and personal possessions had been painful, an experience Vivian had not had before. She had been too young for it when her own mother died, and when she married, her father had sold everything and moved to Florida, where he had lived in an efficiency apartment until his death. But what Vivian saw drew her in, and she stood amazed.

The room might have been occupied. All the furniture was in its proper place, including the bed, a dark, graceful four-poster, which was neatly made up, complete with pillows. Two small rugs had been laid down, one on either side of the bed, and a large one in the middle of the floor. A patched quilt, still folded, lay half out of a carton. Vivian picked it up, smoothed it over her arm. It had been Leonia's favorite, a stylized plume pattern in green and white. The plumes, once a deep green, had faded with wear and time to a soft, delicate green. Vivian laid it across the footboard and contemplated the bed. Its smooth headboard was gracefully curved; the only carving was a band of vines and leaves midway on the slender posts. This bed Leonia had brought with her when she married Harley. Her children had been born in it; she and Harley had died in it. Glancing around the room, Vivian was suddenly struck by what she saw on the dresser. There, set out on the embroidered dresser scarf, was her mirrored tray, complete with her collection of perfume bottles, arranged as she had always done. Looking down at them, Vivian could hardly believe it. There also was the iridescent blue musical powder box that Harry had given her one Christmas. Impulsively, not expecting it would be wound up, Vivian lifted the lid. The tune tinkled out at once, seeming overloud in the quiet house. Startled, Vivian clapped the lid back. At one side was her frilly lamp. She pressed the switch and it came on, its glow barely perceptible in the afternoon light. Vivian stared—the only lamp furnished with a bulb and plugged in in the entire house! In a room that wasn't being used! On a wild suspicion, she jerked open the drawers, one after the other. There were her gloves, scarfs, underwear, sweaters, all neatly arranged. Turning, she threw open the closet door. There hung her clothes, and on a hook on the inside of the door hung a nightgown and matching kimono she had not worn in years. It was of a blue satiny material, with wide bands of a deeper blue on the full sleeves and down the front edges. Harry and Corinne had given it to her on her birthday. While Harry had stood back, smiling, Corinne had made her sit down and close her eyes. Then Corinne had laid the box on her lap and said, "Now you can look!"

Slowly Vivian shut the closet door and sat down on Leonia's bedroom rocker. She was astonished and confused. She had entered where she was not expected. An intruder, she had seen what, perhaps, was not intended to be seen.

In a rather benumbed state, Vivian went downstairs. She paused by the parlor door and surveyed the disorder of boxes and furniture. There were the two plant stands Harley had made to hold Leonia's ferns. She had kept them in the back parlor by the south window, the location, Leonia said, that they were partial to. The back parlor was smaller than the front, the only separation between the two was a pair of glassed-in bookcases that jutted out at right angles from opposing walls. Like the paneling on the staircase, they were of oak and each had a round column on its outer end that extended to the ceiling. They gave a sense of cosiness and seclusion to the back parlor. Leonia liked to sit there with a cup of tea in the late afternoon and watch for Harley to come, either from town or in from the barns, for she had a view of the lane through the front parlor windows and of the backyard through the back parlor windows. After Harley died, Leonia had her tea in the kitchen.

Vivian turned away from the back window, thinking it was time she should go, when her eye fell on a box of photograph albums and large photographs in cardboard frames. On a chair that seemed to have been drawn up for the purpose, another album lay open. Vivian bent to examine it, then sat down and, holding it on her lap, began turning the soft, felty black pages, some of them torn from the little metal spokes through which the cord ran that held them all loosely together. For pages she recognized no one and no place. Faces, clothes and backgrounds— generally farmhouses or front porch steps, favored for small or large groups—were all a pale sepia. Eyes were washed out; smiles dimmed. Print dresses, striped shirts, even dark, tight-fitting suits were faded as if the cloth itself had lost color and worn thin. But there was a young Harley, hair ruffled, with a grin that had endured, leaning cockily against a fence, his arms crossed and one foot braced on the lowest rail. His whole stance expressed triumphant proprietorship. Close beside him, her shoulder behind his, stood Leonia, her glance seeming to distrust the photographer, her clasped hands resting against her thigh to hold down her long skirts that were billowing forward in an invisible wind. There were several more of Harley with the house at various stages in its construction; he was always caught in action, with a saw in his hand or smiling archly as he was about to hammer in a nail. Leonia appeared holding an infant with a shock of black hair, its chin sunk in a froth of lace-trimmed, pleated collar. It had to be Harry.

Vivian pondered the baby's tiny, inscrutable face, then turned the next few pages, past the finished house, a picnic—ladies sitting decorously on the grass, men slouched with hands in pockets and hats on the backs of their heads, Harley beside a car with absurdly thin wheels, and Harry as a toddler in a sailor suit. Vivian smiled. He was no great hand with a rowboat. After a jump in time there was baby Dolly, Leonia with a prize pumpkin, and ten-year-old Harry, grinning like Harley and holding out before him a new football. There were gaps, pictures missing, taken, perhaps, by Dolly when she left home, or sent to distant relatives, no doubt carefully inscribed on the back with date, name, and age to fend off oblivion. There was Shep, tail a-wag, grinning around a stick held in his mouth, and suddenly, though she should have expected it, there was her own face. Vivian bent closer; then she remembered. It had been taken at the zoo, Harry using her Brownie camera. She knew because of the dress and shoes. It had been her best dress, worn to impress Harry. It had short cape-like sleeves, a fitted waist and a full skirt that whirled out when she spun around on one foot. The shoes were very special, black, with a black bow on the cross strap, just like those Eleanor Powell wore when she tapdanced. She had been standing in front of the lion's cage, but Harry had not been interested in the lion, whose head and forelegs were cut off, only his back legs and restless tail showing like a strange extension of Vivian's left side. They had used an entire roll of film that day, taking pictures of each other, Harry clowning, squirting water at the water fountain, she sitting with crossed ankles on the barrel of a Civil War cannon. There was one of them together, courtesy of a passerby. Harry's arm was draped across her shoulders as he pretended to lean on her excessively hard, and they were trying not to giggle as the stranger focused on them. And there was the peacock! Ducks, geese and peacocks, all roamed freely about the park, and as they had tried to sneak up on this peacock, it had turned on them with ill temper and fanned out its gorgeous tail, patterned with iridescent greens and blues. "Take it, take it!" Vivian had exclaimed, and Harry had, catching the full spread of tail feathers, its fiercely haughty eye and arrogant turn of head. Then Vivian had not heard its cry. She raised her head, recalling the insane, piercing cries of the peacocks on the roof that day with Marvel. The woman had called them her watchdogs. Marvel had laughed. Remembering, Vivian squinted slightly as if she were looking down the wrong end of a telescope at something very small and far away. How totally unimportant Marvel was now—not even comic anymore.

Turning a page, Vivian was arrested by pictures taken before their marriage, singly and together. Here they were not clowning. Sobered by their coming marriage, they gazed at the camera with a serene sense of self-importance. Things might go wrong for others, but certainly not for them. For them everything would go well. They were certain of what they wanted and said so, and what they wanted would never change, an assertion which always made Harley laugh good-naturedly and slap Harry on the shoulder.

Vivian studied the two of them—herself and Harry. Her hair was done differently then. It was longer and parted on the side. Her arms and shoulders looked very slim. But her face . . . it was the face of a stranger with whom she had some hidden, mysterious bond, a person whose existence had no reality other than that in the picture, who existed, if at all, on an entirely different plane from that of Vivian's, beyond all reach. And Harry! He had been little more than a boy—not as old then as August was now. She had forgotten how thin and lanky his frame had been, how thin his neck and sharp his jaw. That was not Harry, any more than that girl was herself. He was a young man purporting to be Harry, existing, like a nineteen year-old Vivian, in another dimension.

Vivian closed the album and laid it back in the box with the others. The two parlors, with windows closed, had grown over-warm in the full glare of the afternoon sun. Vivian would have liked to open a window, to breathe in fresh air. Yet as she reached the hallway, her footsteps loud on the bare floors, she was reluctant to leave and sat down for a moment on the steps. When Harley died, Vivian had asked Leonia to come live with her and Harry. Dolly had invited her to go with her back to California. But Leonia had refused, stubbornly, they all thought at the time. She had thanked them but had insisted on staying in her own home.

Vivian was tired. No, not tired, but possessed by a sense of having let slip so many things she should have held onto. She was nowhere; it was emptiness that made her weary. That she might go upstairs and take a nap on Leonia's bed crossed her mind, to be immediately and wryly dismissed. She was vaguely surprised she had even thought of such a thing. She must go before Harry came home and found her there.

The car seat was burning hot from sitting in the sun. The long summer days of penetrating heat and oppressive humidity had begun. Vivian saw as she turned the car and headed down the lane that Molly was dozing, one foot cocked, in the shady angle of the barn.

That evening Vivian sat on the back steps of her apartment and wondered how Harry would ever cope with all that had to be done. So much cleaning, refinishing, unpacking. But he had always wanted to live there and now he was. Probably he would hire the work done. Thinking of the condition of the house and barns, she was scandalized. Harley and Leonia would have been also. Vivian had not realized what a fine house it was. Years ago, when Harry had ventured to suggest they live there, she had been appalled. Then she had considered it not *really* old, but only old-fashioned, unromantic and uninteresting, a place to escape from. Now, herself displaced and seeing the house which held so much of their past in such disorder, she experienced for the first time a communion with it. Harley had put his own strength and sturdiness into it. Between them, he and Leonia had given it a warmth and life that was still there. Vivian had felt it in every room. She understood why Leonia would not leave it. It was part of the fabric of her life.

Vivian wondered at herself for not having understood that sooner. And her thoughts dwelt again on discovering her clothes in the closet and folded away in the dresser. It affected her weirdly, as if, without her knowing, a part of herself were living there. It was ghostly and made her shiver. She had difficulty imagining Harry putting away clothes so neatly—he never bothered to do that with his own things—or choosing a particular gown to hang on the door. Why that one? What had been in his mind? What memory or association? This totally unexpected glimpse of Harry seemed to Vivian so private that she shrank from it. Disturbed and solitary, she sat on until the trees were black silhouettes against the night sky and lights shone out from neighboring houses. Allegra's back upstairs light fell in a pale oblong on the dark ground. Beyond, in the deeper darkness, Vivian could see the fitful glow of wandering fireflies.

EIGHTEEN

Pursuit

Harry's appearance at the office began to be very irregular. Mrs. Brenner, the secretary, never knew when to expect him. Not that Harry didn't keep up with his share of the work. He did. Frequently Mrs. Brenner found that work accumulated and left on his desk at five o'clock would be done and stacked on hers the next morning, including new work for her to do. She could not and did not complain of him in that regard, but she was driven to nervous fits over scheduling appointments. Sometimes he kept them; more often he didn't. On her fell the burden of making excuses and apologies. The disgruntled looks of restless clients who cleared their throats aggressively and made a great show of consulting their watches were hard to bear, implying as they did that it was all her fault. Pushed too far in this way, she would appear in Logan's office.

"Mr. Gamble," (Mrs. Brenner was not one for first names) "Mr. Reinert, who has come all the way from Doylestown, is *still* waiting." Her voice was pained, her hands clasped together against her chest in a prayerful attitude. "Mr. Fox was to have seen him at one-thirty. He promised! But it's two-thirty and Mr. Reinert is . . . he says he *has* to get back. It's not really my fault!"

"Of course not," said Logan. "Send him in. I think I can take care of it." Logan was quite aware of Harry's erratic working hours. Even when Harry was present, Logan had found him strangely preoccupied. He had remarked on this to Jenny.

But Jenny had always seen Harry as preoccupied, and said so. "He looks straight at you, but you can tell he's thinking of something else. Who knows what!" She spoke with a trace of the exasperation she used to feel. As she remembered—and it seemed a long time ago indeed—she had thought him rather like a big cat. "You can never tell which way he's going to jump next!"

Logan laughed and gave Jenny a hug. Quite mistakenly he attributed her testy remarks to her advanced pregnancy, ample excuse for odd notions. He knew Harry very well, and he wasn't a bit like that. Harry was a man of both thought and action, one of the reasons Logan so admired him. When Harry wasn't moving, he was thinking. He was cagey. When he appeared absentminded, Logan knew he was mulling over some tactic. When the time came to act, no one was more decisive. Logan could testify to that. Right now Harry was concerned with something; when he was ready to divulge it, he would do so. Meanwhile Logan would help all he could by taking over extra work at the office and waiting patiently—as in the past, with a good deal of expectancy.

This time Logan was destined never to know what so occupied Harry's thoughts. It was not a matter Harry was ever likely to share with anyone, even Logan, for he was busy tracking down his wife.

He had come home one day and knew the moment he stepped inside the kitchen that something was different. Someone had been there. He glanced sharply around. Perhaps he should have locked the back door. Nothing appeared to have been disturbed, yet the atmosphere was stirred, recharged in a way that made him step cautiously from one room to the next, alert for anything displaced or missing. He almost missed noticing the album because he had gone into the front parlor only as far as the fireplace and was turning with the intention of inspecting the upstairs when his eye registered the fact that there was nothing on the seat of the chair in the back parlor. He had left an album, opened, on it. No one would have taken a batch of old photographs! Then he saw that the album had been put back in the carton with the others.

Harry paused, then went quickly upstairs. Nothing had been touched in his room. Or Dolly's. The bathroom . . . he saw instantly the folded towel and stopped dead. Vivian! It was absolutely characteristic. And in the front bedroom was the quilt, folded over the footboard. She had been there! And she had not wanted him to know. He was sure of it. That she had folded the towel meant nothing. She wouldn't even have realized she had done it.

He had made himself a sandwich, drunk half a quart of milk and after dusk had driven into town. He parked a block away and strolled toward her house. Within sight of the rear apartment windows, he stopped and leaned against one of the Norway maples that lined both sides of the street. The night was very dark under its dense foliage. He could stand there and contemplate her one lighted window—he judged it to be the living room— without being noticed. That is, until Wilder came out the front door with James, who hustled about, snuffling along the hedge until he scented his arch antagonist, Harry. Instantly James stiffened and put back his ears. His fur bristled on the ridge of his spine, and he snarled, outraged at this untoward encounter. Hearing him, Wilder thought he had met another, larger, dog and called him off. James flicked his ears to show he had heard, snarling all the louder, backed as he was by Wilder's presence. Wilder, perceiving a man standing by the tree, called James again, sharply. Reluctantly James backed off; Wilder repeated his command and James ran off at his bobbing, three-legged gait. They went in the opposite direction, and Harry was free to concentrate on Vivian's apartment window.

At seventeen he had done much the same thing. He had haunted the neighborhood where she lived. Had watched for her to come out or go in, appear at a window or turn a light on or off. Now one light was on. As he watched, it went out. It was too early to go to bed. Perhaps she was going out . . . to meet someone. Then he heard a door, but it was the muffled bang of a back screen door. Harry walked around the block and found a spot—it was the other end of the shortcut—from which he could see the back of Vivian's house. She had, as he thought, come outside and was sitting on the back steps. She sat out of the light cast from an upstairs window, and beyond the glow from neighboring windows. But the effect of their joint illumination was such that her figure stood out as lighter than the surrounding darkness; he could tell that she sat with arms crossed on her knees and her chin resting on her arms. Now and then she raised her head and made a sweeping motion with one hand as if brushing away a mosquito. Most important, she was alone.

Had she not been, he would have gone quietly away. Then, because he was facing facts squarely, Harry had to admit that that was not so. He would not have gone away. He would have charged in and beaten whoever it was to a pulp. Just thinking of the possibility his lips tightened and he drew a deep, chest-filling breath. On the crest of that wave of aggression he thought of going over right now and saying, "Come on home!" But what he considered his better judgment dismissed that course of action almost at once. For one thing she might just tell him to go, as she had done before. She might have no intention of ever coming back. For another, there might be someone else. He still had to determine that, even though a small stubborn voice insisted the contrary, that it was not, could not, be true. That she would not have gone out to the farm and through the house as she had done were it true. That he knew her better than that. But there was the catch! He did not know her, not really, not any more. And maybe he hadn't for a long time. When he had been looking through the album, he had taken from his wallet the worn and dog-eared snapshot of her holding Corinne that he had carried all through Korea, and he put it in its proper sequence in the album. That was not Vivian now, any more than it was Corinne now. He had felt a terrible impatience with all those frozen moments, parts and pieces of the past, for they fell short of the present. As if he were solving a puzzle, he had to put them all together to arrive at Vivian now, or himself, or Corinne, the trouble being that he had no pieces for the recent past. He had to find her, see her and himself clearly, as if for the first time, all over again.

Harry stood a long time in the dark before he realized that all the lights had been turned off and there was no longer a shadowy figure on the back steps.

Thereafter Harry, striving to come abreast of the present, spent hours each day observing Vivian's house and following her activities as well as he could. Sometimes he sat in his car and watched, fruitlessly, for hours, seeing no familiar person other than Wilder, his summer-weave hat on the back of his head, hurrying home with his brown paper bag, or the jogger, running now in shorts and T-shirt with a scarf tied around her forehead.

Harry was there when she started out, shoulders back and shirt dry, and still there when she returned, red-faced and panting, shirt clinging damply to her hunched, straining shoulders. Other times he walked about, skirting the immediate vicinity of the house and keeping a sharp eye out lest Vivian should catch him. He even followed at a discreet distance when she walked or drove. She went, he discovered, to very few places: the grocery store, public library, Pete and Lena's bookstore. She walked with no one, except, now and then, that three-legged dog, and no man other than Wilder entered the house.

One afternoon, at the end of June, Vivian walked downtown. She had begun thinking a good deal about Molly and her foal and wanted some books on the raising and training of horses. Harry, on the basis of past observation, guessed her destination and took the opportunity to drop in at the office. On the sidewalk Jim Reeves hailed him.

"Harry, boy! Just the man I wanted to see! Got a minute?"

Reeves always called him "boy" when he was going to ask a favor, a mode of address Harry particularly disliked. Harry set his hands on his hips, aggressively, elbows out, and tilted back his head. He squinted slightly and said, "Yeah?"

For the annual Fourth of July celebration Reeves was organizing a baseball game, Kiwanis against the Junior Chamber of Commerce. "Of course I had to start with you, Warrenville's all-time star. You're the one, Harry boy, who can make it go! What d'you say? You can even pick your own team!"

Harry's gaze slid past him. Across the street Vivian was walking toward the bookstore. She had a graceful carriage and a good straight stride. She didn't walk with her knees bent as so many women did, not even when she wore high heels. Harry had always thought that with her balance she would make a good sportswoman, but she had never been interested in playing any game. "I'll just watch you," she always said. At that thought, he said at once, "Okay, sure. I'll play."

Reeves, pleased with his own persuasiveness, named other Kiwanians he intended to ask.

"Don't forget Logan," said Harry. "He's good at outfielding. He's got a good reach."

Vivian had just passed the courthouse, where several people

had taken refuge from the hot sun in the cool shade of its curved entrance, when she saw Harry standing outside his office. Even at that distance she knew him. Seeing him unexpectedly and knowing that as she neared the bookstore he couldn't fail to see her, she felt a momentary impulse to turn back. But he might have already seen her, and in any case, she would not turn out of her way. She walked on unconcernedly, knowing he could not tell if she were looking at him or not. His hair was very black and his shirt a glare of white in the full midday sunlight. She recognized his pugnacious stance. He never had liked Jim Reeves.

Inside the bookstore, Vivian paused by the low curtain fencing off the window display. She appeared to be inspecting the books, but she was really watching Harry. He had acquired for her that deep fascination attaching to anyone who, supposedly understood, turns out to be, after all, a mystery. Jim Reeves touched two fingers to his temple in the quasi-military salute he affected and went briskly off. Harry stood briefly, facing the bookstore, then went inside his office. Only then did Vivian turn from the window.

When she left the bookstore, Vivian carried several books. Not that she had any definite program in mind. But she knew from Corinne that Molly had foaled and Vivian had an urge to learn what she could about training it. Mr. Farley would help, but Vivian thought she wanted to do this herself.

Later that afternoon she drove out to the farm. She went through the barn into the meadow and called to Molly, who came at once, her foal close alongside. When Vivian reached out to touch it, Molly, expecting the usual treat, pushed between them and nudged Vivian, snuffling impatiently. Emboldened by curiosity, the foal thrust its nose forward by its mother's, and Vivian was able to stroke its neck, though at her touch it quivered and pressed close to Molly. When Molly understood Vivian's pocket was empty, she headed back out into the meadow and the foal, lifting its feet in a stiff, bouncy trot, followed at her heels.

Vivian leaned on the barn door and looked after them. The meadow, level and treeless, was not yet dried out by the summer heat and grazing was good. The foal, suddenly weary, bent its knobby legs and knelt down in the grass, curving its neck around to rest its head on its legs. Molly grazed nearby, pausing now and then to snuff at her foal. In Vivian's eyes the green field with a sprinkling of yellow along the fence, the cloudless blue sky and the two horses were a study in curves and contentment. Dreaming, she filled the meadow with horses and foals; there were roans and chestnuts and blacks with starred foreheads. The barn was freshly painted, an apple green. Inside, the lofts were filled with hay, stalls and floor swept clean. It was a model of a barn, with the name of each horse tacked above its stall. And in the training pen, herself, in plaid shirt, jeans and boots, a lead rope in her hand and a bay filly, neck arched, prancing in circles at the other end. Near the road there was a white sign, "Horses Bred and Trained", and in the turnaround were parked several trucks, with horse trailers and out-of-state licenses.

Suddenly the scene shivered and dissolved, fading as quickly as it had come. Vivian smiled wryly. This time she had caught herself. She would not be misled by a foolish dream ever again. She would, as her father had advised, face facts, and the facts were she knew nothing about horses, their training or the market for horses. She did not have the enormous amount of money necessary; and she could not take over as her own what was Harry's property. Moreover, it meant a long-range, continuing effort—no days off—at work which, to be entirely honest, she must admit had only a romantic appeal. It did not include daily watering, feeding, and shoveling of manure. Or illness and vets' bills, all-night vigils with difficult births or dying horses. Or falls, broken bones, bites and kicks.

Pleased, even amused, by her fine reasoning, Vivian went further. It might even be that since Corinne was no longer interested in horses, Molly and her foal might be sold back to Mr. Farley.

Once again there were two horses in the field and cobwebs in an empty barn. But Vivian was remarkably clearheaded. Tomorrow she would give the books to the library. All the same she wished the barn could be used. Perhaps Harry would. . . .She paused by the car, then crossed to the house. She was drawn to it, had been since her last visit. She had spent hours remembering the way the house had been when Leonia and Harley had lived there, and though she hadn't even tried to explain why, she felt a strong urge to restore everything to the way it had been. Otherwise—and this made her wonder if she were suffering a mental aberration—she had the feeling that something valuable, irreplaceable, would be lost, something she owed it to Leonia and Harley to preserve. Were she to go inside now, she would make herself a cup of tea—if she could find any—and drink it in the sunny back parlor. Then she would clean the kitchen cupboards and start unpacking. In no time at all. . . .The doorknob turned easily under her hand. It was unlocked. Still she hesitated. Perhaps this was just another dream. Besides, it was late afternoon. Harry would be coming home. She could not say to him, "I've come back to straighten up the kitchen." That would be ludicrous. It was his home after all. He had put her things away, but he might have done that because he needed to put them somewhere, anywhere. If he were interested in her help, he would have asked. He obviously didn't need her there. And of course there was Beanna. . . .

Vivian let go of the doorknob, went quickly to the car and drove down the lane, raising a swirl of dust. But she did not drive with her usual verve. Facing facts could be disheartening.

When Vivian had turned out onto the highway, Harry came out of the barn. He had followed her out from town, parked behind the shed so she wouldn't see his car and had hidden himself in the barn while she was in the field with Molly. He had observed her leaning on the barn door, her weight thrown on one hip, her knee bent, foot cocked. Her hair had glistened in the sun, and her face had gone all dreamy. Then she had smiled, the way she sometimes did when things had gone awry. He had watched when she stood at the back door, obviously debating whether to go in or not. He hoped she would, for if she had, he would have gone in too. He could have spoken to her there. But he couldn't come out of the barn, greet her in the middle of the yard. She would have known, then, that he had been watching her and she would have been displeased.

Harry went in the house. He was where he wanted to be, but without Vivian he was living only with memories and ghosts. The continuity with the past was broken, and he could find no purpose in the present. He walked restlessly through the house, his steps echoing dully on the bare floors. The first time he had brought Vivian home formally had been to Sunday dinner. She had sat beside Dolly, across the table from him and to his father's right. His father had complimented him on his exceptional taste in girls and Vivian on her good looks, and his mother had tried to shush him, saying, "Harley, you're making her blush! Let the child eat." His father had laughed. "Only makes her the prettier! But Red doesn't mind a compliment, do you, Red?" And he had put more food on her plate than she could eat. Later, while the dishes were being done, he and his father had stepped out onto the front porch.

"Son," said Harley, and though his tone was jocular, his eyes had shone with that intense brightness they always had when he spoke with conviction, "you hang onto that girl! She'll make you one hell of a wife!"

Harry remembered the very quality of the air that afternoon. And when the women had joined them on the porch and he had invited Vivian to go for a walk, he had felt self-conscious, as if she must know what his father had said.

Harry rummaged in a carton and found a ball and his old baseball mitt. He went outside and threw the ball against the barn, reaching high to make the catch. He threw forcefully, as if to outplay himself, deliberately aiming so he had to stretch sideways, leap up or run back to catch the ball. And as he threw, a course of action took shape in his mind, several, in fact. If one didn't work, another would. He had waited and watched long enough. He would go after her and this time he would not let go!

When he had worked out until his arms were tired, Harry went inside and made himself a dish of scrambled eggs. At peace with his decision, he ate with relish for the first time in weeks.

NINETEEN

Fourth of July

In Warrenville the Fourth of July was celebrated in a very big way. Civic organizations, schools, churches, and the National Guard joined together to put on a show that began in midafternoon and ended with a final burst of fireworks long after dark. The atmosphere was that of a fair. Each year a small traveling carnival set up at one end of the park. There were only a ticket booth and four rides: a ferris wheel, a merry-go-round, high-flying planes and a caterpillar ride, made more exciting by a dark green cover that rose up and curved down over the heads of those riding, plunging the screaming passengers into an exhilarating darkness. When the cover folded back there were always those who were taken by surprise. What the carnival lacked in size was offset by color and noise. The merry-go-round was decorated with flashing mirrors and all rides were lavishly lighted with large colored bulbs. Altogether, the rides set in motion and the jangling calliope created a splendid effect.

At the other end of the park were the baseball diamond with tiers of benches and the football field and grandstand where the fireworks would be set off. In between was the park itself, a large, sprawling area, with small zoo buildings housing a lion, a black bear and a wolf, all elderly tokens of their kind. They looked with jaundiced eyes at those passing by whose repertoire of tricks for gaining attention was so limited and boring. There was a large cage of raccoons who played around an amputated tree trunk and several large pens for a buffalo, a camel and a small herd of deer.

One area—frequented on Sunday mornings by parents with small children—had swings, large ones with clanking chains, often looped back over the supporting legs by teenagers fond of going sideways on the middle swing. For small children there were small swings and for infants, swings like little crates in which they could safely slump while young parents aimed their cameras. There was a pyramidal jungle jim, its top always gained and jealously held by one child who, enchanted by his elevation, refused all orders to share or come down. There were slides of various sizes. One was serpentine and badly rusted, but the prize slide was double, having two descents from opposite sides of a high platform. Mothers did not favor this slide, and fathers issued strict instructions about loitering at the top. One descent was straight and swift, the other wavy and by far the more popular, as evidenced by the depth of the hollow in the ground at its end.

For tired parents who wanted only to sit down, there was a large sandbox where their toddlers could happily dig. Occasionally an encroachment of one on another's territory brought on a bout of sand throwing and gritty tears. The more serious problem raised by the sandbox, however, was the esteem in which it was held by neighborhood cats. This matter was brought to the attention of the city council, whose only solution was to surround the sandbox by a high wire fence, a solution that was met by strenuous objections from parents. They did not want their children penned in or their spontaneity and freedom of action curtailed. There had to be a better way. At their insistence a zoo maintenance person periodically raked through the sandbox with a large sifter.

For those who would wade, a large, shallow cement pool had been provided, paid for by the Rotary. But it had been largely taken over by ducks, dead leaves, crumpled cigarette packs, candy wrappers, pop bottle tops and an occasional milk carton. It also served to float toy boats.

Beyond the pool was a modest band shell, its curved inside painted a sky blue. Before it were rows of park-green benches.

A narrow, one-way road, actually a wide macadamed walkway, meandered through the park. For the Fourth, wooden horses closed off both ends, and stands were set up along its route. There were stands selling hot dogs, without which there could be no Fourth, popcorn, cotton candy and ice cream. Other stalls served a variety of civic concerns. One, manned by young women free to be as flirtatious as they liked, sold kisses for the benefit of the hospital. Another, given what Hester Morris complained of as a marginal and unfavorable location—directly across from a military recruitment booth—sold anti-war buttons and bumper stickers. Marvel Gibson, with the assistance of Calloway Claude, was to hold an auction of donated articles for the benefit of the orphanage. The 4-H'ers had a stall selling homemade fudge, cakes, pies and sweet rolls. Dolphine, to promote the WCT, was ready with a series of charades, for which purpose a wire had been strung across the band shell to allow for the opening and closing of a curtain.

Over all flew the American flag: one from the flagpole by the baseball diamond, another huge one hung across the outside of the grandstand just above the main entrance, a slightly smaller one across the inside curve of the band shell. Medium-sized flags were posted at intervals along the walkway and little hand-waving flags flew from the top corners of every stall, the fronts of which were decorated with red, white and blue crepe paper. Excepting the Army and Marine recruiters, all the men and women manning booths wore stiff-brimmed straw hats banded with red, white and blue, even Marvel, and the men wore elastics around their upper shirt sleeves.

Everyone for miles around Warrenville prayed for clear, sunny weather. For several days preceding the Fourth, the forecast was the constant subject of speculation. People questioned each other about their chances for fine weather. If any pessimist raised the possibility of rain, it was given a moment's consideration then brushed aside as being impossible. At worst there could be no more than a brief, early morning shower. But it was the wrong mind set, just short of being unpatriotic, to grant even that. Whether the hopes of the people of Warrenville rose to a great and generous cosmic ear, or whether Warrenville itself was blessed by lying at a salutary crossing of latitude with longitude, or whether it was all due to a happy conjunction of celestial bodies, is not known, but it was a fact that though it may have poured on the third or been gray and damp on the fifth, the Fourth had been a perfect day for as long as anyone could remember. There *had* been one year when a storm threatened during the last of the fireworks. Drops had begun to fall as people left the grandstand.

Old codgers never forgot that occasion. All day on the third they would squint with watery, suspicious eyes at the sky and take a perverse pleasure in reminding everyone of the one year it had rained on the Fourth.

But their sour intimations once more proved groundless, for this Fourth dawned gently, with a pearly flush of color as delicate as the inside of a shell, and grew to be as beautifully warm and sunny, with puffy, high-riding clouds, as anyone in Warrenville could desire. It was a perfect day.

Perfect or not, Vivian had decided to stay home. To enjoy such festivities one needed a certain lightness of spirit, a certain expectation, and that she lacked. Being thoroughly realistic had made her much too sober. Corinne, stopping by to say that she and August would see her there, was surprised and then indignant to hear that she wasn't going.

"But why not? We always go! Daddy's going to play! He's captain of his team. There was a big write-up about it in the paper. Logan's playing too. You've got to come!"

"Corinne, I don't *have* to come at all! When will you learn not to tell me what I've got to do!"

Corinne shrugged impatiently. "You *know* what I mean." She paused, then looked sideways at her mother. "What will Daddy think?"

"About what?"

"About your not being there!"

"I don't expect he'll think about it at all . . . or even know the difference."

"Mother! You know that's not true. He always shows off for you!"

Vivian sighed audibly. "Corinne . . . !"

"Oh all right! But *we're* going anyway!"

"Fine. Have a good time."

Corinne paused at the door. "Gus got an assistantship for this fall. Isn't that great? I think he'll be a really great architect someday. It's too early to look for an apartment. We don't want to pay an extra month's rent. But we will next month. You'll come and see us, won't you?"

Vivian assured her she would. After Corinne left, she went outside and sat on the back steps.

Corinne encountered Wilder on the front walk and after

saying "Hi," said what was uppermost on her mind. "Aren't you going this afternoon?" No need to say to what, and without waiting for his answer, she said, "Mother says she won't go even though Daddy's going to play!" Her tone was aggrieved, and she looked at Wilder as if he were somehow accountable or could at the very least do something about her mother's obstinate behavior.

Wilder, not adept with a young woman, gave her the sort of vague answer he used to give his sisters, and Corinne went off, thinking him of no use at all, the same hasty, mistaken conclusion his sisters had made years before.

Nearsighted though he was, Wilder was observant. He was by nature a watcher. When he stepped outside he noticed immediately any change in the environment, the weather, a broken branch on a tree, a shutter slipped sideways on a house, a new coat of tar on a driveway. When he didn't understand what he saw, he watched patiently until he did.

When James had barked at a man standing in the dark under a tree, he had been curious because James did not normally bark at passing strangers. Wilder had walked in the opposite direction, but only a short way, returning in time to see the man passing under the corner street light as he rounded the corner. Wilder recognized Harry. He put James inside, then went quietly along the dark side of the house to where he had a view through the shortcut of the opposite side of the block. In a few minutes he saw Harry take up a position where he could see into the backyard. He stayed longer than Wilder cared to observe him.

Thereafter Wilder was quick to notice Harry's car, with Harry behind the wheel, parked on a side street. When sweeping the porch, pruning the hedge or just waiting for James, Wilder saw Harry, day after day, morning or afternoon, wait for Vivian and then follow her, either on foot or in the car. Harry, being cautious, varied his locations, but Wilder, admiring Harry, who possessed all those qualities he himself so lacked, and sympathizing with him, always discovered him. As Harry came to know Vivian's routine, Wilder came to know Harry's. He had begun to wonder to what end all this trailing when Corinne's complaint gave him an opportunity to meddle. He had never meddled before. He disapproved of tampering with other people's lives and besides had never had occasion to do so. But after several weeks of watching Harry, he had become involved, a kind of silent partner. He wished, moreover, to be somehow instrumental in furthering Vivian's happiness. He found her sitting on the back steps and spoke out directly.

"I met your daughter just now. She's disappointed you're not going to the ball game."

Vivian made an impatient sound and shook her head. "She seems compelled to tell everybody what. . . ."

"I'm not everybody," interrupted Wilder. Having decided to speak, he was surprisingly self-assertive.

Vivian was taken aback. She apologized. "No, of course not, it's just that. . . ."

But Wilder interrupted again. As on a previous occasion, he could not stop himself. "She thinks her father will be disappointed not to see you there." Vivian started to speak, but Wilder gave her no chance. His eyes seemed not only larger than ever before, but severe. "I think he will be too. I think you should go."

Vivian was amazed. She doubted this was any concern of Wilder's and said rather resentfully, "*I* don't think he will care one way or the other. And I *don't* see why everyone is making such a fuss about. . . ."

"That's because," said Wilder vehemently, "you don't see *anything*!" His long-buried amazement at her blindness, to himself as well as to Harry, suddenly found expression. "For weeks he's been following you everywhere! I don't see how you could have missed seeing him!"

Vivian straightened up. "Following me! I can't believe it . . .!"

"Yes, he follows you all the time. If you walk, he walks. If you drive, he drives." Wilder might have been speaking of his other self. "At night he stands in the dark and stares at your window! One night he stood over there . . ." pointing toward the shortcut, ". . . the whole time you were sitting here." His sense of outrage, unexpected even by himself, was relieved by being openly expressed, as well as by Vivian's apparent shock.

"You've actually *seen* him?" she asked, frowning in disbelief.

"Yes," said Wilder positively. "I've seen him. Every day and every evening."

Vivian was astounded. She would never have expected this of Harry. "I had no idea . . . I didn't know . . . maybe I should have, but. . . ."

"I thought you should. Otherwise I would not have . . meddled."

Vivian heard at once his acerbic tone, and her words came in a rush, flying, like her thoughts, in all directions at once. She assured Wilder he had not meddled, not at all. She confessed to being foolish. She apologized, though she didn't say for what. She looked at her watch, then asked him what time it was. Without waiting for him to answer, she declared she could not stand there talking. Then, abruptly, she was quiet. She put out her hand but didn't quite touch him. She looked him fully in the face and thanked him. "You have been very kind, very understanding . . . these past weeks. And today you have spoken to me as a true friend."

"That," said Wilder, "was how I intended it." He felt a vast relief. He had regained his self-respect. He could face her now, this woman to whom he had confessed his deepest feelings, without shame or embarrassment, for she too had failings. She was not perfectly attuned. She could hurt without even knowing it. "I hope . . . you will be happy. Always." He felt he had never spoken so well. A sense of dignity swept over him. He called James and went inside.

He had not planned to go to the celebration. Now he decided he would. He put on a fresh shirt and combed his hair. He owed Vivian much—not merely his home, that was the least of it. She had illuminated his life, enlarged it, given it a wider, deeper dimension. His perception of himself and others had been sharpened. What did it matter if in the future the edge once more dulled. She had given him memories to keep. He would see her again, he knew, but they would never again speak on so personal a level. No doubt she would move out as abruptly as she had moved in. He found that the prospect of her going did not bring on that abysmal sense of loneliness he had experienced before whenever she left. He discovered, even as he combed his hair so as to cover his bald spot, that now he could face the loss of her presence with equanimity. He would be foolish to mourn the loss of what he had never had. His life would resume its accustomed placidity, and he could again devote his time to studying the stock market and increasing his holdings.

He put on his loosely woven summer hat. James, excited by the prospect of an outing, brought his leash and dropped it at Wilder's feet. Wilder snapped it onto James' collar and opened the door. They would get to the park in good time. Wilder anticipated with pleasure a hot dog with yellow mustard.

Vivian went inside and stood in a daze in the middle of the room. She breathed as if she had been running; she was conscious of her heart pounding in her chest. Her eyes were wide, envisioning various scenes. Through Harry's eyes she saw herself come out of the house and walk down the street. With Harry she followed along behind, being careful at corners and crossings to keep out of sight should she turn her head. Then from behind his shoulder as he sat at the wheel of his Camaro, she saw him turn out of a side street and follow her Thunderbird, letting other cars come between but never losing sight of the red car ahead. Had he followed her to the farm? Perhaps watched when she went inside the house? She had seen no sign of him, but then, she had not been looking and Harry was very quick and clever. She saw then her own windows from the darkness of the hedge—curtains, a portion of a lamp shade, herself moving past, an actor unaware of an audience. Then the light went out, and she stood with Harry in the dark. When it grew late and lights in neighboring houses blinked out, he went quietly away, stepping carefully so as not to make a noise. On the ride out to the farm, the night air was soft, still warm from the heat of the day. Without turning on a light, Harry picked his way through the rooms, between the eerie shapes of packing cases, up the gloom of the the stairwell to the back bedroom. From the rear window the backyard was a vague pale area of uncertain depth, shadowed by the dark masses of barn and shed. Beyond, the pond was a dull, metallic glimmer, and beyond the pond the dark earth merged with the night sky. Alone, he had thought of her, as she had of him.

Vivian stood entranced, a rapt smile on her lips. All these past days when she had been so confused, felt so cut off and isolated, she had, without knowing it, been watched over, sheltered in Harry's thoughts. A great sense of warmth and security swept over her. Quickly she made ready to go. She had brought few clothes with her; she had an old white pique, sleeveless, with a full skirt. It would have to do. But Harry had always liked her in white.

The parking lots were full, and Vivian had to park five blocks away. When she reached the ball field, the game was already in progress and the stands were full of people. She stepped up to the third tier of benches and squeezed into a space where a batter in position and looking straight ahead would be sure to see her; it was where she had always sat when Harry played. The Kiwanis team was playing the Junior Chamber of Commerce team, who was up at bat. Both teams wore caps with visors and uniforms carrying the badge of the organization they represented. Through her large, rosy-tinted sunglasses Vivian saw that Harry was at first base, his usual position. He was swinging his arms slightly and gently flexing one knee, ready to leap, crouch or run. His attention was fixed on the batter, who at that moment swung and clipped the ball, sending it off at a diagonal. Harry ran forward, scooped it up, touched base and threw the ball to the catcher, who caught a man off third, making the third out. There were groans and yells from the stands as the teams changed places, some of the players trotting into position in what they fancied a professional manner. Harry never trotted. He might run at an easy, graceful lope or, when necessary, at top speed, a pace which always took his opponents by surprise. Otherwise he sauntered. It was his natural style.

Jim Reeves sent out his first batter, Lou Reinert, the paint and hardware store man. Lou was small and wiry, a fast runner and an inveterate base-stealer. Harry sat leaning forward on the bench, elbows on his knees. He appeared to be watching Lou, but he was really scanning the stands. He saw her almost at once, sitting where she always used to sit, third row, sixth seat in. In the sunlight her hair was a burnished gold, and she was wearing those crazy sunglasses. Her hair and white dress set her apart from the crowd around her. He knew she had not been there before the game started. She had come late and squeezed in, shoulders hunched together, in order to sit in that precise seat. Harry's chest swelled with elation. The sharp crack of the bat wrenched his attention from Vivian back to the game.

Lou was on first and Jake Stroud, the jeweler, was at bat. Jake was not a strong batter but, like Lou, was fast, and Harry knew Reeves was trying to load the bases. Jake struck out, but Lou stole second. Reeves glanced at Harry, then, taking a chance, sent out Bert Magill, assistant editor of the newspaper.

Logan was sitting next to Harry. "Whether Bert gets on or not, you'll be next."

Bert did get on. He bunted the ball and it went right past the infielder, whose reach was too short and too slow. Lou stole third and grinned as a howl went up from the Junior Chamber of Commerce fans. Reeves, with a man on first and on third, called Harry to bat.

Harry had been playing routinely, with none of the verve that Logan so enjoyed. Now he rose full of zest. He paused to settle his cap more firmly on his head and give the visor a tug, familiar signs to Logan. Delighted, he sat forward, watching attentively. By the calculating way in which Harry selected his bat—like a fencer testing his rapier while thinking where best to drive its point into his opponent—Logan understood that Harry meant business.

Harry sauntered up to the plate. His eye was on Vivian, but to the fans his slightly squinting gaze, shadowed by his cap, seemed to take in everything at once.

"Bring 'em in, Harry! Bring 'em in!" they yelled. "Send it a mile, Harry!" "C'mon, Harry, show 'em how it's done!"

Harry showed them. He ground one heel into the dirt. He held the bat at an angle, ran his hand down its length and back, then tipped it downward, tapping it twice on the ground. He glanced deliberately at first, around at third, then raised the bat and faced the pitcher. Half mesmerized by Harry's performance, the pitcher, a young man in the County Assessor's Office, came to and began his windup. Unlike others, Harry didn't fan the air with his bat but held a perfectly still, graceful, ominous pose. The fans were hushed and tense. When the ball came, Harry hit it such a crack as to split the bat. The ball sailed up and out, a white pellet against the blue sky. The fans stomped and yelled. "You did it, Harry! Yea! You did it!" The outfielder turned and ran without hope. Lou and Bert crossed home plate one after the other. Harry ran easily around the bases. He couldn't distinguish Vivian's voice or that of Corinne, who was excitedly nudging Gus and exclaiming, "Isn't he great! Isn't he just great!" But he saw, as he reached home plate, that Vivian was smiling and as he crossed it, she raised her chin in the old, familiar salute.

After that the outcome of the game was never in question. In the first half of the sixth, Harry hit another homer, bringing in one man. The other team, quicker now and trying hard, retrieved the ball faster, and Harry barely made home plate, sliding in feet first in a spurt of dirt, just ahead of the ball.

The Kiwanis team won eleven to five. M.T. Reardon was ready with his camera, for the next day's edition would carry photos and articles on all major events. He insisted that both teams group for a photo, and then that Harry and the opposing captain pose shaking hands. As he aimed his camera people swarmed down from the stands, most scattering across the field toward the booths; but a few milled about, congratulating the players. M.T. got a photo of a wife kissing her husband, another of a small boy demanding anxiously to know why daddy hadn't won. The players, hot and dirty, headed toward the one story brick building where they could shower and change clothes.

"I'll meet you by the ice cream booth," Logan told Jenny. "Don't stand. Sit down on a bench. I'll find you." Jenny started slowly in that direction, tipped slightly backward, like a drum major carrying his drum.

Corinne threw her arms around Harry. "Oh Daddy, you were wonderful! Did you see Mother?"

Harry grinned and nodded. Vivian had come down slowly off the stand, observing from a distance as always. Harry gave her a long look before going off with the rest of the team, who were slapping and pulling at him.

Vivian understood. It was a familiar wordless message, sent over the noise and intervening crowd, that said, "Meet me by the hot dog stand." After a game Harry used to consume three large hot dogs and several mugs of root beer. Vivian smiled. She doubted he would eat that much now. As she passed the band shell she saw troops of girl and boy scouts, scarfs neatly around their necks, being herded onto the stage and arranged in rows according to height. They were to present a program of patriotic songs accompanied by a den mother playing on an old upright piano at the back of the stage. Parents were filling up the green benches, and M.T., finished with the ball players, leaned against the front of the stage, waiting for them all to settle into place.

Drawn up near the walkway was a red popcorn wagon with a shiny whistle on top that shot off puffs of steam. Inside, popcorn spilled out of the popper and piled up in drifts against the glass windows. A young man in a white hat and jacket was dribbling melted butter over popcorn in red and white striped boxes, alternately handing them out and making change as fast as he could. Lena and Rilly were in line. Lena waved, and Rilly, seeing Vivian, came running, bursting with news.

"Mrs. Fox! Mrs. Fox! Guess what!" She skipped about excitedly, but as Vivian said, "What? Tell me!" she suddenly stood still, impressed by her own news, her eyes staring. "I'm going to get a dog! Of my very own! He's going to sleep in my room, on the foot of my bed! 'Course he's too young to leave his mother yet, but I've seen him!" Vivian responded with all the right questions. "He's a pug! With a little curled up tail!" Rilly made a twisting motion with her finger. "I'm going to call him Pug, just like in that book where he runs off with a slipper! Do you think that's a good name?" Vivian agreed it was a fine name. "Lena says we can get him in another week. I've got to go now." She started to bounce again. "Later I get to ride the ferris wheel and see the fireworks! Pete promised!"

The area around the hot dog stand was very crowded. Vivian strolled off to one side, away from the drinking fountain with its invariable muddy puddle, toward the wading pool. She watched the ducks snapping up popcorn, but dreamily. At the onset of a totally captivating, all-encompassing dream, Vivian was in a state of suspension. Not a fact was in her head, no thoughts whatever; just a breathless waiting for Harry to appear, for the dream to begin. What they had lost they were on the brink of rediscovering, made all the richer by a wealth of shared memories.

Harry came at a swift stride, swinging out and around a family strung out across the walk, parents pushing a stroller at a snail's pace, a child stopped dead to suck out the last of the ice cream from the bottom of a cone. He saw her before she turned. She seemed to be musing and watching the ducks.

Vivian raised her head, and the sight of him struck her heart like a blow. He came on with an eager, swinging step, his whole attention aimed at her. He was not lanky, as in his youth, nor diffident. He stopped close to her, and the strength of his resolution emanated from him. His deep blue eyes studied her keenly as if to reacquaint himself with her every feature. His face shone with animation.

Vivian waited, not knowing what to expect. What Harry really wanted to do was catch her up and whirl her around, then give her a great hug and a kiss. But he did none of those things. It would have gone against his instinct and fine sense of timing. Instead his intent expression softened into a smile and he said, "How about a hot dog?"

He came back cradling the buns in napkins and carrying two cups of coffee. They strolled along, past the wading pool, eating rather than talking and being careful not to spill their coffee.

"Oh, look, there's Rilly." They were passing a fenced-off circular dirt track, inside of which children were riding ponies that plodded along in a row, moving in step, heads bobbing as if they had been wound up and set going. Rilly, erect and solemn, was astride a milk-chocolate pony with flaxen mane that fell like thick bangs over its forehead. As she passed near them, Vivian called out and waved, but Rilly, subdued by the gravity of her position, dared not raise her hand, and responded only by a roll of her eyes.

At the starting gate a loud wail went up as the owner of the ponies, a dour-faced man in baggy gray pants, lifted a small boy onto the back of an exceptionally small black pony. The boy's face turned red and he kicked frantically. Holding him out at arm's length, the man handed him back to his father.

"Don't think he wants to."

"Of course he wants to!" exclaimed the mother. "He talks of nothing but ponies! He rides his hobby horse all the time!" She turned to the frowning father. "Maybe if you put him on. . . ."

"Ah no!" said the owner. "I put 'em on or they don't get on. He could get hurt or upset the whole string."

"That's silly! Once he got on, he'd. . . ."

"He's *scared*, Lady. Wait 'til next year." Bored, he looked past her. "Next?"

In his father's arms, the child hid his face and clung tightly to his father's neck.

"He is *not* scared!" exclaimed his mother indignantly.

"Lady, please? You're holding up the line."

"C'mon," urged the father and walked off, carrying his son; the mother followed, looking angrily at everyone.

"Poor kid," remarked Harry, amused.

"And poor owner," said Vivian. "Doesn't seem to be enjoying himself."

"What's fun for the kids is work for him."

"Mmmn," said Vivian, wondering if once he had thought it would be different.

Harry touched her elbow. "Come on, let's get some popcorn and take a look at the auction."

As they passed the ice cream stand Vivian saw Wilder, wearing his old summer hat, sitting on a bench. He held James on his lap, steadying him while the dog licked away at an ice cream cone. On the same bench sat Jenny, a drum major resting with drum. She too was eating an ice cream cone.

"Wonder where Logan is," said Vivian.

"Over there, talking with Lou. Rehashing the game. Did you want to speak to them?" He hoped she didn't. Not because of any feeling for Jenny other than what he would normally have for Logan's wife, but because he wanted nothing to interrupt their being together. He remembered years before when he had steered her in roundabout and devious courses in order to avoid chatty friends.

"No," said Vivian. "Let's not interrupt them." She wanted to be just with Harry, the two of them alone in the crowd, and remembered how she used to innocently avert her gaze to avoid encountering girls she knew.

For a moment Harry and Vivian observed Jenny and James, both assiduously licking their cones, turning their heads to one side and then to the other so as to catch every drop, both with the half-closed eyes and deep concentration characteristic of ice cream cone eaters.

"Would you like a cone?" asked Harry.

"No thanks," said Vivian, and they both laughed.

A small crowd had gathered in front of the auction booth. As Vivian and Harry, each with a striped box of popcorn, approached, Calloway Claude was holding up a bedroom clock, dove gray with raised sprays of roses. The stiff brim of his straw hat emphasized the broadness of his face and grin.

". . . offers a real challenge! Make it run and you'll have one beautiful little clock! Five, will you go five? 'Course it's not for everybody! Only a clever fellow can fix *this* clock! Five, five-fifty, six? Seven? Would you go seven? Sold at six!"

Calloway, as the legman, stood outside the stand. Behind him a placard announced that all proceeds were for the benefit of the Warrenville Orphanage. Marvel, behind the counter, handed items to Calloway and sold special ones himself. With his shirt sleeves tucked up and his straw hat at a jaunty angle, he made a slick carnival barker. His attention, Vivian noticed, was taken by a woman at the back of the crowd. She wore a striking dress, stylized red poppies on a white background, and a large floppy-brimmed hat that shaded her face.

"Step right up," urged Marvel, "closer, closer! What we have here is a collection from the best attics in town! Only for a humanitarian purpose would such items ever be offered for sale!" He held up two matching figurines about a foot high, cream colored, a shepherd and a shepherdess. "Here is the perfect pair for any mantelpiece. Having these would be a mark of taste and distinction. Very unusual coloring. We'll start at twenty. Do I hear twenty-two, twenty-two, twenty-five, who'll go twenty-five?"

The woman in the large hat held up her hand.

"Ah, a lady of discrimination, who knows a good thing when she sees it! I have twenty-five, who'll make it thirty? Thirty? Twenty-eight fifty, twenty-eight fifty? Sold, for twenty-five! Would the lady please step to the rear of the booth?"

"See anything interesting?" asked Harry.

"Not a thing," said Vivian. "Let's go over to the band shell. Dolphine's putting on tableaux." As they walked away, they passed the woman on her way to the back of the booth. Vivian, mildly curious, glanced at her and saw with amusement that it was Belvedera. Bel flashed her a roguish look and winked one eye.

The sun had set and though the sky was still a dusky blue, lights were coming on all over the park. The carnival lights showed with increasing brilliance through the trees and above them were the turning lights of the ferris wheel. Strings of bulbs had been hung from street lamp to street lamp along the curving roadway, throwing a kaleidoscope of colors on the people passing by.

A large audience was assembled on the benches before the

band shell, some to see the tableaux, some who were willing to watch while resting their feet, others who were simply waiting until it was dark enough for the fireworks. The lights that arched above the stage and the footlights were on, and sporadic clapping had just risen from the audience as the curtain was pulled shut by two little girls who met in midstage. They stood importantly, side by side, looking out and blinking, waiting for a signal from within to draw the curtains open again.

Harry and Vivian sat down, mindful, without appearing so, of leaving a little space between them. All afternoon, from the moment of Vivian's appearance at the ball game and on into the evening, they had been drawing closer together. Neither would have suffered anything to separate them, yet the moment to acknowledge that had not yet come.

A faintly heard note sounded on a pitch pipe set the little girls in motion. They walked to opposite sides of the stage, pushing the curtains ahead of them to reveal the tableau. There was a cardboard fireplace, several chairs, a footstool. Two men in colonial dress, wearing white wigs curled up on the sides and with beribboned pigtails in back, stood, tricornered hats in hand, regarding a woman sitting in a rocker. She wore a ruffled cap and on a table beside her was an open sewing basket. A flag lay across her knees; she held up its corners for the benefit of the two men as well as for that of the audience.

Recognition was instantaneous. One irrepressible young voice near the front cried out, "It's Betsy Ross! It's Betsy Ross!" The audience gave Betsy a modest hand clap, the pitch pipe sounded, and the little girls promptly drew together, like figures on a Swiss clock.

The sky had now turned a deep, vibrant blue, like that of butterfly wings set in plastic trays. One star could be seen to the right of the band shell. The metallic jangle of merry-go-round music floated out on the evening air. Harry offered Vivian more popcorn.

"No thanks," said Vivian, not quite looking at him. "You're probably hungry. You have it."

"Have some," urged Harry affably. "Then I'll eat the rest." They both smiled. Daintily Vivian took several kernels. Harry tipped out what was left, ate it and dusted his hands.

The curtain pushers were signaled, the curtains were pushed

back and there was a wintry scene, complete with a fierce wind provided by an offstage fan. A row boat was stage center and around it were fiberboard cutouts of waves and floating ice cakes, alternated to give the effect of choppy water. Heavily clad men strained at the oars, and standing near the prow, in a wig, tricorn and billowing cape, was Swanger. He stood majestically, one knee bent for balance, his raised chin thrust forward. An appreciative murmur rose from the audience. Then, without altering his heroic stance, Swanger reached into his hip pocket, drew out a bottle and raised it like a trumpet to his lips. There was an immediate audience reaction, exclamations and laughter, and a frantic peeping of the pitch pipe. The little girls pulled the curtains, then, confused, opened them again. The rowers had dropped their oars and were looking about for direction. Swanger, perceiving the curtains open once more, stepped regally out of the boat. Standing between the waves, he swept off his hat and bowed to the audience, to the left, to the right, and, as the curtains at repeated hissed urgings were hurriedly drawn closed, to the center. There was an enthusiastic outburst of applause, catcalls, whistles, and one "Attaboy, George!" The little girls stood close together, staring uncertainly out over the footlights, one nervously pleating the side of her skirt.

The audience, now thoroughly attentive, waited eagerly for the next tableau. Strange clomping sounds and loud insistent whisperings could be heard from behind the curtains. The little girls exchanged glances and were almost overcome by a fit of the giggles. When the pitch pipe sounded again, rather forcefully, they hurried to push back the curtains. There was an expectant, attentive hush on the part of the audience. This scene, more elaborate than the last, featured a fiberboard church, painted white, with painted-on windows and a high, pointed steeple with a cutout window. A man appeared in the steeple window, holding up a lantern. At a short distance from the church stood, or was supposed to stand, a chestnut horse (live, courtesy of Mr. Farley). Mounted on his back was Swanger, in buckled shoes, white stockings, cloak, wig and tricorn. The horse, alarmed at finding himself treading on hollow-sounding boards and in front of glaring lights, jerked on the reins and rolled his eyes. Swanger tried to hold him steady as he gazed up at the steeple. Swaying dramatically with the restless stomping of the horse, he threw out one arm and exclaimed loudly, "But soft! What light through yonder window breaks? It is the east and. . . ." At that moment M.T. Reardon at the front edge of the stage took a flash photo, and two boys, hunkered down in the shadows at the end of the band shell, busy hatching more mischief than they knew, tossed onto the stage behind the horse a lighted rocket. With a loud hiss it zoomed up and looped erratically above the stage. As if touched by a hot iron, the horse reared and leaped forward, knocking over the supports for the church, which came crashing down, bringing man and stepladder with it. Swanger dropped the reins, and the terror-stricken horse plunged off the stage with Swanger clinging to his neck and yelling, "Heigh-ho, Silver, awaaaaaay!"

Dolphine rushed onto the stage, crying after him, "Come back, come back!"

People yelled, grabbed up children, and scattered from before the galloping horse. Swerving to miss the drinking fountain, it loosened Swanger's grip, and with cloak flying out behind him, he sailed off into the wading pool. Veering away from the noise and lights of the carnival, the horse, pursued on foot by a panting Mr. Farley, ran toward the now darkened zoo buildings, and there Mr. Farley found it, trembling and standing with head pressed against the buffalo's enclosure, where it smelled the comforting odors of animals and hay.

Swanger, dripping wet, and the man who crashed with the church were both taken to the hospital in an ambulance called by Sergeant Sidney Kemp. It came with blaring siren and flashing lights. A large crowd gathered, and Officer Travis had to ask them all to stand back. M.T. Reardon, taking press privilege, stepped forward and got a photo of the two men being lifted into the back of the ambulance which was almost spoiled by Swanger. Like one transported, he rose from his stretcher yelling, "Idiot! Idiot! You should be locked up! You bloody fool!" He grabbed for M.T. to throttle him and had to be restrained. M.T. was bundled off, proud that freedom of the press had triumphed. Swanger was treated for a broken leg, the steeple hanger for concussion and assorted bruises. The two boys were never identified. The audience never saw what would have been the climax and the grandest tableau of all: the signing of the Declaration of Independence. But it is doubtful that, had they been given the choice, they would have exchanged the one experience for the other. Swanger said later that except for the leap off the stage, the ride to the hospital was the most exciting of his life, and well worth a broken leg.

Fortunately, Sergeant Kemp remained in that general area of the park. That morning, when assigning duty, he had put two men on the parking lot detail, two others, including Officer Travis on pickpocket detail, and himself in the area of the recruitment and anti-war booths. "If there is trouble," he had said, "that is where it will start." He was right. He was also grateful to Harry, for had he not acted quickly, what was an ugly small incident might have become a major disruption of the peace and a blot on the celebration of the Fourth.

People were drifting away from the carnival and the booths toward the football stands, heads tipped back to judge the degree of darkness. Harry and Vivian, strolling in unspoken accord, paused to speak with Hester Morris at the anti-war stand.

Hester, unmarried and childless, had volunteered her time so those with families could enjoy the celebration. She had sold more pins and bumper stickers than she expected, but she had also taken the brunt of hostile looks and asides intended for her to hear, such as: "She ought to be ashamed!" "The cops ought to run her off!" "If she were *my* wife, you bet I'd set her straight!" *"Our* boys are over there fighting and dying! *Hers* has probably run off to Canada! Probably got a yellow streak a mile wide down the middle of his back!"

Hester, tired and a little nervous, admitted to Vivian that she was glad the day was about over. She was looking forward to the fireworks and had begun packing up. As they spoke, a thin young man with long wiry hair held down by an embroidered band fastened around his head stopped and, digging down into his pants' pocket, said he would like to buy a "Vietnam: Love It or Leave It" sticker for his car.

"Look at that kid! He oughta be held down and have his head shaved!"

Harry turned slightly. The speaker was a man about forty. He grinned at Harry and laid a hand on the young man's shoulder. "How about it, kid? Shave your head for you?"

The boy glanced around, shrugged off the man's hand, but said nothing.

"Huh," said the man, inviting his companion, another, slightly older man, to be witness, "another one thinks he don't have to answer when spoken to. No respect, that's what, not for anything."

"Why don't you lay off," said Harry quietly.

The man looked at him belligerently. "Why should I? This is *my* country, and I'm behind it all the way! Anyone isn't, should get the hell out!"

At that the young man turned. "If you're so eager to get blown up, why don't you go?"

"Why, you punk! You dirty, stinkin' punk!" The man spun him around and smashed his fist into the boy's face. His arms flew up and he reeled backward from the blow. The man socked him in the stomach and as he fell, fell on top of him, hitting him again in the face.

Harry threw himself forward. He straddled the man and grabbed for his arms.

"Harry!" cried Vivian.

"Stop! Oh, please stop him somebody!" cried Hester.

From the recruitment booth across the roadway a young man in Army uniform came running. Harry had pinioned one of the man's arms behind his back and was grabbing for the other. The man's companion picked up a stone and was about to smash it down on the back of Harry's head when Vivian screamed and the Army private leaped forward, caught his upraised hand and twisted it back and up, forcing him to drop the stone.

Sergeant Kemp, who had been helping restore a lost child to its parents when the shouting began, came at a run through a gathering crowd. He found an Army private holding one man immobile and Harry sitting astride a man who was lying on top of another. Harry held the man's wrists crossed behind his back. At his slightest move, Harry gave them a painful, upward jerk. The boy's bloody face was close to that of his assailant, who grimaced and tried to spit at him.

"Go on!" Sergeant Kemp ordered the crowd. "Get moving. Fireworks are over there. Nothing to see here. Move along! Now, you," addressing the man held by the private, "you stand there, back to the booth, and don't move." Then, addressing Harry, "Let him up." Harry released his grip and stood up and back. "You, on your feet." The man got up slowly, flexing his wrists. "Stand there, beside him, and don't move." Officer Travis, just arrived, bent to help the young man onto his feet. His mouth and cheekbone were split and bleeding. "What happened?" asked Sergeant Kemp of Harry, who told him as briefly as possible, the Army private adding his part.

"You have the right to prefer charges," Sergeant Kemp told the young man. "Do you wish to do so?"

The boy was standing, but unsteadily, hunched forward, his arms crossed over his midsection. He shook his head and mumbled without looking up, "No . . . no charges."

The man who had hit him snorted in disgust and looked defiantly at those few people lingering to watch.

"Are you all right?" Kemp asked the boy sharply. He nodded again, but even as he did so, his knees bent. He slumped and would have fallen had Officer Travis not caught him. "Put him down easy and call the ambulance," ordered Sergeant Kemp. He turned to the two men standing sullenly with their backs against the red, white and blue crepe paper decorations. He took down their names and addresses, then snapped his book shut and tucked it away in a pocket. "I should take you both in for disturbing the peace. I'll let you go with a warning, but I can bring you in any time! Any further disturbance, any at all, and you'll be booked! Now go, but remember—I have my eye on you!"

They all waited until the ambulance came. Officer Travis folded his jacket and put it under the young man's head. He had come to, but Travis told him to lie still until the medics came. As they waited, the National Guard marched out onto the football field and all in the stands rose to sing the National Anthem, their voices carrying strong and clear on the evening air, tinged with the sadness that space and distance lend to human voices. The carnival lights and the strings of lights along the walk were out. Only the street lamps were still on, turning the leaves that overhung them a yellow green and throwing circles of light on the macadam. The musky odor of the zoo hung faintly on the dampish air, and there was a deep, unidentifiable bawl of an animal settling to sleep.

As the National Guard shot off a salute, the ambulance came, lights whirling. The medics looked at them all curiously. "A busy night, huh," remarked one. They loaded the young man into the back, snapped shut the doors, and drove off. Officer Travis dusted off his jacket and put it back on. As Harry, Vivian, Hester and the two policemen walked across the dark field toward the stands, the first burst of fireworks flared out against the sky, an immense chrysanthemum, and a drawn-out "ah" rose from the stands.

Sergeant Kemp and Officer Travis stopped at the entrance to speak with a guard, Hester joined some friends, and Harry guided Vivian to a seat near the top of the stands, where they had a fine view. With the lights of Warrenville low in the background, the fireworks rose against the night sky. There were rockets that described a high arc, then burst into a shower of multicolored, falling stars; and there were rockets that went off in three separate stages, each larger than the preceding one. Others exploded into a thousand points of light and hung, trembling in space before suddenly disappearing. One took the form of a long-stemmed rose, another the profile of a woman with long, wavy hair. The dull, thunderous reports of each rocket vibrated across the land. At the end, on a large, rectangular framework at one end of the field appeared a representation of Niagara Falls, all in white, falling lights, and then, as the National Guard played "America" and the audience stood up and sang, it changed to a representation of the American flag, rippling in the breeze.

The audience waited, standing, while the National Guard marched out. Then they crowded into the aisles and gradually, with a minimum of pushing and shoving, made their way through the two main exits. Cars were already leaving the lots; flashlights, swung by parking attendants and policemen, traced arcs of light in the dark as cars were directed to right or left.

"I had to park the car five blocks away," said Vivian.

"We can go home in mine," said Harry. "It's over here, near the shower house." He spoke quietly, almost in an undertone, and after a brief silence during which they reached his car, he added, "We can pick yours up tomorrow."

Once they were out of the congestion around the park, the fifteen-minute drive to the farm was easy, with little or no traffic on the country roads. They rode with the windows down, the breeze created by their motion blowing their hair. Vivian looked at Harry obliquely, admiring his strong profile against the moving dark. As if aware of her regard, he glanced around and smiled.

"Too much wind?"

Vivian shook her head. "No. No, it's fine."

Harry parked the car short of the shed and got out. Vivian

followed rather more slowly. They walked in silence to the back porch. Vivian felt skittish. Even on the night they had paused outside this same door and had given each other a reassuring kiss before going in to announce to Leonia and Harley their intention to get married, she had not been so nervous. She was almost ready to back off and run.

Harry, indicating the door, said, "It's unlocked."

"Yes, I . . . I know," said Vivian.

"You do? How?" Even in the dark Vivian could see his eyes widen comically. He seemed to be amused.

"Oh well, I . . ." she shrugged, "I just guessed it was."

"Hm. Well, no need to stand here. Let's go in." He opened the door and preceded her, mumbling something about a light. Suddenly there was a crash as of a falling chair. In the dark Vivian, startled, could just make out Harry's arms flung out and then the sound of a heavy thudding impact and a metallic clash as Harry and some pans fell to the floor.

"Harry!" cried Vivian, moving forward, hands outstretched. "Harry! Did you hurt yourself?" There was no answer. "Harry! Oh damn!" Vivian stumbled over what turned out in the morning to be a frying pan and a kettle. Bending over, she felt about, touching the floor, a kitchen utensil, a shoe. Guided by that, she discovered Harry was lying on his side between the table and the cupboards. She knelt and pulled him over so his head and shoulders were in her lap.

"Harry, Harry, are you all right?" Quite forgetting her nervousness, she cradled his head against her breast, stroking back his hair. "Oh, Harry!" she whispered and kissed his forehead, his eyebrows, and laid her cheek against his.

Harry groaned briefly. After a moment he groaned again, raised one hand, which accidentally happened to land on the back of her head. He pulled her down just enough that her lips, pressed to his cheek, touched his. "Oh, Harry," she exclaimed, kissing him again and again, "speak to me!"

"This is lovely," said Harry softly, sliding his other arm around her waist, "but I think we'd be more comfortable upstairs." Vivian drew back in surprise, but Harry tightened his grip and again pulled her head down to his. Vivian uttered a strange incoherent sound, sniffed and pressed her face against his neck.

"If I can lean on you," said Harry, "I think I can make it

upstairs." Vivian braced him as best she could as Harry, with surprising alacrity, got to his feet. He put one arm close about her shoulders and leaned on her, not too heavily but just enough that she put an arm around his waist. Close together, they moved through the dark without the least difficulty, out of the kitchen, through the dining room, into the hall and up the stairs.

"There," said Harry, as they successfully reached the bedroom door, "and we didn't even need a light."

TWENTY

Jogging Home

The morning sun, its intensely brilliant face promising a long hot day, shone across the vast flat land of corn and soybeans, striking sharp points of light from gilded spires and domes, and setting the windows of its cities afire; from a distance they wavered and gleamed, magical cities in the promised land. From the Warrenville Airport, a plane lifted effortlessly like a fish through clear water, its wings flashing in the light. The stolid row of silos by the railroad tracks and the flared stacks of the ironworks were stained a deep pink and stood with ephemeral beauty against the pale blue sky.

In the municipal park the tops of the trees were a sunlit green, and the bars of the zoo cast oblique shadows across the floors of cages. The lion yawned and shook his scruffy mane, but didn't yet deign to rise. A duck stretched up on its toes and flapped its wings. Immediately the others rose and began waddling toward the wading pool, stopping here and there to poke into a crumpled wrapper or a carton that seemed promising. The park maintenance crew were already busy taking down strings of lights, dismantling booths and stabbing up litter into large brown bags. The carnival, its gleaming, gaudy colors of evening now merely tinny and garish, was being rapidly skeletonized, its metal frame fitted compactly into vans.

The entire front of Harley Fox's house, facing east, was bathed in sunlight. It had been his conviction that all houses should properly face east, and through the curtainless bedroom windows the sun reached halfway across the room. It shone on Vivian's face and woke her up. She blinked, stretched, and her upflung hand came in contact with the bedpost. Her fingers traced its carved pattern. It was a beautiful bedstead, hand-crafted and painstakingly finished. Like the house, it was solidly built. It was not plastic, padded or tufted. It did not fold up or roll away. It did not have shelves with built-in clocks or radios or plugs for instant coffee. This bed had already cradled three genera-tions, and could last through three more. One day soon she would give it a good polishing. There was so much to be done. But she was in no hurry because she was, finally, at home. This, she was certain, was where she belonged, and for the first time, although this did not occur to her, her dream did not revolve solely about herself, nor was it all in the future. For now she saw herself and Harry as rooted in the past. Everything they were, everything they had of any value, was a continuation of the past, like the bed and the house. There was no necessity to hurry because all they needed was right here, in the present, requiring only nurturing.

She turned her head and looked at Harry, his face half in the pillow, his black hair tousled. He was still asleep. She would get up quietly, go down and start breakfast. She wondered what, if anything, was in the refrigerator. She turned back the covers and was sitting up when she was caught from behind and pulled back.

"Where do you think you're going?"

"I thought you were asleep," said Vivian. She could see the deeper flecks of blue in his eyes. "I was going down to get break-fast."

"Breakfast," said Harry dreamily, "can wait."

"How is your ankle?"

Harry, intent on his own line of interest, blinked. "What?"

"Your ankle. Does it hurt?"

Harry's eyes opened wide, then they crinkled at the corners as amusement spread over his whole face. She felt his chest shake with an inward laugh. Suddenly understanding, Vivian looked at him accusingly.

"You didn't!"

Harry chuckled. "I was always better at falling than anyone on the team. You didn't know that, did you? See, there's lots about me you don't know yet."

"And about me too," said Vivian, rather primly.

Harry sighed contentedly, "Well . . . let's get acquainted."

Marvel always dressed before coming down to breakfast. A certain stiffness of character prevented his enjoying eggs, toast and coffee if he were still lolling about in a robe. When he did come downstairs, he saw the shepherd and shepherdess on the mantel where Bel had put them. Not a bad buy, he thought, but placed a bit too far apart. He was moving them closer together when Belvedera rushed in from the kitchen and peered out the front window.

"Oh, Marvel! There goes Louie, right toward the street! I'm not dressed—would you go out and get him?"

The point was made because walleyed Louie in no way considered Marvel to be his equal. If he jumped up on their bed, he purred on Belvedera's chest while his tail twitched in Marvel's face. He took over Marvel's favorite chair. He refused to eat any food that Marvel set down. It was doubtful that he would come back to the house peacefully with Marvel, but at Bel's request, Marvel went out to try.

Louie was strolling toward the sidewalk, his plumy tail waving gently from side to side, when down the street came the jogger. Louie stopped dead, in midstep. Then, as the jogger came near, his fur rose, his tail stiffened, and he arched his back, hissing more fiercely than when he had first met Bel's cousin's German shepherd.

The jogger was returning from her long morning run and was hot and pushing hard. The folded handkerchief around her head was damp; her short, spiky hair stuck out wildly above and below it. Her stained sweat shirt bagged, revealing no definitive shape. Her arms were bent at the elbows and worked like pistons. Her shorts were short, but her legs, leather-tan, lacked any shape save that of ropy muscle and tendon. Her face was flushed, her legs pumped, her arms swung. She breathed with mouth open, and her eyes stared straight ahead, focused on some distant, forever receding point.

Marvel scooped up a stupefied Louie. Cat and man, they stared as the jogger passed; for once they were in accord. Astonished, Marvel shook his head. He couldn't tell if it were man or woman.